SCARLESS & SACRED

The Chicago War, Book Three

BETHANY-KRIS

Published by Bethany-Kris

www.bethanykris.com

eISBN: 1-988197-02-9
eISBN 13: 978-1-988197-02-9
Print ISBN: 1-988197-05-8
Print ISBN 13: 978-1-988197-05-0

Cover Art © Jay Aheer
Editor: Dominique S.

For the people with pasts that are painted a little black.

CONTENTS

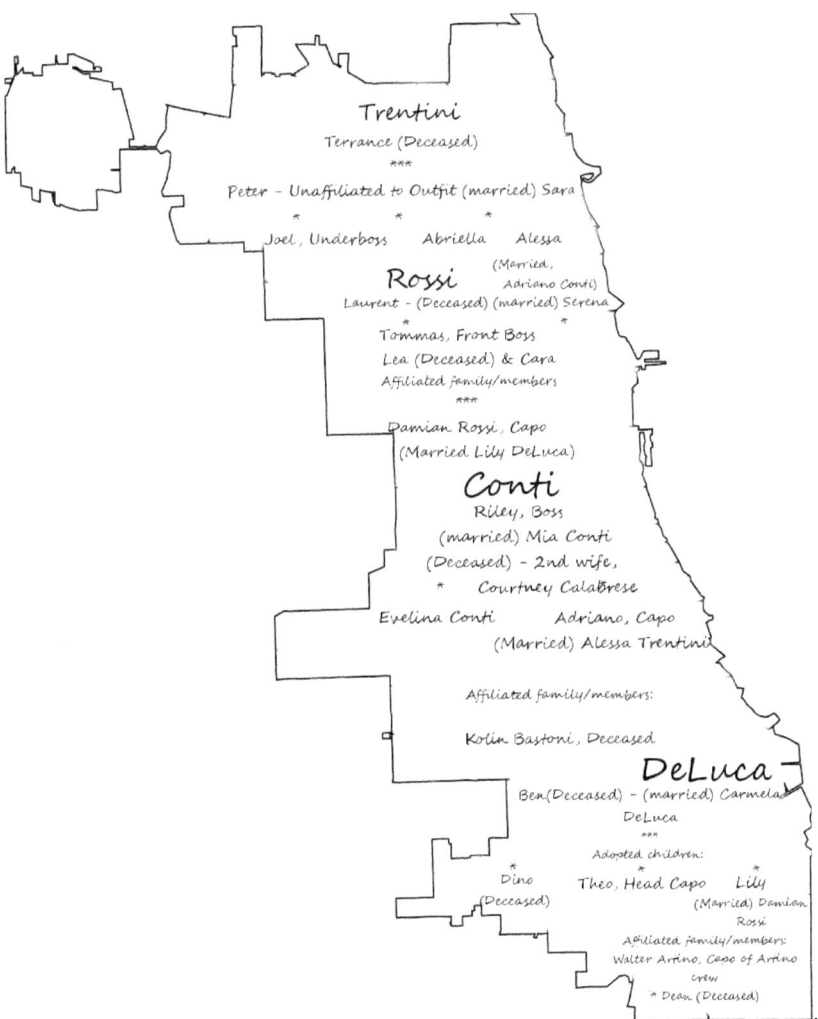

Trentini

Terrance (Deceased)

***

Peter – Unaffiliated to Outfit (married) Sara

*   *   *

Joel, Underboss   Abriella   Alessa

(Married,
Adriano Conti)

Rossi

Laurent – (Deceased) (married) Serena

Tommas, Front Boss

Lea (Deceased) & Cara

Affiliated family/members

***

Damian Rossi, Capo

(Married Lily DeLuca)

Conti

Riley, Boss

(married) Mia Conti

(Deceased) – 2nd wife,

*   Courtney Calabrese

Evelina Conti   Adriano, Capo

(Married) Alessa Trentini

Affiliated family/members:

Kolin Bastoni, Deceased

DeLuca

Ben(Deceased) – (married) Carmela
DeLuca

***

Adopted children:

*   *

Dino   Theo, Head Capo   Lily

(Deceased)   (Married) Damian
Rossi

Affiliated family/members:

Walter Artino, Capo of Artino
crew

* Dean (Deceased)

PROLOGUE

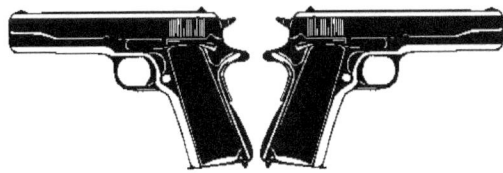

Parties should bring happiness. Evelina Conti felt anything but happy as she watched the guests at her eighteenth birthday mill around with drinks in one hand, laughter abound, and all eyes on her. She knew what they were thinking.

The Conti *princess*.

Finally of age, ready for the Outfit, and just waiting for the right last name to come along.

Evelina found her mother and father in the crowd. Her parents had thrown the biggest bash the Outfit had seen this year. They'd gone all out for Evelina's birthday. Mia stood at her husband's side with an honest smile for the crowd and an eye on her husband. God knew if she didn't keep an eye on him, Riley would run to the first good-looking piece of ass he could find.

Sighing, Evelina leaned against the wall and tried to keep from being noticed. It was hard when the party was for her, and she was supposed to be front row and center for all the people.

When it came to these families, the Trentinis, Rossis, DeLucas, and her own, the Contis, nothing was ever *real*. It was all for show.

The Outfit had always been like that. Who had the most of what, who was trying to step over who, and who could stay on top for the longest. Sure, they played a good game and made nice at the dinner table like all good mafia families did, but jealousy, greed, and violence were always right around the corner.

Evelina felt like her birthday was nothing more than another day. Only this time, she was her family's prize. She was their one thing to show off. The only daughter, a *perfect* daughter. She was at a prime age for her father to begin looking for someone to marry her off to. She could be the Conti family's way to the top in the Outfit, or another crime Syndicate elsewhere.

Her future was uncertain.

This was not a happy day.

"Hey," Adriano said, sliding in beside Evelina.

She gave her younger brother a false smile. "Hey."

"I was outside admiring your new wheels, at least Dad went with a good brand."

"I guess."

Riley had handed Evelina over the keys to a beautiful electric blue two-seater BMW that morning. The car sported a huge pink bow on the hood and white leather on the inside with blue highlights. It was stunning. It was also another way for her father to control her.

The car wasn't freedom as Riley could easily take it away. It probably had trackers on it. Turning eighteen didn't mean a damn thing, as she was still under her father's thumb.

"Mom looks happy," Adriano noted.

"As long as Dad keeps his hands and stares to her, sure."

Adriano chuckled dully. "Truth. Where's your friend?"

"Hmm?"

"Lily. Shouldn't she be here?"

Lily DeLuca had been Evelina's best friend for as long as she could remember. The two went to the same private schools growing up and had always been close. But graduation had come and gone. The girls had left the boarding school to come back to life. Evelina was the only one to return to Chicago.

"No, she's not here," Evelina said.

Adriano frowned. "Where in the hell is she?"

"Dino let her go overseas. She's backpacking and stuff. Traveling."

Being free, having fun, and getting away from here.

Evelina loved her friend, but she was jealous of her, too. Lily's circumstances were not the same as Evelina's. Lily's two older brothers raised her while Evelina was forced home, made to pick a college in Chicago, and do her duty as her father's daughter. Lily's oldest brother, Dino, had set his sister free to do what she wished.

"She'll be back," Adriano said, shrugging. "You can't stay away from family for long."

Evelina doubted it. Lily hated the Outfit for leaving her an orphan.

"Whatever," Evelina said, pushing off the wall. "I'm going to take a walk."

"Don't go far."

Right. Because their father would still want to show her off as much as he could.

"Dad was talking about having a dance with you later or whatever," her brother added.

Evelina shot Adriano a look from the side, taking her brother in. Adriano looked older than his sixteen years. But that wasn't what Evelina noticed the most about her brother. He seemed tired of the day, guests, and party.

Since she had returned home from boarding school, she also noticed

Adriano was beginning to dip his fingers in the family business. That was the thing about the mafia. Once you got your fingers wet, they pushed you right in the pool head first.

Evelina couldn't help but wonder if anyone had given her brother a choice in the matter. Had Adriano stepped into *la famiglia* because he wanted to, or because their father had shoved him into it? She hoped he was better than that and better than this. She hoped Adriano was better than making his wife cry, wonder, and wish.

Better than their mother and father, anyway.

"Don't be like Dad," Evelina said.

Adriano's brow shot up high. "Hmm?"

"You heard me."

Don't be like him, she wanted to say again. *Don't be an asshole. Don't run around on your wife. Don't put your children on show for this stupid game they all play. Be better than Riley Conti.*

"Be a good man, Adriano," Evelina said quietly.

Adriano smiled. "I'm trying."

"I hope so. Cover for me if Dad comes looking?"

"Sure, Eve."

Evelina slipped away from the crowd when she was sure nobody would notice. She wasted no time slipping into the attached garage for a breather away from the people. The garage should have been empty except for her parents' vehicles, but it wasn't. She walked into a glaring contest between two men.

Dino DeLuca stood toe to toe with his brother, Theo. There was a five-year age gap between the two brothers with Theo being the younger brother at only twenty-three. Both had an arm and leg inside the Outfit, considering their uncle Ben DeLuca was the boss's underboss for the operation and the DeLuca side of things had a great deal of power. Evelina could count on one hand the amount of times she had witnessed the two DeLuca brothers share a conversation. Usually, they stuck to opposite sides of the room, did business in passing, and said very little to one another.

She didn't know why they weren't close, but she couldn't remember a time when they had publically fought, either.

"Christ, Theo," Dino hissed, taking a step closer to his younger brother with his fists clenched at his sides. "You just fucking got the goddamn button and already, you're going to screw it up. I can't clean any messes for you, all right. Not anymore. You're in with the family, you clean up your own issues. But use your head. And that does *not* mean sliding in with another family's crew, especially not the Trentinis. Jesus."

Theo sneered, not backing down for a second. "Is this about business or something else?"

"Don't walk that line, Theo."

"I think I want to."

Dino's gaze narrowed. "Don't forget where you came from, little brother. Don't forget who made it possible for you to get in with the Outfit, keep your last name and be proud of it. I did that—don't fuck it up for us, Theo."

"Why in the hell are you so focused on what I'm doing, huh? You didn't give a damn before, Dino."

"Stick to the DeLuca side of the Outfit, Theo. Snakes like Joel Trentini will only bite you when you're not looking."

"Who I do business with is none of your concern, bro."

Dino scoffed. "Right. You keep thinking that."

With those words, Dino stalked past his brother and opened up the side door on the garage that led to the outside. He slammed the door so hard, the wall shuddered. Evelina's legs finally caught up to her brain and she turned around to go back inside the house.

Theo DeLuca's dark tenor stopped her. "Didn't anyone ever teach you that spying on people can get you in trouble, princess?"

Evelina scowled as she met Theo's brown gaze over her shoulder. "Don't call me that."

"What, does it offend your sensibilities, *princess?*"

"Stop," Evelina warned.

"Well, does it?"

"No, but does it look like I'm wearing a crown?"

"Princesses wear tiaras. Crowns are meant for queens, babe." Theo smirked wickedly, his gaze taking her in from the heels on her feet to the dress that fell just above her knees. "But that's all right, too."

Evelina swallowed the lump forming in her throat. "Why is that?"

"Queens make all the rules—they don't get to have much fun."

Damn.

Evelina was unnerved under Theo's stare. The guy had never paid her much attention when they spent time near one another. He was Lily's older brother, sure, but he stuck to his own family and Evelina stuck to hers. Plus, he was five years older than her. They never had anything besides Lily to talk about and he didn't seem interested in chatting about his sister to Evelina.

"Are you always this quiet?" Theo asked.

"No."

"Can you speak more than a few words at a time?"

Evelina glared. "You're an ass."

Theo grinned. "Not always."

She didn't like how his amusement made his features darken, like something wicked was right on the tip of his tongue. It only added to the sexiness that Theo seemed to sport alongside his aloof attitude and quick tongue. With sharp cheekbones, an infallible smirk, a cut-from-steel jaw, and brown eyes that were almost black, Theo was downright fucking gorgeous. There was enough stories about Theo DeLuca and women to go around, as far as that went. Evelina didn't want to be one of them, but she couldn't deny that something about Theo was interesting.

That was a problem.

Evelina couldn't afford to even consider getting mixed up with someone like Theo. For one, because she wasn't allowed to. Dating was a no-go with her father's rules, as was any kind of behavior that would shame her family. Two, because Theo irked Evelina.

In a really good way.

Just standing there watching him watch her, Evelina was curious, anxious, and bothered. All kinds of bothered. She liked it.

"I should go back—"

"Inside?" Theo interrupted with a cock of his brow.

"Yeah."

"Happy birthday, by the way."

Evelina cracked a smile. "Thanks."

"Eighteen, right?"

"Like you don't already know," she said.

"Oh, I know." Theo tipped his chin in her direction, smirking in that way of his. "College in the fall?"

"That's the plan."

"A dorm?"

Evelina fidgeted on the spot, unsure of what Theo was getting at. "Hopefully."

Theo shoved his hands in his pockets in the most unconcerned fashion Evelina had ever seen. He walked the length of the garage and stepped up beside Evelina in the doorway. His fit, tall form crowded her against the doorjamb without even trying. He was tall enough that she had to look up slightly to see his eyes.

"Make sure you get a dorm," Theo said. "No matter what you need to do to get out from under your daddy's thumb, do it."

Evelina nodded. "I'm trying."

"Lily always said you never got to have any fun."

She didn't have a response for that because it was the truth.

Apparently, Theo wasn't expecting one. "Even in boarding school, where Riley couldn't see you, she said you followed the rules."

"You're not a girl," Evelina said.

Theo chuckled. "No."

"And you're not Riley Conti's child."

"Good thing."

"Why?"

"Because that would make this really awkward," Theo murmured, still watching her like she might bolt at any moment. "Get the dorm, Evelina."

"Eve."

Theo flashed his white teeth in a sinful smile. "Get it. Have some fun. Just be smart about it."

"What kind of fun?"

"The bad kind. It's the only kind of fun there is."

"Princesses get to have all the fun, huh?" she asked.

"Whenever the king isn't looking, babe." Theo's right hand left his pocket, and before Evelina realized what happened, he'd caught her bottom lip under the pad of his thumb. "And do me a favor."

Evelina caught his gaze and held it, trying to figure out Theo's game. "What is that?"

"Give me a call after you've gone out and had that fun. You know, once you've had enough."

"Had enough of what?"

Theo's thumb swept her lip before he dropped his hand and stepped inside the house.

"Evelina!"

Her father's shout echoed through the house as Theo DeLuca disappeared down the hall.

"Had enough of what?" she asked again.

Theo ticked a finger in the air, never turning back. "Of acting like a princess."

CHAPTER ONE

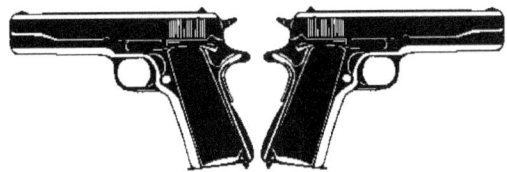

Family is everything.

Theo let those words bang around in his thoughts as he watched the Conti boss kiss his soon-to-be bride on the steps of a familiar church. A church where Theo's older brother had been killed just months before.

Riley Conti's wedding rehearsal had apparently been a small affair. Theo went to check it out before he could talk himself out of it. He knew better than to get caught keeping an eye on the boss, but his mistrust led him to doing things like this a lot lately.

Letting his gaze wander, Theo could still see some of the aftereffects lingering from the bomb that blew up Dino's car. Shaded spots on bricks where the blast had hit. Damage on the parking lot corner where the Bentley's roof had come off and smashed so hard into the ground, it tore the pavement up. Where there had once been beautiful rose bushes planted along the brick fence, dirt now rested as it was early December and occasional flakes of snow had already started falling.

But mostly, the spot looked normal. Except to Theo, it couldn't possibly be normal again.

Family hadn't always been everything to Theo, but it took him too long to realize his errors. He'd figured out a lot since then.

Family was the people who protect you even when you don't give a damn about them. It was the shared blood, the common name, and the memories of a time long past. It was missing what could have been and what should have been, but keeping close what you had.

Family was the weak spot.

It was not a pillar of safety and protection. It was not a comfort and promise of something good. It was the anxiousness slipping through your veins and the worry that it might go away. It was holding on tight because when you let go, it might not come back.

Family was the bomb ready to blow—the one you didn't see coming until it was too late. It was blood on the ground and your heart in your throat. It was terrifying.

Sometimes family hurts.

Sometimes it was the familiarity seeping into a cold heart. Because you don't ever want to lose something that couldn't be replaced. Family shouldn't have been any of those things at all, but it still was.

Family was *sacred*. Something pure, something that should have been held close and protected at all costs. Something untouchable; something loved.

Theo DeLuca had come to the conclusion that his family had been broken long before he could keep it safe. And then suddenly, without warning, their family had been ripped apart again like it had when he was younger. Someone—more than one—had stepped into the holy grounds of his family and spilled their blood without a care.

They'd killed his brother. A long time ago, they'd taken his mother and father, too. *Family* did that. The Outfit had always been family to the DeLucas, after all.

It ached in his soul, but it burned in his heart even worse. When had the DeLuca name that their family worked so hard to keep in power, to keep from being stained again from past mistakes, turned so weak? When had their family been looked at like they were an easy fucking target? When had family turned into something bad?

Theo felt a million miles away from the Outfit and had for a long time. The Outfit had cut too many scars into the people it called family, Theo included. Everyone had marks to show.

No one in this life walked around scarless.

"You're not eating."

Theo glanced up from the steak and potatoes on his plate to find the familiar brown eyes of his sister watching him intently. Her husband sat at the other end of the table, cutting into the steak on his plate, quiet as always. Damian Rossi didn't know how to be loud.

"Theo," Lily said. "Are you going to eat or let your food go cold?"

"I'm eating," Theo replied.

"No, you're pushing your food around on your plate and staring at it."

Damn it.

Lily was far too observant for her own good. When she was a kid, Theo used to think that perceptiveness would be a good thing for her. Then again, five years separated the two siblings with Theo being the oldest at twenty-seven, so he'd always kind of hoped Lily had something inside to keep her going. God knew her brothers wouldn't be able to carry her forever.

Dino was already gone, after all.

Theo's gaze flicked in Damian's direction. The man wasn't watching anything but his wife. It was the one thing Theo took solace in over the last few months. Lily was okay and despite how crazy it was that her marriage to Damian worked out in her favor, she had someone who could keep her safe in the hurricane that was the Outfit

Yeah. A *hurricane*. It was an apt description for their lives and the craziness around them.

"Theo," Lily said again, quieter the second time.

"What, little one?" Theo asked.

"What is up with you?"

A lot.

Mostly, it made Theo feel ten different kinds of awkward whenever he entered Dino's house. His older brother was marked over every inch. It reminded Theo that he'd spent a lot of time trying to be someone else other than Dino DeLuca's brother. By the time he understood none of that was important, it was too late.

"Lily, go get us a couple of drinks, huh?" Damian asked.

Frowning, Lily nodded and pushed out of her chair. Once she was gone from the dining room, Damian turned his attention on Theo. The slate-blue eyes of Theo's companion barely flickered with any emotion or care. Theo didn't mind. The only time Damian cared to show emotion was toward his wife.

"There's a difference between grief and anger," Damian said.

Theo leaned back in his chair. "Oh?"

"Yes, but it's a very fine line."

"So I'm learning."

"Have you learned yet that they often walk hand in hand?"

Theo chuckled dryly. "What are you, the resident therapist, Ghost?"

Damian smirked. "No, just your brother-in-law."

It was automatic. Theo couldn't stop it. He flinched at the word brother, but Damian didn't say a thing. Theo wanted to get the hell off this topic and fast.

"How's the Rossi crew coming?"

"Tedious," Damian replied.

That was life as a Capo.

Damian had finally gotten a crew to control when his cousin Tommas stepped up as the front boss for the operation. With nobody else familiar enough to run the Rossi side of things in the Outfit as a proper Capo, Damian was the first nomination to get the seat.

"I never wanted to be a Capo," Damian said, shrugging. "Someone always fucking needs something. Someone else is whining about this or that. And then you've got all the little pricks on the streets testing your patience at every turn."

"Take a few out," Theo suggested.

"Out?"

"Yeah, whack them, D. Clean it up and spill some blood. Make them afraid. Scare them into compliance. You know this game. Killing is your thing, isn't it? So go on out and do what you do. Trust me, they'll catch on quickly enough and cull the nonsense."

Damian's cool expression didn't change. "Taking a few men out isn't likely to do me any good when I want a strong crew, Theo. Unless, of course, you think dropping my numbers is a good thing to do when there's still a lot of unrest between the families."

It was a valid concern. There was little to no love between the three highest men in the Outfit currently. The boss, Riley, couldn't get his underboss and front boss to work together. Joel Trentini faced off with Tommas Rossi at every chance he could. Tommas brushed Joel off with his usual nonchalance and disinterest.

It made for a bad boss when he couldn't handle his men.

"Bad apples will infect the rest," Theo warned.

"There is no such thing as a bad apple. By nature's course, something will come along and pick up the discarded ones."

"True."

"Have you picked up a few of your own along the way?" Damian asked.

"What is that supposed to mean, D?"

"I think you know, Theo."

"Let's say fuck the runaround and get straight to the dirty point of it all, huh? Besides, I didn't come over here to play word games with you, Damian. I came over here to have dinner with my sister."

Damian chuckled. "Then why aren't you eating?"

Before Theo could answer, Lily slipped back into the dining room with two bottles of beer in hand. She set one in front of Theo before giving her husband the other and then taking her seat.

"As you were saying," Theo said, waving at Damian.

"Maybe you've let a few of the bad apples bleed their way into your good ones."

"I'm not an idiot. There are a hell of a lot of rumors about Dino's death. And I certainly haven't tried to hide my blame and contempt for Riley where that is concerned."

"But you can't deny the whispers of other men's involvement, either."

Men like Joel Trentini.

There were issues with Dino's death and Riley's possible involvement. Dino's murder did little to move Riley along in gaining power and position other than inciting fear in the Outfit. Any person's death would have worked just as well. It didn't make sense. Theo was waiting patiently. Someone was bound to fuck up. Someone, on their way to the top, was going to screw up something and fill in all the blanks.

He would be there waiting when they did.

"Do you think I'm stupid, Damian?" Theo asked.

Lily clicked her tongue chidingly, but both men ignored her quiet warning.

"No, Theo. Not stupid. I think you're grieving."

Theo's jaw clenched. "Maybe so, but let's be real here. Say whatever it is you're chewing on."

Damian passed his quiet wife a look and then said, "What was it that Dino always used to say when we were kids and dipped our hands in other families' games?"

"Stick to our side of Chicago and stop playing with snakes," Theo said.

"Yeah, so maybe you should do that, Theo."

"I am."

Damian cocked a brow. "Artino."

Theo's cheek twitched as he tried to hold back his aggravation. Ever since Dino's passing, Walter Artino had tried taking the DeLuca reigns more and more. It was starting to get annoying. Theo couldn't let the DeLuca name be sullied by the Artino cause.

Simple as that.

"What about him?" Theo asked.

"Not him. The family. The entire bunch."

"Again, do you think I'm stupid, Damian?"

Damian's lips flattened into a grim line. "You need to be careful, Theo. Nobody is out to help you right now. Once people get in, you can't get them out."

Theo laughed, brushing off the comment and his sister's curious look. "There's always a way to get them out, Damian. It's called a bullet."

"And this feud your guys have with the Conti crew," Damian added.

"I don't know what you're talking about."

Damian scoffed. "Sure."

"I show up to tribute. I give Riley his dues. I follow the fucking rules, D."

"And you keep letting blood spill all the while. Stop that before it gets out of hand again, Theo."

"I am not the one fighting with the Conti crew."

"Theo," Lily said softly. "Things are quiet with the families right now.

Let them stay that way."

"Things have never been quiet," Damian replied before Theo could. "Too much has been left unsaid for the families to be quiet, sweetheart."

Lily frowned, but didn't respond.

"Where is this coming from, anyway?" Theo asked.

Damian cut a piece of his steak and kept his eyes down on his plate. "A friend to a friend, Theo. Besides, you know me. I take care of what's mine. Family is important."

Sure.

Except Damian was a Rossi.

"Which family is that?" Theo asked.

"The only one that matters, of course."

That answered everything, didn't it?

"Are you going to the wedding tomorrow?" Lily asked.

Theo scowled. "No."

"But—"

"Riley Conti doesn't need me at his wedding, Lily. Walter is going, anyway. That's enough for our side of things."

"Is he the only one going?" Damian asked.

"Yes," Theo answered.

"You're making a pretty bold statement there, Theo."

The world didn't revolve around Riley Conti.

"Adriano—"

Theo held up a hand, stopping Damian before he could get in another word. "I'm not concerned about Adriano Conti's little feud with some of the DeLuca crew. I told him on the night Riley became boss that I wanted nothing from him."

"Your men's actions on the street say differently," Damian said.

"That's my men, not me," Theo replied coolly.

"Yours or Walter's?"

"Exactly."

Damian didn't move as he took in that statement. "I guess you're not as blind as I thought."

"I like this, though," Theo said.

"Taking the blame for Walter's revenge because of his son's death?"

Theo laughed darkly. "No, making Riley uncomfortable. He's probably wondering when I'm going to strike him."

"Are you going to?"

"I haven't decided yet," Theo answered honestly.

"What if I told you that Riley didn't order the hit on Dino," Damian said.

"It wouldn't make a difference."

"Why not?"

"Because right now, it's more than just Dino. And even if it was just about him, there are only a few men who I can point the finger at. They're all pretty high right now, Damian."

"Your point?" Damian asked.

"Sometimes you have to take out the top and wait for the rest to crumble in on itself. It's the only way to get out clean."

Theo didn't want to be the boss. It wasn't about that at all. People could believe what they wanted. The war wasn't over.

Not even close.

"Here, let me help you," Theo said, grabbing the pile of plates his sister was balancing.

Lily smiled and let him take the dirty dishes. "Gentleman, huh? No wonder there are all those rumors about you and a dozen different women. They can't say no to the charm, Theo. You should put that to use and find yourself someone to settle down with."

Theo barely held back from scoffing. He was not a gentleman. A little rough around the edges. Cold in his heart. Bloodthirsty on the streets.

DeLuca born and bred.

DeLucas didn't make nice, pillow-talking, sweet-touching bedfellows. A good, hard fuck that was sure to leave him satisfied, worn out, and dirty? Sure. But being a gentleman didn't fall into that category at all.

Theo wished his sister didn't hear anything about his bedroom activities. Lily didn't need to be concerning herself with who he was or was not fucking. He wasn't nasty enough to tell her to mind her business, though.

"No, but you're my sister and all," Theo settled on saying. "So maybe you stick to bothering me about keeping my bachelor apartment clean and not who I should be filling it with."

"Hey, I was just saying."

"I don't need you to, Lily."

Lily hummed under her breath like she didn't believe him. "Whatever, Theo. Someone's going to come along and you won't even see them coming."

"Not everybody wants someone, Lily."

"Keep telling yourself that."

He would.

The last thing Theo needed was some female inserting herself into his life and getting him caught up in a mess he couldn't clean. He had enough of that going on with the Outfit and his streets, never mind his family.

Women?

Not anytime soon.

Theo followed Lily into the kitchen, deposited the plates where she directed, and then he proceeded to help Lily rinse them off before filling the dishwasher. The two siblings stayed quiet as they worked. Damian had excused himself after supper saying he had phone calls to make.

"It's the house, isn't it?" Lily asked quietly.

She didn't take her eyes off the dishwasher as she pressed the buttons. She'd left her crystal wine glass sitting on the counter to wash by hand.

"What about the house, little one?"

"It reminds you of Dino. Right?"

Theo shifted restlessly, leaning back against the cupboard. "Why would you think that?"

"You don't come over much anymore."

"I didn't come over much when Dino was alive."

It was the truth.

Theo had spent too many years trying to get out from under Dino's name. He hadn't wanted to be just Dino DeLuca's younger brother growing up. He wanted his own name being carried through the streets and the men in the Outfit.

He'd gotten his wish.

In all the wrong ways.

Before Theo realized all the good his brother had done by actually giving the DeLucas a well-positioned, safe spot in the Outfit, it was gone. And so was Dino.

Theo felt the ice slip back into his veins like a familiar friend giving him comfort. It wouldn't leave now.

"You were coming around a little bit more," Lily said.

"Like any good brother would do."

Dino was dead. The brothers never got the chance to fix their burned bridges.

"It's better to leave the dog where he is than wake him up and beat him," Theo told his sister.

Lily's lips pursed like she wasn't pleased with his answer, but thankfully, she didn't push him on it. "Fine. Are you going to stay a while?"

"No, I need to head out. Big day tomorrow and all that."

"I thought you weren't going to the wedding."

Theo smirked. "I'm not. That doesn't mean I won't be around, Lily."

Riley Conti wasn't the only man Theo had to keep an eye on, after all.

"Thanks for helping me clean up, Theo."

"Of course."

Pushing off the counter, Theo's eye caught sight of a familiar bottle of red wine. He'd brought it over for his sister because he knew she liked red wine with her steak. Plus, it wasn't nice to show up to someone's home without bringing some kind of a gift.

"Is that not the brand you like?" Theo asked, plucking up the bottle to read the label.

"What are you going on about?"

"The wine, Lily."

Lily's gaze widened as she noticed the bottle in his hands. "Shit, I meant to put that away."

Why?

Theo glanced down at the bottle again. This was Lily's brand, circa 40s and specially imported from Sicily. It was expensive as hell, but his sister was worth the money.

"Saving it or something?" Theo asked, amused.

Lily's teeth caught her bottom lip, and Theo knew right then a lie was on the tip of her tongue. She wasn't any good at lying and her brothers had always known when she did tell one.

"Lily," Theo said quietly, "you were drinking from a wine glass tonight."

"Yes."

The glass was a blue colored crystal and still sitting on the counter.

"Not the wine I brought you."

Lily sighed. "God, why can't you leave things alone?"

"Because you're my sister and I worry," Theo replied.

"About which brand of wine I drink?"

"No, about why you wanted me to think you were drinking this wine. If you didn't want it, you could have—"

"I can't drink wine, Theo, and I didn't want to be rude."

Theo's brow shot up high. "Excuse me?"

"I can't drink wine. Not for another eight months."

It took Theo far too long to realize what his sister was saying. He grew still as his gaze flicked between the wine in his hands and the smile playing on Lily's mouth.

"We're not ready to start telling people, Theo," Lily added softer. "There's a lot of unhappiness between the families and problems happening. Plus, Adriano and Alessa just announced their pregnancy a few weeks ago and that's still sinking in."

"Yes, but you two are married and weren't sneaking around behind your families' backs," Theo said, trying to figure out how Adriano Conti and Alessa Trentini's pregnancy made any difference to his sister's.

"I know that," Lily replied. "The fact still remains, they shouldn't be shamed any more than they've already been by the Outfit, Theo. It's a baby, people should be happy. They're getting married next month. It's all settled. I'm not the kind of woman who will flaunt my pregnancy for others to use it, and say that's how it should be, not how theirs happened to come about."

Theo rubbed at his temple as he set the wine bottle down. "The whispers won't stop after they get married, Lily."

"Maybe not, but I still think they should be able to enjoy this time and have a bit of happiness just for them."

"Selfless girl."

"She is," Damian said from the kitchen entryway.

Theo tried to not to react to his brother-in-law's sudden presence. Damian did that shit far too often. "Congrats are in order, I guess."

"Thank you," Lily said, smiling.

"It didn't take you two very long."

"Theo!"

Damian chuckled, but stayed quiet.

Theo shrugged. "Just saying it like it is."

"I'm sorry for lying about the wine but I'll put it in the cellar."

Winking, Theo ticked his sister under the chin.

"Do that," he said, "and the day my niece or nephew is born, we'll bring it out and celebrate. I'll even sneak it into your hospital room."

Lily grinned wide. "Yeah?"

"Absolutely."

"That's awful," Damian said under his breath. "I'm going to pretend like you two aren't planning something like that."

Theo flipped his brother-in-law the middle finger.

The baby might carry the Rossi name because of its father, but it was still half DeLuca, too. Family was everything. The only thing Theo knew to hold close. He learned that lesson the hard way.

CHAPTER TWO

Evelina poked her head into the living room entryway to find Alessa rifling through another bag of baby clothes with tags still attached. "Adriano drop that off earlier?"

Alessa glanced up, grinning. "Yeah."

That was kind of cute. Adriano didn't seem to be freaking out over the fact he would be a father in just a few short months. The two were prepared.

"But he just picked this up for me, he didn't go crazy again," Alessa informed.

Her voice was soft and quiet as she spoke. It wasn't unusual. Alessa Trentini, soon to be a Conti when she married Adriano in a little over a month, wasn't a loud person. She tended to stick to herself, keep a low profile, and was a pretty happy person even on her bad days.

"Oh?" Evelina asked.

"Abriella picked up some outfits, I guess."

Oh.

"And Adriano had to play middle man and pick them up from someone, I take it?"

Alessa nodded. "She passed them off to Tommas and he gave Adriano a call."

Evelina didn't want to make Alessa sad by acknowledging the fact that Abriella wasn't permitted to spend time with her sister. The two were close, but ever since the debacle Alessa and Adriano created with the pregnancy, Joel Trentini was pretending as if his youngest sister didn't exist. Like he was trying to wipe away the shame.

There wasn't very much to be ashamed about. It was a baby with young parents who needed support and love in this new stage of their lives. Besides, the pregnancy had done a lot for Joel. After all Joel had done to Evelina's father, Riley, the guy should have been killed by the Outfit standards. Instead, to apologize for the wrongs Riley's son had done with Joel's sister, Joel was given a high position, respect for having the seat as the underboss to the Outfit, and more control than he needed.

Riley was asking for trouble doing that.

"If you see Abriella," Alessa said, "tell her I said thanks."

"You'll see her tomorrow at the wedding," Evelina replied. "Tell her then."

"Joel will be there."

"Don't let him shame you into a corner like you've got a big scarlet letter painted on your forehead, Lissa."

Alessa sighed and dropped the cute mint green sleeper set into the gift bag. "Listen, it's not about Joel, it's about Adriano. I don't give a shit about my brother, but I don't want to cause Adriano any problems by making a fuss. Abriella calls me when she can, sometimes we see each other here and there, and that's fine. I also don't want to cause problems for my sister. I know what Joel is like, Eve."

"Yeah, you've told me."

Joel was an asshole. A manipulative snake was more like it.

"So there you go. Until Joel feels like we've all paid enough for embarrassing him—"

Evelina barked out a laugh, interrupting Alessa. "He's done enough of that for himself, babe."

Even Alessa cracked a sly smile. "I know."

"Anyway, I get it. I'll pass the message on directly tomorrow, but you should really do it yourself. Screw Joel, he'll probably be too busy raking in attention as the new underboss."

Alessa snorted. "Yeah. Typical Joel."

"Where is my brother?" Evelina asked.

"Work."

Alessa didn't offer anything else, and Evelina knew better than to press for more information. Adriano was secretive about his position and work in the Outfit. He tried his damnedest to keep it from coming home. Evelina had to admit, she was proud of her younger brother. Adriano hadn't turned out like Riley Conti, after all. He was better than their father. A better man; a more loving, caring one.

"Is he going to be back anytime soon?" Evelina asked.

Alessa shrugged. "Tonight, maybe."

"Do you want to come over to Lily's with me so you're not alone?"

"No, I'm good, thanks." Alessa waved at the gift bags full of baby stuff. "Priorities, you know."

"Well, at least you've got them figured out. The rest of us don't have a fucking clue."

Alessa laughed. "It's sad how right you are."

Evelina recognized the cherry red Stingray parked in Lily Rossi's driveway the second it came into view. Lily hadn't said anything about her older brother Theo coming over. Riley had made it clear to Evelina that she was to steer clear of Theo at all costs. Her father hadn't given much of a reason why, except to say that there had been some unresolved issues between the DeLucas and Contis after Riley became boss.

Regardless, Evelina didn't mind following her father's demand to keep a distance. While Riley's temperament had gotten better over the last couple of months since he became boss, Evelina couldn't shake the reminder that her father was not the man he appeared to be. She still refused to go back home because Riley wouldn't allow her to go back to her dorm. So, she stayed with her brother. Her father conceded.

It didn't change a thing to Evelina. Riley Conti could dress himself up all he wanted, but to Evelina, he was just a king wearing a stolen crown. How long would her father be able to last as the boss of the Outfit before someone else realized it, too?

Evelina parked her BMW beside the Stingray, got out, and pulled the garment bags from the back seat. She barely made it half way across the paved driveway before the home's front door opened. Theo darkened the doorway with Damian Rossi. Neither man noticed Evelina standing just thirty feet away.

Theo DeLuca didn't seem to age. Just like the day of Evelina's eighteenth birthday when she'd accidentally stumbled on him and his brother's argument, he still stood with an uncaring confidence that oozed with learned arrogance and cockiness. The man's features were still as striking as ever with sharp cheekbones, a strong jaw and hair that looked like some female had been wrapping her hands in and pulling on the blond strands. The shadow of a smirk still kept the corner of Theo's mouth twisted upward, even with the sadness darkening his brown gaze.

Evelina supposed the man had a lot to be sad for, now. His brother had been murdered and his uncle, too. Even his sister had been taken in a way what with her marriage to a Rossi. The Rossi family was closer to the DeLucas than the rest, but Lily was still settling into her new life.

Who did Theo have left? Himself. His crew, considering he was the head Capo with Dino DeLuca dead. The Outfit … maybe.

Evelina suspected Theo blamed the Outfit for a lot of what was happening to his family. Who wouldn't? Maybe that was why her father demanded she stay away from him.

A grieving man was a dangerous man.

"You've got a guest, Ghost."

Theo passed Evelina a look. His glance was almost dismissive in nature, like he had taken her in and then pushed the picture of her right back out again.

"Yeah, Lily and clothes, you know. The wedding," Damian muttered. "I'd say see you tomorrow and all, but we both know you're not going to be there."

"Nope."

With that, Theo tossed his hands in his pockets and turned away from the door to make his way down the front steps. His strides were smooth and quick, and he held his head low like he was looking around but no one could see his eyes. It made Evelina think that maybe Theo liked to have people wonder about him and never really know a thing.

But who was she to say?

"Eve," Theo murmured as he passed.

Cordial. Polite.

Stressed.

Tense.

Evelina caught all that in her name coming out of his mouth. She also caught the sweep of his brown eyes looking her over again and the way his smirk deepened. She didn't like how that one look seemed to slap her skin without him ever raising a hand.

A memory bled into her mind with the slowness of syrup.

"You never gave me that call, princess," Theo said.

Evelina pursed her lips, sipping on the wine in her glass as people milled around at her friend's homecoming party. Lily DeLuca smiled and chatted with the guests, but she was pissed as hell. Evelina knew it. After all, who wanted to be married off like cattle to a man you didn't know? Even if that man was a half decent one.

"Don't call me that, Theo," Evelina warned.

Theo chuckled. "Still sore about that?"

He called her a princess every damn chance he got. Yes, it bothered her.

"No, but I'm not one, so quit it."

"What did I tell you, huh?" Theo asked, turning his shoulder to the wall so he could face her while she watched the crowd.

Evelina smiled, unable to hold it back. She couldn't deny the fact she liked Theo's attention. He was damned gorgeous, especially wearing a fitted suit that accentuated the fact he was in shape, tall, and every inch of him gave off dangerous vibes. He was tall, dark, and sexy and he fucking knew it. That was the worst part.

"You're smiling," Theo said smugly. "That means you like me."

"You're crazy."

"Get tired of acting like a princess, yet?"

Evelina took another sip of wine and swallowed it down. "Have I called on you, yet?"

"I'm starting to think women like you need a little shove," Theo said, grinning.

Oh, Christ.

Evelina could practically feel her father's eyes watching her from wherever he was in the room. Riley Conti was always keeping one eye on her, or he had someone else doing it.

"You're going to get me in shit," Evelina told Theo quietly.

"For having a conversation?"

"For flirting with me, Theo."

Theo chuckled. "This isn't flirting. However ..."

Evelina eyed him from the side. "What?"

He took a step closer. Close enough for her to smell the fresh scent of his woodsy cologne. Theo's tongue wet his bottom lip where his thumb was touching as he moved closer again. Her arm brushed his chest and she swore every muscle jumped under the simple touch. Evelina fought the hot shiver working its way down her spine as Theo reached up and dragged the pad of his thumb down her arm. He stopped at the inside crease of her elbow. She didn't even realize it until he pressed his thumb into her skin again, but his digit was wet from his lips and he'd made a pathway on her arm. She felt almost sensitive under that caress. Because no doubt, it wasn't innocent at all.

"Now this," Theo whispered, "might be considered flirting."

Evelina's cheeks heated. "What game are you playing tonight, DeLuca?"

"What do you mean?"

"I'm not a conquest for you to take to bed, Theo."

Theo cocked a brow. "I don't chase after women, Eve."

"Funny. That's not what I hear."

"Maybe you shouldn't believe everything you hear," he responded quietly.

Evelina felt his thumb sweep the inside crease of her elbow again.

"I don't run after women," Theo repeated. "They either come to me or they don't. I don't go pussy chasing every chance I can to add new names to my list."

"Then what in the hell are you doing right now?" Evelina asked.

"Good question."

"Excuse me?"

"There's something about you, Eve. It makes me want to find out what it is."

"Like a chase," she said.

"Just like that."

"Why?" she asked.

"Why are you still acting like a princess?" he asked back.

"You don't know me at all, Theo, not if you think that." Evelina searched through the crowd again, looking for her father. "You are going to get me in trouble."

"Babe, I'm a terribly careful man. It's my job to be careful. Otherwise, I'd be dead."

Damn.

Evelina didn't want to show how his words affected her, so she lowered her gaze to the wine in her glass. "Is that so?"

"Yes."

"Hmm."

"Tuesday," Theo said. "The thirtieth."

"What about it?"

"Giselle. The ballet. Go with me."

Evelina clenched the stem of her wine glass a little harder. There was no twinkle in his eye, no smirk left on his lips. Not a thing to suggest it was an option or a joke. In fact, Theo watched her like he was waiting for her to bolt.

She had news for him—she wasn't a scared little doe. But she was terribly careful.

"You're serious," Evelina said, taking that in for a second.

"Very. Go with me."

"I didn't give you the call you wanted, Theo."

"I'm giving you a shove, Eve."

"Why me?" Evelina asked.

Theo shrugged. "I told you, there's something about you I want to know."

"That's not a very good answer."

"Then give me a better one."

Evelina jerked back into the present at the sound of a car door slamming shut. She turned on her heel in just enough time to see Theo smirk as he revved his engine.

She was standing in front of his car and blocking his way from turning out as he couldn't back out with her car blocking the turning section of the driveway. Evelina stared into the windshield, catching Theo's eye. His face was passive, other than the cocky grin he wore, but a fire still glimmered in the darkness of his irises.

Maybe he hadn't quite forgiven her for flaking out of that date a while back. She hadn't meant to, but her father demanded she go to the Rossi restaurant for dinner. And then her mother was murdered in a drive-by shooting the same day.

"Hey," Evelina mouthed.

She didn't want Theo to think she was ignoring him. He'd never really asked her why she cancelled that date, but she figured he knew what with her mother's death and everything. It wasn't a secret that she had been at the dinner, too.

A ghost of a smile graced Theo's mouth before it disappeared. The coldness was back in a blink, hardening his handsome features. Evelina couldn't help but notice how Theo seemed older than his twenty-seven years sitting there in his car, watching her.

"Move," Theo mouthed. "Now."

Evelina tipped her chin up, defiant. She didn't know why, but Theo always irked her in that way. He made her want to push back. There wasn't a lot of people who could get under her skin like Theo had. It was too bad that she never got the chance to explore it.

Theo revved his car again, the engine roaring loud enough to make Evelina cringe.

She moved.

"Did you see Theo outside?" Lily asked.

Evelina cleared her throat and tossed the garment bags over the bottom of the bed. "Yeah, but he didn't say much."

Lily frowned and passed a look toward the doorway of the bedroom. Evelina followed her friend's stare to find Damian standing there, but he walked away. He didn't say a word to his wife or Evelina before he went, either.

Evelina liked her cousin, as far as that went. Damian was a pretty easy-going but quiet man. He didn't like to make a fuss and he adored his new bride. That much was evident. But there was also a darker side to Damian Rossi, one that a lot of people didn't get to see.

"What's up with him?" Evelina asked Lily.

"Damian?"

"Yeah."

Lily shrugged and pawed through the garment bags, taking her time to unzip each one and peer inside. "Theo's visit put him on edge, I think."

"He's your brother, Lily."

"I'm aware."

"Damian should get used to him being around."

Lily laughed, standing straight to face Evelina. "It's not that he doesn't like Theo. Friends since they were kids, remember?"

"I know."

"Damian is worried that his friend is going to do something crazy because of all the crap he's been put through these last few months," Lily said.

"Oh." Evelina sighed. "My father?"

"Partly, but there's other stuff, too. I think, anyway. With Theo, it's hard to tell. Sometimes you think he doesn't know a thing about anything around him and then other times, he opens his mouth and shocks you silent with what he's learned. I just ..."

"What?" Evelina pressed.

"This isn't Theo. That quiet, cold person. It's not Theo. He's happy and loud. He's a charmer through and through."

"That he is."

Lily raised a single brow high. "And how do you know?"

Shit.

Evelina grabbed the first bag she could reach and opened it up, wanting to try and distract her friend from delving too deep into her statement. "I'm just saying, Lily. We all know Theo likes his women."

"Actually, I think my brother likes to let people believe what they want to believe. Is that to say he's a saint? No, but he's never been a big personal sharer, either."

"Maybe," Evelina agreed.

Leave it alone, Lily, Evelina begged silently.

Lily sighed softly, grabbing a bag for herself. "And how are you doing?"

"Fine."

"You sure?" Lily asked.

"Yep."

"Your father is marrying a woman only a couple of years older than you tomorrow, Eve."

Barely even that, actually. Evelina forced back her scowl and opinion of Courtney, her father's new and very young fiancée, and pulled the black dress out of the bag. It looked nice and appropriate.

"Oh, my God," Lily said, laughing. "Please tell me you didn't bring all black dresses to choose from to wear tomorrow."

Well, Evelina considered it. Black was fitting. Tomorrow felt like a funeral instead of a wedding.

"I don't like her," Evelina murmured, never taking her eyes off the dress.

"Courtney?"

"Who else?"

Lily tugged on the dress, drawing in Evelina's attention. "She's young."

"She's spoiled," Evelina shot back. "She's bitchy and needy. Every time I go over there, she gets even clingier with my father like she thinks I give a damn about them and she has to over compensate for something. And she's nasty, Lily."

Lily snorted. "You can handle her."

"I can."

And Evelina had, repeatedly. That didn't mean she liked Courtney Calabrese.

"Isn't she the half-sister of Matteo Calabrese from the New York family?" Lily asked.

"Yeah, she's Carl's daughter from his second marriage. She was here for school. Her family here is kind of low down on the totem pole for the Rossi crew or whatever, but they're mixed up in the Outfit."

"Huh," Lily said faintly.

Evelina wasn't surprised that her friend didn't know a lot of the connected people in Chicago. Lily had always been sheltered by her brothers in that way. Evelina wished she had been, too, but with a front boss for a father, she had the best seat in the house day after day.

"Talk to me," Lily said, drawing Evelina out of her thoughts.

"I'll be fine."

"You mean to say you'll plaster on a smile, make face, and do the right thing tomorrow."

"Essentially," Evelina said.

"So tell me how you really feel."

Evelina bit the inside of her cheek before whispering, "My mother has only been dead a few months and he's already marrying someone new, Lily. He didn't give a damn at all. My father doesn't care about anyone but himself. But this is how it goes, right? This is the way the Outfit works and we just follow the rules."

"The boss needs a wife," Lily replied, sadness coloring up her tone.

"He does. So help me pick out a dress. I can go to my father's wedding tomorrow, pretend like I give a damn about him and his spoiled little wife, and not look like I'm going to a funeral at the same time."

Lily nodded. "I can do that."

Best friends. Lily had been right all those months ago, Evelina realized. The two women slipped right back into their old routine without even a bump. How long would it last before they were torn apart again by someone else's desire to get higher in the Outfit?

In this life, peace was a goddamn myth.

"Smile," Lily told Evelina as she slid in beside her friend.

Evelina tried her damnedest not to glare at her father and Riley's new bride as the two kissed on the steps of the church in front of guests. Lights flashed and shutters of cameras clicked repeatedly as pictures of the day were captured for the happy fucking couple.

"I'm smiling," Evelina said.

"With a kill-kill-kill look in your eyes," Lily replied, giggling.

Evelina caught sight of Adriano as he exited the church with Alessa at his side. Like usual, her younger brother's hand was firmly attached to Alessa's slightly rounded stomach and all of his attention was on her. Adriano nodded in his father's direction as he whispered in Alessa's ear and hugged his fiancée tight. It was sweet. A far sweeter, more honest love than Riley and Courtney's show.

Evelina wondered how long her father had been actually messing with the girl. Probably a while. Maybe even when her mother was alive. That just burned like acid was being poured straight into her veins.

Sighing, Evelina shook off the annoyance.

"People were going on about Alessa and Adriano again," Lily noted.

Evelina heard the whispers. She sat beside her brother and Alessa throughout the ceremony, wanting to give them some sense of support in the vapid harshness that could be the Outfit and its people.

"Smile and tell them to eat their fucking hearts out," Evelina said, smiling coldly. "Half of them are just jealous that Adriano and Alessa got what they wanted in the end—each other. The rest just want something to gossip about because they're bored."

"Truth." Lily hummed, scanning the parking lot of the church. "Oh!"

"What?" Evelina followed her friend's stare to find Theo leaning against his cherry red Stingray at the very edge of the parking lot. "Didn't you say he wasn't coming?"

"Theo said he wouldn't be here," Lily replied.

"There he is."

But he didn't look happy. In fact, he looked like ice—beautiful like crystal and cold all over. Theo watched Riley Conti kiss his bride again.

Evelina had a feeling whatever this was … this war, the fighting that had quieted down, and the peace that had been made … it was just about ready to blow up again.

She didn't even care.

CHAPTER THREE

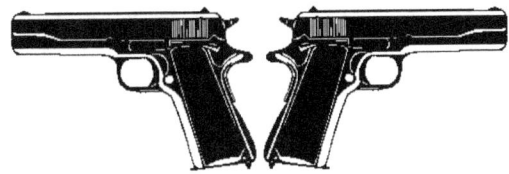

Politics.

The mafia was all about the politics.

Theo considered those words as he watched the crowd from Riley Conti's wedding party and guests flood out to the steps of the church. By the size of the gathering crowd, most of the Outfit and the connected families had shown up to give their well-wishes to the couple. The politics of the Outfit demanded these people show up and give their boss well-wishes and respect, even if they hated the man and didn't think he deserved it at all.

Theo knew Riley would be taking a trip out of the city with his new wife for a week and a half, although where exactly was a mystery. Anger burned heavily in Theo's gut, like a poison killing him slowly.

Theo found his sister in the crowd of people. Evelina Conti was at her side, talking.

Evelina had always been a bit of an enigma to Theo. She was younger than him by five years and the daughter of a man he hated. She'd caught his eye back when he was twenty-three, and she'd just come home from boarding school.

Theo liked trouble back then. Evelina was sweet, good-natured and followed all the rules. Seeing if he could make her break them would have given him all the trouble he wanted. She never even batted an eye at him. Theo loved a good challenge, but as the Outfit took over his life, his interests in that sort of thing faded.

She was still there in the back of his mind, though. *Waiting.*

Theo didn't know what to do about that. He'd never understood his curiosity with the Conti *principessa*. Except maybe her loyalty to the life and her family, even when she clearly wasn't happy with them, reminded him of what the Outfit was supposed to be about.

No divides, or families working against one another. *Famiglia* was most important.

But Evelina wouldn't happen, not with Theo. He'd given her a chance months ago and she didn't take it. While he knew the details about her mother's murder and why she had cancelled their date, the girl never contacted him back. Theo didn't give second chances and she was on the other side of the divide.

The cold chill of the December air bit into Theo's cheeks and exposed skin. Shoving his hands into his pockets, he watched the people for a little while longer. He wondered what would hurt them the most, like he had been hurt, but mostly, he wondered what would make them change. What would make them understand that they were no longer *la famiglia*, they were foul and untrue?

Yeah, politics.

Follow orders.

Make money.

Obey the boss.

Make money.

Pay the boss.

Make more money.

Stick to the rules.

That was enough for Theo. He was tired of these people. Tired of their games. Tired of the goddamn *politics*. The Outfit was more than just the people. And when the people forgot about loyalty and honor, it all went to shit anyway.

They all thought he was fucking stupid. Like he was blind to their tricks. The young DeLuca *principe* who was unable to stand on his own or hold his spot.

Theo had news for them.

"I didn't see you at the wedding," Walter mumbled around the rim of his scotch-filled glass.

Theo eyed his companion, hoping his blank expression was enough to make Walter drop the topic of the Conti wedding. It'd been two days since the nuptials and as far as Theo knew, Riley was off with his wife on their honeymoon to wherever.

"I'm talking to you," Walter said, cocking a brow.

"I was around."

That was the most Theo would give the Artino Capo. Theo didn't hide his contempt for the Outfit boss, so he wasn't about to show an ounce of support for him, either.

Walter, on the other hand, had gone to the wedding with a suit on, fake smile plastered to his face, and good-wishes rolling off his snake tongue. Yeah, Theo knew. Walter talked a big game where the boss was concerned, especially considering his son Dean Artino had been killed by Riley's son, but Walter was a snake all the same.

Slithering up to the side of any man who would keep him there and then biting the asshole when the guy wasn't looking. Snakes couldn't be trusted.

Walter swirled the scotch in his glass, keeping his stare on Theo all the while. Sitting across from one another in Walter's home office, the DeLuca Capos were supposed to be discussing business. Instead, Walter kept poking at Theo regarding Riley.

Theo wasn't interested.

"Streets were quiet this week," Walter noted.

"I noticed."

"Heard you pulled that synthetic coke off before the guys could run with it."

"It's dangerous."

"And real coke isn't?" Walter asked, oozing with sarcasm. "Listen, Theo, it is easy money. You might as well get the dealers' hands full of it, sell as much of it as you can, and make some cash instead of losing out by getting rid of it."

"It's dangerous," Theo repeated simply.

Walter sighed heavily. "Hey—"

"Seven out of ten people overdose or have extreme reactions to it. Do you really think that's the kind of attention the Outfit needs right now? You would have a dozen different officials all over the streets looking for the pricks putting that shit out there and it'll lead right back to the Outfit. We don't need to be in the news for anything else this year, Walter."

Walter's lips drew thin in his frustration, but the fool stayed silent.

This was Theo's main problem with the head of the Artino family. They had long since worked with the DeLuca side of the Outfit, especially Walter. Given the familial ties between Walter's wife and Theo's deceased uncle Ben, the two families were close. Walter had run the DeLuca crew as a second Capo alongside Dino when he was alive.

Theo worked under Dino, for the most part. But now, with Dino dead, Walter seemed to think he had some kind of control over Theo and the DeLuca crew. It was almost like the man thought he could run it all and Theo would just blindly follow along.

It was sickening.

"Do you think I'm a fool?" Theo asked, standing from his chair.

Walter placed his glass to the desk and crossed his arms. "I beg your pardon?"

"Do you think I'm a fool? It's a yes or no question."

"I think you're young, like my boy was," Walter said.

Theo barked out a laugh. "Dean is not comparable to me, Walter."

Except maybe in Walter's eyes. Father's always did see no wrong in their children, especially their sons. And in doing so, those boys turned into spoiled rotten little brats. Kind of like how Dean Artino had been.

"It's called the DeLuca crew for a reason, Walter."

"I'm aware of what the name of my crew is."

My crew.

Right there.

Signed, sealed, and fucking delivered.

Theo was done.

"I didn't mind all that much, you know," Theo said as he did up the buttons on his suit.

"Didn't mind what?" Walter asked.

"All that bullshit you were causing and the trouble you stirred. Out there on the streets, I mean. I get it, you were pissed off about Dean and you wanted some kind of action, so you had it whispered on the streets that Theo DeLuca was going to the mattresses with the Conti crew. A little bullet sharing here, a man down there ... no one really knew because no one ever saw until it was too late. And of course, it came back to me because I'm the easy target, Walter."

"I—"

"Oh, shut up with it," Theo snapped.

Walter blinked, anger heating his gaze as the man stood fast. "I think it's just about time for you to go, Theo. You've clearly forgotten which Capo in this room is the highest between us and which one of us has the connections to the throne."

Theo smiled, cold and slow. Mistake number two. "Do you?"

"You heard what I said."

"Riley Conti has the throne and he wouldn't look twice at you, Walter."

Walter clenched his fists at his sides. Panic. The man was looking for an acceptable excuse. He'd already given too much. Mistake number three.

"I was going back and forth between Joel, too, these last few months," Theo informed as he grabbed his Stingray keys off the side of Walter's desk. "But I was so stupid and stuck inside my own head because of Ben and Dino being killed that I couldn't focus on anything else. It made sense for me to push my anger at Riley and side myself with the only person who I thought would give him a challenge for the boss's seat. And you were right there, too. Weren't you?"

Walter swallowed hard. "You know I was. I still am. What is your point?"

"Still are," Theo echoed.

"So?"

"I was good with it, Walter. I didn't mind taking the blame for your revenge on the Conti crew in the name of your son. I didn't mind my name being thrown out there to put Riley on edge. I didn't mind being the fall guy for a time."

"I never—"

"You're a liar, so don't even bother to start," Theo cut in. "Everyone thinks I'm too young to handle a crew the size of the DeLucas on my own. They think I'm too wild because they don't know a fucking thing about me. They all think I make decisions with my heart."

"You have before," Walter pointed out.

He had and Theo learned his lesson. His heart and pride demanded distance be put between him and his older brother. The shared past they had growing up under Ben and Carmela DeLuca after their parents' murder was forgotten. All that tough love and ass kicking's from their uncle because they weren't men enough, and they weren't cold enough had been pushed to the side.

Ben's way of making the DeLuca brothers comply with whatever he wanted had always been physical, violent, and bloody. Theo thought with his heart back then. Dino ended up killed. Theo never corrected his heart with his head. He wouldn't make that mistake again.

"I can't have you fucking this up for me," Theo said quietly.

Walter's brow rose high. "Me? Theo, your brother was killed right under your nose without you even knowing a thing. You were both at the church that morning yet neither one of you noticed anyone putting the bomb on the Bentley. Do you realize the kind of effort it takes for a radio timer bomb like that to be set up? You're too focused on everything else to realize it's more than just you. Maybe, had you paid more attention, Dino would still be alive. A crew like the DeLucas cannot be run by someone like you—someone young and rash and incapable of leaving his heart behind."

Theo only heard three words in that whole diatribe: *radio timer bomb...*

Rage was a beautiful feeling. It was almost as good as being high. It had the ecstasy of sex and the sweetness of candy. It filled Theo like nothing else. He held it tight and didn't let go.

"What did you just say?"

Theo's voice had dipped threateningly low. It dripped with a warning that any intelligent man would be able to hear. Standing still and quiet, Theo could feel his rage flooding every inch of his body.

"About what?" Walter asked sharply.

"Radio timer bomb," Theo said. "*Radio. Timer. Bomb.*"

"What about it?"

In the Outfit, trust was a goddamn myth.

"That was unreleased information," Theo said coolly.

The coldness was back in a blink. Comforting. Safe. Good. Theo liked the iciness. It kept him alive.

Walter's gaze widened. "I-I ..."

"Keep mumbling and you might come up with an appropriate excuse to explain away how you know that information. I've never told a soul. Lily has kept quiet about the exact bomb used and so has her husband. No one knows what kind of bomb timer was used to kill my brother, Walter. Except you do, I see. Somehow."

Walter stood stunned and silent.

Theo didn't mind.

Then, as fast as a burst of lightning, Walter reached for something under his desk. Theo didn't have a single doubt that the man was reaching for a gun. Before Walter could get to his weapon, Theo withdrew the magnum he liked to keep safely tucked in at his back.

Never keep a fucking gun on you, Dino used to say. *Keep one close. Keep a dozen guns close, but never keep one on you.*

Sometimes, his brother had been right and sometimes he was wrong. Theo didn't usually keep a gun on him. But he did around men like Walter Artino.

Theo cocked back the hammer on his magnum and aimed, putting a bullet directly into the oak desk only inches from Walter's hand. Walter's arms flew high as he backed into the wall with frightened eyes and an opened mouth.

"I didn't miss," Theo informed.

Walter bumbled and rambled, his eyes zoning in on the barrel of Theo's gun. "I did not know, I didn't. I just said—"

"Radio timer. Unreleased information, Walter. Don't treat me like a child, I've had enough of that bullshit. Radio timer, you cocksucker. That's what you said. How did you know that?"

"J-Joel," Walter stuttered.

"Joel."

"Joel did it."

"Why?"

"I don't know—"

Theo pulled the trigger and watched as a bullet entered Walter's raised hand. Blood spilled as pain lit up the older man's features. Walter shouted, holding his hand to his stomach and cussing a blue streak.

All the while, Theo didn't say a thing.

"Why?" Theo asked again.

Tears crawled down Walter's puffy cheeks as the man held tighter to his bleeding hand and glared up at Theo. The tears were a disgusting sight. A weakness. Never cry. Never beg. Theo wished he could be surprised that Walter had met his breaking point, but he wasn't.

"You know why," Walter hissed, his spittle flying. "Or are you too focused on your heart again, DeLuca?"

Theo's anger flared again, but he tampered it down. It took him all of a few seconds to realize that Joel had gotten one of the strongest Outfit families aligned with him by taking out their head Capo. Dino had been the sacrifice. It wasn't about the DeLucas being an easy target, after all. It was just about gaining more power by sacrificing one man.

"I told him to kill you instead."

Theo grinned wickedly. "Because Dino was going to prison, right?"

"Yes."

"And you knew with him gone and me gone, there would be no one left to fight you for the DeLuca crew."

Walter didn't answer.

He didn't have to.

"Where's your wife, anyway?" Theo asked.

Walter swallowed audibly. "Gone to Florida to visit her sister."

Good.

Theo stepped forward, fiddling with the tip of his gun. Walter watched him all the while with a wariness in his agonized gaze. Stepping around the corner of the oak desk, Theo grabbed the heavy bronzed paper weight from the top and slammed it into Walter's face before the man had a chance to react. Bone crunched under the force, drowning out Walter's shriek. The old man tried fighting back, but he wasn't any match for Theo's younger strength.

Forcing the man to the floor, Theo grabbed Walter's hand and wrapped it around his gun. He then turned it on Walter as he forcibly wrapped the fool's finger around the trigger. Bloodied, broken, and looking like he'd had the hell beat out of him, Walter stared into the barrel of the gun with hazy, watery eyes. Blood dripped from his battered mouth and his face was beginning to swell.

"Go to hell, Theo," Walter spat.

Theo laughed. "I've already been there for a while."

Then he forced Walter to keep the gun steady, pointing it at his already broken face, and made the man pull the trigger. Theo took the paper weight and his gun with him when he left.

Theo tightened his leather jacket around his frame as he walked through the quiet Wicker Park neighborhood. Wicker Park was known for its artistic feel and for being one of the safer parts of Chicago. He kept his head down low as he strolled through the streets, not wanting to draw attention to himself by someone who might recognize his face.

It wouldn't be unusual for him to be in Wicker Park. The Outfit was everywhere, not just in Melrose. Everyone had business with someone else. Theo's reasons for being there could be excused if needed.

Coming up to the playground where children, bundled up warm in the early December air, played and squealed happily, Theo leaned against a bright green metal fence and watched. Theo wished he could remember a time when his childhood wasn't tainted by one thing or another. His parents' murders were always forefront, but he'd conceded his feelings on that long ago knowing his father had turned on the Outfit.

The death was justified.

Move on.

Theo preferred being in open spaces and the outside usually gave him the freedom he craved. Outside, he could think of Dino and not be bombarded by his unshakeable guilt at never seeing his brother clearly enough. Or for not giving Dino the confirmation that he cared, that Theo knew what it felt like to keep secrets, and that he was sorry his loyalties had been given to the wrong people.

People like Ben DeLuca and Joel Trentini.

Dino worked hard when he was alive to keep his siblings safe. Sometimes, that included sending Lily away so she didn't have to experience the things her brothers sometimes did growing up in Ben DeLuca's home. Thinking about that time, when he was on the cusp of being a teenager growing into a man, was hard for Theo.

Ben had been a cold, hard man. He'd favored locking his nephews, no matter their ages, into small, dark places after they were beaten by a few of his favored men. He'd turned the DeLuca brothers into molds of himself and never batted an eye. His uncle had rarely spoke of his past actions, either.

While Theo could push it out of his mind if he wanted, he knew Dino had often suffered aftereffects of the abuse. Like being anxious in small spaces or needing to work himself to death before he could fall asleep at night, because the darkness would creep into his mind and wouldn't let go.

Never tell Lily.

That was Dino's only demand. Theo understood why as he felt the same way. Lily had been protected from that, and when Dino had enough control of his own, he'd started fighting back until Ben backed off. Theo was at a point then where he blamed his older brother, but at the same time, he felt like he owed his uncle something.

Wrong.

So, so foul.

Sighing, Theo watched the children. Silently, a familiar woman bundled up in a bright red jacket saddled up beside Theo. She leaned against the fence like he was, keeping her eye on a particular blond-haired, brown-eyed boy trying to crawl over the top of the monkey bars.

"He's a dare devil," she said, laughing softly.

Theo watched her from the corner of his eye. In her early thirties at least, she was pretty featured with soft lines and an honest smile. Her eyes lit up when she laughed and a special glimmer seemed to form whenever she watched the little boy.

Maybe he understood then ... Maybe Theo got it then how his brother had fallen in love with a woman and wanted to keep her safe from their life and the Outfit.

She wasn't like them.

"Careful, J!" she shouted as the boy nearly tumbled off the monkey bars.

J.

For Junior. Dino Junior, actually.

Theo hadn't known about the boy until a few months ago when he'd stumbled on some paperwork in his brother's office after Lily had come home. Dino tried to brush it off, but Theo wouldn't relent.

"Oh, my God, he's going to fall," Karen grumbled.

"He'll be okay," Theo said, as his nephew scrambled even faster across the bars.

"Oh, you think?"

"Sure. He's a DeLuca. We're tough as steel inside and out."

Karen smiled. "Maybe."

"The accounts are all signed over for him," Theo said.

"Yeah?"

"Sure. Just go have a chat with the lawyer we talked about and he'll give you access to the banks and accounts. I sold out a few of the business, too, because I don't need them. It was all liquidated and added to the pool. You can do whatever you want with it for him. Get out of this fucking city, even. That's what I'd do."

Karen scoffed. "I don't want to leave, Theo. This is my home, too. Even if he's not here anymore."

"Doesn't it hurt?" he asked.

"Everyday."

"Do you feel like his secret?"

"Like a dirty one?" she asked quietly.

Theo shrugged. "I guess. You said it, not me."

"No, I didn't feel like his secret."

"That's it?"

Karen sighed. "That's it, Theo."

The paperweight in his pocket drew his attention for a moment. Tugging the heavy bronzed piece out, he set it on the edge of the fence. He'd cleaned the blood off it the night before after he arrived home. It took Theo a while to settle everything he now knew.

He needed a new plan.

Something else.

Riley wasn't necessarily all at fault, but he wasn't innocent in a lot of things, either. As far as Joel went, Theo had to be careful. He'd get out of killing Walter easily, but the new underboss of the family wasn't going to be the same.

That could cost Theo his life.

His nephew had already lost one man.

"What is that?" Karen asked, looking over the paperweight.

Theo smirked. "A gift."

"Oh?"

"Yeah. Keep it."

Theo thought it appropriate his brother's lover have some sort of souvenir for the deaths of at least one of the bastards who'd taken Dino. Walter Artino might not have set or ordered the bomb on Dino's car, but he knew about it. That was enough.

Morbid? Maybe. Karen didn't know the difference, but it made Theo feel better.

Karen shook her head. "You're so strange sometimes, Theo."

"I'm aware."

"Say hello to J before you go. He asked about you this week."

An ache started in Theo's chest. He was still trying to settle his feelings. He didn't think he could sit with his nephew and talk. The coldness felt better than hurting.

"Not today," Theo said, backing away from the fence.

Karen didn't push him for more.

"Next week same time?"

"Yeah, sure."

Without a goodbye, Theo started his stroll back down the quiet streets until he was far from the park and lost in the people beginning to flood the streets. Wanting coffee before he walked another twenty minutes to where he'd parked his Stingray, Theo slipped inside the first coffee shop he came to.

And walked straight into Evelina Conti.

CHAPTER FOUR

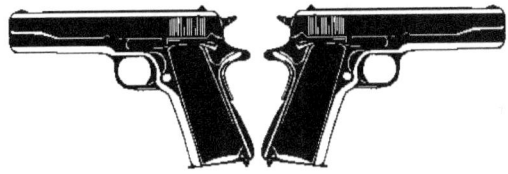

Evelina cursed under her breath when she rammed into the hard body of a man. Her chai latte went flying from her hand, splashing all over his leather jacket and up his neck and cheek. Embarrassment filled Evelina to the brim.

"Oh, my God. I'm so sorry," Evelina said, refusing to look the frozen stranger in the eye. She used the napkins she'd taken to wrap her hot drink in to wipe at the mess on his jacket. "Sorry, so—"

"Stop."

The familiar voice sent a shiver running down Evelina's spine. She glanced up only to find Theo DeLuca's brown eyes staring right back into hers.

"Theo."

"Eve."

"I made a mess of your jacket."

Hello, Captain Obvious.

Theo cleared his throat and wiped at his cheek. "There's frothy shit on my face."

"It's a latte, so there's supposed to be froth on the top."

"Mmhmm." Theo's posture was rigid, like someone had shoved a metal rod up his spine. Even his stare seemed disinterested and detached. Evelina couldn't remember this man ever being so distant and cold. "Well, I don't think it's supposed to end up on someone's coat and face, Eve."

"Sorry," she muttered, her cheeks turning red all over again. "I wasn't looking where I was going."

"So you're clumsy."

"No, I just—"

"Clumsy," Theo repeated, his tone darkening as he cocked a brow.

Evelina felt her hackles rise to the occasion. What was it about this man that got her defensive, edgy and willing to battle it out every time he opened his sexy mouth?

"I am not. I have a lot on my mind and was checking my phone in case Alessa needed something," Evelina said heatedly.

"Alessa has a sister."

"And a useless prick for a brother. What is your point?"

Theo's expression didn't waver, but something unknown flashed in his eyes. "That we can both agree on."

Glancing around, she noticed that people were standing behind them, waiting to get out of the café as they were blocking the door. Two more people stood outside the door behind Theo, wanting to get in.

"We should move."

Theo didn't budge. "Why?"

"We're in the way."

"You know, this would be the perfect time to make up for never calling me back, princess."

Evelina pursed her lips and forced back the irritation. "Are you ever going to stop calling me that?"

"If the title fits …"

"And what is yours? Asshole?"

Theo frowned. "Ouch. My ego."

"I doubt it even felt a thing."

"You don't know that. Maybe I'll go home and cry my damn eyes out tonight because you called me names."

Evelina didn't like that Theo almost seemed to be joking with her, never mind the impatient people who were beginning to make noise behind them.

"If that were the case, I'd think you're a terribly sensitive man in the wrong kind of business," Evelina said.

Theo chuckled. "And what kind of business is that?"

"Uh …"

Public, she reminded herself silently. *We don't talk about family business in public.*

"Eve?"

"The different kind."

Theo hummed under his breath. "Good save."

"I try."

"Let me buy you a coffee," Theo said.

"I don't drink regular coffee."

"Yeah, well, I don't think I can handle watching you lick froth off the rim of a cup while I'm still wearing the last bit you spilled."

What was that supposed to mean?

Oh.

Oh.

Like maybe he wanted to see her licking froth off him.

Sweet Jesus.

This man was such a mind fuck. One minute, he seemed like he didn't give a damn if she was alive or dead. The next, he was doing a complete one-eighty. Strangely, the distant attitude he sported was still firmly in place. If it wasn't for his suggestive words, she wouldn't know if he wanted her to disappear or get on her knees and open her mouth.

The visual of her on her knees, sucking Theo off, was dark and heady. It followed right behind her thoughts, making an ache start up between her thighs. She needed to get as far away from those thoughts as fast as she possibly could.

Trouble.

Theo screamed it all over.

Evelina's throat constricted heavily with a sudden rush of desire as Theo looked her black wool dress and high boots over.

"Your father still out of town?" he asked.

"Yes, thankfully."

Theo nodded. "Are you still staying with Adriano?"

"Yep."

"There, the small talk thing is done. I was polite, appropriate—"

"What is your definition of appropriate?"

"—and I didn't try to kill you," Theo finished with a smirk.

Evelina sighed. "You don't frighten me, Theo."

Not in the way he might think he did, anyway.

"It's not me you have to worry about. No frothy drink, Eve."

Somehow, she managed to say, "Coffee it is."

Evelina held onto her hot mug of coffee as Theo slid into the small booth across the table. He'd taken off his jacket and cleaned what mess he could from his face and neck. At least her chai latte hadn't ruined his silk dress shirt.

Without the jacket, Evelina had the perfect view of Theo's muscular chest moving under his shirt. The fabric stretched across his pecs with every movement, and she was positive there was a ring in his right nipple. The top of whatever tattoo he had inked on his lower neck peeked out as he adjusted his frame on the bench seat and picked up his coffee to take a drink.

With a dry mouth, Evelina glanced away. She took a drink of her own black coffee, wanting to get away from those thoughts. The coffee was terrible and she cringed.

Theo chuckled. "That bad, huh?"

"It's not bad," she tried to lie.

Theo arched a brow high and took a sip of his own coffee. With just that single look alone, Evelina caved.

"Yeah, it's terrible."

"Thought so."

Theo grinned and just like that, his hardened features softened in his amusement. The grin on his face faded fast, but it had been there nonetheless. She saw it. It reminded Evelina of a time when the DeLuca *principe* hadn't always been so serious and stoic.

It wasn't all that long ago, Evelina thought.

But it felt like decades.

"I see you're still wearing that tiara," Theo said quietly.

"You just had to go and ruin it, didn't you?"

Theo didn't even blink. "Ruin what?"

"You smiled. You were being nice. And then you had to go and ruin it with all that princess nonsense again."

"Wrong," Theo said.

"I am not."

"Boy, you really like to argue, don't you? I'm not one for the combative types, but it's pretty interesting whenever your hackles get rattled and you get all huffy."

Evelina stiffened in the booth. "Actually, no. I don't like to argue."

"Funny, you turn into a pretty little cactus whenever I come around."

She heard pretty and cactus.

But mostly, she heard pretty.

Goddamn him.

"Maybe that's because you like to tease me, Theo. I'm not a little kid and neither are you. Stop with the teasing."

Theo shrugged and set his cup to the table. "It's not teasing, Eve. I was just saying that any normal person would tell someone they didn't like the drink. They wouldn't try to lie or hide it for the other person's benefit. They'd just politely say it wasn't their kind of thing. You get what I'm saying?"

"You told me no froth, Theo."

"You're missing the point, Eve."

Evelina crossed her arms, going on the defensive again. "So enlighten me."

"That princess crap, it's like a habit you can't break. I'm not saying there's anything wrong with some of it, but most times, it's not to your benefit. What were you always told growing up? Be quiet, stay in the corner, look pretty, and never offend or bring shame to the family. It's a goddamn cup of coffee, Evelina."

She liked the way her full name rolled off his tongue.

Not Eve.

Not Conti.

Not *princess*.

Evelina.

"It is just a coffee," Evelina agreed, feeling warier than ever.

"Tell me you don't like it."

"I did."

"Tell me again," Theo demanded.

What game was he trying to play with her?

"I don't like the coffee, Theo."

Without a word, he grabbed her steaming mug and pulled it across the table. Theo then picked out a couple of packs of sugar from the glass dish in the middle and three creamers in the small bowl. Evelina watched him curiously as he ripped the packets of sugar open one by one and poured them in slowly, followed by the three creamers. All the while, Theo kept his stare firmly leveled on her under his hooded lids.

Theo plucked a brown stir stick from the stack in the middle and dipped it into the mug, spinning the liquid around and around until it was a creamy beige.

"You're welcome," Theo said, pushing the cup back to Evelina.

Unsure, Evelina didn't touch the mug. She had never liked the taste of coffee and because of that, never went as far as using milk, cream or sugar as a way to sweeten it up. She just figured it was one less unhealthy thing she was putting into her body. No dependence and all that good stuff.

Besides, she was already addicted to caffeine through the other coffee-like drinks she enjoyed.

"Try it," Theo urged.

Picking up the coffee, Evelina smiled before taking a hesitant sip. It wasn't bad at all. Sweeter thanks to the sugar and smoother thanks to the creamers. The heavy taste of coffee was still there but lessened.

"It's good," Evelina said.

"I know."

Laughing, Evelina took another drink of her coffee. Theo let her enjoy the drink in silence as he occasionally lifted his own mug to his lips and drank while they passed looks across the table. Before Evelina realized it, half of her cup was gone and Theo's knowing grin had grown into a full blown smile.

"I get it," Evelina said.

"Hmm, what is that?"

"The princess thing. Or … some of it."

"Do tell," Theo said.

"It's about everything, right? Not like how everyone treats me, but how I am about everything and everyone else. Proper. Appropriate.

Respectful. Correct."

"Follow the rules, chin up, smile for the crowd, and be a good girl," Theo added when Evelina grew silent. "It's not your fault, really. We're all made some way, Eve. This just happens to be the way you were made. Sometimes, I don't even think you know you're doing it."

"Breaking the mold is good."

"Sometimes."

Evelina grinned down at her mug. "I don't always follow the rules."

"Nothing wrong with that, either," Theo muttered around the rim of his cup.

"According to my father, there's a lot wrong with it."

Theo shrugged. "Only because your good behavior benefits him, and believe me when I say, Riley Conti has been waiting for his moment in the Outfit for a long damn time. What he doesn't need right now is an unruly daughter that he has to chase after when he's trying to settle the conflict inside the Outfit."

Evelina wanted to get off the topic and fast before it got too deep. "I saw you at the wedding."

"Outside," Theo corrected. "I didn't actually go."

"It was enough."

"I like to keep an eye on things."

"Like what?" she asked.

"Everything. My family, most importantly."

That was kind of sweet, even if his frown didn't give off the impression he meant it that way.

"Lily, you mean?"

"The Outfit," Theo replied simply. "But she's a part of the Outfit, so yes, she gets put in that category as well."

"Oh."

"What?"

Evelina lifted a shoulder in explanation, saying, "I guess I just thought with everything that happened lately, I figured family would be the last thing you considered the Outfit to be."

Theo chuckled. "The people and the Outfit aren't the same thing. Two different entities. Maybe once they were, but now it's just four families throwing stones at each other's glass houses whenever they get the chance."

Sad but true.

"And I've been caught in the crossfire enough," Theo added darkly.

Evelina cringed. "You mean with your uncle and brother being killed."

"Brother, mostly. My uncle isn't all that much of a loss. Trust me."

"You always seemed close to Ben."

At least, that's how Evelina remembered it. Whenever she had seen

Theo with his uncle before the man's death, the two seemed to have a better relationship than any of the other siblings had with their uncle.

Evelina waited for Theo to respond to her statement, but he offered nothing at first. Actually, he just stilled and rubbed his right wrist as he rotated it against his palm like it was hurting or something.

"Ben was fond of me," Theo said finally.

Evelina's brow furrowed. "And he wasn't fond of Lily or Dino?"

Theo scoffed. "Lily maybe, but that was only because she wasn't around a lot. Dino, on the other hand, didn't follow the rules very well, so no, Ben wasn't all that fond of him."

Unsure of what to say to that, because she didn't have the first clue about what it meant, Evelina chose to stay quiet. Theo rubbed his wrist once more as he glanced down at his coffee.

"Did you hurt your wrist?" she asked.

Just like that, Theo's cool demeanor was back in a blink. He dropped his hand to the table and moved his right arm underneath where she couldn't see it.

"No," he said, "I didn't hurt it."

"What's wrong?"

Theo smiled a charming sight. "Nothing."

Deflection.

Evelina could recognize that shit from a mile away.

"Theo—"

"I like my coffee black," he interrupted smoothly.

Evelina lifted a brow, confused. "I can see that. I can't imagine why. It tastes disgusting."

"No, it tastes bitter. It's dark, it's heady, and it leaves a thick taste on my tongue. And I like the harshness of fresh black coffee, because I like the way it feels when I drink it down. A little pain is a good thing, as the saying goes. After a while, you don't even notice the taste anymore because you learn to like the bite it leaves behind and how it wakes you up."

Something wicked settled in Evelina's stomach like a heavy weight pressing her down. Maybe it was the way Theo's mouth curved with a sensual flair or how his gaze caught hers and held it, completely unashamed.

It was coffee, for fuck's sake.

He was talking about *coffee*!

So why did she feel like he was talking about something else entirely?

"The only thing that reminds me of what it feels like when I drink coffee is sex," Theo said.

Christ.

There it was.

Evelina wasn't even surprised.

"And why is that?"

"Because I like my coffee how I like my sex. Harsh, hot, and with a little bite of pain lingering behind. So I drink it black, Eve. I don't need the sweetness or the cream. I just need the feeling."

Evelina let out a slow breath. "Huh."

"You should have called me after your mother was killed," Theo said, changing the conversation altogether.

She was feeling far too hot to want to get into that discussion. Evelina guessed Theo probably wasn't going to give her a choice.

"I would have, but you, like everyone else, had a front row seat to Riley's mess after it all happened, Theo. He was crazy as hell and getting worse every day."

"So?"

"So I didn't want to push his buttons. Blatantly dating someone without his approval certainly would have pushed my father in the wrong direction. Just showing up at Lily's wedding left me with bruises that lasted for a week."

Heat flashed in Theo's gaze.

"He hit you for that?"

"No, Adriano stepped in."

Theo sucked in a hard breath. "Well, at least your brother is finally learning to fill his own boots."

"I think so," she agreed.

"I'm not a second chance kind of guy," Theo told her.

Evelina shrugged. "That's too bad."

"Why is that?"

"Because I was thinking maybe it was time to stop acting like a princess."

Theo's gaze narrowed briefly. "This is a bad idea, Eve."

"Maybe."

"No, it's a bad idea," Theo said. "Not because it's a bad time, or there's unresolved shit between our families. It's bad because you're an opening and I might use it."

Evelina didn't have the first clue about what he meant.

Theo pointed at her face, likely seeing the confusion written across her crumpled brow. "And that right there tells me it'd be goddamn easy, Eve. I don't know if I want to be that guy."

What guy?

Evelina didn't get the chance to ask.

Theo stood from the table and pulled out his wallet before dropping a few one-dollar bills to the table.

"That's it?" Evelina asked. "We're done talking?"

"My coffee is gone and I have business to do."

His cup was empty.

Evelina's was almost gone, too.

"I imagine I'll see you around," Theo said.

"Probably," Evelina agreed.

She sipped from her cup, wanting to hide the hurt she felt over his rejection. Around the rim, a dusting of sugar crystals scratched her bottom lip. She licked the sugar off before draining the remaining contents from her cup.

Theo's gaze caught hers out of the corner of her eye. She'd still licked the damn rim and there wasn't a bit of froth in sight. Evelina laughed when Theo shook his head.

"I know you didn't do that on purpose," he said.

Evelina grinned. "Well, as far as you know."

"Where is your car parked?" he asked.

"Just down the block."

"I'll walk you to it if you're done in here."

Always the gentleman, even when he was rejecting a woman.

Evelina wanted to decline and save a bit of her pride, but when he held his hand out to help her from the booth, she took it.

Theo tucked Evelina's hand into his elbow as they walked down the street, keeping a firm hold on her as people swarmed around them going to wherever they were going.

"I can stay upright on my own two feet, you know," she told him.

That, and being close to Theo made her body react in ways she would rather it didn't.

Theo shrugged. "So you say, but your earlier mess says differently."

"I told you, I was looking at my phone."

"And now, you're looking at me. Imagine that."

Evelina scowled. "You're incredibly difficult."

"Funny, I've been told I'm incredibly charming."

"Until someone gets too close. And then you bite them—"

"Like a snake?" he interrupted.

Evelina made a face. "Bad choice of words."

"I'd say so." Theo glanced around the street as they got closer to the parking lot where Evelina had taken her car earlier when she had some shopping to do. "Where are your enforcers?"

"Somewhere."

"Don't they stay close enough so that you can see them?"

Evelina laughed bitterly. "Why would they do that? Then they can't report back to Riley about all the bad shit I might be doing."

Even Theo laughed at that. "I hadn't thought of that."

"Well, it's either that, or sometimes they just can't keep up."

Theo's grin was downright sinful. "Best thing about having that BMW of yours is the horsepower in the engine."

"And I do favor the highways."

"Do you ever notice when you lose them?" he asked quietly.

"If I don't see their cars every so often, then yeah, I pretty much know. Sometimes I get a call from one of them, but I don't answer. It doesn't matter, really."

"Why?"

"GPS on my car," Evelina informed frankly. "Dad has his ways."

"That only works if you're actually in the car when someone comes searching for you, Eve."

She hadn't thought of that.

Theo bumped his shoulder with hers in a playful manner as he added, "I'm being a bad influence, aren't I?"

"Is that what you're concerned about?"

"Not really."

Pointing at her car in the parking lot across the road, Evelina let Theo direct her through traffic once they had the chance. He only let her go once she was standing beside her BMW and was searching for the keys in her messenger bag.

"Thanks for having coffee with me," Theo said.

His voice turned uncharacteristically quiet. The distance on his face, like he was somewhere else entirely, said that maybe he had something on his mind.

"Thanks for asking me," Evelina replied. "What were you doing around here, anyway?"

Theo cleared his throat and tossed his hands in his pockets. A fond smile took over his features. "I had some business to do. Someone to see."

A heat flashed in Evelina's gut. She didn't recognize the feeling at first, but it didn't take long for her to clue in to what was wrong. She didn't like how he smiled about the person he visited like they were important. Like maybe he cared about them.

What in the hell was wrong with her?

She had no claim on Theo DeLuca and the attraction she felt was entirely unfed. She had no reason to be jealous of someone she didn't even know.

No claim.

None.

"Oh," Evelina said.

Theo glanced around the parking lot. Evelina had parked her car close to the exit of the road, so they had a view of the cars going back and forth down the street.

"What were you doing around here?" Theo flashed his charming smile again. "Seeing as how you asked me, it's only fair."

"Shopping. I needed a break after ..."

"After what?" he pressed.

She didn't want to admit how much she disliked her father's new bride, or say how having the woman as her stepmother was literally vomit-inducing.

"It doesn't mat—"

Theo's gaze cut into hers fast, stopping her words up. Evelina knew what he was going to say. It was right on the tip of her own tongue. Princess.

She was still acting like the proper little Conti princess. Protecting her family, even if it hurt her and she was lying about her own feelings. Making sure her father wasn't shamed and doing exactly what Riley wanted and needed from his daughter.

Yeah, the proper Mafioso *principessa*.

"Eve?" Theo asked quietly.

The truth could set you free, after all.

"I needed a break after the wedding. Something to get my mind off my power hungry father and his sugar baby bride."

Theo snorted. "Sugar baby. Now there's one I haven't heard used yet."

"I bet you've heard everything else."

"Pretty much," he admitted, not even looking the least bit ashamed.

"It's all true," Evelina said, sighing.

Everything they heard whispered about her new *stepmother* was true.

Theo eyed Evelina silently. She fidgeted under his heavy regard.

"You asked," she said before he could say anything.

"I did. Honesty is the best policy, too. I kind of warned you earlier, right?" he asked. "Bad thing with us and all."

"Yeah, you warned me."

What did it matter?

Evelina didn't need to be told again.

Theo nodded. "As long as you know."

Evelina laughed under her breath. "I got it, Theo."

"Good. But I wouldn't be opposed to doing this again."

Wait ... what?

"Are you saying—"

Theo held up a hand, stopping Evelina from saying any more. Once again, his gaze was drawn to the road where cars were still zooming on past. Evelina didn't notice anything particularly odd as a black car with tinted windows slowed down like it was going to turn into the parking lot.

Except it didn't turn.

Theo moved so fast he was a blink. His arms encircled Evelina with enough force to hurt as he took her thrashing to the ground. At the same time they hit the pavement, she heard the rain start.

No, not water.

Bullets.

CHAPTER FIVE

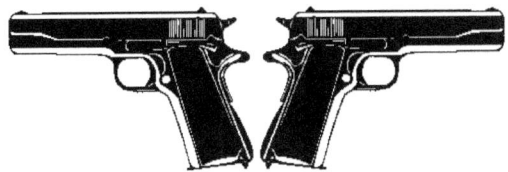

Theo wrapped a wide-eyed Evelina into his embrace, tucked her head into his chest, and rolled them both as close as he could get to the car. The BMW was too low to the ground for them to roll under it completely, but Theo had Evelina firmly tucked between the tiny gap, the ground, and his body. His back faced the onslaught of bullets shredding the air.

Not a single one hit him.

Evelina shook like a leaf in Theo's strong hold, but he refused to let her go. He couldn't afford to turn his head and get a look at the vehicle, either. Maybe, if they were lucky, whoever the shooter—or shooters—was might think they had hit their target with the two being prone on the pavement.

"Stop moving," Theo hissed into Evelina's hair.

She whimpered. "I'm trying."

Just before he'd left the coffee shop, Theo had an odd feeling that raised all the hair on the back of his neck. He'd only experienced that twice before. Once, when his parents were murdered and then again on the day of Dino's bombing.

Those had been two entirely different days, years apart, but they'd imprinted their memory inside his mind and soul. They had, essentially, changed his life in their own ways. Stained with violence and grief, they were moments Theo didn't want to relive. So, when he felt that again, he took note of it.

Theo asked Evelina to let him walk her to her car, despite wanting to get on with his day and not feed the curiosity he felt about her. It was only liable to get him into trouble, anyway.

And then he'd noticed it.

Once, the black car passed the coffee shop as they were coming out. Again, it came from the opposite direction as they hit the first block. The final time he'd noticed it was when it passed them again from the opposite direction as they walked into the parking lot.

A black car was easily overlooked. There was probably hundreds of thousands of black vehicles in the city. Theo probably would not have given the car any mind either had he not felt odd and noticed the black car driving a little slower than the rest down the busy street.

Tires screeched loudly. He refused to let Evelina up from the pavement as he kept his head tucked down and his arms snug around her frame.

He felt her shiver. The goddamn pavement was cold as fuck and all she had on was a wool dress and knee-high suede boots.

"Theo?"

"What?" he barked.

Evelina swallowed audibly. "It's over."

Yeah, he figured that, but he wanted to be safe. Tipping his head up, Theo glanced around. Sure enough, there wasn't a black vehicle in sight and the road had all but turned silent. Traffic had stopped and sirens blasted in the distance. People were getting out of their cars, a few with stunned expressions and some others had phones pressed to their ears. A couple began to make their way closer to Theo and Evelina.

"You can move now," Evelina whispered.

Theo met her green eyes and everything he thought he knew wavered in that split second. She was terrified with tears welling and her bottom lip trembling. Her fists had wrapped tightly into the sides of his leather jacket, holding him firmly against her like she didn't want to let go. Theo had somehow managed to turn them both on their side with his back facing the road, but her legs were wrapped tightly around his waist.

Intimate.

Way too intimate.

But he could still see it in her eyes. The fear, the uncertainty. She didn't want him to move. She didn't want him to let go. Not yet.

"You're all right," Theo murmured.

Evelina nodded, but she fisted his jacket tighter all the same. A panicked, wild look colored up her eyes that were focused on only him.

"What is it, Eve?" he asked.

She wouldn't answer.

Theo immediately went back to the last shooting Evelina had been involved in—her mother's. He hadn't seen the aftermath of Mia Conti's shooting, but he'd heard enough to know it was violent, bloody and unforgettable. One side of the woman's face had been unrecognizable, blown off from rapid assault gunfire.

Eve had been just seats away from her mother. Could she still hear the gunfire? Could she still smell the blood? Did she dream of it?

When it came to his own memories, Theo was a yes for all three.

He still remembered what it felt like walking up to his Melrose home to find police and a crowd gathering. He could still feel the uncertainty when he'd been shoved into a car and driven away from the scene of his parents' murder.

And then there was Dino.

The heat …

The screams …

The bomb.

Theo glanced down at Evelina again as the voices of people got closer. How much time had passed? Thirty seconds, maybe a minute or two?

It felt like forever.

"You're okay," Theo told her.

He wished someone had told that to him years ago.

"Not okay," Evelina replied in a breath.

Pretending was better. Nobody knew then.

Theo didn't think Evelina would understand. She wasn't quite like him. She didn't have a history with a man who beat the fear out of a person. She didn't have a job that labeled her a criminal and killer or the button in a family that demanded he never fail.

Evelina sniffed, trying to blink away the wetness in her eyes. It didn't help. Her tears coated her bottom lashes, threatening to fall. Women shouldn't cry; they deserved men who never caused them pain.

In this life, that was impossible.

Theo sucked in a hard breath, wishing he wasn't so aware of how much of Evelina Conti's tight, toned body was pressed to his against that pavement. He wished that her dress hadn't ridden up and that the heel of her boots weren't digging into the back of his legs. He really wished that her body didn't fit so well with his.

But mostly, he wished she didn't look entirely vulnerable underneath him. Like being under his weight put her in a weak position. Exposed. Unprotected. Fragile. Like he had control.

With her, he probably did.

Evelina wouldn't know any better. He didn't want to be that man; the one who would use someone like Evelina to his own benefit even if it was to the determent of her heart.

This was not the time. It was never going to be the time. They would be a bad thing.

"Oh, my God," someone mumbled, coming closer to the car. "Are you two okay?"

Theo didn't look away from Evelina, nor did he answer. Her lip was still trembling. Her eyes were still watery. She was still scared.

The sirens got louder.

"Fuck," Theo groaned.

The very last thing he wanted was a run in with the cops. There was no hiding the fact he was heavily involved with the Chicago mob. This would be more attention on the families, and considering the drive-by that just happened, it wasn't over yet.

"Who would do something like that?" the frazzled woman asked.

"We know nothing," Evelina said.

Her words mirrored Theo's thoughts. That's how kids like them grew up.

You know nothing.

You saw nothing.

You heard nothing.

Walls didn't talk and windows didn't see. Learning how to turn cheek and be a blind eye had become a mastered art form for people brought up in the Outfit.

"Nothing," he echoed.

Without another word, he pushed up from the ground and away from Evelina. She held onto him until she couldn't anymore, but then he helped her up, too. Once she was standing, her dress was fixed, and they had a few inches between them, Theo felt like he could breathe.

Who had been the target, him or her?

"Who did that?" Evelina asked.

Theo didn't have a clue.

But he intended on finding out.

Theo stepped out of the police precinct feeling dirtier than ever. He did a lot of bad shit on a daily basis. But when he stepped inside a police station and sat down with detectives? Theo shuddered and wiped his hands on his slacks.

Dirty.

Fucking filthy right down to his core. He couldn't get that feeling off no matter how hard he tried. And God knew he tried damn hard. It wasn't normal for people like him to be making nice with police in any sort of way.

Stay away from cops.

Don't talk to cops.

Never involve cops.

Pretty goddamn simple.

How his father had ever turned rat all those years ago and made nice with the officials like they were old friends, Theo didn't know. Of course, he knew why his father had done what he did, but Theo just couldn't relate to it.

Sighing, Theo took the stairs leading down from the front entrance of the precinct two at a time. The faster he could get away from the police station, the happier he would be. He wondered how Evelina had fared in her interview with the cops.

Because his car was still over in Wicker Park, Theo needed to catch a cab. When the detective offered him a drive to wherever his vehicle was parked, Theo laughed in the man's face. What did the guy want, to get Theo killed?

No fucking way.

Theo didn't get the chance to hail one of the cabs across the street. A black Mercedes pulled up to the side of the road with windows tinted so dark, Theo couldn't see inside. He recognized that car as it was the source of debate over the last few months between the Rossi and Conti family.

It belonged to Serena Rossi. Serena was not the person inside, however. When the back passenger door was pushed open, Theo found Tommas Rossi waiting.

"Get in," Tommas demanded.

Theo hesitated. "Why?"

"I didn't realize my requests were up for debate as the front boss for the Outfit, DeLuca. Get in the fucking car."

That was that. Theo jumped in the backseat and before he'd even gotten the door closed completely, the car was speeding away. Tommas was the kind of man who barely let an emotion flicker across his features. He was serious in all things—business, family and life.

Tommas waved his hand at the driver, catching the man's attention in the rear-view mirror. "Nate, take us around the block a few times. I'll let you know from there."

"Will do, boss."

With the driver's attention focused back on the road and not the two men in the back seat, Tommas turned to Theo again. For the most part, Theo liked Tommas. The two weren't all that far off in age and had been friends when they were younger men in the Outfit. Plus, the guy was Damian's first cousin, so Theo afforded Tommas a little more trust than he would to others in *la famiglia*.

"Isn't this your mother's car?" Theo asked.

Tommas scoffed. "I took the car away from her when she tried to drive it into one of Laurent's old restaurants in one of her many spells since his ... unfortunate end."

Unfortunate end. That was one way to put it. Another would be to tell it like it was and say Tommas killed his father.

"I might as well put it to use," Tommas added. "And Nate prefers driving this instead of my two-seater."

"Makes me feel like an actual fucking driver," Nate muttered from the front. "How am I supposed to act as a driver and enforcer for you when you're sitting in plain view in the front seat, huh? Christ."

"Shut up and drive, Nate."

"Got it, boss."

Theo shifted in the seat, wondering why in the hell Tommas had shown up at the police station. "What is this all about, Tommas?"

"We've got a problem," Tommas said simply, never taking his gaze off the front windshield. "Well, you've got a problem and I'm here to explain some of it to you. Evelina is now at a dinner with her brother and his fiancée, by the way. I had someone pick her up and drive her over there."

"Her car—"

"Is being held by police, of course."

"Figures," Theo muttered. "This problem you mentioned."

"Things were settling down, Theo. People had quieted about Riley and even the little feud between your crew and the Conti crew had stopped these last few days. Everything was perfectly *fine*."

Tommas growled the final word. Theo didn't blink at the show of anger. Tommas was not a man to cross. He could be cold and calculating, but mostly, Tommas liked to spill blood to make a point. He'd done that a few times over the years with his own crew and family. He'd earned respect by instilling fear. The man wasn't all mouth. He was a hell of a lot of action, too.

"I'm not sure I get—"

"What in the hell were you doing with Evelina Conti?" Tommas interrupted.

"What in the hell is that supposed to mean?"

"Answer the goddamn question, Theo."

"I had business in the Park and happened to run into her. We had a coffee. I figured instead of acting like an ass, I would walk her to her car. Then, someone decided to shoot it and us up. What more do you want, Tommas?"

Tommas' jaw tightened. "Her car wasn't shot up."

"I beg to differ."

"I saw the car. There wasn't a single bullet hole in it. All the cars around hers? Yes. The cement wall at the far end of the lot? Littered with bullet holes. Evelina's car didn't take a single one."

Confusion settled heavily in Theo.

"That was rapid assault fire, Tommas," he said quietly. "Like a fucking Uzi or something. Someone with very terrible aim had to have fired that gun and missed her car."

"Or someone with very good control," Tommas replied.

"I feel like I'm missing something here."

"You know you're getting the blame for this, right?"

Anger flared in Theo's gut. "I was there, too! Why in the hell would I order someone to light up a place with me right there, huh?"

Tommas shrugged. "Maybe that's why the car didn't have a single bullet hole in it, Theo."

"Or maybe someone wanted it to look like something else, and they used someone they knew would really get to Riley. Someone like his daughter. It works just the same way, all right."

"Still could have been you."

Theo clenched his fists against the leather seats, willing away his irritation. "Are you fucking serious right now?"

"As a heart attack." Tommas sighed heavily, leaned forward, and tapped his driver on the shoulder. "Take us to Wicker. Theo can direct us to wherever his car was parked. We'll drop him off there and follow him down to the other end of Chicago."

"Sounds like a plan, boss."

"Follow me down to the other end?" Theo rubbed at his forehead, willing the headache away. "I need a babysitter now?"

"No, you need to stay at your end of Chicago." Tommas turned to face Theo again with a grim frown. "When the boss got word of this shooting, the first person he blamed was you. I was on the phone with him while his little bride giggled in the background. Nice thing, that was. Nonetheless, I didn't even finish getting the words out and you were the one he put the responsibility on. Your issues over the last couple of months with the Conti crew is coming back to bite you, Theo. Today was just the final straw that broke the camel's back, so to speak."

Theo swallowed hard, forcing himself to stay quiet. He hadn't been the one to cause those issues on the Conti streets against Adriano's crew. Walter had done it and Theo let the man put the blame on him because at the time, he hadn't cared.

Theo couldn't out the fact he'd killed Walter. As far as Theo knew, no one was aware of Walter's dead body in his home office while his wife was still away in Florida. The woman was due home within the week, so it wouldn't be long before Walter's corpse was found. To keep from getting killed over whacking a made man without the boss's permission, Theo needed to keep all suspicion off himself for that nonsense.

"I'm giving you a heads-up, basically," Tommas continued, seemingly unaware of Theo's silent war inside his head. "This is your one pass, Theo. At the moment, you're on Trentini territory and Joel has already put word out that if even one man from the DeLuca crew steps beyond their lines, he'll light them up like New Year's Eve."

Jesus.

"And to make matters worse, Riley was extremely annoyed to be getting a call like this while he's away on his honeymoon," Tommas added, a bitterness twisting the final word.

Shit.

"When is he getting back?"

Theo was not looking forward to dealing with that. He had enough shit to deal with. Riley Conti was not supposed to be one of them until Theo was ready to deal with the man.

In a very permanent way.

"He's not," Tommas said, smirking. "He's finishing out his honeymoon with his wife like he originally planned to, and he hopes that whatever this is will be settled and everything will be back to normal by the time he returns."

Theo almost laughed. "Really?"

"His words, not mine."

"He's so concerned about his family and his daughter being shot up, he's pissed off at me like nothing else, but he can't manage to crawl out from between his twenty-something-year-old wife's legs to handle it?"

"Careful, Theo. Respect, remember?"

"I was there today, Tommas," Theo said again.

"I'm aware."

"I didn't put myself in the middle of a shooting, for Christ's sake!"

Tommas didn't act like Theo had said a thing. "As of right now, Adriano is staying quiet on his end of things. But the kid is always like that and better for him, I suppose. He's got a pregnant fiancée and he's never been very active in this feud."

"Your point?"

Tommas laughed dully. "Thank your lucky stars that your territory lines straddle his."

Theo clenched his teeth so hard, his molars ached. "This is ridiculous."

"Maybe so, but you have no one to blame but yourself. What in the hell were you doing on this side of Chicago, anyway?"

"Business, like usual. What does that matter?" Theo had no desire to out the fact he had been checking on his nephew. Since Dino was dead and couldn't look after his son, Theo was left to the task. He didn't mind, but Dino hadn't wanted J to be dragged into the Outfit's games. "I do business up here all the time."

"Actually, you don't," Tommas replied. "You have very little reason to be on this side of Chicago, which was the first thing Joel spat out when he found out you were on his territory."

"I've not had any problems with Joel."

Well, Theo hadn't before. Now that he knew the truth ... he'd get to Joel one way or another.

"This is your one pass from me, Theo," Tommas said coolly. "Things were calm, they were okay. If anything, you've just given certain people in the Outfit a reason to blow it all up again."

People like Joel. Theo didn't miss Tommas' unspoken words for a minute. Rage simmered through Theo's veins on low, but it was getting hotter with every passing second. How likely was it that Joel had been involved somehow with the shooting today?

Very.

"He's going to start a war with me just to get at Riley," Theo said.

"I have no idea what or who you're talking about," Tommas murmured. "Be careful about who you run your mouth to, Theo. You never know who you can trust in this family."

Right.

His one pass.

Yeah, Theo got it.

"You know I won't take this shit lying down, right?" Theo asked, a dangerous edge sharpening his tone. "If Joel comes at me or even one of my guys, I will slaughter him, Tommas. He's asking for it then. Joel Trentini isn't ready to go to the mattresses with a crew like mine."

"You've got two other crews' territory to get through before you hit Joel, Theo. And you won't find a lot of sympathy from the Rossi crew at the moment, considering we've got our problems with the Bastoni side of the Conti crew."

"Then you better get out of the way. I won't be someone else's fall guy or their way to the top. Someone already used my brother for that."

Joel.

Again.

"Have you ever thought that maybe your brother is the reason for all of this?"

What in the hell was that supposed to mean?

"My brother is dead," Theo growled.

Tommas nodded. "So he is. And if you're not careful, DeLuca, you're going to end up in the same graveyard that he did."

Theo ignored the biting chill of the December wind whipping through the city. He ignored the stares he got as he strolled through Melrose, too.

Stay away from Trentini territory.

Theo wasn't scared, he was pissed.

Tommas and his driver had dropped Theo off at the spot where he'd parked his Stingray with a warning to get out of Trentini ground. Tommas promised to follow behind to make sure Theo followed through, and the man had. It was just too bad Theo didn't follow the rules.

The black Mercedes parked a little ways down the road behind Theo as he continued his stroll down the quiet street, heading for a familiar restaurant. A couple of phone calls was all it took to find out where Joel Trentini was playing the good little underboss.

The whole day felt bad to Theo. He didn't want to end up like Dino because someone wanted to make a point and Theo would be the sacrifice. He planned on nipping that shit in the ass quickly.

The only thing Joel Trentini had going for him was his underboss position. It was the one thing keeping him safe. A street war was one thing, but going after the underboss of the Outfit was something else entirely. Theo had to be careful. Extra careful. But if Joel wanted to play games, Theo was up for that.

Starting now.

CHAPTER SIX

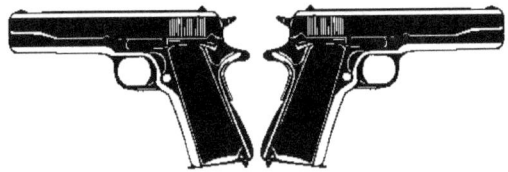

"I have a hard time believing that Theo DeLuca would put himself in that kind of situation," Adriano said. "So no, Joel, I won't start another street war with the DeLuca crew when everything is finally quieting down."

Joel scoffed. "That, or you're afraid you don't have the man power to finish it out."

Adriano's jaw ticked. "Or maybe I would simply like to see this all come to an end."

"I think it makes perfect sense that he was there today," Joel replied. "Think about it, Adriano. Would he put himself in that situation? Would he risk being shot? Any sane man would say no, but no one said anything about Theo being sane. It's the perfect distraction for your father. He expects Riley to look everywhere else but at him. You have to be careful and pick the right sides."

"Listen," Adriano practically spat, "if you want to go head to head with Theo on something, then do that. It was your territory, after all. Don't, however, bring me into it, too. Don't use my name and my sister's name as a reason to justify your vendettas. I won't do that shit, Joel. I've got better things to do than share bullets with another Outfit family."

Evelina passed Adriano a small smile, thanking him silently. Joel and her father blamed Theo for the earlier shooting. No matter how many times Evelina said that meeting up with Theo in the café had been nothing more than coincidence, Joel brushed her words off like she was a silly woman.

Adriano listened, thankfully.

Evelina appreciated that.

"You've found out the gender, right?" Abriella asked suddenly.

"Another four or five weeks, and that's only if the baby cooperates," Alessa said quietly.

"Oh, I thought you would know by now." Abriella pouted before breaking out in a wide grin. "You want a girl, right?"

"Of course, not," Joel said as he poured gravy over the potatoes on his plate. "They want a boy—a Conti *principe* to follow after his father. Every man wants a boy to carry on his name, Ella."

Evelina forced herself to stay quiet. This dinner was one of the only meetings between the Trentini and Conti families since Adriano and Alessa's pregnancy had been announced publically. Joel had shunned his sister and Evelina's brother without a backward glance.

Why Adriano was even sitting down with the man, Evelina didn't know. Well, maybe she could understand a little as she watched Alessa smile at her sister from across the table.

"A boy, am I right?" Joel asked Adriano.

Adriano shrugged, unbothered. "Either gender is fine by me as long as the child is healthy and happy like its mother."

Joel chuckled dryly. "How sweet."

"I'm sure you'll understand someday, Joel."

"Children are the very last thing on my mind currently," Joel replied.

"That's too bad," Adriano said, frowning. "At your age, most men are married and starting a family. I'm surprised my father hasn't brought up the issue to you, yet."

Joel's gaze narrowed. "What issue?"

Someone's form passed by the large bay windows at the front of the restaurant and caught Evelina's gaze. She stiffened in her seat, unsure if that was who she thought it was or not. Surely *not*. He wouldn't be that stupid, right?

Joel had put out word on the street that he would kill any man from the DeLuca crew who dared step into his territory because of the shooting. Surely that wasn't Theo.

Yeah, it was.

A spike of dread drove straight into Evelina's spine as the restaurant door opened and Theo stepped inside. With his hands shoved in his pockets and a disinterested expression, he surveyed the restaurant floor until he found the table he was looking for. Quickly, Theo crossed the restaurant with a confident stride and a bitter smirk.

The anxiety settled a little deeper into the pit of Evelina's stomach. *Not here*, she wanted to say. *Don't do this here.*

It wasn't what Theo would do that Evelina worried about, but rather, what Joel might do. The asshole had proven that the safety and happiness of others, even his own family, didn't matter as long as he got what he wanted.

Adriano took note of Theo as the man came closer to their table. With a sigh, Adriano tossed his napkin to the table and stood, drawing in Joel's attention, too.

"Well, well," Joel said with a grin. "Who do we have here?"

Theo bypassed Adriano with barely a glance. Even when Evelina's younger brother tried asking Theo to step into the back of the restaurant with him, Theo ignored the request.

"There are a lot of people inside this restaurant," Abriella said quietly.

"Try not to act like a bunch of gun toting fools. One shooting connected to the Outfit is enough for today."

Always the voice of reason, Evelina thought.

Abriella never hesitated to stick herself in a situation where women usually weren't invited when it came to the mafia.

"Yes, thank you, Ella," Joel said as he stood from his seat.

In one step, Theo had passed Evelina by and was standing toe to toe with Joel. A pin could have dropped on the other side of the restaurant and they would have heard it.

"I heard we have a problem," Theo said, taking his hands out of his pockets.

It showed he had nothing. Not a gun or a weapon on hand. He hadn't come with men, either, considering the outside of the restaurant was vacant of people.

"We do," Joel replied.

"Well, you have a problem," Theo said, chuckling. "Seems when I was being a gentleman and walking Evelina to her car because her enforcers are too useless and can't keep track of her, someone wanted to use her as target practice."

Joel opened his mouth to speak, but Theo held up a hand, silencing the other man.

"No, listen, Joel. Maybe it was me they wanted to use as target practice, I'm not sure. What I do know is that not one single bullet hit Eve's car. It was almost like someone wanted her to be caught up in a drive-by just to rock the boat. Between the two of us, we know who likes to rock the boat, Joel."

Joel's fists twitched at his sides. "What are you saying, DeLuca?"

"I think you know damn well what I'm saying. The first thing you do when you get wind of a shooting is blame me. You want a fall guy. Someone else to pick up the crap you leave behind. If you're looking for another way to mess with Riley Conti, look elsewhere from me. You won't like what happens if you try to use me as your middle man on your way to the top. I did that once, and look what you did to me."

"I—"

"Don't," Theo interrupted sharply. "Don't lie, don't open your mouth and speak, and don't even think whatever bullshit you're getting ready to spit. I know better. Everybody else might be too busy shoving their heads up someone else's ass, but I'm not, Trentini."

Joel took a step forward. "You know, huh?"

"About the radio timer?" Theo asked.

Evelina caught the corner of Theo's profile as he grinned coldly.

"Yeah, Joel, I know."

"Then maybe you ought to be a little more careful, Theo."

Theo let out a low, dark laugh. "You have no idea. None."

"Of how stupid it was of you to show up at this dinner inside Trentini territory?" Joel scoffed loudly. "Oh, I think I know."

"Keep tossing your threats. They're always empty."

"Do you want to count on that?"

"Hey," Adriano said sharply, stepping in between the two men. "This isn't the place or time for this. People are watching. We're already on the news today, like Abriella said. Handle this another time."

Once again, Theo seemingly ignored Adriano's warning.

Theo pointed at Joel over Adriano's shoulder. "Blame me for this— go on ahead and do it. Give the boss someone to come at while you sneak in from behind. You're a fucking snake and you've always been slimy like one, too. This shooting has you marked all over it. If Riley Conti is too pussy-blind by the new broad he's fucking to see what you did, then that's on him, Joel. And he can suffer for his stupidity however the Outfit deems fit. But me and you? We'll do this. Go on and come at me on the streets like any good made man would do to defend his territory, Joel. Put that mouth of yours to action and actually do something instead of talking about it. Give me a reason to put you down. I dare you. *Come at me.*"

Joel barked out a laugh. "You don't know what you're asking for, DeLuca."

"I absolutely do. Unlike Dino, I'll see you coming."

Adriano turned fast on his heel to face a stone-still Theo. Without a word, Theo nodded at Adriano and spun around to leave just as quietly as he had come. Just like that, the confrontation was over. Theo hadn't even raised his voice. With a two finger wave over his shoulder, Theo disappeared back out the front door.

Evelina finally took a breath.

"Shit," Adriano muttered under his breath, still watching the windows.

Joel was already on the phone when the other women at the table finally decided to start moving again. Abriella pushed her plate aside and made a grab for the red wine. Alessa didn't take her eyes off Adriano for a second, but the worry she must have felt wrote heavy lines across her brow.

"Yeah," Joel said into his phone, "what do you think?"

A brief moment of silence passed.

Even Adriano turned to stare at Joel with a blank expression.

"Then that's what we'll do, boss," Joel said. "He did this, so he asked for it ... You're right, nobody else had a reason."

Evelina didn't know what to think. Not about Theo showing up at the dinner, or Joel's strange conversation with who she suspected to be her father. Joel might have been Riley's underboss, but the two weren't friendly. They certainly spoke like they were now.

When had Hell frozen over and how did she manage to miss it?

Evelina slammed the door closed on her BMW and tightened her messenger bag over her shoulder. After a week with no car of her own and a driver taking her back and forth from school, she was glad to have her car back. The cops had released it after Riley made a few calls and cash was handed out.

Frustrated, Evelina stared at her father's large home from the driveway. She didn't want to play nice with her new stepmother. Riley and his bride had finally gotten home from their honeymoon just a couple of days after the shooting. When her father invited her over to dinner that following Monday after Evelina's classes were out, she'd wanted to say no. Riley didn't offer the dinner like it was a suggestion, but rather, an order.

Steeling her nerves, Evelina walked across the paved walkway and up the front steps. She used her own key to unlock the door. Kicking her shoes off and tossing her coat and bag in the closet, Evelina followed the smell of food cooking in the kitchen.

Sadly, the old vintage-styled Victorian home no longer felt familiar to Evelina. It had been this way ever since her mother died. Nothing about the home felt … well, like home. It was even worse now that Courtney had taken up residence in the place.

"I'm here," Evelina said the moment she walked into the kitchen.

Courtney, with her bottle blonde hair and her big blue eyes, faced Evelina. Courtney scowled, but quickly replaced it with a fake smile and a flighty wave of her jeweled fingers. One of those rings in particular, Evelina recognized. It happened to be her mother's.

It was another thing for Evelina to put on her list of why she disliked this spoiled, young woman. Courtney didn't mind that the jewelry she wore was once a woman's who had been married to the girl's husband for over twenty years, or the fact he had two children, both of whom were close to Courtney's age.

No, the girl just liked things. Flashy things, pretty things, sparkly things. Any kind of thing.

Evelina had to swallow back the rising bile as she thought about the fact her father had been messing around with Courtney for some while. Long before Mia had even been killed. Courtney was nothing more than a mistress who had won her man's last name by default.

Mia had been a much stronger and better woman than this one would ever be. Evelina sincerely hoped her father realized that.

"Hello there, Eve," Courtney said, still smiling far too wide for it to be true. Turning back to the cook who was busy checking the items in the oven, Courtney gestured at the gray-haired woman. "Corrine is just finishing up some things and we'll be able to eat."

"That's fine." Evelina didn't have much of an appetite whenever she was around Courtney anyway. "Where's my father?"

"Busy and you shouldn't bother him. Riley gets testy when people interrupt him while he's busy in his office. You know that."

"I'm aware. I just wondered where he was."

"Did Rhonda let you in?" Courtney asked. "I didn't hear the doorbell."

"No, I let myself in."

Courtney slapped the counter with her palm. The woman eyed Evelina like she was the stupidest thing to grace her presence.

"See, this is what I keep telling your father about," Courtney said.

"I beg your pardon?"

"This—you letting yourself in! You don't live here, Eve. You're old enough to know that it's rude to just walk on in to someone's home without even shouting a hello when you enter. Come on, you know this."

Evelina arched a brow and bit her inner cheek to keep from spewing all the vile things she thought Courtney needed to hear. "I didn't realize I had to hand over the keys to my childhood home just because my father married a new woman."

Courtney's cheeks pinked. "What did you just say to me?"

"We both know you're not deaf and I didn't mumble."

Ouch. Even Evelina had to admit, there was a hell of a lot of bark in her tone.

"Where do you get off—"

Corrine dropped a steaming glass casserole to the counter, interrupting the two women's glaring contest. "Mrs. Conti, the food is ready. Please let your husband know."

"Yes," Evelina said, letting her tone ooze with false sweetness. "Go let my father know his daughter is here to have supper with him, *Mrs. Conti.*"

Huffing under her breath, Courtney stormed from the kitchen. Evelina let the woman's anger and attitude bounce off her. It wasn't the first time the two had words with one another and it surely wouldn't be the last.

Corrine waved Evelina over and gave her a piece of peanut butter fudge from the glass center piece that held a dozen different sweet treats. "Here, a gift for your bravery."

Evelina snorted indelicately. "There's nothing brave about honesty, auntie."

The cook had always been close to the Conti children. For as long as Evelina could remember, Corrine worked in their home. She'd helped the kids with homework, cleaned their faces, and sometimes stayed long after supper was served just to spend more time with them.

"My God, you are working on her nerves something awful," Corrine said with a quiet laugh. "Be careful, or you'll find yourself under your father's wrath."

Evelina shrugged. "I didn't do anything."

"Sadly, that's true. But it doesn't change the fact your father has eyes for her and everything she says is golden to him right now, my Eve." Corrine offered Evelina another sly smile as she added, "And I know Courtney is a very ... *special* young lady, but she does keep your father's attention diverted to her instead of the things you're doing."

"You're not actually defending her, are you?" Evelina asked.

Corrine scoffed. "God, no. She is rotten on her good days, but she has a way with Riley's temper. I like not having to deal with that when I'm working. Did your brother not want to come?"

"He had work to do."

"What about Alessa?"

Evelina passed Corrine a look. "What about her?"

"Yeah, never mind. Riley doesn't treat her particularly well, does he?"

"That's putting it mildly. He treats her like garbage, and she won't spend a second near him when Adriano isn't there to put Dad in his place. I don't blame her."

Corrine frowned. "Me, neither. She doesn't deserve that, poor girl."

No, Alessa certainly didn't.

"Maybe he'll ease up after the baby comes," Corrine suggested.

"Maybe," Evelina echoed.

"Let's eat!"

Riley's shout echoed through the house followed by high feminine laughter, and the low chuckles of another man. Nobody said a thing about someone else joining them for dinner.

"Oh, I forgot to mention," Corrine said.

"About what?" Evelina asked.

"Your father has a guest."

"Who?"

"Tommas Rossi."

Evelina helped Corrine load the dishwasher with the dishes from supper. Her father and Tommas had disappeared after a quiet dinner. Actually, it was kind of nice. Riley hadn't bombarded Evelina with demands like he usually did. He asked her about college and how Adriano had seemed that week.

A loud sigh drew Evelina's attention to the kitchen entryway. Courtney stood there with her arms crossed as her pink pumps tapped a beat to the tiled floor.

"Eve, you're not required to assist the help in cleaning up. You can leave if you'd like, since the dinner is over and everything."

Evelina straightened to a standing position as Corrine quietly put the last few cups into the top of the dishwasher. "It's never actually been Corrine's job to handle the cleaning after meals."

"Is that so?" Courtney asked, her nose crinkling.

"Don't," Corrine said far too softly for the fool across the room to hear.

Evelina ignored her. "It is. Our mother used to have us help her because it taught us some sense of value in ourselves and respect for those who work for us. It also taught us how to take care of ourselves because not everyone can afford cooks and maids."

Courtney was the perfect case in point. She hadn't been very much except Riley Conti's mistress in a paid-for apartment before Mia's death.

"Well, your mother isn't here anymore and I am. Corrine knows her place."

Her place?

What in the honest *fuck*?

"The only reason you are here is because my mother isn't," Evelina said, struggling to keep her tone level.

"Eve," Corrine murmured, placing a hand on Evelina's arm gently. "It's fine, dear."

No, it wasn't.

Someone needed to clue Courtney into the truth, and Evelina really didn't give a good goddamn what her father would think about it.

"Oh, let her have her words," Courtney said, laughing sharply and waving a hand dismissively. "God knows if I have to sit through another dinner pretending to give a damn about Riley's spoiled little bitch of a daughter for one more minute, I will scream."

Evelina scoffed so loudly it echoed. "Spoiled? Spoiled? Courtney, you are the definition of a well-paid whore. The only thing you were worthy enough to do in my father's life was step into the role of his wife after my mother was dead. You wear her jewelry, you sleep in her sheets, and you drive her goddamn car. And that black mink coat you adore so much? Even that was hers. So you know what? You're second place and that's the first bitch to lose. You're a man's second pick. The hand-me-down wife, Courtney. You might wear my mother's rings, but you're absolutely nothing like her. And you could never be. Everybody knows it, even my father. You're the only one playing house here, sweetheart. The rest of us are just making due with the replacement."

Courtney gaped with what could only be described as a fish-face.

Evelina didn't give the woman a chance to respond and instead, gave Corrine a tight smile. "Thank you for dinner, it was lovely. As usual."

"Eve ..."

Even Corrine didn't know what to say.

"It's perfectly fine," Evelina whispered, aching in her heart. She'd let out a lot of anger and resentment. A great deal of it probably should have been directed at her father, but Courtney was the easy target. "I should go."

Corrine nodded.

Evelina wasted no time getting out of the kitchen. Courtney glared as Evelina passed by. Unbothered by the woman's attitude, Evelina glared back. Sometimes the truth hurt. Courtney had to learn that little fact of life.

Evelina had.

At the closet where she'd dropped off her things earlier, Evelina stopped to gather her stuff. The sound of familiar male voices coming down the stairwell from up above echoed inside the closet. It was one of the oddities about the large, old home. In some places, the walls were paper thin.

"A marriage," Tommas said, dragging the last word out.

Evelina felt the blood freeze in her veins.

"It's my last resort," Riley replied.

"Well, I think there are a dozen more ways to correct the issues rather than that, boss."

"Perhaps, but this will suit me well, too. After all that Adriano did with Alessa, the stains he left are hard to clean, Tommas. And now we have a mess with Walter Artino ending up dead in his house. Did you see the autopsy photos?"

"I did. He'd been dead quite a while before his wife came home from her vacation and found him."

Evelina shuddered.

"Another problem, Tommas."

"You've already got allies where you need them. I'm sure the DeLuca mess will clean itself up on its own. That's how it usually works."

"And if it doesn't?"

Tommas sighed and the footsteps above Evelina's head stopped. "Have you given consideration—"

"I don't need to. This works, Tommas."

"All I see is another problem. You might push everyone right over the edge here, Riley."

"A marriage will solve that," Riley replied sharply. "And if Joel is willing and you're not, then he can take the arrangement."

"You're willing to marry your daughter off to Joel Trentini just to keep him in line?"

"It's more than that!"

Evelina couldn't breathe.

No way in hell.

She couldn't marry Joel!

Joel?

"And I know he'll take it, and in a few years, that will make him look all the better for the seat, Tommas."

"Fine," Tommas muttered heavily.

"Hmm, what was that? A little louder, please."

"Fine," Tommas repeated, "I'll take the marriage."

"Good choice."

Evelina felt her fingernails cut into her palm.

She couldn't marry Tommas Rossi, either. While her mother had been adopted by David Rossi and his wife when Mia was just an infant, making the cousin relation between Tommas and Evelina only through marriage, she had grown up knowing him as her family. But even she could overlook that. What she couldn't overlook was her friend.

Abriella …

Why would Tommas agree?

"Give me a week or so to think it all over before I officially say yes or no," Riley said.

"I thought this was the yes or no," Tommas replied, chuckling.

Even the sound of the man's amusement was strained and sad. Tommas had never settled with a woman because he had one he loved. Evelina knew it, and that stabbed at her heart as she thought about what that could mean for him and her.

Why agree? Evelina didn't waste any more time thinking about it. As the footsteps began to move down the staircase again, she simply yanked her coat on, closed the door, and left the house.

Anywhere …

She had to go anywhere but there.

CHAPTER SEVEN

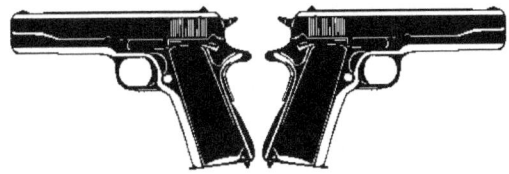

"Riley is back."

Theo didn't look up from the stack of money he shoved into the cash counter. The machine spat the bills out on the other side and lit up the screen with a digital number in the thousands. Whenever Friday rolled around in any given week, the members of Theo's crew who handled cash flow, because their hands could be trusted not to steal, dropped off their cash, took their shit, and ran with it. Theo's cut was always ninety percent of whatever somebody brought in to him whether it be from dealing, stealing, or scheming.

Or hell, even all three.

Theo wasn't picky as long as money was being made and his crew was being productive with their methods of making cash on the kind of streets where everybody had something to sell. But out of Theo's ninety percent, seventy of that went to the boss.

Sighing, Theo slapped the cut owed to Riley into an envelope and slid it into a drawer in the old, weather-beaten desk. Regardless of his feelings toward the boss, or the problems he was facing with the Trentini crew, the head of the family was the head of the family.

"Nice pile," his guest appraised from the doorway.

"My boys follow through," Theo said, grinning.

"How much do you have there, anyway?"

"This is just from the early ones. I've got the better payments coming in tonight."

"That's not what I asked, Theo."

"One-fifty."

"One-hundred-fifty?"

"Thousand," Theo confirmed.

Damian whistled low. "Jesus Christ. How are you making that in a month?"

Theo glanced up from the pile of cash that was his. "My take is only forty-five grand, D."

"Still … you said this was the early guys. What else are you waiting on?"

"Rackets from the pier and the construction companies come in checks and a couple of my bookies pay on Saturdays."

Labor rackets sometimes happened to be a hard thing to get on. A Capo needed to find the right company willing to pay out employees on the payroll when they actually didn't even show up to the job.

Damian frowned. "The Rossi crew is barely touching one-hundred in a week."

"Maybe the Capo thing just isn't for you, D."

"That's what I fucking told Tommas, all right."

Theo chuckled. "Or maybe you're not watching the hands that are feeding you close enough, man. Tommas always had a high earning crew. He's got a hand in just about everything. Weapons dealing with some gangs here, drug selling there ... shit, he even managed to get a racket in on that road crew when they were tearing up the new highways. Seven flaggers were hired and never missed a day, but then again, they never showed up. He's got a smooth talk and people fall in line with that."

Damian's face turned unreadable as he surveyed Theo's cash again. "It's not that I dislike the title and job, man."

"Then what is it?"

"I'm still getting used to the spotlight."

Theo hummed. "Ghost, huh?"

"Well, I used to be."

"You know, you have to give it time, Damian. Being a Capo is tedious and slow. It takes years to build a decent name and reputation on the streets and five minutes to lose it all. As far as the DeLucas go, this pile used to be split between Dino, Walter, and me. Just like how Bastoni used to divide his with Adriano, or Tommas with his father."

Damian cocked a brow. "I hadn't thought of it that way, although they didn't kill their partners."

Theo kept his expression blank. Walter's death wasn't necessarily being blamed on Theo, but people weren't not blaming him, either. He also wouldn't be attending the funeral, whenever it was had.

"I have no idea what you're talking about, Damian."

"Sure you don't."

"We're not discussing whatever it is you want to discuss, D."

"You did hear what I said when I first came in, right?" Damian asked.

"Yep. Riley's back. Here." Theo pulled open the drawer, grabbed the item he put in there earlier, and tossed the envelope to Damian. The other Capo caught it easily and the money disappeared in Damian's jacket pocket. "Take that to the bastard and deliver it to him. I have no plans for my next tribute to be my last when it's accompanied by a bullet to my skull."

"Sure, I'll make sure it gets to Riley."

"Let him know another one will make its way to him, also."

"Whatever."

"What are you doing down here in the Heights, anyway?" Theo asked.

"Giving you a heads-up, old friend."

Theo scoffed. "About Riley's return? I've known about it for a week. Word travels fast when the boss is back in town and all that interesting shit."

Riley had returned home and hadn't sent a single word along to Theo. Sure, rumors flew about what the boss had to say, but very little of it was likely true. The shooting incident that happened nearly two weeks before had practically faded into obscurity. Nothing had happened since and Joel Trentini had yet to act on anything he promised. Once again, Joel's mouth was a hell of a lot bigger than his actions.

Theo wasn't concerned.

"No, not about the boss," Damian said. "Although he has a lot to do with it. Some people are getting antsy, that's all."

"About what?"

"The fact you're being so quiet."

Theo smirked, unable to hide it. "Being quiet is a problem?"

"It is when a couple of weeks before, you were confronting the underboss at a family dinner."

"Joel asked for that."

Damian tossed his hands in his pockets, seemingly unconcerned. "Maybe he did."

"So what's the problem?"

"The problem is that maybe I'd like to make sure you don't end up like your brother, Theo," Damian said quietly. "With Lily being pregnant and all, it just reinforces this belief that she should be happy and her family should be happy. I'm sick and fucking tired of watching my wife suffer because of the selfish men surrounding her."

Theo's jaw ticked; his only show of agitation. "What is that supposed to mean?"

"You know what it means. Don't play dumb. Lily doesn't need another one of her brothers ending up dead because of his own stupidity."

"Are you suggesting that Dino—"

"I'm not suggesting anything, I'm stating it."

Theo didn't like what Damian was playing at. Like fire, it was probably going to burn. Theo had his suspicions about what Dino had been up to before his murder, but no proof. Every finger that Theo pointed at Dino for certain things could be pointed at other people for the same reasons. In fact, the Outfit did blame others for certain things. The shooting that killed Mia. The shooting of a Conti business. The shooting at the Trentini home that killed Theo's uncle and a Rossi twin.

Dino had been a quiet man, but for the months leading up to his death, Theo noticed his brother had turned more solitary in nature. When Dino called Lily back from traveling, Theo really took note of the changes in his brother. Then he found out about Dino's son.

Clearing his throat, Theo slammed the drawer shut on his desk and stepped out to face Damian. "What do you know about my brother, huh?"

"More than I want to," Damian admitted.

Tommas Rossi's words from nearly two weeks before rattled around in the back of Theo's mind. *Have you ever thought that maybe your brother is the reason for all of this?*

Had the scars of the DeLuca brothers' raising under their uncle's demanding, cold eye finally opened back up for Dino? Had he finally bled out all that pain and all his secrets with a few bullets and some bloodshed?

"Revenge is a dish best served cold," Damian said. "But never forget, your hand is the one holding the plate as you deliver it and that'll leave you feeling like ice, too."

Theo chuckled, feeling deader than ever inside. "Thanks for the heads-up."

"You didn't even hear a word I said, do you?"

"I hear what I want to hear," Theo replied.

"Which is what, man?"

"That you know a lot more than you should, D."

Damian stiffened, but he didn't look away from Theo. "Yeah, I do."

"So how much of this mess was you, too?"

"The part of the mess that keeps me breathing, Theo."

Lily.

Theo let it go.

A knock on the office door broke the men's staring contest.

"Yeah, it's open," Theo said to whoever was waiting behind the door.

One of his younger guys pushed the door open when Damian moved out of the way. Eighteen-year-old Cole Artino looked Damian up and down. He likely didn't recognize the hitman turned Capo, but anyone who came into Theo's strip club and who got invited to the back offices wasn't just a regular patron. But the kid knew better than to ask questions.

That's why Theo liked him for certain things.

"What?" Theo asked.

"I need the key for the holding room," Cole said.

"Why?"

"Pick-ups."

Theo grunted his approval and pulled the keys in question out of his pocket before tossing them to the kid. "Make sure every pound is marked and counted, and that every man who takes a brick has paid me for the week and for his spot."

Cole nodded. "I will."

"I'll be right behind you to look over the books, kid."

"I know, Skip."

With that, the kid disappeared.

Damian laughed when the door shut. "Is he even legal to be inside this joint?"

"Barely. Three months past his eighteenth. He can't drink or serve liquor, so I don't let him. No need to have the cops in here going batshit crazy over a kid with a liquor bottle in his hands. They've got enough to watch me for without adding him to the mix."

"Yet, you're letting him handle business for you."

"Some," Theo agreed. "He needs to learn the ropes somehow and I don't have time to be hands on for every single little detail, so he's learning what respect means through trial and error."

"Sounds a lot like how we learned this business, Theo."

Theo tensed. "Without all the beatings, sure."

Damian knew what it was like to be under the control of men like Ben DeLuca, after all. Theo didn't need to add to his statement.

"What is the kid doing for you exactly?" Damian asked.

Theo grinned. "In here? He's my middle man, D, the one I wouldn't mind giving a button even if that meant he'd take my seat. Every good Capo needs one."

"This looks good, Cole," Theo said as he checked the black notebook the kid had spread out over the pool table. "You're getting better with the numbers. There's nothing short this week. That's three weeks in a row."

Cole grinned, happy with the praise. "I learned my lesson the last time."

"Good."

Unlike Theo's lessons as he learned the trade of a Capo, Cole didn't get quite the same treatment. Theo would have received a beating for messing up, but Cole had shit he liked taken away from him so he could think about what he did like a child who had misbehaved.

Simple? Yes, but effective.

Ben DeLuca's lessons for his nephews hadn't just been about business, but also things like violence, numbness, being untouchable, and having no fear. Sometimes the brothers didn't even know the beatings were coming. Inside this very room in the strip club, Theo had taken a beating from Riley Conti. The man hadn't always been the front boss. Once, he was just a Capo.

Theo learned quickly that fighting back when Ben leveled down one of his lessons would only earn him a far worse punishment. It finally stopped for Theo once he'd gotten his button. Theo still had a scar that ran from just below his neck to his right pec from the incident with Riley. He'd gotten it covered up with a tattoo of a tribal owl with sharp eyes and an even sharper beak.

Back to business, Theo reminded himself. *Leave that shit in the past.*

"I see Jonas took an extra ten pounds," Theo noted.

"Yeah, but I didn't see the issue seeing as how he said he sold out before mid-week, and had the cash to prove it."

"If he's short once, he goes back to the regular ten without the extra."

"Sure, Skip."

Theo pressed in the false top on the broken pool table and lifted it up. Bricks of cocaine, taped, marked and ready to sell, rested inside. Theo tossed the notebook in with the bricks and closed the top back up.

Not a second later, someone knocked on the storage room door.

"It's open," Theo said.

Karver, a bouncer for the club and bodyguard for the strippers, pushed the door open. "Boss, there's somebody out front asking for you."

"Oh?" Theo asked, fixing his suit jacket as he turned to face the man. "Yeah."

That wasn't anything unusual, but Theo had been terribly careful about not letting his whereabouts be known for the last week or so. He didn't want to run into another shooting situation or something else that might end up getting him killed.

"Who is it?"

"Not sure," the bouncer answered. "But I think this is the first time I've ever seen a female walk into this place who wasn't looking for a job and didn't already work on a pole."

Theo caught sight of Evelina the moment he stepped on the strip club's floor. It wasn't like she stuck out in the crowd, but she was mighty hard to miss in her tight black dress, silver sky-high heels and radiating a grace any woman would be envious over. She didn't look like the place offended her high-class sensibilities as she took the drink a server offered and turned to watch a woman grind on the pole only ten feet away.

What in the hell was she doing here?

Theo's throat tightened when Evelina's tongue peeked out to lick the rim of her glass. The reddish colored liquid inside swirled as she twirled her hand and grinned at the woman working the pole. Did she enjoy watching the woman dance? There wasn't a lick of disapproval or judgment on Evelina's pretty face.

In fact, her nose crinkled upward as she smiled and drew her full bottom lip in between her teeth.

Christ.

Theo's pants turned snugger at the sight of her biting her lip. He couldn't help but wonder what Evelina would look like if he shoved something else between her lips while his hand was under her dress.

Evelina cocked a brow and tilted her head to the side with a look of interest as the girl slid lower on the pole while upside down. Good *God*. Who was this girl? Where had she come from?

He liked it a lot.

A lot more than he was willing to admit.

Theo shook those thoughts off and steeled his spine. Regardless of his curiosity towards the Conti princess, the woman couldn't be in his club. Hell, she couldn't even be in his territory.

And didn't she say there was GPS on her goddamn car?

Strolling across the floor, Theo ignored the curious gazes of the patrons. Rarely did he come out of the back offices during business hours. He wasn't there for the girls or their moves on stage. That wasn't his scene. But the joint brought in good money. The girls knew how to keep their mouths shut about some of his more illegal activities during certain weekdays, and that was hard to find in an employee.

Someone always talked.

No one in here ever did.

Evelina turned her head just enough to catch sight of Theo. The small grin she'd been sporting as she watched the woman dance melted into something far sexier. She seemed ready to be out at a club with her dark makeup accentuating her green eyes and her hair piled high in a messy chignon, showcasing delicate collarbones and the soft lines of her features.

No doubt about it, Evelina was a beautiful young woman. Theo would need to be stupid, blind and an idiot not to see it. She was also ten shades of trouble that he didn't particularly need at the moment.

"Eve," Theo greeted as he saddled up beside her at the bar.

"She's very good," Evelina said, nodding at the dancer.

Theo shrugged. "I suppose. I'm not the one who vets the dancers before they get the job."

Evelina glanced at him. She was only shorter than him by a couple of inches in her heels, but it was enough to make her need to look up through those thick lashes of hers. "You don't watch them while they work?"

"No."

"Why?"

"Because I'm here to work, Eve, not get my rocks off on lap dances and strip teases."

Evelina smiled a tiny smile. "Huh, imagine that."

"What?"

"I think all those rumors about you and women are a load of crap, especially if you spend a lot of your work time in a strip club and can't even be bothered to taste the spread. I'm sure they would be willing."

Theo laughed deeply. "Probably."

He'd had a few offers.

Not that he took any of them.

"Since when do you frequent strip clubs?" Theo asked, curious.

Evelina winked. "Since someone told me to have a little fun a few years ago."

Well, damn.

"Strip clubs was where you found that? This isn't necessarily the kind of place where an Outfit daughter should be hanging out, Evelina."

"Not necessarily, but I learned that everybody has a job to do, Theo. This is just one of them, and it's a paycheck like anybody else's nine-to-five."

"True."

"Are you going to send me away now?" Evelina asked.

Theo watched her from the side, taking in the curves of her body underneath her black dress and the way her legs looked to be a mile long standing in those heels. The demure look she wore only added to the fact he found himself reacting to her just by being close. The scent of whatever perfume she wore was a mixture of heady and sweet, and it soaked into his lungs instantly.

Yes.

Yes, he was going to send her away. Because she looked like sin and she was standing in a place meant for it. Theo did terribly well with sinning.

"Yes," Theo murmured.

"That's a shame."

"Why?"

Evelina flashed her white teeth in a sinful smirk. "Because you never gave me the chance to thank you, Theo."

His confusion climbed higher.

"For what?"

"Keeping me from getting shot."

"Eve, there's no need to thank me for that."

"I know," she said, "but it seems like everyone wants to blame you for it and I wanted you to know that I don't. I wanted to tell you directly, so you could know, Theo. People think I'm deaf or something, or maybe they just think I won't repeat what I hear. It doesn't matter really, because when you showed up at the dinner, I figured out enough from that, anyway."

Theo blinked, surprised. "How did you find out I was here tonight?"

Evelina lifted a single shoulder in response, and tilted her glass up to her lips to take a sip.

"Eve," Theo pressed.

"Maybe I got Alessa to get some information out of Adriano. But who knows?"

Theo chuckled. "Yeah, who knows?"

"Not me."

"You shouldn't be here, Eve," Theo warned quietly.

"I know. I left my car a couple of blocks into the Conti side of the territory line and grabbed a cab. So even if someone comes looking, they won't find me. Thanks for that advice on the GPS, by the way. It came in handy after all."

Theo swallowed hard, wondering what kind of game this woman was trying to play with him. "Did you think that this might get me into a hell of a lot of trouble, too?"

"Maybe, but I just needed to do something different tonight."

"And you came to me."

Evelina shifted on her heels, still watching the stage and the dancer. "Why not?"

"I have a dozen reasons why not, Eve."

She tilted her head just enough to catch his gaze again. Evelina held it, her stare never wavering. There was something in the hard expression she wore that told him something was wrong.

Theo wouldn't ask.

He couldn't care.

Not right now.

"They're going to turn me into someone I don't want to be," Evelina said quietly.

He didn't even have to ask what she meant. Theo knew. The Outfit. It was always about the Outfit where they were concerned. Someone did that to Theo once, too.

"I learned to like the changes," Theo murmured.

Evelina sighed. It came out breathy and tired, but it still made Theo ache. No, he couldn't deny his attraction to Evelina Conti. But what he could do was control himself in her presence.

Never think with your cock or heart.

DeLuca rule number one.

Evelina wet her bottom lip as she looked him over. "I think I figured something out way too late."

"Oh?"

"Yeah. I don't want to be a princess."

Theo pushed away from the stools, grabbed Evelina's drink from her grasp, and set it to the bar top without a word.

"That's too bad," Theo said.

"Is it?"

"Yes."

He snagged her wrist in his palm and pulled Evelina away from the bar without a word.

"What are you doing?" she asked as he tugged her through the club and closer to the front.

"Taking you back to your car."

Evelina yanked hard, stopping Theo. "Why?"

"Because you don't seem to get it, Eve. You're right, it's too damn late to try and change shit now. And I will not be the sacrifice you bleed out in an attempt to feel better. I've got enough people as it is waiting in the wings for me with knives already sharpened."

Her gaze darkened. "Is that why you think I came here?"

"To get some kind of rebellious streak out? Yeah, I do."

"Wrong," she spat.

"Then what is it?"

"I just wanted to spend five minutes with someone I thought might understand."

Theo forced those words away. He didn't want to hear that.

"I'm sorry, Eve, but I can't do that, either. Not with you."

"Why the hell not?" she asked.

"Because I might like it."

Theo had never been good at denying things he liked.

Evelina just stared at him, saying nothing.

"I'll take you to your car," he said again.

Evelina didn't argue.

CHAPTER EIGHT

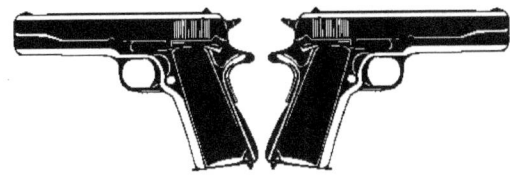

"Where are your enforcers tonight?" Theo asked.

Evelina fidgeted in the passenger seat. "I told Adriano I was going to the store to pick up some junk food. They don't follow me down the street."

"Seriously?"

"Well, Adriano tells them to back off sometimes, too."

Theo shook his head. "Jesus. Useless. That's what they are."

Maybe. But Evelina got out without someone noticing.

"I didn't see you at church last Sunday," Evelina said.

The corner of Theo's mouth lifted wickedly, but he didn't take his eyes off the road. "Did you seriously think I'd be going to church with all this nonsense going on?"

"Let me correct that then."

"Please do."

"I haven't noticed you at church since your brother's funeral."

Theo tensed in the driver's seat and his hands gripped the steering wheel tight enough for his knuckles to turn ash white. "I'm not ready, I suppose."

"I get that."

Chuckles answered her back.

"No, Eve, I don't think you do. I've got a few things left to get finished, and when I go back, I'd like to get all of my confession out in one good, long sitting instead of three or four. Besides, confession is meant for those who don't wish to repeat their sins. Mine are ones that won't go away until others leave, too."

Evelina's brow furrowed as she took in his words. He spoke about it so candidly, like he'd been thinking about it for a while.

"Are you talking about my father?"

Theo's gaze cut to her as he took a corner sharply. "And if I was?"

Evelina shrugged. "Look elsewhere for someone who cares, Theo."

"You care. Trust me, you do. Even the people we hate always manage to pull some sympathy from us, even if it's just a little bit. Regardless of whatever you feel is wrong with your father, he's still your blood, he still

81

helped to put you on this earth, and you still love him, Eve. Simple as that."

"He didn't care much about my mother these last few months."

Theo blew out a slow breath. "You're not Riley. He's not you."

"Is that how you feel about your brother or uncle?"

"Hmm?"

"Your brother and uncle. You were close to Ben but not really Dino. Is that how you feel about them, like your sympathy is greater for one, but still there in some way for the other?"

Theo's hands tightened on the wheel. "You ask a lot of questions."

"I'm a curious girl."

"Woman."

"What?"

"You're a woman, not a girl. You stopped being a girl years ago, Eve."

Evelina shivered in the passenger seat. The shadows of the passing street lights darkened Theo's features. She couldn't have hid the reaction even if she tried. Just the way his voice dipped into a lower cadence, and he passed her another silent look that said he could see she was very much a woman and not a girl was enough to make Evelina ache.

And *wet.*

"You did that on purpose," Evelina accused.

Her voice was weak.

Or turned on.

Theo raised a brow high. "I beg your pardon?"

"That ... *that* ... right there," Evelina struggled to say as she waved at him.

Theo laughed under his breath. "Babe, I have no idea what you're mumbling about, but all right. Whatever makes you happy, I guess."

"Stop it. You did do that on purpose, Theo. Just to distract me."

When his tongue snaked out to wet his lips as his hands slid across the steering wheel smoothly to take another turn, Evelina's throat went dry. He handled his car easily, like he was holding onto feathers when in fact, the Stingray had one hell of an engine under the hood. She couldn't stop the thoughts slamming into her one after the other as she watched him drive.

Is that how he touches a woman? What do those hands feel like when they grab hard enough to hurt? Is that how he would touch me?

Jesus.

Evelina made a noise under her breath and turned her attention to anywhere but Theo DeLuca for a moment.

"Eve?"

"What?"

Evelina had all she could do to ignore the heat between her legs and the air in her voice. She completely refused to even look at Theo again until she could manage to do so without contemplating how she could get his hands on her while he drove at the same time.

Stop that right now.

"I kind of did that on purpose," Theo admitted.

"I knew it!"

Theo chuckled a dark, lovely sound that rocked Evelina straight to her core. "So you can show up at a strip club looking for a man, and enjoy the show all the while, but you can't spend thirty minutes alone with him in a car without being embarrassed? That's a little strange."

"It is not," Evelina retorted hotly. "And you're well aware that it's not the same thing—we're not the same thing."

"Oh?"

"No."

Theo pulled the car over to the side of the road, threw it in park, and unbuckled his seat belt without any warning. Then, he turned to face Evelina with a slowness and grace that reminded her of a predator who might have just caught a prey in his sights.

"Then do tell, Eve."

"W-what?"

Why was her throat so goddamn dry again?

"Tell me what is so different about us. I'd love to know."

Theo's brown stare was practically black as he watched her under the lamplight shining into the Stingray. They weren't very far from where she'd parked her car, maybe only a block or two away. His side-crop peaked style hair seemed a little messier than normal, like maybe he'd been running his fingers through it.

Was he stressed?

Why?

"You know," Eve said, willing away the thickness in her tone, "… a while ago, I probably would have asked you if some girl was pulling on your hair just because it always looks like you were fucking somebody."

Theo's lips drew thin. "Mmm."

"Yeah, and all that charm you've got is a mighty good deflection to keep people's attention on where you want it to be." Evelina shifted in the seat so her back was pressed to the door and she could watch him, too. "We've all got walls to keep people out, and I think your charisma and distractions are yours. It lets you keep people close, but only as close as you want them."

"Interesting," Theo said. "But what does it matter?"

"It doesn't. Not to anyone else. But maybe I want to know why you're doing it to me, too."

"I'm not."

"Liar," Evelina whispered.

Theo's gaze flitted away briefly before he sat back down in his seat and threw the car out of park. Evelina couldn't let him do that. It was just another deflection. Before she'd really thought her actions over, she leaned across the seat and grabbed his wrist as he placed his hands on the steering wheel.

"Stop," she demanded.

The muscles in his arm jumped under her touch. She grabbed tighter, squeezing his wrist.

It was a blink.

Just a blink ... Evelina found herself pushed back to the door roughly. It didn't hurt, but it was shocking. There was nothing sweet in Theo's angry, dark stare. His jaw was clenched tight, teeth bared. A hissed cuss was right on the tip of his tongue as Evelina gasped.

She let him go.

Theo swallowed hard and rested back into his seat, rubbing his wrist in circles with his other hand. Her small squeeze couldn't have possibly hurt him, but pain marred his features all the same.

"I'm ... sorry," Theo rasped.

Evelina's eyes widened and her heart raced.

What just happened?

"It's okay," Evelina said.

"Don't grab me, not like that."

"Not there or not at all?"

Theo's shoulders stiffened.

It wasn't the first time Evelina had noticed Theo's strange quirk of rubbing his wrist whenever he turned quiet or a certain subject was brought up. A subject like his brother or uncle.

"Theo," Evelina said softly.

He closed his eyes, sucked in a breath, and then stared out the front windshield. The anger was gone, but so was everything else. All that was left on Theo's handsome features was a cold, blank expression as he grabbed the steering wheel, and the car pulled out onto the road.

"Theo, there or not at all?" she asked again.

"There."

"Okay." Evelina filed that info away for later. "Why?"

"Because I don't like it, all right," he said harshly.

"You rub it a lot, I noticed. I asked and—"

"And I told you it doesn't hurt, I just don't like it."

Like a vice, she realized. He used it like a vice. Or maybe a memory. Evelina wondered what Theo was hiding.

"This is why, Eve."

Evelina watched him warily. "Why what?"

"I don't date."

The words might as well have been spit through his teeth. He didn't take his intense, burning stare off the road for a second. Evelina was grateful because she was sure if he turned it on her, it would surely hurt.

Evelina blinked, confused. "At all?"

"No."

"Hookups is kind of like dating," Evelina said. "I mean, in a way."

"In a way," he echoed. "Only if you keep seeking out and fucking the same person."

"And you don't."

Theo cringed. "I don't mind having a dozen women hanging around. I don't mind sweet-talking them or letting people believe whatever they want about my relationships with those women. I just don't care."

Evelina cleared her throat, feeling more uncertain than ever. "Why?"

"Because then I don't have to explain why I don't have a girlfriend or a wife yet, or even a few kids running around under my feet when I'm twenty-seven-years old. I don't have to explain why I don't want those things. Instead, people just see what they want to see about me and they draw their own conclusions. I am more than fine with letting them do that."

"Theo—"

"Why did you come looking for me tonight?" he asked sharply. "*Why?*"

"I told you."

"A bunch of bullshit."

"It is not!"

Theo glowered at the windshield. "I think it is. I don't know what you're looking for when it comes to me, but look elsewhere, princess. You won't find it here."

Evelina glared right back at him, even if he wasn't looking at her. "You sought me out first, Theo. Remember? Several times."

"Stupidity," Theo spat.

"Yours or mine?"

"Mine, obviously."

Evelina sighed, over the entire conversation. "You know what, I'm done."

"There's nothing to be done about."

Wrong.

He was so wrong.

"There's something," Evelina said quietly, crossing her arms and watching the buildings pass them by. "There was something."

"You have to start something to finish it, Eve."

"You started it with me!"

Theo's hand smacked the wheel hard. "You don't get it, do you? I'm

85

not in the right spot or frame of mind to give you anything and even when I thought I was, I still couldn't. I was playing stupid, just like my fucking brother. Hiding bad things and keeping the lights on at night. I won't keep doing that, Eve. Look elsewhere."

"I didn't come looking for anything!"

"Yes, you did," Theo said heavily. "You did because you came to me tonight. Don't do this. I can't do this, Eve."

"I don't understand."

"Of course you don't. Princess, remember?"

"DeLuca *principe*, isn't that what they call you?"

Theo laughed, dark and hateful.

"Yeah. And the king should have kept me locked in the tower, Eve."

Before Evelina could respond, Theo cursed under his breath and cut the lights on the Stingray. The car jerked to the side of the road again.

"Where did you say you left your BMW?" he asked.

Evelina followed Theo's stare, noting the flashing red, blue, and white lights reflecting off the buildings down the block. The police cars—there had to be more than one with the amount of lights going—couldn't be seen from their position.

"Eve?" Theo asked.

"I parked it in a twenty-four hour spot where it wouldn't get ticketed or towed."

"Where those lights are coming from down that street."

Evelina nodded. "Yeah."

"Shit."

"This is bad, right?"

Theo scoffed. "No, this is perfect. Great, even."

"Sarcasm looks awful on you, Theo."

"Liar, I look goddamn good when I'm being an arrogant ass and everybody knows it."

Evelina didn't bother denying it. Because he did look good when he acted like as asshole. Well, he looked good all the time.

"Shut up, Theo," Evelina muttered, unwilling to give him the last word.

A faint smile curved his lips as he shook his head. "That all you got?"

"For now."

Theo pulled the Stingray back on the road silently and turned the lights back on.

"What are you doing?" she asked.

"Quiet."

"Theo—"

"Eve, sit there and be quiet, goddammit."

He didn't act like anything was amiss as they drove closer to where the lights were flashing down inside the street. A block had been put up at the end of the street where police officers stood, huddled in groups. A few people gathered around the road block, looking down the street.

Evelina couldn't help herself; she leaned forward and looked down the road when Theo slowed the car down. If her heart had been racing before, it now felt like it was going to jump right out of her throat.

"Oh, my God," Evelina whispered.

"That your car?" Theo asked.

Was.

Was her car, she wanted to say to him.

Now, it looked like black, twisted metal. It was still smoking. What in the hell happened? Evelina glanced around the people down in the street, but couldn't discern the faces. It couldn't have been a random attack. Not her car. And by the looks of it, that was a pretty big bang.

When a police officer noticed Theo's car slowing down, he stepped away from the group of officials to approach. Theo hit the gas and sent Evelina flying back into the seat.

"Sorry," Theo muttered.

"S'okay."

It wasn't.

Nothing was okay.

"That was my car," she said faintly.

"Looks like it."

"No one knew where I was, Theo."

"So you said."

"Where are we going?"

"Away from here." Theo rubbed at his temples. "Is your phone turned on?"

"No."

"Why not?"

"GPS," she explained.

Just like the GPS that was in her car. The one her father liked to use to track her. Evelina couldn't breathe. Did Riley do that? Why would he do that if he even did?

She found it hard to blame it on anyone else when her BMW wasn't exactly the only one in the city, she'd parked it in a decent, quiet location, and her father would have been the only person who could have found it.

Theo watched Evelina from the corner of his eye like he could read her thoughts. "Take a breath or something, babe."

"Don't call me that."

"I kind of like it."

Evelina frowned. "Me, too."

"Breathe," he repeated quietly. "You're sure no one followed you, right?"

"Positive," Evelina said, wishing it was a lie.

The truth hurt.

"GPS was still on your car, yeah?"

"Yes."

Theo cursed lowly.

"Why would someone do that?" she asked.

Someone.

Evelina choked on the word. Theo didn't answer. The last shooting, he had been given all the fault for it.

"Will they blame you for this, too?" Evelina asked.

Theo blew out a harsh breath. "Probably."

"Why?"

"Someone wants me gone."

"Someone?" she asked.

"I thought it was Joel," Theo admitted. "But I don't know anymore."

"That was my car," Evelina said.

She felt like a parrot, repeating one thing over and over as if to make it true.

"Yeah, it was."

Evelina glanced out the window when Theo pulled a U-turn right in the middle of an empty road. "Where are we going?"

"Somewhere."

"Somewhere," she echoed.

Theo passed her a look, the darkness filling his features again. "Just don't say I didn't warn you, Eve."

"Here." Theo tossed a cell phone to Evelina. She let it fall to the king sized bed between them instead of catching it. "Eve, call your brother and let him know you're okay."

Evelina took inventory of the hotel room. The Hilton suite wasn't anything to scoff at with its leather furniture, huge flat screen and entertainment space sporting among many things, a pool table, plus the wet bar, and an enclosed, heated deck with a hot tub outside.

Thirteen floors high.

Evelina felt like she was floating up above, looking down.

"Eve," Theo said again.

"Call my brother, I heard you."

"All right. I'm going to go have a smoke or something."

"Is the phone safe?" Evelina asked.

"It's a phone I use to keep in contact with someone I don't want others knowing about, so yes, it's safe."

Evelina wanted to press him for more information, but she chose not to. Once Theo stepped outside onto the enclosed deck and shut the glass door, Evelina picked up the phone and dialed Adriano. Her brother picked up on the second ring.

"Conti speaking."

"Adriano, it's me … Eve," Evelina said, willing away the shakiness and confusion still lingering in her tone. She didn't want him worrying or freaking out, but chances were, he already was. When Adriano stayed quiet on the other end, she added, "I'm okay."

"Jesus Christ," Adriano mumbled. "Eve?"

"Yeah."

"Where are you?" her brother demanded. "I'll come get you."

"No, don't. I'm okay right now."

"You were supposed to go to the store!"

Evelina flinched. "I know."

"Do you? Because when you didn't come back to the apartment, I had to send guys out looking for you. When they couldn't find you, I had to call Riley to get a trace on your fucking car."

"I saw the car," she said softly.

"Before or after somebody burned it to the ground?"

Yikes.

Adriano did not sound pleased.

"After," Evelina said. "I don't know when that happened. Somebody burned it down? I thought it looked like somebody blew it up."

"No, it looks like gasoline or some kind of accelerant was used to burn it. By the time the firemen got there, it was pointless. After I got the last location from Riley, Alessa and I took a drive over there and found the mess. Where in the hell are you, Eve?"

"I just … needed to get away for a night."

"Why? Do you realize how fucking worried I was?" Adriano grumbled something unintelligible and then said, "Listen, I don't know what is going on with you, but no matter how awful shit is, you don't get to just disappear like that."

Evelina nodded even though her brother couldn't see it. "I know, but I did, so drop it."

"Somebody burned down your car."

"Yeah."

"Stay away for a couple of days," Adriano said, a sadness lacing his words. "I'll cover for you. Somehow. Even if I have to lie about it, whatever."

She was not about to argue with that.

"Okay."

"Where are you, Eve?"

"With somebody," she admitted.

"Who?"

"Somebody I shouldn't be with."

"Christ," Adriano muttered. "Don't tell me."

"I won't."

She never would.

Evelina waited for over an hour, but Theo didn't come back inside the hotel room. No, he just stayed outside in the enclosed deck. Never once did he light up a cigarette, either.

Frustrated at being ignored, she stalked across the room and opened the glass door. The warm heat blasting into the space hit Evelina instantly. The hot tub was covered but she could hear the hum of the heater and jets working. With the glass windows overlooking a rather busy part of Chicago, the lights thirteen floors down seemed to almost flicker like sparkling diamonds.

Heights bothered Evelina.

She shouldn't have stepped out on the deck.

"Yes?" Theo asked from where he stood leaning against one of the floor to ceiling windows.

"Um ..."

"Come on, you can do better than that."

Evelina's hackles rattled at his teasing. "Don't do that, Theo. You only do that nonsense to get a rise out of me."

"And it works." Theo smirked, adding, "Go order something to eat, or whatever. There's no need for us to bicker with one another tonight."

What was he trying to prove?

Evelina ignored how high she knew she was above the ground and stepped a little further out on the enclosed deck. "You're a walking cliché, aren't you?"

Theo cocked a brow. "I beg your pardon?"

"You are a walking cliché. The bad boy with issues, maybe you think you're irreparable or something, and you have to warn everybody off that gets too close. It's like your defense mechanism. That's why you're always poking at me like you do. Because I get close and you feel like you need to push back. What, is the pretty woman going to come along and fix all the parts on Theo DeLuca that don't work right? Is that it?"

Theo stared at Evelina and not an inch of him moved. He didn't even blink. Evelina was sure he didn't breathe, either.

"Well," he drawled.

Evelina shifted in her heels, letting her hands fall to her sides. "Well, what?"

"That's a first. I've never heard that before."

"People don't get close enough to tell you."

"Maybe," he agreed.

She felt almost uncomfortable under his heavy stare.

"Stop it," Evelina muttered.

"Stop what?"

"Looking at me like that; like I'm crazy or something."

Theo laughed. "I don't look at you like you're crazy, Eve. I look at you like I don't know what's going to come next."

She took another step forward. "Is that a bad thing?"

"Yes. This is all bad."

"All of it?"

Theo hummed his agreement. "I already told you this."

"That we would be bad."

"So bad," Theo said quietly. "Go back inside."

"I really don't want to."

"Bad," he repeated.

Evelina wondered if he even cared about his own warnings. Guessing by the way his jaw tightened, his gaze traveled down her black dress, and his balled fists stayed on the railing attached to the glass walled windows, she didn't think so. She was pretty sure Theo wanted her.

What would it hurt?

Who would it hurt?

Evelina moved forward until she was standing close enough to reach out and touch Theo if she wanted. A heat flared in his eyes. He'd taken his suit jacket off and tossed it over one of the plush chairs on the deck. The silk dress shirt he wore stretched across his chest with every little movement. It showcased defined muscles, and the hint of a tattoo peeking out on his tanned skin where the top two buttons on his shirt were undone.

Theo was the very definition of tall, dark, and gorgeous.

"I'm not good at denying things I like," Theo said, his tone dripping deep with sex. "You should listen and do what I say."

"Go back inside," Evelina said.

"Yeah. I've got enough problems without adding a woman to the list."

Evelina didn't even feel offended by his statement. "And I'd be a problem—"

"I just said that."

"—because you like me," she finished.

Theo turned slightly, just enough to face Evelina. "I'm not a cliché, but that was a good try. I don't think I'm broken, I just have no interest in trying to pretend like I'm perfect. I'm not looking or waiting for a woman to fix me, either, but I also don't need one to make me better, Eve. So good try, but not quite."

"Deflecting," she said.

"No, not at all."

"You warned me."

Theo pushed off the glass wall window and straightened to his full height.

"I did," he said.

"But you still brought me here. You didn't have to that, Theo. You could have taken me anywhere, dropped me off, and made a call. But you didn't. We came here."

"You're right."

"So why?" she asked.

Theo shrugged, a hint of a smile edging at the corner of his mouth. It was sexy and sinful, almost playful in nature. Except he moved forward again, crowding Evelina as his thumbs ghosted along her trim waist. The touch was light enough to make her shiver and to make her wet at the same goddamn time.

"I already told you why, Eve."

He wasn't very good at denying things he liked.

They wouldn't be bad.

She didn't care what he said.

Evelina didn't get a warning from Theo before his hands grabbed her waist hard. His fingertips dug into her sides, making her ache from the pressure. It didn't hurt, even if it stung. He held her so tight, she was sure his fingerprints would imprint on her skin under her dress.

"I heard a rumor the other day," Theo murmured, his gaze zoning in on Evelina's lips as she let out a shaky breath.

"Oh?"

"Someone said there might be a marriage on the table soon. No talk about who, just that there might be one coming."

Evelina's shoulders fell. "Maybe."

"You shouldn't have looked for me tonight, not if something like that is being discussed."

"You shouldn't have brought me here, Theo, not if you heard about it."

He didn't respond. Not in the way she thought he would.

No, he kissed her instead. Hard, fast, and demanding. His hands fisted into her dress and yanked her close before one traveled up into her hair and rooted her in place with enough force to make her scalp sting. Evelina sighed, letting Theo's tongue snake between her lips and find hers, owning the kiss. His teeth scraped her skin and lips, taking more, and his five o'clock shadow left a lovely ache behind.

There was no give in Evelina's kiss.

Theo just took.

She didn't mind.

All over again, Evelina couldn't breathe. When she finally got air, Theo forced her head back, his thumbs finding her cheekbones as he stared down at her.

This couldn't possibly be *bad* when it felt entirely fucking *good*.

"Tell me to stop."

Evelina shook her head.

Theo's fingers on her cheek and neck pressed a little harder. It was lovely and wicked. She wanted more. More of his roughness, more of his touch. "Tell me to stop."

"Do you fuck like this, too?" she asked instead.

Theo's gaze darkened. "*Eve.*"

"Do you?"

"Yes."

"Wonderful. Don't stop."

CHAPTER NINE

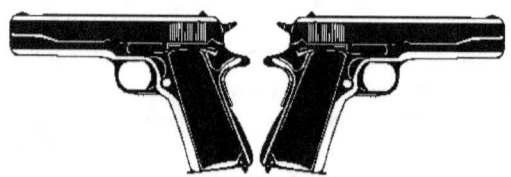

Theo dragged his thumbs from the high lines of Evelina's cheekbones straight to the corners of her painted red lips. She caught the pad of his left thumb with the strike of her tongue before it disappeared back into her mouth.

It was enough. Enough for him to feel the heat and wetness of her saliva. Enough to make his cock ache.

"I wondered," Evelina hummed out.

"Wondered what, princess?"

Evelina's grin was downright scandalous. "What you'd taste like."

She was pushing him, testing him. Her voice was demure, promising sex. She watched him through thick lashes with hooded eyes and the patience a God would give a Saint. There was nothing innocent about Evelina Conti.

"And what about tomorrow, huh?" Theo asked.

"What about it?"

"When you have to go back, Eve, and tonight goes away."

Evelina blinked, her smile fading slightly. "You mean to say when I have to go back and act like a princess."

"You said it."

"I guess I don't have to worry about that for a while since Adriano told me to stay away earlier."

Shit.

Theo wet his lips, feeling the silky smoothness of Evelina's skin under his palms and fingertips. She caught his thumb with her mouth when he swept the digit over her lips. Instead of flicking it with her tongue like she had before, she sucked the tip between her lips and bit down with just enough force for it to sting.

"Christ," Theo muttered heavily.

Evelina grinned around his thumb, her tongue swirling at the top of his digit.

She might have been pushing him, but he was no better. Theo was trying to give her an excuse to run. They could both just forget this almost happened, and he could go back to pretending like she didn't exist. It was easier to act like Evelina didn't matter than to admit she did. Because if he did admit she mattered, he'd be fucking stuck like that.

He didn't want to give someone else the chance to open up his scars again, or that more could be made.

"Stop overthinking," Evelina said.

Theo wouldn't deny a woman who knew what she wanted. Pushing Evelina backward until she hit the sliding glass doors, Theo leaned down until their noses touched and he could see the fire in her eyes. When Evelina squirmed under the weight of his body pinning hers, Theo pressed harder, catching her wrists in his right hand and moving them above her head. His cock throbbed beneath his pants, the hard length of his erection digging into her pelvis. Evelina's tongue peeked out to wet her lips, a wariness settling in her features.

Without warning, Theo grabbed the hem of Evelina's dress and bunched it up her legs until he could look down and see black cotton trimmed with navy blue lace at the junction of her thighs. Evelina's stare caught his and her lashes fanned her cheeks when Theo swept his thumb over her bare thigh. With each stroke, he came a little closer to her cotton covered sex.

Theo grinned. "Just remember to breathe, babe."

Evelina swallowed audibly, her pink lips opening with a shuddering whimper as Theo drove his hand between her thighs. He spread her legs wider, and rubbed his palm against her pussy.

"Breathe?"

"Breathe," he said.

"Remind me every once in a while, Theo."

"I'll try. Are we good? Because I'm done with the talking thing, now."

Theo stroked the pad of his thumb across the soft fabric of her panties directly above her clit. Evelina shivered. Already, the cotton line of her panties covering the slit of her sex was damp and hot. Theo wanted to feel her wet sex bare, and hear all her pretty little sounds. He bet Evelina sounded damn good when a man's name was in her mouth, and she was begging.

"We're good," she said, a heat coloring up her tone.

"Good," he echoed. "Do you like to beg for it, Eve?"

"Hmm?"

Theo slipped his thumb under the slip of her underwear and found the lips of her pussy wet to the touch. She was also smooth-skinned and trembling. Driving his thumb between the fleshy lips of her sex, he smeared the juices of her arousal up to her hard little clit, and then right back down to her sex.

Evelina froze under Theo's weight. He refused to let her move from the glass doors as he touched and learned her body for as long as it took.

What he wanted most was to see the perfect Evelina Conti lose a little bit of her control.

Even better if she lost it to him.

"Do you like to beg for it?" he repeated.

Evelina didn't say a word.

"Have you ever begged for it, Eve? Ever found a man that made you so fucking wet, got your blood hot and your muscles aching without even touching you that you just wanted to beg him to fuck you? Has a man ever put you on your knees and made you ask for it? Have you found a man that made you *want* to get on your knees and ask for it? Tell me you've had the pleasure of looking up at a man and asking for him, Eve, begging to suck his cock or to be fucked good and hard because you wanted him that badly. *Tell me.*"

"I—"

"It's a yes or no question, babe."

Evelina's eyes darkened. "Never."

Theo cocked a brow. "That's too bad."

"But I think I might have found one now."

Fucking perfect.

When his thumb slid back down from her clit again, Theo let the digit sink into Evelina's tight, slick channel. Her sex hugged his thumb hard. It was just a touch—a taste. He could have added more, or fucked her sex harder with his fingers, but he just wanted to test her body, see her reactions, and hear her sounds.

"How's this?" Theo asked. The silkiness of her arousal smeared to his palm. "Eve?"

Evelina's teeth cut into her bottom lip as Theo thrust his thumb in and out of her sex with a measured slowness. Leaning down, he kissed the reddened, plump flesh of her lip and nudged her bite to release with his own mouth.

"Don't do that," Theo warned.

"W-why not?"

"Because then I can't do it. I have a feeling you'll like it when I bite your lip a hell of a lot more than when you do it."

Theo punctuated his words by removing his thumb from her clenching pussy and slamming two fingers in just as fast. Evelina's knees buckled at the new sensation, but Theo didn't relent in the faster, harder pace as he forced her to stay upright against the window. Evelina gasped, her hips canting into Theo's hand over and over.

"There, Eve. Feel that, babe? Christ, you're fucking soaking me now."

"*God.*"

Theo released Evelina's hands and grabbed her chin just under her jaw. Her skin pinked under his roughness as he tilted her head up and back, looking down on her with heavy lidded eyes. Evelina didn't seem to mind, and she didn't shy away from his handling.

"Does it feel good?"

Evelina whined in the back of her throat. "*Yes.*"

"Are you going to come?"

She nodded, her eyes squeezing shut as her sex hugged him tighter.

"Words, Evelina. Use your fucking words."

"Yes," she groaned low, "yes, I'm going to come, Theo."

"Eyes open and watch me when you come, Eve."

His demand came out harsh and throaty. Evelina's eyes flew wide instantly to find his. The very next moment, Theo learned forward and pressed his lips to hers, taking a kiss from her mouth that burned him all over.

He'd never chased a woman once before, but he had a long time ago with Evelina. She'd been worth the effort, even if he had stopped his conquest before anything had come of it.

So worth it.

She was fucking *bellissima* under his control like this. Sexy. Needy.

"Nothing like a princess," Theo growled against her lips.

Evelina laughed but it melted into a breathless moan when Theo flicked his thumb up to drive into her clit in time with his fingers still stroking her pussy. Instantly, her juices seemed to flood his hand even more. Theo knew it then; he could feel the way her body clenched around him, like the muscles tightening in her stomach, and how her frame swayed.

"Shit ... *Theo!*"

Theo caught Evelina's bottom lip between his teeth and bit down hard. Her sharp mewl was high and broken as she came undone with tremors rocking her entire form. He always thought that sex worked well with a little bit of pain. The sting made the bliss that much better.

Releasing his bite on her lip, but keeping his hold on her throat, Theo slowed the thrusts of his fingers back to his previous measured, teasing rhythm.

"Oh my God," Evelina breathed. "I ... I can't ..."

"Sensitive," Theo said for her. "You're sensitive, but you can."

He could feel the way her hips jerked every time he even grazed her pussy with the lightest touch. Theo didn't relent. He liked her like this.

Wanting him. High on him.

Just like this.

"Theo ... Theo, just ..." Evelina's words trailed off with a shuddering exhale. Her hips rolled into every gentle drive of his fingers. "I want ..."

"Hmm?"

"Let me, Theo."

Her body arched off the glass door, pressing to his. Theo could feel the way her stomach muscles tightened with her need to come again and how her nipples had hardened under her dress.

"Let you what, Eve?"

Theo didn't really need to ask, he knew. She was close to orgasm again. Being sensitive like she was, he expected it. But instead of chasing that high, she wanted to give something to him.

Evelina wanted to beg for it. She was hot, trembling, and probably ached from her head to her toes. Theo didn't need to hear her say any of those things because he knew just by looking at the desire swimming in her eyes.

"Eve?" he asked, his tone low and husky.

"I ..." Her bottom lip, plump and red from his kiss and bite, found its way between her teeth again. Theo used the pad of his thumb to draw the tender flesh out.

"Tell me, Eve. Get on your knees and beg for it."

She didn't need to be told again. Just like that, Evelina dropped down to the ground on shaky legs. Theo's hand slipped out from between her legs as her fingers coasted over the line of his erection through his pants and down his thighs. She grabbed him tight, her sweet nails digging into his skin through his slacks.

Evelina looked up at him, her eyes wide but dark, and her lashes fanning her lids. Theo's mouth went dry. He couldn't remember a time when a woman had looked quite as good as Evelina did when she was on her knees.

"Do it," he said, his throat tight.

His cock downright ached.

Evelina reached for his belt.

"Do it," Theo repeated.

She wet her lips, still watching him silently. Theo let her work his belt until it was hanging loose and her quick fingers were undoing his button and zipper. Evelina pushed his pants and boxers down around his hips until his cock sprung free. Evelina didn't say a word, simply grabbed the base of his shaft and squeezed with enough pressure to make Theo's blood thicken.

"Shit," he hissed when her fingernail glided down his length. Shivers of pleasure danced down his spine, chasing the sting of her nail pressing into his sensitive cock. Theo loved it. He wanted more of it. He was pleased that Evelina hadn't forgotten what he told her that day in the café. "You remembered, huh?"

Evelina's lips arched sinfully. "Like black coffee, right?"

"Harsh, hot, and a little bit of pain, babe."

"Do you want me to beg for it, Theo?"

"Of course. Anything worth having is worth working for, as the saying goes. And I'd love to hear the kind of music you can make, so hurry up and get on that, Eve."

Her fingernail slid down his length again as she stroked his cock from tip to base.

"Be nice," she warned.

Where had this girl come from all of a sudden?

Theo liked it a lot.

When she opened her mouth again to say something, Theo traced her bottom lip with the fingers he'd used to fuck her. Evelina took the digits into her mouth without question, her tongue flattening to his skin and then licking all the way around to clean them of her taste and come. With his free hand, he rooted her in place by fisting her hair tight in his grip.

"Tell me what I want to hear, Eve, and I'll let you have a taste."

Evelina released his fingers with a soft sigh that came off needy and sweet. "Please, Theo."

"Hmm? Better, louder."

Her tongue snaked out, hitting the head of his cock with a wet heat that seared him instantly. Theo kept his stance firm, refusing to move or release her hair so she could try and get more of him in her mouth. It damn near killed him to do it. He wanted to see Evelina sucking him off and then he wanted to find the closest flat surface that he could to bend her over and fuck her hard.

"You're making me wait here, Eve, and that isn't a good thing."

Evelina met his gaze again, unashamed and beautiful. "I want to taste you, Theo, please. Let me taste you."

Theo grinned and loosened his grip on her hair. "One more time, Eve."

"*Please.*"

It was a whisper that practically crawled over every inch of Theo's skin. Breathless, thick, and desperate. That's how Evelina sounded on her knees in front of him. Nothing had ever sounded quite so good before. With her lips parted, her eyes hazy and hooded like she was drunk on her want for him and nothing else, it was perfect.

Dangerous for him.

Bad because Theo knew he wanted to see her like this again.

But still perfect.

"There we are," Theo said, tugging her hair and bringing her closer to his cock. The heat of her warm breath washed over his length and he ached to feel her soft lips take him in. "Suck me off, Eve. I don't have to tell you how I like it, do I?"

"No. I think I know."

Hot and hard.

Theo felt the silkiness of her lips on the head of his dick before

Evelina took him in her mouth. It was just a fraction of a second, her lips tightening to his cock, teeth scraping along his shaft, and her tongue flicking into the throbbing vein, but it was enough to make him shudder and groan.

Evelina's hand tightened around the base as she sucked harder, keeping her gaze locked on his all the while. Theo swore under his breath, deciding to let her do whatever it was she wanted. She'd clearly wanted a taste of him and he didn't mind providing that. Evelina's free hand crawled up his stomach under his dress shirt. Her nails scored into his abdominal muscles the harder she sucked on his cock. Every time she would come back to the head of his cock, her teeth would graze the tip. It gave him just enough of a shock to send sparks bursting straight down into his balls while her tongue lapped up the precum leaking from his dick.

His breath was gone.

Just like that.

"Jesus fucking Christ."

Evelina winked up at him as a wicked heat curled in Theo's stomach.

Innocent?

Yeah, right.

Who in the fuck ever said this girl was innocent?

They were *wrong*.

Theo let her stroke and suck his cock until his balls were tight and a pressure had started to build in his back. When he liked something, she seemed to take notice immediately and repeated it just to see if she could get another reaction out of him.

Evelina liked sucking him off. Theo could see it in the way her breaths had picked up and the way her lips curved, pleased and happy, around his cock the more she sucked and stroked. Coming was going to be far too easy for Theo if he didn't stop her and soon.

"Stop."

His order came out growled and clipped. Evelina stared up at him with wide, confused eyes as she released his cock and bit her lip. *Fuck*. She was going to send him straight to hell doing shit like that.

"What'd I say about that, huh?" Theo asked, reaching down tap her lip with his thumb.

Evelina let go of her lip. "Not to. I liked it better when you did it, anyway."

"I told you that you would." Theo could see the hesitance and confusion in her eyes. She was probably wondering why he had made her stop when he'd clearly been enjoying it. Tugging gently on her hair, and earning himself another one of her pretty little gasps, he said, "Up, babe. Get up here, now."

Theo yanked Evelina to her unsteady feet before shoving her back to the glass door.

"What—"

He interrupted her question with a bruising kiss as he tugged at her dress. He wanted that off; he wanted to see what Evelina looked like in nothing but her skin while she was hot for him and wet between her legs.

Tilting her head back, Evelina sighed. Theo nipped a path down the throbbing pulse point in her neck, tasting sex and salt on her smooth skin.

"Oh, my God," she breathed.

"Turn around," Theo growled. He kept yanking her dress higher until he had it bunched around her stomach. "Now, Eve."

She did, watching him over her shoulder all the while. When he pulled the dress up, Evelina lifted her arms and let him discard the clothing. She wore no bra under her dress. Bending down to his knees, he pulled her panties down until Evelina stepped out of them.

Standing, Theo hummed in approval at the sight of Evelina's unmarked, peach-toned skin under his fingertips. He ran his hands from the tops of her shoulders all the way down to where her ass melded into her thighs.

She shivered. He did it again just to make her shake.

"Fucking beautiful."

Evelina made a soft noise that had Theo's stare snapping up to meet hers. "Thank you."

Theo cocked a brow. "Haven't you been told how beautiful you are before, Evelina?"

"Nobody has ever said it quite like you did just now."

"That's a damn shame. Again?"

Evelina nodded silently.

"Beautiful," Theo murmured.

Her smile was a brilliant, bright sight.

Theo placed his hands to the glass on either side of her body and moved forward until his chest was pressed tightly to her back. It allowed him to kiss and taste her shoulders with quick pecks and fast strikes of his tongue.

"Please," he heard her whimper. "*God*, Theo, please fuck me."

Her pleading shattered any resolve he had left to keep her waiting longer than he already had. Yanking the glass door open, Theo shoved them both through the hotel room. He didn't even bother to close the door as they stumbled across the hardwood. Evelina turned on her heels to face him, grabbing at his shirt to pull the buttons apart with enough force to pop a couple off the silk fabric.

Theo reveled in her coarse actions, and the feeling of her fingernails dragging over the tribal owl tattoo that covered almost over half of his right side. When her legs hit the back of the couch, Theo forced her to lean over it. He dragged his hand down between the valley of her chest and straight between her thighs. Her pink nipples were tight, hard little buds while her sex was hot and slippery under his hands.

The tip of her index finger traced the ring in his right nipple, directly over where the eye of the owl had been tattooed.

"Why an owl?" she asked, breathless and rocking into his touch.

As much as he didn't want to stop playing with her pretty little pussy, he did. Theo's cock rested between their bodies, and he stroked his member while he dug for a condom in the pocket of his undone slacks. "Not important."

"I'm curious."

"Owls see everything at night."

"Oh?"

"And they're not afraid of the dark, Eve."

"I suppose not." Evelina quieted as Theo found the condom, tore it open, and covered his cock in latex. He went back to teasing her sex with light caresses that had her sighing and moving against his fingers with every stroke. "Jesus, that's wonderful."

"You know it'll get better. Fuck, you're so wet."

Evelina mewled softly, her spread legs trembling as he stroked her slit over and over. "I want to come again."

"So hard. You'll come so fucking hard you'll see the goddamn stars behind your eyes, babe."

Theo's punctuated his promise by flipping her over onto her stomach. Evelina's hair billowed out around her as her body bent over the back of the couch and she grappled for purchase. He didn't give her a chance to find anything to keep her steady. As quick as he flipped her over, he pulled her ass high until she was standing on tiptoes inside her heels and positioned his cock at the slit of her glistening sex.

"Oh, God."

"We'll start there," Theo said.

Evelina laughed, her desire darkening her tone as she glanced over her shoulder. "Oh?"

"Yeah, but we'll end it with you screaming my name only."

"Make sure of it."

Theo's fingers dug into her hips a second before he yanked her back onto his cock. He'd entered her hard and fast, taking her deep with the first thrust. He felt her wet heat encompass his dick and squeeze him tight. Her cry was a broken, wonderful sound that bounced off the walls and heated his blood to a boiling point.

Fuck, no, she wasn't a virgin. But she was tight as fuck and it seemed like she just kept getting tighter with every second.

"Damn," Theo grunted.

He felt the flutters of her orgasm rippling through her inner muscles the second time he pulled her back, harder and even deeper. It wouldn't take much for Evelina to come undone around him.

Over and over, he bet.

Theo started a pace that was harsh and brutal. Skin on skin while his fingers dug rougher into her body, leaving his marks behind. Letting go of Evelina's left side, he fisted her hair and tugged just enough to make sure there was a sting. The harder he fucked her and the tighter he pulled, the more she shook and the better her rolling crescendo of cries sounded.

"I ..." Evelina's air caught in her throat, the words dying before she could get another thing out.

"Breathe," Theo demanded.

She sucked in a harsh breath of air. "It's better when I don't."

Yeah, he knew that, too.

Her honey practically soaked his cock as she came, shouting his name to the dark, quiet room. Theo didn't relent in his pace for a second, not even when he felt a tremor rocking his calves or the tightness returning to his back, promising his release. He could fuck Evelina all night if she kept moving like she did and calling his name like she was.

All. Fucking. Night.

"More," Evelina pleaded, fisting the cushions on the couch. She backed her beautiful, tight ass into his cock with every thrust, taking him as hard as he gave. "Harder, Theo. Again, *please.*"

She liked it rough, then. Rough got her off. Rough made her weak and let her be free. Theo could do that, it was easy. He wondered if walking away would be, too. But with the way she looked under him, how she begged him for more and the needy gleam in her eye ... he doubted it would be.

Right then, he didn't give a damn.

Theo pulled on Evelina's wavy hair, forcing her body straight so her back was pressed to his chest and he had access to her shoulders again. Biting her skin, he left more of his marks behind. He could taste the remnants of her perspiration on her flesh and the way her body had heated under their fucking.

"Sin," he rumbled, holding her tight to his cock. Like this, with him, she tasted entirely of filth and lust. "You taste like sin."

He wanted more of that from her.

Evelina had offered.

Theo took it.

CHAPTER TEN

Evelina's scream died in her throat the very second the bullets entered her chest, and her breath was taken away. Blood poured into her waiting hands, and then it was over. She bolted up in the bed, clutching the sheets in a death grip as she released a shuddering exhale.

Just a dream.

The mantra never really helped with the nightmares, but she repeated it to herself anyway.

"Breathe," she heard murmured from the corner of the room.

Evelina's body heated instantly at Theo's rich, dark tenor. Somehow, she managed to be turned on and thoroughly embarrassed at the same time. She never had to worry about sharing a personal space with someone, so no one had ever witnessed her nightmares. It wasn't that she used to have them a lot, but ever since her mother died, she'd had one almost every single night.

Feeling unsteady and fidgety, Evelina tried to avoid the man in the corner. She could feel his stare on her, watching her through the darkness. She'd fallen asleep when he demanded she go to bed, even though her body hadn't felt the least bit tired.

"You can fuck a woman but you can't share a bed with her?" Evelina asked quietly.

From the corner of her eye, she watched Theo raise a dark eyebrow in contemplation.

"That's what you want to ask right now?"

Evelina nodded her response, keeping the sheet firmly over her naked chest.

"It has nothing to do with sharing a bed, Eve," Theo said. "I typically don't share a *space* with anyone."

Curious, Evelina watched her companion as he began disassembling a handgun one piece at a time. He pulled a small red bag from the inside pocket of his leather jacket and opened it up to expose what looked to be a cleaning kit.

"Is that what you do at night, clean your gun?" she asked.

"*Guns*, and no."

Theo's clipped tone offered no room for discussion.

"What time is it?"

"Three," Theo said.

He emptied the clip of bullets, dropping them to the glass coffee table with several clinks. Evelina took the chance to admire the fact that Theo hadn't buttoned his dress shirt after she'd yanked it open earlier in the night. Peeks of his tattoo contrasted against his lightly tanned skin, the black ink licking across the cut definition of his muscles. She hadn't given it much thought before except to take note of the piece, but the tribal art was beautiful and suited his body. It looked to be the only tattoo he had, actually.

The memory of the tangy taste of metal as she'd bitten onto his nipple ring when he'd flipped her back over to her stomach and grabbed her throat flashed in her mind. He'd seemed to like that if the way he'd fucked her harder after she did it was any indication.

"Did that hurt?" Evelina asked.

"Hmm, what, princess?"

She let the title brush off her shoulders. For once, it didn't sound like Theo was calling her that to make fun of her for whatever reason.

"The piercing."

Theo chuckled, his tongue snaking out to wet his bottom lip as he started polishing the metal pieces of the handgun. "For a quick second it did, but nothing worse than what I'd already had, I suppose."

"The tattoo, you mean?"

"No, not the owl."

Evelina's brow furrowed. "There's nothing else there, right?"

Theo didn't answer.

"When did you have that tattoo done?" she asked.

"Shortly after my twenty-first birthday. Dino took me out to a guy who was good at covering scars."

Evelina blinked, taking his words in slowly.

Nothing worse than what I'd already had … Not the owl.

Clearing his throat, Theo rotated his right wrist like he was trying to crack it or something. Evelina wondered if he wasn't holding the gun in his left hand, would he be touching his right wrist like she'd seen him do at other times. She filed her thoughts away for another time, but already, things were adding up and she didn't like what they might mean at all.

Especially not for Theo.

Before Evelina could say a thing, Theo said, "The nipple ring was my idea. I didn't realize all the aftercare that came along with it. I probably wouldn't have had it done if I knew beforehand."

"I like it."

The words slipped through Evelina's lips before she could stop them.

A slow smirk curved Theo's mouth at the corners as he glanced at her from the side. The one look heated up her blood in an instant, promising something wicked behind his eyes. She knew for a damned fact the man would follow through, too.

"You're a thrasher," Theo noted, picking up another dismantled piece of weapon.

"What?"

"When you have a nightmare, you thrash around. At least you're quiet, though."

Evelina's cheeks heated. "Oh."

"I know better than to wake someone when they're having a nightmare like that. It usually just makes it worse, or it did for Dino."

"Your brother had nightmares?"

"Slept with the light on every night," Theo said like they were discussing the weather. "Even when he was well into his thirties, he still dreamt of the same fucking shit. I think he found it easier to manage if he worked out a lot before bed and kept the light on. Then, his mind was too tired to dwell on things that happened a long time ago and with the light on, the memories weren't as bad."

Owls are not afraid of the dark, Eve.

His words from earlier banged around in the back of Evelina's mind like a warning bell. She added it to her growing pile of assumptions and curiosities. What was this man fighting to keep hidden; was it something he was ashamed of? Evelina wondered if Lily knew that her brother had some kind of demon he was trying to hide.

Theo sighed, drawing Evelina from her thoughts. "Everybody has their own way of dealing with that sort of thing."

"I just try not to think about it all. It's not real, so it shouldn't scare me or anything. I'm an adult, not a child."

"You should talk about it, Eve, not brush it off. There's no reason for you to pretend like it's not happening. You have nightmares that obviously bother you."

She didn't try to deny it.

"Do you talk about your nightmares?" she asked softly.

Theo's shoulders tensed briefly, but loosened just as fast. "No, I don't."

Evelina was shocked that he even admitted he had nightmares.

"Why not?"

"Because unlike yours that aren't about real things, as you said, mine are. And some things, the things I can't forget, are better left in the past where they no longer bother me."

"But if you dream of them, doesn't that mean they still are bothering you?"

"I'm surprised," Theo said with a quiet chuckle.

"About what?"

"You, Eve. I'm surprised about you. I mean, you were always around Lily whenever she was home from boarding school and whenever the families got together for whatever, you were there, too. I just saw you and thought that's all there was."

Ouch.

"That was kind of unnecessary," Evelina said, hiding the hurt she felt over his words. "I'm not as dull as dust, Theo. I'm a living, breathing person, okay."

"Well, I was wrong. I started wondering about you when you caught me arguing with my brother way back when. You had me curious, I guess. What made you like that—quiet, compliant, and sweet. Lily is so fucking stubborn and defiant, or she was, and you were the complete opposite. It interested me."

His confession took her off guard.

Evelina knew exactly what Theo was doing. "You're trying to distract me again. You're giving me something else to get me off a topic you don't want to talk about."

Theo grinned down at the table. "See, much more than I gave you credit for, Evelina. Others wouldn't even notice."

"Maybe you make me curious, too."

"What is that old saying about the cat?" Theo asked, shaking his head.

"The cat must have been a fool. It had nine lives."

"We only have the one, Eve. Just one chance to get it right."

"You won't tell me about your nightmares, will you?"

"No." Theo glanced up from his work, meeting Evelina's wary stare. "What do you dream about?"

"Why should I tell you?"

"Because you're the kind of person who talks. I'm not. It's not about who you are, but who I am, Eve."

"It's just dreams."

"To you," he replied just as fast. "My monsters are real, and I won't feed them like my brother did."

"Will you tell me about his nightmares?" she asked.

"No."

Evelina frowned. "You're not a very open person."

"They're not my stories to tell and like I said, it's just who I am, Eve."

Well then … Theo was right. Evelina didn't fault him for his character.

"Honestly?"

"I asked, babe."

Evelina ignored the shiver crawling down her spine at the affection in his tone. Fucking someone didn't necessarily mean that person cared about you, too. Lots of people had physical relationships, and emotions never got involved. She didn't want to let herself believe that Theo might actually have some kind of feelings for her. It wouldn't lead to anything good.

"I dream about dying," Evelina confessed.

Theo drew in a slow breath. "Dying."

"Usually."

"Any particular event?"

"Being shot. Most times it's in the chest, for whatever reason, but I've had a few where it's in the face, too."

"Like your mother."

His tone had dropped to a gentle volume, quieter than Evelina had ever heard it before.

"I had these nightmares long before she died," Evelina replied. "But they're more frequent since the restaurant shooting."

Theo's brow furrowed. "What bothers you the most about the nightmares?"

"The dying thing isn't enough?"

"After you have the same nightmare so many times, you know what to expect, Eve."

She refused to look at him again, hating how he seemed to see right through her words to the troubles she truly felt.

"I don't like how I feel it, mostly."

"Feel it?" he asked. "Like the gun shot?"

"No, my blood. I always try to reach for it, like I want to hold it or maybe I'm trying to stop it. But when I do, I feel it."

"Warm," he said.

"Wet, too."

Theo didn't seem as though he found her nightmares odd at all. In fact, he picked up his wipe and small plastic jar of oil and began to clean his dismantled gun without another word.

"Theo?"

"Yes, Eve?"

"Are you not going to sleep at all?"

Theo stilled, his hands freezing. "Probably not."

"It's not because of ... us, right?"

"No."

"Me?" she asked.

"Partially. Like I said earlier, I don't usually share a personal space with someone at all."

Evelina eyed his tattoo again.

Owls weren't afraid of the dark.

She was pretty sure Theo didn't like it, for whatever reason.

Silently, she clamored out of the bed and crossed the space between them. Theo went back to wiping down the gun as Evelina settled into the couch beside him. She tucked the sheet around her shoulders and leaned into his side. He didn't tell her to go back to bed.

The quiet sounds of the buffing cloth sweeping over the metal mixed in with Theo's rhythmic breathing quickly lulled Evelina back into a peaceful state. She barely noticed her eyes turning drowsy, and the sleep edging around her senses.

Theo leaned back on the couch, and moved Evelina's head into his lap. She caught the sight of his amused smirk as he worked above her to stick a Q-tip down the barrel of the gun. The cut of his jaw was as strong as ever, but he seemed more relaxed than he usually did. It made his handsome features all the more gorgeous.

Evelina wondered if Theo realized how sexy he was when he was calm and content.

"You're disgustingly good-looking."

Theo laughed under his breath. "That's a first. I've heard a lot about my looks, but I don't think anyone has ever called me disgusting for it."

"Well, I'm special."

"You are."

Evelina grinned, feeling his fingers roll through the waves of her dark hair a second after metal clicked on glass. "Are you done cleaning your gun?"

"It doesn't need to be cleaned at all."

"Then what were you doing?"

"Distracting myself."

Evelina frowned. Through the shadows of her lashes, she couldn't help but notice the distance in Theo's features. "You can turn the light on, Theo."

Seconds passed. He said nothing and did the same. Then, Theo leaned over and hit the remote to turn the lights on dim.

"Eve?"

"Hmm?" she asked softly, close to drifting off to sleep.

"I didn't think we'd end up like this tonight."

"Us having sex?"

"No … this. Talking and shit. I've been thinking about fucking you for a while, as far as that goes. Don't blame a guy for wanting it."

Evelina smiled. "I won't."

"Definitely worth the wait. Worth the trouble, anyway."

Maybe …

"This is okay, too, Theo. I don't expect anything."

She wasn't lying.

Theo didn't respond to that. Instead, he said, "I think I'm going to end up being that guy."

Evelina struggled to know what he was talking about. "The one who uses me to get what he wants?"

"Yeah, that one."

"Huh. What is it you want?"

Theo sighed. "I'm not even sure yet."

"Ugh, stop moving, pillow."

Theo's dark chuckles rocked Evelina more. "Sorry, but I have to make a call."

"God, what time is it?"

"Six."

"Who in the hell do you call at six in the morning, Theo?"

"People. Go back to sleep, *bella*."

Evelina felt his palm ghost over her cheek. "Did you just call me beautiful?"

"You can speak Italian."

"I can."

"Then don't ask me something you already know."

"Asshole."

"Sometimes," Theo agreed. "Let me up and I'll be back in a few for you to sleep on again."

"Okay. Deal."

Theo was a hard pillow, but a good one all the same. Evelina had woken up a couple of more times only to find Theo still awake and lost in his own thoughts. She hadn't bothered him, but simply fell back asleep feeling his hands on her skin under the sheet she'd wrapped up in.

"You're still not moving, Eve."

"Boo, you suck."

Theo laughed. "I'll be right back."

Evelina grumbled and forced herself to wake up just enough to move for Theo. Once he was off the couch, she turned into nothing but legs, arms, and a sheet curled into the couch. Without Theo's warm form to snuggle with, the coolness of the room wrapped around her body. Evelina didn't care. She was already halfway to falling back asleep.

She'd never been much of a morning person.

"Yeah, hey," she heard Theo say in the background. "Sorry, I know it's early."

Evelina perked up, but tried not to move. She knew better than to eavesdrop on Theo's conversation as his voice became muted and the bathroom door clicked shut, but she couldn't help it. There were only a few times Evelina had heard Theo's voice turn gentle like it had just then. Whenever he talked about Lily, for one. And earlier, when she'd woken from her nightmare.

Sitting up on the couch, Evelina strained to hear the muffled, one-sided conversation.

"Not this week," Theo said, "and probably not next. I know I said I'd come see him but … Yeah, Karen, I get that, but it's not smart for me to be running up there right now."

Karen?

Something awful welled in Evelina's gut, making her feel sick and terrible. She was sure Theo wasn't involved with any other woman. He'd given her the impression he didn't have any romantic relationships that were serious. She didn't want to think he had lied to her, but she didn't want to be that woman for a man, either.

"Listen, there's a lot of shit going on right now, and I don't want to draw any attention to him or you. I'll be around … Yeah, I'll send over a video for him to watch or whatever. He likes that … Okay, later."

Evelina barely dropped back down to the couch before the light from the bathroom filtered into the large hotel room. She heard the phone hit the table before Theo's hands were roving over her sides, urging her up from the couch again. Evelina kept the groggy, half-asleep act up as he took his spot on the couch and laid her head back into his lap silently.

All of the questions were suddenly burning on the back of Evelina's tongue. She couldn't have stopped them from coming out even if she wanted to.

"Theo?" Evelina whispered.

"Sleep, Eve. I'll have hot coffee and breakfast for you when you wake up again."

Evelina gazed up at him, dropping the pretense of sleeping. She was wide awake now. A heat curled in her middle as his palm found the curve in her waist and then moved down to her thigh under the sheet. She said nothing as he fixed the tangled sheet around her legs as the tips of his fingers roamed her skin. His dark gaze traveled over her breasts before he fixed the sheet there, too.

She felt hyperaware and so fucking alive with this man. It was strange and dangerous.

"What, Eve?" Theo finally asked.

Pushing away her nerves, Evelina asked, "Who is Karen?"

Theo sucked in a hard breath, a warning darkening his features.

"Someone you don't need to worry about."

"But—"

Evelina's words cut off as Theo's hand found her chin. He caught her chin and bottom lip between his forefinger and thumb, tilting her head back enough that all she could see was him leaning over her. At the same time, she felt his hand on her thigh snake between her legs. With a little snap of his palm against her skin, she opened her legs to his silent request. Two fingers slid along her sex, teasing and touching. With just a few quick strokes, she was wet and hot, and her breath felt shallow.

"You-you're …"

Evelina couldn't get the words out. They were swallowed by her moan as his fingers slid inside her pussy and curled hard into her G-spot. His thumb, still pressed to her lip, pushed a little harder. Through hooded eyes, she watched his lips twist into a smirk as her legs began to shake.

"What, Eve?" Theo asked.

"Distracting me," she breathed.

Theo nodded. "I am."

It was good, though.

So fucking good.

Theo seemed to know just how to play her body without any prodding at all. Fast, rough strokes of his fingers that stretched her open and hit every goddamn nerve she had. Evelina didn't know what else to do except open her legs wider for him when he told her to do it, and pant her way through the first orgasm.

"Oh, my God, Theo."

Theo cocked a brow and pressed his thumb hard into the hood of her clit. "Again, Eve."

She couldn't breathe. Sensitivity walked hand in hand with bliss and he didn't relent for a damned second. If he kept going like he was, fucking her roughly with his fingers while his thumb jarred her clit over and over, she was going to come again and fast.

"Again, Eve," Theo demanded. "My name in your mouth while you're shaking and coming all over my hand."

"You're distracting me," she accused, still wanting his hands and fingers.

Anything.

She'd take anything from this man.

"She's not important," Eve heard him say as the pleasure rocked her for a second time.

"I—"

"Stop it, Eve. I told you."

"Not important."

"Yes."

That was enough for Evelina.

Her throat felt tight and dry as he pulled her up and caught her cry with a kiss that was sure to leave more of his marks behind.

"Again," Theo repeated, growling the words against her lips. "Give me that again, Eve. Let me feel it, babe."

Everything he did was to feel—wasn't that what he had said once?

What control she regained was lost.

Evelina didn't mind.

"You're not ready yet?"

Evelina jumped at the sound of her father's voice. Fixing the curls back around her neck to hide the mark she'd been looking over. It was one of the few reminders of her three days holed away in a hotel with Theo. She pretended like her father hadn't scared her.

"I'm ready," Evelina said, turning to let her father look over the silver, knee-length sparkly dress she'd chosen.

As the boss of the Outfit, Riley had decided to throw a Christmas party for the families. Maybe it was some attempt at a peace offering, or a way to bring everyone together and try to make peace. Evelina wasn't exactly sure what games her father was playing with the people around them, but he'd invited everyone as far as she knew.

Riley looked her over, sighing quietly. "You look …"

"What, Dad?"

"Grown up."

Evelina tried not to let the sentimental tone her father took on weed its way into her emotions. The last few months couldn't be ignored, and Evelina had very little trust for her father, now. Not after all he'd done, and how he acted after her mother's death.

"Thank you."

Riley took another step forward. "Courtney will be on her best behavior tonight."

For once, Evelina held back from saying.

"Okay."

"I expect for you to do the same," Riley finished firmly.

"I will."

No need to piss her father off, after all. There was only so much the man would take, and acting like a fool in front of his people was not one of them.

"And if anyone happens to mention your little disappearing act last week, you're not to say a thing," Riley said.

Evelina swallowed the lump that lodged in her throat. "I won't."

"I understand your brother's reasoning for panicking and hiding you away, but it looked terrible on me when I was unable to account for my daughter, Evelina."

"I'm sorry."

But she wasn't.

Not at all.

"As far as the BMW ..."

"What about it?" she asked.

"I have a new one ordered, but it'll take a few extra days what with the holiday and everything. We'll call it your Christmas gift, I suppose."

Evelina didn't like this at all. Nothing was right about her father's behavior. He'd been this way ever since Evelina had returned home with no one any wiser about her days away with Theo DeLuca. Her father hadn't thrown a fit about her disappearance, that she sneaked away from her enforcers, or that she lied to Adriano the night her car was burned. Riley had been nice, good-natured, and had even kept Courtney's attitude on a leash. It was almost like her father was trying to soften Evelina for whatever reason.

No, she didn't like this.

She didn't trust Riley.

"I wanted to have a chat with you before the guests start arriving, which was why I asked you to come here and get ready," Riley said.

Evelina stiffened at her father's admission. "About what?"

"After your brother's mess with the Trentini girl—"

"Alessa, Dad. It's Alessa."

Riley waved her words off. "Whatever. He made a damned fool of me, Eve. And at the worst possible time. I have to fix it. You've always understood the rules before; you understand this life and how it works."

A sickening sensation washed over Evelina. He couldn't possibly be talking about what she thought he was. He wouldn't ... right?

"Groomed and understand are two entirely different things," Evelina said quietly.

Riley's gaze narrowed. "Yes, well either way, you know what is expected."

She did, sadly.

"What is it?"

"Tonight, I'll be announcing your engagement."

Evelina's heart stopped. "My engagement."

"Yes."

"To who?"

"Tommas Rossi, of course. He's got the proper name and the best position to back him up. It'll give my family the appearance of solidarity with another family we've had previous issues with, and should hopefully quiet whatever unrest remains. The Rossi crew has always been partial to the DeLuca side of the Outfit. My hope is that the marriage will settle the feuds between everyone. No one wants problems simply because they dislike the Conti boss. It would only add more enemies to their list."

Simple, but effective.

It still didn't make much sense to Evelina. Someone had still shot at her while Theo walked her to her car. Someone burned down her damned car. People like her father and Joel Trentini blamed Theo and his family for those things, but she knew that just wasn't possible. Theo had been with her. Her father knew that as well.

So, if her father was trying to force the crews into peacefully settling down whatever issues they had with someone else, maybe Riley didn't believe Theo was the actual perpetrator of those incidents.

"The DeLucas or someone else, Dad?" Evelina asked.

Riley smirked. "Well, we'll use young Theo as a stand-in for now. He's a good example to make to the rest. I don't mind the sacrifice."

A good example? Sacrifice? What in the hell was that supposed to mean?

"Someone is always waiting to fill in, as the saying goes," Riley added.

"Tommas is my cousin," Evelina said harshly.

"Through marriage only." Riley smiled coldly. "It's well known your mother was adopted into that family through a close friend when she was an infant. There's no blood to be shared between you and Tommas. Hell, your mother hated Tommas' mother as well, so even when people were told they were sisters, most wouldn't believe it. There's nothing that says it shouldn't happen."

Except the way Evelina felt.

"I know him as my cousin," she argued weakly. "Others do, too."

"And soon, you'll know him as something different."

Before Evelina could respond, a knock on the bedroom door drew her attention to the man standing there. Tommas Rossi offered Riley a polite, tight smile that spoke of respect and very little else.

"Boss," Tommas greeted quietly.

"Rossi. I'll give you a second with her to discuss what you'd like." Riley turned back to Evelina, his lips tight and his expression severe. It was almost like he could see the fight in her eyes and how she wanted to refuse. "What have I always told you, Eve?"

"Be a good girl."

Riley nodded. "Smile for the crowd, Evelina. Make your parents proud, beautiful girl. You were always so good at that. Don't fail at it now."

Never shame me.

The Conti *Principessa.*

Evelina felt sick and cold all over, but she said nothing as her father left. Tommas closed the door behind Riley and took a few short steps into the bedroom.

"What do you want?" Evelina asked. "I know the deal, Tommas. I know how to act. You don't have to worry about me embarrassing you later or whatever."

Tommas nodded, smiling grimly. "Thankfully, that is one thing I do know about you, Eve. The rest is a mystery."

He sounded tired and lost, like this was the very last thing he wanted to be doing, too. She wasn't surprised.

"Turn around," Tommas ordered, "I have a gift for you."

Confused, Evelina did as she was told. He came up behind her, and she watched him in the large dressing mirror as he pulled a long, thin jewelry box from the inside of his suit jacket.

"Have you told her, yet?" Evelina dared to ask.

Tommas stilled on the spot, his gaze darting to hers in their reflection. "I have no idea who you're talking about."

"Yes, you do."

"Eve—"

"Have you told her?"

"No," Tommas admitted.

Evelina shoulders dropped. "She's going to hate me."

"Actually, I suspect Abriella will hate me a great deal more than you, even if she doesn't understand why I have to do this right now."

"I don't understand why you're doing it so why on earth would she?"

"Because you don't have to, but she should know better."

Tommas popped open the jewelry box and pulled out a strand of ivory colored pearls. Sweeping Evelina's hair to the side, he placed the necklace around her neck and fastened it without a word. His fingers grazed the back of her neck, but it did nothing for her. His hands certainly didn't bring forth any feelings or desire. Tommas was a handsome man with his strong features, blue gaze, and his dangerous nature, but she wasn't his.

He was already taken. She would never fill that spot for him.

"Abriella should know better," Tommas repeated, "because everything I do is for her, Evelina."

"Marrying another woman is for her? I don't think Abriella will be very agreeable to that, Tommas."

"I simply need the idea of it, Eve, and nothing more. For both of us."

His vague words did nothing but confuse Evelina further.

"Is there a ring, too?" Evelina decided to ask.

"I'll hand it over later when we announce the engagement."

"Fantastic."

"One more thing …" Tommas pulled Evelina's curls to the side a little further, but he kept his gaze locked on hers in the mirror.

"What is that?" she asked.

"Who has touched you?"

Evelina froze. "W-what?"

The pad of his finger pressed to the mark on her neck with the gentlest of pressure, almost like he didn't think it was his to touch.

"Someone has left his mark behind, Evelina," Tommas murmured. "Men who leave marks like these on a woman's body tend to do it because they want it to be found, and because they want other men to know they're to stay away. I'd like to know who it is that left his on you."

"I—"

"The best thing to do right now would be not to lie to me. If you don't want to answer that question, I'll ask another. Is there any more that could be noticed without you realizing someone has seen them?"

Evelina had to think about it, but only briefly. Theo's marks were hidden under her clothes, beneath her bra and panties where only a lover would find. It was just the one on the side of her neck that she had to be mindful of.

"No," Evelina finally said.

Tommas gave her a slow smile and fixed her hair, hiding the mark. "Good."

Evelina didn't know what to think. "Good?"

"Yes. As I said, I don't expect you to understand this, Eve. You don't need to. And you, like Abriella, will figure it out in due time. Her anger I can withstand, I'm sure. Will you tell me who left these?"

"No."

"Be mindful and let whoever it is know that he isn't to leave another that I, or someone else, can find."

Evelina blinked, stunned speechless. Without another word, Tommas turned on his heel and left the bedroom, leaving Evelina behind.

Who was that man?

CHAPTER ELEVEN

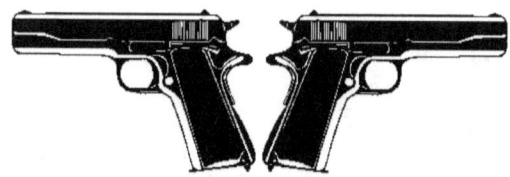

Theo just opened the front door to his sister's and brother-in-law's home in time to see Damian draw Lily in for a quick hug and a kiss on the top of her head. Damian's hand dropped to Lily's stomach momentarily before coming back up to tug on one of her curls.

"Better?" Damian asked.

Lily nodded. "You make it that way."

"Good, sweetheart. No tears on Christmas."

Theo felt like he'd somehow intruded on a very private moment between his sister and her husband. Clearing his throat, Theo opened the door a little wider and stepped inside to announce his arrival and interrupt the couple.

"You came!"

Theo hid his frown as his sister wrapped him in a tighter hug than she normally would. "Of course, little one. Why wouldn't I come?"

Lily shrugged and took a small step back. "I don't know. I guess there's just been a lot of nonsense happening and maybe I thought you would—"

"Be smart and lie low," Damian interrupted.

Theo offered his old friend a nod that Damian returned. "Hey, man."

"Evening. And Merry Christmas, I suppose."

"Merry Christmas."

Lily eyed her husband over her shoulder before saying, "He was invited to the party at Riley's, wasn't he?"

Damian nodded. "He was."

"Then what's the problem, Damian?"

"There's no problem," Theo said. "Riley passed word that all was forgiven."

Although, Theo didn't know what in the hell there was to forgive. He'd had no involvement in the drive-by shooting or the burning of Evelina's car. As far as he knew, and he was pretty damned sure of it, none of his men in the DeLuca crew had stirred that mess up, either.

Theo didn't entirely trust Riley and his motives, whatever they were, for inviting Theo to the Christmas party. Nonetheless, rules were rules.

Theo wouldn't refuse a boss, even if he despised the very breath that boss breathed.

"If there's no problem," Lily said, jutting her fist to her hip, "… then why does my husband keep acting like he's going to jump out of his damn skin every five minutes?"

"That's just Damian. He's twitchy."

"Fuck off," Damian muttered under his breath. "Just be good tonight, Theo, and don't cause any shit."

"Who said I was planning anything like that?"

"Hard to say with you, man."

"Give me a bit of credit." Theo smirked. "It's Christmas, after all."

"Oh!" Lily threw her arms high and turned fast on her heel. She disappeared out of the foyer in a flurry of blonde hair and happy laughter.

Theo tossed Damian a questioning look. "What is that nonsense all about?"

"Happy day," Damian said, waving it all off. "The hormone thing is crazy with pregnancy. Today is a good day. I don't question it, I'm simply grateful for it."

Theo decided to take his friend's word for it. Pregnancy and babies were not something Theo could see in his near future, never mind the far future. It just wasn't his style. He didn't want to see his kids ending up being raised the way he had, or the way he watched others grow up. There would be no abuse behind closed doors in his home, and certainly no show for the watchers. He wouldn't give someone the chance to do that to his children.

And Theo knew if he had kids, they would forever be known as DeLuca kids. Mob kids. Mafia *principes* or *principessas*. Their father would always be the gangster—the Outfit mobster. What kind of heritage was that to have to carry around? No, Theo wouldn't do that to his blood. Kids weren't even a thought in his mind.

"The guy who dropped it off said there was big bonus for the carrier who would deliver it on Christmas," Lily said as she walked back into the foyer. In her arms, she held a small package a little bigger than a shoe box. "We haven't opened it."

She dropped the box to the decorative table.

"But it was addressed to you and Lily," Damian said.

Theo could see who the package was addressed to, and he recognized that messy scrawl on the top, too. Suddenly, his lungs wouldn't work and his fingernails were biting into his palms.

"It's from Dino," Lily said quietly.

"He expected to be serving time right now, right?" Damian asked.

Theo nodded, but stayed quiet.

"So maybe he got something ready for us so we could have a gift from him at Christmas." Lily tugged on Theo's jacket, pulling him closer. "This is a nice surprise. Aren't you happy, Theo?"

He was. Or he was trying to be. But as he stared at the box, all of his anger and guilt came rushing back tenfold. There was no escaping the tidal wave of grief that washed through his bloodstream, and cracked his cold heart all over again.

Theo had been doing okay. He'd pushed a lot of his anger aside and was trying to think about moving forward, and not the wrongs that had been done to his family, Dino's death included. He hadn't forgotten or entirely forgiven what happened, but he didn't have a lot of choices in the matter to fix the situation, either. The package was just another reminder to Theo that his brother had expected to still be alive, if not a little more confined than before. He still expected to see his family grow and succeed after all the work and pain he'd gone through to give the DeLucas someone to be proud of.

And his boy … Dino's son …

Theo refused to even go there.

"Open it," Theo said gruffly.

His feelings were not his sister's burdens to bear. Lily was clearly excited over the surprise and Theo understood why. She'd taken Dino's death especially hard. She still had a great deal of guilt for the years she'd pushed her brothers away, and all the time she wasted. Theo wasn't going to ruin her happy moment with his anxiety.

"Yeah?" Lily asked. "If you want to wait, we could do it after the dinner party."

"Nah, just open it up, little one. Let's see what's inside."

Damian crossed the foyer, pulling out a small pocket knife. When Lily tried to take it from her husband, Damian clicked his tongue chidingly and then sliced the top of the box across the tape.

"I could have done that," Lily grumbled.

Damian chuckled. "Pregnant, not disabled. I'm aware. You're clumsy, though. You'd probably end up slicing yourself or something. And on Christmas, no less."

"I am not!"

"You kind of are," Theo said.

Lily made a disgusted noise, waving the men off as she popped open the top and stuck her hands into the box. She pulled out a box of chocolates that Theo knew happened to be her very favorite, and in the other hand, she had two envelopes.

She passed over the envelope that had Theo's name marked across the front. His was much bigger and looked stiffer than Lily's did. His had to be at least ten inches long and eight wide while hers was standard size.

"You first," Theo said, eyeing the envelope Lily held with her own name marked on it.

"Why not you first?"

"Because I'm the oldest between us, and I make the rules."

"Yes, but it's her house," Damian put in.

Theo flicked his hand in Damian's direction to silence him. "Be quiet, you're not a DeLuca. You get no vote here."

"Neither is she, not on paper, anyway."

"Oh, shut up, both of you." Lily grinned and winked at her brother before ripping off the side of the envelope. She tipped it over and pulled out what looked to be a letter and several photographs. "Is that …?"

"Let me see," Theo said, moving closer.

The pictures were old, certainly. He recognized himself and his siblings in the photographs almost immediately. Dino was well into his teenaged years while Theo was just beginning to get there and Lily was still little.

Lily flipped through the photographs silently. Each one had the siblings together in some variation, and a couple had them with their parents.

"Those had to be done—"

"A month before Mom and Dad were killed," Theo interrupted quietly.

He remembered the day the photos were taken with vivid detail. His mother had been ecstatic for the photographer because the person was apparently the best in Chicago at the time. Their father had paid a lot of money for the shoot. Dino and Theo had been their usual rowdy selves while Lily soaked up the attention as the baby of the family.

"And the letter?" Theo asked.

Lily handed the letter off to Damian without a word. Theo didn't miss the tremor rocking his sister's fingers before she went back to flipping through the photographs all over again.

"The strip of negatives are folded up in here," Damian said. "If you wanted to have a few sized larger, we could go do that, Lily."

Lily didn't say a thing. Theo supposed his sister was in a similar state as him.

"What does the letter say?" Theo asked again.

His own letter burned against his palm. He was stuck between wanting to open it and wanting to hide it.

Damian glanced down at the paper he held, reading, "Merry Christmas, Lily. Have you forgiven me for Damian, yet? I suppose being separated by a few states, cement walls, and bars will give you all the time to work through your anger. I'll see you when you're ready, little one. In the meantime, I was cleaning out some things in storage while I was getting the house ready for when I was sentenced and found these. What do you give a woman who has everything, or everything that she wants, anyway? You give her memories she didn't even know she had. I went back for these and a few other things like Mom's rosary. I'm sure you'll do something amazing with them, something better than hiding them away in a box. Love, Dino."

"You hated that dress," Theo said, pointing at the one his sister wore in the pictures.

Lily sniffed and wiped at her eyes quickly. "Did I?"

"Yeah, but Mom loved it and you loved the way Dad treated you like a little princess, so you wore it for them. It was a nice day and you managed to stay clean somehow. Usually you were dirtier than sin, because you were always chasing after me back then."

Damian folded the letter up and stuffed it into the envelope. "Do you want me to put the pictures away in the office for now just to be safe?"

"In a second," Lily whispered. "What is inside yours, Theo?"

Tension crawled over Theo's shoulders. He hadn't known Dino planned anything like this. They were speaking at the time, barely, and yes, Theo knew about Dino's son, but that was about it. He didn't know what would be inside.

"Open and read it for me?" Lily asked quietly.

Theo couldn't deny his sister a damn thing when she was lit up like she was, so he opened his own envelope from Dino and pulled out the contents just enough to get a glimpse at what was inside. In his hand, pictures of a boy and his father—Junior and Dino—stared up at Theo with wide smiles and pride.

Lily reached for the pictures instantly. Theo slammed them back into the envelope. Why had his brother sent him these? Why would Dino do that knowing Lily would be right there, too?

Dino's main goal when he was alive was to keep his son as far away from the Outfit and that mess as much as he possibly could. At least, that was how he explained it to Theo. Dino didn't want their family's past, or their uncle, to stain his son.

"Theo?" Lily asked. "Let me see the pictures."

"They're the same as yours," Theo lied.

Damian's brow furrowed, but the man stayed quiet.

"The backs were new prints, Theo," Lily argued.

"He had some done up from the negatives." Theo's lies came like running water. "Later, okay?"

Lily opened her mouth to speak, but Damian beat her to the punch. "We're going to be late, sweetheart."

"Fine. I forgot my purse in the kitchen."

Theo could see it in the set of his sister's pursed lips that she was pissed off, and didn't believe a word he was saying to her. Even so, she left in search of her purse, and Theo took the chance to escape the house at the same moment.

He had planned on going to the dinner party with Lily and her husband. It would have looked good on Theo to show up with the head Capo for the Rossi crew, even if that Capo was married to Theo's sister. It would have showed he was agreeable to settling down the feuds.

Mostly, Theo was sick of getting blamed for shit that wasn't his fault or causing.

Right then, he just didn't give a damn.

"Hey!"

Theo hadn't even gotten the chance to close the driver's door of his Stingray before Damian was yanking it back open.

"What in the hell, man?" Theo growled.

His anger was spilling like hot lava into his veins. Dino had put Theo into a terrible position with his sister. Theo was the one left protecting Junior, not Dino. The last thing he wanted to do was hurt Lily by lying to her, or worse, telling her the truth and then refusing her access to her nephew.

Theo made a move to toss the envelope into the backseat, away from Damian, but the man grabbed it right out of Theo's hand. Damian took a couple of quick steps away from the car as Theo jumped out, reaching for the item to take it back.

"Give that to me, you asshole," Theo practically snarled.

"What—" Damian's words cut off as he pulled the pictures out. "Jesus Christ."

"Give them to me right fucking now, D."

Damian's gaze darted between the pictures and Theo's face. No doubt, the man was drawing his own conclusions. Damian had never been stupid.

"He had a fucking kid?" Damian asked.

Theo sucked in a hard breath, willing his rage to subside. "It's none of your damned business."

"Wrong. Anything that affects my wife is entirely my business, Theo. Your attitude in there bothered her, and I knew you were trying to hide something, but this? This, man? She … Oh my, God, Theo, he had a fucking kid!"

"Lower your voice," Theo snapped before he snatched the items from Damian's outstretched hand. "And it's *has*, okay. He has a kid. Dino might be dead, but my nephew is very much alive and I intend for him to stay that way, D."

Damian turned as still as stone. "And you knew."

"Not until a few months ago."

"But you knew, Theo!"

Theo tossed the envelope back into his car as his sister walked out of the house and began locking the door. "Keep your fucking mouth shut about it, D, or I swear to God."

"You swear what, huh? I won't lie to my wife. I did enough of that for your goddamn brother in this whole mess, Theo."

There it was again. Someone else with their vague comments about Dino and the war.

Theo didn't know what to think. "Tommas said something like that to me, too. Do you have something you want to fucking tell me, Ghost?"

"You're not a stupid man. You figure it out."

Theo was pretty sure he already had. "Keep out of this, Damian."

"Don't ask me to lie to my wife."

"I'm not. But you know nothing about that child in those pictures other than who his father is. You don't know where he lives, who his mother is, or even his first name. And if you go looking for him, I promise you won't find a goddamn thing. So go on ahead and tell my sister the good news; tell her she has a nephew she can't see or spend time with; tell her that, D."

Damian's jaw clenched. "You're an—"

"Asshole?" Theo scoffed. "Figure out something new. Everyone else has used that one up on me, Damian."

Lily started walking down the steps after finally getting the front door locked. Theo needed to end this conversation and fast.

"Let it go, D. Don't lie, just let it go."

"As Lily has told me, omission is the same thing. She feels guilty all the damned time about Dino, how he died, this fucking house, and the time she spent away. I would like to take that away for her. Knowing he's got a kid for her to love and watch grow up would help Lily more than I can explain. Give this to her, Theo."

"I'm sorry, D. I can't. Not yet."

"He's just a kid. He's not a part of this life or these families."

Theo pointed at his chest. "I was just a kid. I didn't have to be a part of this. They dragged me kicking and screaming into it whether I wanted to or not. Just like my brother, just like my sister, and just like you, D."

Damian swallowed hard. "I know when you were younger—"

"If you say I had a rough go of it like everyone else does, I'll feed you your fucking teeth, man. And you're not to ever tell Lily about that shit, either."

Damian looked like he was ready to choke Theo or kick his ass. It wouldn't be the first time the two friends had fought and it probably wouldn't be the last.

"Damian, didn't you say we were going to be late?" Lily asked as she opened the door to the blue Porsche.

"Yeah," Damian called back.

Neither man took their eyes off one another.

"Forget about it," Theo murmured.

"Give me a guarantee she'll know that boy someday."

Theo beat back the nerves he felt at the demand. "Someday, D. Not today."

"Good enough. Lock your car up. You'll look better showing up with a Rossi."

"A Capo, you mean."

Damian chuckled. "Well, you need all the fucking help you can get."

Just like that, the two men softened in their stances. The argument was over and Theo felt his anxiety and anger bleed away. It was why he kept Damian Rossi close. The man might be a killer and a Rossi at heart, but he was fucking loyal to the people who mattered most to him.

"We good?" Theo asked.

Damian shrugged. "Yeah. We're good."

"Shit, and I thought they whispered about me," Adriano said with a chuckle.

Theo tossed back the remainder of his rum and coke. "You're just the stain on your daddy's reputation, Adriano."

"Thanks for that."

"But I'm the bomb they're waiting to see blow."

Adriano's gaze swept the crowd of guests at the dinner party and found his fiancée across the room. Theo wasn't surprised. The kid was always watching that girl and making sure no one was bothering her. For good reason, too. People could be assholes sometimes.

"You never let me apologize for Artino and—"

"Not necessary," Theo interjected quickly.

"Isn't it?"

"No. I figured it must have had something to do with Alessa."

"It did," Adriano said quietly. "He got physical with her after the first time. I couldn't let it go down like that. Your other guy just happened to be in the way. I was pissed that night. I might have done it differently on another night, but I can't say for sure."

"You did what you had to."

Theo would slit the throat of any man and watch the fucker drown in his blood for putting his hands on a female he cared about. He didn't blame

Adriano for his rash choices a couple of months earlier when he killed Dean Artino and another one of Theo's guys. Frankly, Artino's attitude had that one coming.

"Thanks, I guess," Adriano said.

Theo smirked. "Oh, I'll cash in the apology someday, to be sure."

Adriano frowned. "Even better."

Adriano Conti was a damn good kid. He was young, sure, but he was golden, too. Loyal to a fault. Protective over what was his. Smart on the streets.

"How much shit did the crew give you when you took Kolin's spot?" Theo asked.

Adriano laughed dryly. "Enough. Not as much as I expected, but I'm just a kid to them."

"You're a kid to me, too."

"Nobody else has much to say about it," Adriano said, shrugging. "The important people, you know. I'm not sure if that's because my father is the boss or what."

"No, it's because they know you, Adriano."

"So why do people feel like they have to run their mouth over your title, huh?"

"Because I wasn't like Dino and everybody knew it. Makes a person wonder, that's all."

"Well, with Walter Artino dead, you've got nothing to worry about now," Adriano said.

Theo watched Riley Conti dance with his young bride in the middle of the room. The man had made a point of talking to Theo in front of the guests and shaking his hand. He was making every effort for it to appear like nothing was wrong.

Something definitely was. Theo just couldn't pinpoint what it was.

"Sometimes worries just switch from one thing to another," Theo replied simply.

Adriano eyed Theo from the side. "You don't trust anyone, do you?"

"No." Theo hummed under his breath, adding, "Well, a couple."

"Not my father."

"No, he isn't one of them."

Adriano cocked a brow and found his fiancée in the crowd again. "Yeah, me, either."

"I thought I saw you come in with Lily earlier."

Theo tensed at Evelina's sudden presence at his side, but quickly relaxed. She was damned sexy in a slinky, sparkling silver dress that fell above her knees and showcased fine legs in black pumps. Theo always did have a taste for women in heels.

Tonight wasn't a good time for that.

He'd always had an attraction for Evelina, as far as that went, but feeding it and admitting to feeling it were two entirely different things.

"Eve," he greeted. "No enforcers or bruises, I see."

Evelina's brow furrowed as she glanced up at him. "Pardon?"

"There are no enforcers three feet off your ass or any bruises on your arms, which means I can safely assume your father took your return back to real life better than you thought he would."

"Strangely, yes."

Theo kept one eye on the guests and one on Evelina at his side. With their backs to the wall as they stood side by side, there was nothing suggestive about their postures or conversation. Nothing that could be twisted into something bad, anyway.

Even still, being this close to Evelina reminded Theo of what she felt like under his hands and how his name sounded coming out of her mouth while she was shaking and needy. The slinky dress gave a hint of her curves and body beneath the fabric, but Theo's memory wouldn't let him forget what she looked like with nothing on at all.

That kind of attraction was so fucking dangerous.

"Don't you have a crowd to dazzle for Riley?" Theo asked.

Evelina snorted under her breath. "He's got Courtney for that now."

"Lucky you."

"Besides, he'll get to show me off later," she said bitterly.

Knowing he shouldn't but unable to stop the urge to soothe Evelina's irritation, Theo reached between them with his hand and stroked her side with his pinky. Evelina visibly shuddered at the touch and sighed softly. Clearly he wasn't the only one struggling with the attraction he felt.

"We'd be bad," Evelina said, swallowing hard. "Wasn't that what you told me, Theo?"

"I did."

"Does that mean we won't get to fuck again?"

All it took was that word coming out of Evelina's pretty little mouth, and Theo's dick was as hard as steel under his slacks.

Jesus.

"Don't play that game, Eve," he warned.

"I don't play games like these people do." Evelina nodded across the room, drawing Theo's attention to where Damian stood with Lily at his side and Tommas Rossi on the other. "But I figured that it would only be right for me to let you know that Tommas asked you not leave another mark on me that he can find."

Theo's chest felt like someone had just hit it with a sledgehammer, but on the outside, he remained passive and unbothered. "What is that supposed to mean?"

Evelina reached up and brushed her curls to the side. To anyone else, it might have looked like a normal gesture but Theo's eyes were immediately drawn to the red mark he'd left behind on her neck. He knew there were a few other love bites on her body from his mouth, too.

"Shit," Theo muttered, not knowing what else to say. A heavy realization settled in his gut. "Your father is going to show you off tonight because he's going to marry you off, right?"

Theo didn't even know how he felt about that except for the fact that he didn't like it at all. This was the Outfit life, the mafia way, and Evelina was the daughter doing what she was told. Theo still felt like hot lava had been injected straight into his gut.

What in the hell was wrong with him?

"Tommas Rossi," Theo said. "He's going to marry you off to Tommas."

"Bang on, Theo. Tommas wasn't even angry about the mark. He basically told me to be careful and nothing else."

None of that made sense at all.

"Why?" Theo asked. "Why in the hell would Tommas say that?"

Evelina shrugged and lifted her wine glass for a sip, although she didn't take a drink. It hid her mouth from being seen by others as she murmured, "I'm wondering that myself. I thought maybe you could work it out and let me know."

Theo scoffed lowly. "Right now, I'm a fucking disease to these people."

"Can you tell me something?"

"What, princess?"

"Why would my father call you the sacrifice?"

It felt like ice had suddenly been poured into Theo's veins. He didn't have the first clue what that could mean, but in general, nothing good could come of that word.

"I didn't think it was a good thing," Evelina added quickly, "and the way you just froze up tells me I made the right choice."

Theo forced the tightening in his throat away so he could speak. "What choice is that?"

Evelina smiled. "That girl, Theo."

"That girl?"

"That girl who tells the man using her what he wants to know because she's got things she wants, too."

"And what is it you want, Eve?" Theo dared to ask.

This conversation felt ten shades of wrong, and he knew better than to indulge whatever was going on between him and Evelina. The hookup was enough of a mistake. The two days in a bed with Evelina that followed that mistake was even worse.

Except it hadn't felt bad at all.

"I already told you what I want," Evelina said, pushing off the wall.

A deja vu sensation passed over Theo. Like maybe they'd done this thing or something like it before at a different time.

"Which is what, Eve?"

Her finger ticked in the air over her shoulder.

"To not be a princess, Theo."

CHAPTER TWELVE

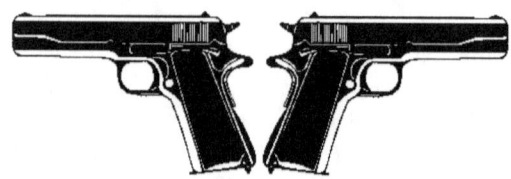

"Eve, could you let the head server know we're getting low on wine out here?" Courtney asked. "They seem to like you more than me."

Sweet as sugar, her stepmother smiled like the poisonous snake she was.

"Have you wondered why that is?"

Courtney's fake smile melted away. "Just do what I said."

Riley's words from earlier, reminding Evelina to be on her best behavior where her stepmother was concerned, rang loudly in the back of her mind. "Fine."

Not wanting to spend more time than was necessary with Courtney, Evelina left the dining room. Tossing a glance over her shoulder as she entered the hallway leading to the kitchen, Evelina noticed Theo was still standing where she had left him.

Games, he'd said.

Evelina wasn't trying to play games, but she wasn't going to lie down and take whatever these people threw at her. She wasn't going to watch them as they tore apart someone else like Theo, either. He'd done no wrong.

At the same time, Evelina felt a kindred connection to Theo. They were both being used as pawns in the games around them without having any say at all. Neither of them even knew what the game was yet, except for the fact that they were someone's pieces to move.

The Outfit was dirty like that.

In the kitchen, Evelina found a dozen more guests swarmed around the table of finger foods that had been placed out earlier. She quickly relayed the message to the head server of the catering company and then turned to leave.

"Eve!" Abriella gave her sister's hand a squeeze and left Alessa's side to join Evelina. It took all the willpower Evelina had to fight off the rush of guilt suddenly swarming her insides. "How are you?"

Evelina fidgeted with the silver bangle on her wrist. "I'm okay, Ella. You?"

"Better. Still not back at your dorm?"

"No. You back at your apartment?"

Abriella smirked and shook her head. "Not after you know what."

"Alessa and Adriano?"

"Joel doesn't trust his left pinky right now, let alone me. I think if he could figure out a way to do it without getting my fist shoved down his throat, he'd be forcing me to the clinic every week to get a pregnancy test."

Evelina cringed. "Yikes."

"Yeah. It's pretty bad."

Without needing to ask, Evelina had the feeling that also meant Abriella wasn't getting to spend any time with her long-time lover, Tommas Rossi. The guilt over the engagement that would soon be announced came back with a vengeance.

"But you know Joel," Abriella said, a hint of bitterness coating her tone. "He's happy to use others misfortune to get him what he wants."

"My father."

Abriella shrugged. "Adriano did the deed."

"But you're the one who gave the secret away," Evelina said quietly.

"Did Alessa tell you that?"

"She did."

"Did she also tell you why I did it?"

Evelina nodded. "You did it for her."

"Then tone down the judgment a little, Eve."

Evelina checked her attitude. "You're right. I'm sorry."

Abriella glanced down at her hands and said, "I know I went about it in a shitty way, but I didn't want my sister to suffer because she found someone she loved. I didn't think it was fair and Adriano is …"

"A great guy," Evelina finished for her old friend.

"For Alessa, yeah."

"Well, my brother is nothing like my father. I'll give him that."

"Truth." Sighing, Abriella smiled a little. "Listen, I know we've been at opposite ends of this whole thing with the families and whatnot, but I don't want to be like that, Eve. Their issues aren't our issues. Okay?"

Evelina's throat closed around the lump that formed there. She didn't know the first thing to say to Abriella. She wanted to agree; she wanted her old friend back in her life like they had been as teenagers. A bigger problem remained. Evelina knew some of Abriella's secrets, like Tommas. How would Abriella feel about Evelina when she found out Riley was going to use the one thing Abriella adored just to keep peace between the families?

"Eve?" Abriella asked again.

Her mouth opened, but no words came out. Should she tell Abriella, or—

A familiar voice broke Evelina's inner turmoil. Lily Rossi wrapped her arm around Evelina's and pulled her friend close. "Where have you been all night, Eve?"

"Around," Evelina answered, giving what she hoped was a real enough smile. "I see Damian let you away from his side for more than five minutes."

Abriella laughed. "I bet he's right around the corner."

Lily tossed a look over her shoulder. "Probably. Give him a break. He's ..."

"Overprotective?" Evelina asked.

"Special?" Abriella supplied.

Lily flashed a brilliant smile. "Mine. And all of that other stuff, too."

Evelina joined in on the girls' laughter. It seemed like with Lily's entrance, Abriella had dropped their previous conversation. She was grateful.

"This is a first," Abriella said.

"Hmm, what?" Lily asked.

"You're at an Outfit gathering and for once, you're not drinking."

Evelina took note of the water in Lily's wine glass. "Wow. And it's Christmas, too."

Lily's cheeks turned pink as she said, "Uh, I'm going to go find my—"

"Whoa, now." Abriella grabbed Lily's wrist, keeping her from running. She gave the wine glass and Lily's embarrassed smile another once over. "You're not the kind of girl who bolts, either. Don't tell me you're—"

"Shut up, Ella."

"What am I missing?" Evelina asked.

She always felt so out of the loop, now. Like everyone around her knew some giant secret about someone else that she didn't know.

Lily waved a hand as if to dismiss Abriella. "It's nothing."

"Are you?" Abriella asked quietly.

"Is she what?"

Abriella rolled her blue eyes and mouthed, "Pregnant."

For a split second, time stopped.

Then, Evelina found her voice. "What?"

"Shut up, shut up," Lily grumbled, sticking her hands up to cover both her friends' mouths. "Shut up right now ... good *God*."

"So you are?" Abriella asked, her voice muffled.

Evelina couldn't help but giggle.

Lily raised a single brow. "Not a damn word."

"But—"

"Not a word," Lily interrupted Evelina sharply.

"Congrats," Evelina whispered.

"Okay, that's one I'll accept."

Evelina laughed when Lily finally dropped her hand.

"How far—"

Lily's stare cut to Abriella, quieting her instantly. "Not here, okay?"

"Aren't you happy?"

"Very. Damian is over the moon, too. But right now, I don't want the kind of attention this announcement might bring."

Evelina understood instantly. "Because of my brother and Alessa."

Abriella's shoulders dropped at the statement. "Oh."

"I could only imagine how they'd feel to see someone being praised and whatever else while those same people shame them for their joy. That's not okay with me." Lily frowned and added, "So I just want to give it a little more time. I like that only a few people know right now, anyway. Our family gets to enjoy this privately before the rest of the Outfit knows, too. That's how it should be, all right."

"Who all knows?" Abriella asked.

"Tommas, Theo, and now you two. Damian and I don't have a lot of people we're close to. Theo figured it out on his own when he came over for dinner one night. Tommas was the first person Damian called after I told him because he had a moment."

Evelina laughed. "A moment?"

Apparently, Lily's statement wasn't meant to be funny if the way her expression darkened with sadness was any indication.

"He never had much of a father growing up. It's a scary thing, you know, having to worry about raising a child when you never had someone to raise you. He's got nothing to go on, and he needed someone who wasn't me to tell him that it'd be fine."

"He'll make a good father," Evelina assured her friend.

Of course, Damian would. Because when the man loved, he loved. There was no in-between. Evelina had seen it well enough when her cousin fell in love with Lily.

"He will," Lily agreed. "So, lips sealed."

"Sealed," Abriella agreed.

Evelina made the motion of a zipper closing across her lips.

"Thanks." Lily turned to Evelina with a curious glint lighting up her gaze. "I heard you went AWOL last week."

Oh, crap.

"I heard something about that, too," Abriella said. "I couldn't believe it. Evelina Conti skips out on her enforcers and doesn't call home? No way."

Evelina brushed their teasing off. "I called my brother."

Abriella pursed her lips. "Joel said Riley was saying Adriano sent you away because someone burned the BMW."

"That's the story," Evelina said. "Two incidents involving me makes for a bad situation."

"But it's not the truth," Lily murmured. "Not one bullet hit your car during the shooting, and you weren't in your car when someone burned it down. I hear things just like anyone else does, Eve. You're not telling the whole story, are you?"

"Sounds to me like someone is getting just close enough to you to bother your father," Abriella noted quietly. "And maybe you used that chance to skip out of life for a few days."

"Sometimes we need to get away," Evelina said with a shrug.

"Is that all you're going to give us?"

"Yes."

"Damn," Abriella said, pouting. "You're no fun. This would have been a much better story if you'd included something interesting."

"It was interesting," Evelina replied before she could stop herself.

Lily's gaze widened. "And why was that?"

Evelina wasn't entirely sure how Lily would take the fact that she'd slept with Theo. Or that she stayed with him in a hotel room for several days after and kept sleeping with him. Or that Evelina still wanted to sleep with him.

"I felt free," Evelina settled on saying. "For a few days, nobody else mattered but me and what I wanted. I got what I wanted and then I had to come back down to real life."

It wasn't a lie.

Lily sighed. "It's a nice place to be, isn't it?"

"Yes. I mean, it wasn't like you and Europe, but it was freeing."

"You know what I learned from Europe?" Lily asked. "I learned that being free doesn't always mean not being confined. Sometimes it's coming home and being freed here, too."

Evelina didn't know what home was anymore. Was it the friend she was about to betray when she became engaged to Abriella's lover? Was it the friend she would hurt by her lies when Lily found out what had happened between Evelina and Theo? Was it the greedy father and the new stepmother? Was it the Outfit with its dirty ways and confusing games?

Where was home for Evelina?

"Being home is a freeing thing?" Abriella laughed under her breath. "I can't say that my home feels anything like that right now."

"Truth," Evelina agreed before gulping down the last bit of her wine.

"No," Lily said simply. "There's a difference. Home is what makes you feel free, and freedom is the home that doesn't confine you."

A brown-eyed, rich-voiced man with a magic touch and demons on his back had done that for Evelina. But she and Theo were still worlds apart, even when they stood side by side.

Evelina stayed close to the wall and behind the backs of the guests as her father took the head of the room. With a glass of red wine in his one hand and a handful of Courtney in the other, Riley looked as though he was king of the world. For the moment, Evelina supposed he was.

"Thank you all for coming to celebrate this holiday with my family," Riley said, his voice carrying over the murmurs.

"This house always looks better when there's lots of people filling it," Courtney said, her giggles following her statement.

"It does." Riley lifted his glass higher to the guests, smiling widely. "We've had a rough few months together, this family. We shouldn't be fighting with one another. Our families have always been above that sort of nonsense and tonight, my family would like to cement our happiness and extend our loyalty to this life and its ways in the best way we know how."

Evelina's chest tightened. She had all she could do not to run for the door. Tommas Rossi slid into her side wordlessly. She hadn't even noticed he was nearby until he was staring her right in the face with a sad smile.

"Ready?" he asked quietly.

No, she wanted to say.

"He's making a terrible show of this, isn't he?" Evelina whispered.

"He's making a point." Tommas shrugged. "Let him make it, Eve. The idea of this is all we need. Smile, please."

"What does that even mean?"

"Smile."

His fingers locked around her wrist like he knew she was about to bolt.

"Evelina, Tommas?" Riley called out.

People turned, staring. Evelina could practically feel the eyeballs searing into her and Tommas as her soon-to-be fiancé kept holding her in place and watching her closely.

Movement from the corner of her eye drew in her attention. Theo cocked his head just enough to catch Evelina's stare and hold it. He tipped his glass up for a drink, but not before she caught the sight of his frown.

He stood alone.

Theo was always alone.

"Eve." Tommas squeezed her wrist. "Smile for me, please."

"I—"

"The idea, Evelina, is the most important thing you need to

maintain," Tommas murmured. "You have always been good at this. Do not give them anything different."

An idea was not a guarantee. Evelina was finally starting to read between the lines. Tommas didn't need to tell Evelina to smile again. She put on her best smile as his hand slid from her wrist into her palm. As her father called out their names again, Tommas turned around and tugged Evelina forward with him. She went without a fight.

At the head of the room, Evelina focused her stare on a painting at the far wall. She didn't want to see the hurt this would cause her friend. She didn't want to know who would be happy and who would be angry.

"When my deceased wife was alive," Riley said, his tone dripping with false sadness and heartbreak, "... the Rossi and Conti families had always been close. Our familial relation kept us that way, and when Mia was buried, I think both sides felt the cracks begin to form and the divide widen."

Coughs echoed from one corner of the room. Evelina found the person making the noise—Serena Rossi. At least she seemed sober tonight. That was a first. Tommas stiffened beside Evelina, tossing his mother a cool look from where he stood. Serena quickly quieted.

"When one family started to divide, the others followed," Riley continued. "I want to begin repairing that crack and moving us all back together again. And I will start doing that with another marriage."

"Marriage."

"A wedding."

"Tommas ..."

"Evelina ..."

She heard all the words and quick whispers that followed her father's statements, but Evelina didn't move her eye off the painting at the back of the room for a second.

Riley lifted his wine glass toward his son and Alessa in the corner. "In a couple of weeks, my boy will solidify our relationship with the Trentini family through his marriage to Alessa. The Rossi family has already become acquainted with the DeLucas through their recent marriage. It is time that the ones who are left wipe what slates remain so that we can all start out clean."

The idea, Evelina told herself over and over. She kept repeating those words even when Tommas pulled out a jewelry box. Like the proper gentleman she knew him to be, he got down on his one knee. Her smile never fell. Her voice never wavered.

It wasn't easy.

Evelina swore the change in the room was instant. Like a shock of realization had settled over the thirty or so guests standing frozen in the dining area and they were finally waking up from it.

The flurry of movement from the side was the only thing that broke Evelina's concentration as Tommas slid the ring down her finger. The flyby of dark hair and a black dress was all Evelina saw of Abriella before the girl was gone.

Taking her attention off the important goal at hand was the wrong thing to do. Evelina was quick to gage the rest of the people and their reaction to the announcement as well. One person stood out to Evelina above the rest.

Joel Trentini.

Clenched fists. Tight jaw. Burning eyes.

The conversation between Riley and Tommas that Evelina had overheard rang heavily in the back of her mind.

You're willing to marry your daughter off to Joel Trentini just to keep him in line?

What had her father done?

Glancing back at Riley, she could see her father was watching his new underboss carefully. Riley wasn't missing Joel's visible rage for a second. Chances were, he'd just played another hand. Evelina just happened to be the damn card he put down.

"Riley!"

Joel Trentini's sharp hiss gave Evelina the chance she needed to get away from her father's side when Riley turned to Joel with a scowl.

"It's Boss, Joel."

She didn't wait around to hear what else would be said as Joel and Riley moved off into a more private section of the room where less guests were. Evelina left the dining area without a second look back.

She needed to breathe.

Just one damn breath.

Not a minute after Tommas had put the ring on her finger, the man disappeared. Riley hadn't seemed to mind Tommas taking leave like that, but it left Evelina unsettled. She didn't want to face all those people alone after the big announcement but that was exactly what she'd been left to do.

With her father and stepmother, of course. She might as well have been fed to the damn wolves. Like a *sacrifice*.

Doing her best to hide the tremor in her hands, Evelina slipped down the first hallway she came to. It led to the downstairs section of the Conti home where extra bedrooms, a couple of bathrooms, the laundry room, and an entertaining room with a bar and pool table could be found. Guests were rarely allowed into that section of the home unless directly invited. Evelina figured that would be the safest place to go if she didn't want to be found for a few minutes.

She was wrong.

The moment her foot hit the bottom step leading into the lower floor, she heard voices echoing from down the darkened hall. They might as well have been spitting hatred and rage with just their tones alone.

"You're a fucking coward, Tommas," Abriella said.

She almost sounded like she was goading him.

Evelina cringed and turned on her heel to go back upstairs but Tommas' next words stopped her.

"I am not, Ella. It was me or Joel. Don't you fucking get that, girl? Is that what you want, for your friend to be married off to someone like your brother? And for that matter, it's never going to even hap—"

"Shut up," Abriella hissed. "You couldn't even give me the decency of telling me first. You could have called me or at the very least, sent me a message, as low as that would have been. It would have been better than this. At any time tonight, you could have taken me aside and told me, Tommy! Why didn't you tell *me?*"

Tommas didn't say a thing.

"Because you're a fucking coward, that's why, Tommy."

"I am not. But what I couldn't do was hurt you, Ella. I couldn't do that."

"You already did!"

"Stop it. You know I love you to death, Ella. I'd fucking do anything for you—I'm doing it now."

"By marrying my friend," Abriella said in a scoff. "That's rich, Tommy."

"You're not getting it," Tommas muttered, a heat coloring his words. "There is so much shit at play here. More than you can possibly understand, and here in this house is not the time for us to get into it all. I haven't been able to tell you a lot because you've not been around. Phones aren't safe, not like we think. I couldn't refuse and give your brother the option of stepping higher."

"Is that all it is for you? Who has the better position? You'll marry Eve, your cousin—even if it is through name only—and one of my very best friends, just to get yourself higher in the Outfit?"

"No!"

"I'll be your whore then, right? I've always been your little slut in the bedroom, so why not take it outside, too, huh?"

Evelina heard a thump followed by a sharp gasp right after Abriella finished her tirade. Concerned, she peeked her head around the corner to see what had happened. Tommas had Abriella pinned to the wall with her two wrists caught in his one hand and placed high above her head. His other was holding under her chin tightly, forcing her head up so she had to stare at him.

If it wasn't for the way Abriella twisted closer into Tommas' hands, moving toward the man, Evelina might have stepped in. But instead, she didn't. Abriella didn't look like she wanted help when Tommas kissed her and Abriella bit him hard on his bottom lip.

"Fuck," Tommas snarled under his breath.

"Coward. All you've done is made me your whore, Tommy."

"Stop it. You don't ever get to say that about yourself."

"Just you, right?"

"Five minutes, Ella," Tommas pleaded. "Just give me five minutes with you alone, outside of this house, and away from these people to explain."

"I'll give you nothing. Not anymore."

"Ella—"

"I hate you," Abriella whispered, her voice breaking. "I hate you for doing this to me. And you know what you've done to me. I've let you own me because you got me, Tommy. It's so much more than tonight. You fucking know. I'm so ruined now. You did this. I hope you're happy."

"Five minutes," he pleaded.

Abriella got one of her hands free and struck Tommas hard. Evelina jumped at the sound the slap made.

Tommas didn't even flinch. "Is that how you want to do this, then?"

"Useless," Abriella spat.

"Stop."

"Asshole. Coward. *I hate you, Tommy.*"

Those four words shook Evelina straight to her heart. She suspected this situation would hurt Abriella, but she hadn't realized quite how much in the end. Clearly the two had a relationship that was complicated and delicate in a way Evelina couldn't possibly understand.

Tommas pushed Abriella harder against the wall and kissed her until she was forcing him away with tears streaking down her cheeks.

"You never could say it, Ella. Come on, baby, just fucking say it for me once."

Abriella glared. "No."

"Tell me, Ella, tell me you love me. We've been doing this for almost four years and not once have you said those words to me even when I begged you to fucking do it. You try to hide it, but you can't. Lie to me, even. Tell me you love me."

"Go to hell."

Evelina sucked in a breath when Tommas pushed Abriella into the

139

closest room. It was one of the bathrooms at the far end. She heard another slap echo, and then the slam of the door followed.

She didn't want to get closer to the couple and their fight. She didn't want to interrupt them, but at the same time, she didn't want someone else to find out what was happening, either. Stepping down into the hallway, Evelina moved to the opened laundry room which just happened to be directly beside the bathroom that Tommas and Abriella had entered.

The front loading washer was running through the final couple of minutes. The quiet hum of the machine was near silent as it turned the towels inside slowly to get out the remaining water. Evelina grabbed the knob and turned it back on a heavy spin cycle.

The noise would block out whatever sounds came from the bathroom and the couple. Mostly. She heard a soft cry and a thump, followed by Abriella's demand for more. She didn't want to hear those things at all.

Evelina finally understood why Tommas overlooked the mark he found on her body. He had his own to make on another woman and he simply wanted the idea of the marriage. Evelina hoped he got the chance to explain that to Abriella. For now, Evelina would keep Tommas' secrets.

Because he kept hers.

Evelina turned to flick on the exhaust fan for the room and froze right where she stood. Theo leaned in the doorway with dark eyes trained on the wall. Without a word, he leaned over and hit the fan switch. The noise finally drowned Tommas and Abriella out.

CHAPTER THIRTEEN

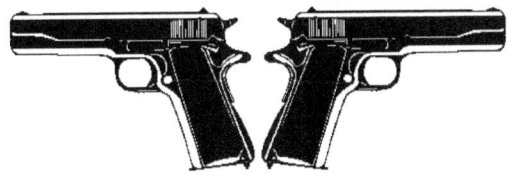

"Who is in the next room?"

Theo's question was answered with silence from Evelina.

Who was she trying to protect?

Despite the hum of the fan and the noise of the washing machine as it vibrated through a loud spin cycle, Theo could still hear the telltale sounds of what was happening in the next room. Repeated thumps to the wall and muffled voices. Whoever it was liked it rough and hard. The noise was muted, and no one upstairs would hear, but he could.

"Eve?" Theo asked again.

"Did you follow me down here?"

"Yes."

"Why?"

Theo wasn't sure how to answer that, honestly. "You seemed upset."

"So you followed me?"

"I thought—"

"Thought what, Theo?" Evelina cut in, her lips drawing thin and her gaze narrowing. "You told me not to play games with you, remember?"

"I did."

"Then don't do this, okay. This is the same thing. It might make me think you give a shit about me and neither one of us needs that nonsense. Go back upstairs."

Theo cocked a brow. "No."

"No?"

"No." Taking a step further into the room, Theo closed the door behind him. "Not thirty minutes ago you basically asked me when we were going to fuck again. Now, you're trying to shove me off quickly because you don't want me to know who is in that room fucking, Eve. Isn't that right? Because someone is in there, and that's exactly what they're doing. Deny it."

Evelina twisted her hands together. "Yes."

"Who is it?"

"Tommas."

Theo's stance softened instantly. "Tommas?"

"That's what I said, Theo."

She'd just gotten engaged to the man and Tommas couldn't wait five minutes before sticking his cock into the closest wet, warm hole that he could find? It wasn't like a lot of guys in the Outfit were faithful to their wives, because they weren't. People in the Outfit didn't marry for love, mostly. They married to strengthen their families and do their duty. The lucky ones like Adriano and Alessa were far and few in between.

Theo didn't agree with infidelity, but another man and woman's choices weren't his to speak about. But hell, why here and now? Didn't Tommas have even an ounce of respect for Evelina?

Jesus.

"And who else?" Theo asked quieter.

"It's not—"

"Listen, I don't give a damn about your precious little morals here, Eve. If you want to act like the Conti princess with everybody else, feel free. With me, you give me Evelina or fucking nobody. Got it?"

Evelina scowled. "It has nothing to do with being a princess, okay."

"Then what?"

"It's my friend, Theo. He's with my friend and I already betrayed her enough tonight with this whole thing. The least I can do is protect her from being hurt more or keep her from getting caught because she is hurting."

Theo ran through a quick list in his head of people Evelina was close to. Only three females stood out and two were taken.

"Abriella Trentini."

"Yes." Evelina crossed her arms and leaned against the loud washer. "You didn't know?"

"No."

Obviously not.

Theo had heard rumors that Tommas Rossi was involved with a woman, but that was all he knew. Theo wasn't the kind of man who pried into personal shit and Tommas didn't offer info. Everybody assumed Tommas didn't want a wife. Apparently, it wasn't a matter of not wanting one, but being unable to have the one he wanted.

"Damn," Theo mumbled, running a hand over his face. "How long?"

"As far as I know, since she was eighteen."

Shit. Almost four years.

There was an eight year age gap between Abriella and Tommas.

"It's not a casual thing then, is it?"

"No," Evelina whispered. "They even have an apartment together that they stayed at a lot when Abriella had her apartment with her sister."

"Do a lot of people know?"

"I don't think so. Just people who are close to Ella and maybe Tommas, too. They've been really careful and quiet."

Theo had to agree.

"For good reason," he said. "Joel would kill Tommas for this. Abriella is the only thing the Trentini family has left to get them anywhere. She'd make Joel look like a damn fool."

"He already does."

"Still …" Theo didn't really know what to say. "I'm sorry."

"What for, Theo?"

"I thought you were protecting him or some shit because that'd be your thing, wouldn't it? You know the rules, and you know how to turn cheek like a good little mob wife." Theo took another step forward, close enough to reach out and stroke a finger down her bare arm. "It's got nothing to do with being what they want you to be, does it?"

"I care about Ella. And Tommas, too. He kept my secrets. I won't tell his."

Evelina understood loyalty a hell of a lot better than most Outfit men did. And she was a damned woman.

Theo couldn't stop the heavy feeling in his chest from spreading. He liked that she was that kind of woman. That even with Abriella's and Tommas' actions putting Evelina in a bad situation, and probably even hurting her, she still protected them in the only way she knew how.

"He's intended to be your husband," Theo said. "You can be angry about this, Eve."

"I don't think he intends to be my anything."

Theo's brow furrowed. "Why is that?"

"The idea of a marriage is what he asked me for. That is not a guarantee for one, Theo."

"The idea," he echoed.

What in the hell was going on around them? Theo felt confused with a giant target on his back that he didn't even understand how it had gotten there.

"And I also think that's why he didn't care about the mark he found on my neck," Evelina added softer. "Because he doesn't intend to follow through with this at all, so he's willing to let me do what I want as long as I'm careful about it."

"Until he can find a way out of this whole thing," Theo said.

"Maybe." Evelina shrugged. "That nonsense upstairs with my father sure seemed like a good show for the crowd and nothing more, didn't it?"

"Riley would not put the offer of an engagement on the table, Eve, not if he meant for it to be followed through to the end."

"Tommas isn't Riley."

"You're very right about that." Theo's mind drifted to the scene he'd seen before he followed Evelina downstairs. Joel had approached Riley with clenched fists and whispered words before both men disappeared into the upstairs section of the home. "Remember when I asked you at the hotel about the marriage rumors?"

"What about it?"

"Was it only Tommas?"

Evelina shook her head. "I overheard my father talking to Tommas a few days before I approached you at the club. Riley had talked to Joel and Tommas about the offer of an engagement to me. Tommas took it for whatever reason. I don't know why."

"Or maybe Riley didn't give Joel the chance to accept."

"It doesn't matter, Theo. Not right now."

The noise from the next room had died down to practically nothing at all before another thump landed against the wall. Theo eyed Evelina silently, taking in the way she didn't seem bothered by what was happening all that much.

"You're too good for these people," Theo told her.

Evelina looked up at him through her dark lashes, amusement dancing behind her green irises. "Actually, I think I'm kind of perfect for them."

"Oh?"

"I'm a liar just like everybody else and apparently I'm too loyal for my own good."

She was.

Theo liked it all, too.

"Not exactly a liar," Theo said.

"Sometimes."

"Not to me."

Evelina smiled. "Not yet, anyway."

Chuckling, Theo asked, "Are you planning on lying to me anytime soon?"

"No."

"That's all that matters, babe." Theo reached up and caught Evelina's chin between his forefinger and thumb. Tilting her head up, he watched a varying range of emotions flicker over her features. "And I still think you are, Eve."

"What?"

"Too good for these people."

Evelina bit her bottom lip. "Don't say stuff like that, Theo."

"Why not? It's true. I speak only the truth, Evelina."

"But—"

"Hey." Theo took another step closer, crowding Evelina's body to the frontloading washer. Her hand grabbed onto the buckle of his belt and her eyes widened. "Don't start with that nonsense, Eve. Don't let what others do and think affect who you are."

"See, stuff like that, Theo."

"I have no idea what you're talking about."

Evelina's hand tightened on his belt when his hand settled on the curve of her waist. Theo knew better than to be messing with this girl at all, but especially inside this house. Frankly, right then he couldn't find it in himself to give a damn. Evelina was upset and he didn't like that at all.

"Stop frowning," Theo murmured. "Your smile is a much better sight."

"That, Theo." Evelina shook her head and said, "That right there."

"What?"

The truth?

She didn't like the truth?

"When you say stuff like that and do … this," she said, waving between them. "We hooked up, right? That's all it was. If you keep doing shit like this, you're going to start messing with my head. No games, that's what you said. Don't play them with me, either. Don't go on making me think you care about me in some way and getting me mixed up in that craziness. We both know it won't end well."

"Bad," he said quietly. "We would be bad. That's what I said, Eve."

"Exactly."

"But I said nothing about not caring for you. Not once did I say something like that."

Evelina stilled under his heavy stare. "Oh."

"I do care about the things that happen to you. It also bothers me that twice now you've been involved with an incident that has been blamed on me when we both know I didn't do a damned thing. It concerns me entirely that someone is using you as a means to get rid of me. Or at least, that's how it seems."

"So, you don't care about me, Theo, you're just worried about the things around me."

"It's the same thing, isn't it?"

"I don't think so," she whispered.

Theo tightened his grip on her waist to keep her in place. Evelina didn't try to move, but he didn't want to give her the chance to run. He needed to think for a second. He couldn't do that if he was chasing after her again.

Again …

Because he'd chased this girl in his own way for a long time.

"I think if I didn't care, I would have given up trying to know anything about you a long time ago," Theo said, chuckling. "Back when you were eighteen and never gave me a phone call. Or during all those dinner parties when you brushed me off. How about the date you refused and another call you never made?"

"I—"

"I never said I wasn't interested or that I didn't care, Evelina."

"No," she admitted. "Just that we would be bad."

"Yeah."

"Are you interested?" she asked softly.

Theo wet his lips. Evelina looked up at him with a vulnerability in her eyes. "I hate your father. I don't trust him, we've had issues long before he became boss, and I can't see my problems with him changing anytime soon. You're involved in a fake engagement with a man who can't seem to keep his eyes on the right woman for long enough to make people believe what they need to believe. You've got a brother who made quite a scandal with the sister of a man who is as stupid as they come, and is probably at least one of the people who would like to get me in a makeshift grave."

"Your point?"

"I have enough problems, Eve. I have so much shit to worry about and take care of that bringing someone else into it all seems really selfish of me. What do you want from this, huh? Do you want someone to take you out on dates and give you some kind of happily ever after of your own making? Do you want a white wedding and children? That's not my style. I don't do that kind of nonsense."

"I didn't say anything like that, Theo."

"No, but it'd lead to that eventually. Everybody gets to that point at some time in their life. So yeah, I think it'd be really fucking selfish of me to even try to start something with someone only to have to end it when I couldn't give them more than what I have now."

Evelina blinked, her green eyes glazing with water. "Who made you feel like that?"

Theo cleared his throat, surprised. "Pardon?"

"Who made you feel so entirely worthless, Theo?"

"No one."

Lies.

Lies were so much easier to speak than the truth.

"Someone did," Evelina said quietly. "Someone made you feel like you're not worth more than what you are right now. Alone. By yourself. Surviving. Who did that to you?"

"Drop it."

"Is that why we would be bad, Theo?"

"Yes," he admitted.

It was the only thing he would give her.

Evelina pointed her finger hard into his chest. "I never asked you for anything more than what you already gave. And keep in mind, Theo, you're the one who approached me and handed over exactly what you wanted to give me. So, if you don't want to do this with me, then don't fucking do it."

"Don't do it, huh?"

"No. Don't. At all." Evelina dropped her hand and sighed. "Don't give me mixed signals, don't make me think you might care, and don't approach me again. It's that simple. Just stop it. All of it."

Theo opened his mouth to agree, but something kept him from doing so.

"What?" Evelina demanded. "What is it now, Theo?"

"You're still not asking for anything," he said.

"What could I ask you for?"

Nothing.

She extended him loyalty and trust. She'd given him nights with her and then asked for nothing when it ended. Nothing more. Everybody else always wanted something from Theo.

"The only thing I want is for you to leave me alone if that's what you need to do, Theo. Don't make me believe there's something here that could turn into something else. Don't lead me to believe that putting myself at risk for someone who doesn't give a damn about me is worth it. Don't do that. It isn't fair."

Theo glanced away, taking in her words and letting them settle in. "But you're not asking me for more, right?"

"No. Where could this even go?"

"If I didn't leave you alone, you wouldn't ask me for more, right?"

Because he wasn't entirely sure if he was going to leave her alone.

Evelina tightened her grip on his belt again. "No."

"I don't want to be selfish, Eve, but I'm very interested in you and who you are."

"It's all right to care, Theo." Evelina tugged on his collar, forcing him to look at her. "You're not going to leave me alone, are you?"

"You make it easy, even if it's stupid."

"What does that even mean?"

"Who you are makes it easy for me to care, Eve."

"I'm not asking you for anything, Theo."

But she might … someday.

Evelina poked his chest again. "Stop overthinking this, okay."

"Okay."

Without warning, Evelina stood on her tiptoes and pressed a kiss to his mouth. It should have been quick and done, but the moment her lips touched his, he wanted more. He figured that out during their stay at the hotel.

A little bit of Evelina Conti was not nearly enough to sedate a man.

She could satisfy him.

She could please him.

She could fuck him dry.

But Theo wanted more.

Like he was the goddamn addict and someone had just handed him the needle, he needed more of this woman. Just a little touch made his cock hard and her sweet kiss was enough to make his chest tight with need. So when she kissed him, he couldn't just leave it at that. No, he pinned her harder against the vibrating washer, drove his hands under her dress to feel the smoothness of her thighs against his palms, and soaked in the taste and heat of her mouth as her tongue battled with his.

"Fucking hell," Theo groaned into her mouth.

Evelina sighed when his hands skimmed around to her backside and he grabbed tight. The lace of her panties covered his fingertips as he slid his hands under to feel more of her. Theo shuddered when Evelina drove her hands under his belt and pulled at his shirt, tugging the material out of his pants.

"Not the right place at all," Theo told her.

She tossed a look over his shoulder. "We're not the only stupid ones, apparently."

"I don't like fast, Eve."

"What about fast and hard, Theo?"

Christ.

Evelina canted her hips forward, allowing him to drive his erection into her pelvis. With the taste of her flavored lip balm still edging at the corners of his mouth, Theo gave into the urge that demanded he find more of that taste. Kissing Evelina harder until she was begging for a breath, he yanked her away from the washer and turned her around fast.

Before either of them had even blinked, he had Evelina sitting up on the small counter. She opened her legs for him instantly, not even waiting to be told. The action drove her dress higher, flashing the black lace under her silver dress.

"Fuck," Theo growled as he bunched her dress around her hips. "Do you always wear this kind of pretty, delicate shit under your clothes?"

"I was going for sexy, not pretty."

"Oh, it's sexy."

So sexy.

Theo stroked his palm over her sex before tapping his fingers down right over the spot where her clit was covered with lace. Evelina's sharp gasp was swallowed by Theo's mouth catching her sounds. He'd quickly learned that he enjoyed her sounds, but he did not want to be interrupted by the couple next door, or the people upstairs.

"Quiet," he warned.

Evelina nodded. "I will."

"Make sure of it."

"Can you stop talking, Theo? The washer only has another few minutes on spin before it's finished again."

"Cute. Ass up, Eve."

She did as he demanded. Theo hooked his fingers around the hem of her panties and yanked, pulling them down over her thighs and legs easily until the scrap of fabric fell to the floor. It took him all of thirty seconds to find the damned condom in his wallet and then shove his pants down just far enough to get his cock freed from his boxer-briefs.

Evelina reached out and stroked the head of his dick with the tips of her fingers. Then, she let her fingernails drive down the side of his shaft. It was enough to send a wicked cascade of shocks straight down his spine.

"Can I?" she asked, reaching for the condom.

Theo hesitated. "I usually do it, Eve."

"Why?"

She'd always given him the truth.

"Because I don't trust anyone."

Especially not women who might have ulterior motives. But he handed the condom over to Evelina without a worry. She tore open the package and slid the latex down his length with a slowness that could have killed him. She took her time to squeeze the base of his cock hard as her other hand slipped beneath his pants to find his balls.

"Jesus, Eve, I thought you wanted fast."

"I do."

"Then stop that."

Evelina grinned. "You like it."

"Yes, but then I'll put you on your knees, make you suck my dick, and you won't get what you want from this when you leave this room with my come down your throat, and nothing more."

Evelina let his balls go, fisted the bottom of his shirt, and yanked him closer. "Don't be an asshole, Theo."

"Then shut up and let me fuck you, Eve."

Her hand smacked his chest hard. Her gaze narrowed and her lips pursed. Theo had all he could do right then to stop himself from pulling her off the table and making her get on her knees so he could fuck her mouth. He was pretty sure watching Evelina sucking him off while she was in a mood would be one hell of a beautiful sight.

Instead, he teased her pussy with two fingers, stroking her slit over and over until her wetness was smeared all over his digits and she was shaking. Evelina looked damn good when she was trembling all over, too.

"*God*, Theo."

Theo laughed under his breath. "Do you know how fucking hot you look when you're pissed off, babe? It makes me want to stick my cock in your mouth and give you something to be really pissed off about. You wonder why I get you all worked up by calling you a princess? There's why,

Eve. Nothing fucking hotter."

Evelina sucked in a harsh breath. "Jesus. Your mouth, I swear."

"You like it."

"I do," she mumbled when he stroked her slit again.

"We just don't have the time."

"No."

Evelina's hands found Theo's shoulders as he drew her ass to the very edge of the counter. The head of his cock pressed at her slit, the urge to slam as deep and as hard into her depths as he could thrummed hot and fast into his bloodstream.

"Don't make a sound, Eve."

"Then keep me quiet, Theo."

His fingers dug deeper into her thigh, giving her a shock of pain as he slammed into her sex. The first seconds of entering Evelina was bliss for Theo. Even with the condom on, dulling some of the sensation, he could still feel the heat of her pussy surrounding his cock as her inner walls hugged every fucking inch of him tight.

Evelina's mouth popped open, a cry right on the tip of her tongue. Before she could get it out, Theo reached up and covered her mouth with his palm. He felt her breath puff against his hand in a huff as her tongue stuck out to taste his skin.

"Fuck," Theo hissed, drawing out until only the tip of his dick was inside her sex.

Evelina bit his hand just hard enough for it to sting. Theo didn't move his hand off her mouth. But he watched the desire darken her eyes, and the way her cheeks curved with a smirk beneath his hand.

"You good?" he asked.

She gave him a single nod.

That was all Theo needed.

He pushed her back until her head was resting against the wall and he could bury his face into her neck. Quick, hard thrusts drove them both into the wall, but his hand on her shoulders kept them from making any noise. Theo shivered when Evelina's fingers scored into the back of his neck while her other hand drove up into his hair and pulled hard.

Short, harsh breaths answered each one of his thrusts. The sounds of skin slapping to skin as her hips met his was near drowned by the hum of the washer beginning to finish its final spin cycle. The tips of Evelina's spiked heels pressed into the small of Theo's back, urging him on.

He wanted to come. He could feel the way the fast pace and her wandering hands were urging him to a quick finish. But mostly, she needed to get what she wanted from him in this.

"Come on," Theo said in her ear. "Shake for me. Get me wet with you. Chase it, Eve, and get it for me. You're goddamn hot when you're pissed but you look even better when you're being held down and fucked, babe."

Evelina whined a sweet sound beneath his hand, her thighs beginning to shake with telltale tremors. She was close, and the harder his thrusts became, the more she rocked into his pace, matching him every step of the way.

"God, you fucking love this," Theo said, grabbing her face tighter until her skin pinked under his fingertips. "Come for me. Milk me fucking dry, babe."

His tone had turned rough and gravelly. There was nothing like fucking to make Theo feel alive. It was the only thing that really did that for him now. And strangely, Evelina had been the only female in a long while that made Theo want to even fuck at all.

Evelina bit his hand as the tension in her body released and her scream of pleasure was muffled enough for no one to hear. Theo hissed, the pain of her teeth cutting into his skin was far sharper than before. It was more than enough to send him straight over the edge with her.

With her under his control, the feeling of her body coming undone around his cock, and the idea of someone catching them together, Theo couldn't hold it back. He let the clenching muscles of Evelina's pussy take him to the finish. He came hard—far harder than ever before. It was still a shock to his system. The intensity of the sensation coursing down his shaft and into his balls was enough to send him to his knees.

Theo held tight to Evelina to keep him upright, dropping his hand from her mouth to grab onto her hips with both hands.

Jesus.

He couldn't fucking breathe. Evelina touched his jaw with a tender sweep of her fingertips. It was too tender. Too sweet. But she didn't ask him for a fucking thing, so Theo let her touch him until his own tremors ceased and he could pull away from her without feeling like he was going to topple over. She didn't ask for him to hold her or snuggle or even have sweet talk after they'd finished. She simply touched him with gentle sweeps of her fingers until they were both settled and calm. Theo didn't realize that he'd needed what she did until Evelina gave it to him.

Quickly, he stuffed his semi-hard cock still covered in latex down into his trousers and fixed his pants and belt. He found Evelina's panties on the floor and helped her put them back on before smoothing out her dress and curls.

Evelina still looked like she'd just been handled by someone.

Theo was all over this girl.

Damn.

Why did he like the sight of this so goddamn much?

"God, you look …"

Evelina wet her lips, her gaze dropping. "What?"

"Like you're trying to kill me. Get down from there," Theo said, offering Evelina his hand.

She jumped down, her heels clicking softly to the tiled floor.

"Will you be careful?" Evelina asked.

"With what?"

"My father. Tommas, maybe. Everybody, Theo."

"I still don't understand what in the hell is going on enough to know who or what I should be careful of, Eve," he said honestly.

Evelina frowned. "I know."

"But I'm going to work on figuring it out."

"Good."

Theo froze as the sound of a door opening resounded out in the hallway. He'd closed the laundry room door, thankfully, but he was still in a very compromising situation with Evelina just being alone with her in a room.

"Fuck you, Tommy," Abriella hissed out in the hallway.

"Ella, wait—"

"You can't fix this. Don't you get that? So done, Tommy. We are so done."

Theo caught the sight of Evelina's flinch, but he stayed quiet.

"Ella … *fuck!*"

Theo cringed at the sound of Tommas hitting the wall with something. Probably his fist. The sound of running water echoed from the bathroom before the door clicked shut again.

Then, before Theo could try to react and hide, not that there was anywhere he could do that in the laundry room, the door was opened. Evelina turned to stone behind Theo as Tommas stood on the other side with a white facecloth pressed to the corner of his mouth.

Tommas looked the room and Theo over and quickly found Evelina behind him. There was no hiding what it looked like. The goddamn room smelled like their sex, and Theo still had smudges of Evelina's red lip balm on his mouth and jaw.

No, it was obvious.

Tommas didn't look like he gave much of a damn.

"Well," Tommas said, dropping the facecloth to his side. "You were not who I expected to find messing around with Eve, Theo."

A nasty scratch bled at the corner of Tommas' mouth.

"You might want to do something about that before you go back upstairs," Theo said, pointing at the wound.

Tommas nodded. "Working on it. I was looking for another facecloth, actually. I knew this was the laundry room."

"Tommas," Evelina started to say.

"Give Abriella some time," Tommas interjected quietly. "She's going to need a cool down period before she'll give anybody a chance to talk, Eve."

Theo felt like someone had just picked him up and dropped him off in the Twilight Zone.

"Okay," Evelina said quickly.

Tommas looked Theo over again. "This changes things."

"Like what?" Theo dared to ask.

The man didn't answer him.

Instead, Tommas held a hand out to Evelina. "Come, you'll walk back upstairs with me, Eve. It'll look better. Theo can make his way up in a bit when some time has passed."

"Thanks," Theo said.

Evelina stepped around Theo and took Tommas' hand. "The idea, right?"

"Right," Tommas echoed. "Theo, have a good evening."

What game was this man playing?

Theo didn't like how it seemed as though Tommas was using Evelina for something. Secrets were not safe in this life as they rarely stayed that way for long. How far could Theo trust Tommas to keep his secrets?

"Are you good?" Tommas asked Theo.

"I don't know, man. Am I?"

"As long as you play along."

Well, what tune were they all playing?

"Cat got your tongue, Theo?" Tommas asked when Theo stayed quiet.

"I'm just surprised; that's all."

"Don't be. You know very little about me."

"I know enough now," Theo said.

"Theo, Tommas," Evelina said sharply. "Stop it."

"Exactly. You know enough to cause harm, Theo." Tommas waved a finger over Evelina's head. "As do I."

"We're going to have to sit down and chat about this soon, man."

Theo wanted some answers.

None of this made sense.

Tommas shrugged. "Not tonight."

CHAPTER FOURTEEN

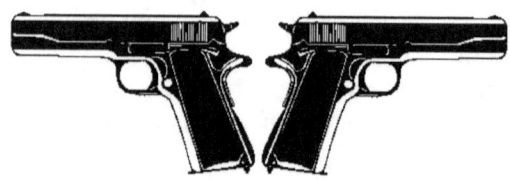

"Stop for a second," Tommas said.

His hand on Evelina's side tightened, keeping her from rounding the last few steps. The muted voices of the guests still echoed down the hallway, leading her to believe that no one had missed their absence.

Thank God.

"What?" Evelina asked.

"Let me see you for a moment before we face everyone again."

Why did it matter?

Tommas urged her to turn and with his steel-blue gaze that was usually emotionless and detached, he looked her face over. Silently, he pulled out the cloth napkin from his suit pocket and wiped at the edge of Evelina's mouth. Heat pinked her cheeks.

Tommas chuckled. "Don't be embarrassed, Eve. It was just a couple of smudges from your red balm, I think. Nothing too noticeable."

"You noticed."

"Yes, well, I knew what you were doing. I drew a conclusion. The rest of your face is fine, by the way. Theo only messed your pretty mouth up a bit. I'm sure you didn't mind."

Evelina dropped her gaze. "I shouldn't have done that at all."

"In this house?" Tommas laughed loudly. "Probably not, Eve. Neither should I, really. We're in the same boat, you and I. Attached to people we can't have."

"I'm not—"

Tommas cocked a brow, quieting Evelina instantly. "You're going to deny what you were doing when you know exactly what I was doing in the very next room?"

"No."

"Then what were you going to say, hmm?"

"That I'm not very attached to Theo. We're not a thing or whatever. Not like you and Abriella are."

Tommas scoffed. "I beg to differ. Maybe it's not the same thing, but no woman of your name and status would risk herself the way you did a few minutes ago with a man like Theo DeLuca unless you were looking for something, Eve. It doesn't have to be love—"

"It's not."

Of that, Evelina was most sure.

"—for it to be something," Tommas finished quieter.

"What is your point, Tommas?"

"Things have a way of growing something bigger, Eve. Be mindful you don't end up in my situation."

"I'm not even sure what your situation is."

"A difficult one." Tommas offered her an easy smile. "But that isn't for you to concern yourself with. I did want to ask, though, did you follow me downstairs?"

"No. I wanted a break."

"Good. I didn't mean for you to walk in on … that."

Evelina frowned. "I knew she would be mad."

"That isn't what I mean."

She knew what he meant.

"You're not mine, Tommas," Evelina said simply.

Tommas' smile faded slightly. "I'm not. You're right."

"And I don't expect you to be."

"Well, thank you for not making a scene and for turning on the washer. I suspect that was your doing, yes?"

Evelina nodded. "It was."

"As for Theo …"

Shit.

"What about him?"

"Was he the one you went missing with last week?" Tommas asked. "Please don't lie. It won't make my choices any easier."

"What choices?"

"Just answer my question."

Evelina blew out a quiet huff. "Yes."

"And the mark I found. Is that his, too?"

"Yes."

"And there's no other man you're involved with?"

"No!"

Tommas' eyes widened at her outburst. "I just wanted to be sure."

"I'm not a whore, Tommas. I don't run around with every man that will have me."

"I didn't imply that. But, even if you did, I still wouldn't use that word to describe your choices. They're not mine to make or judge you for, Eve."

"Funny, all the other men in my life wouldn't say the same thing."

Tommas shrugged and placed the napkin back in his pocket. "They're not me."

Something nagged at Evelina's thoughts. The words she heard Abriella spit at Tommas rang heavily in the back of her mind. "Abriella said—"

"Nothing," Tommas interrupted sharply, anger clouding his features. "She said nothing."

Evelina's spine straightened. "I'm … sorry. That was a private conversation, and I had no right to bring it up."

Tommas softened in his stance, but barely. "She was angry and hurt. We've always had a different relationship behind closed doors than most people do. That, what you heard, is just a small part of it."

"Oh. I don't understand."

"I don't expect you to. However, tonight made Abriella feel like I brought that private side of us into a very public forum, even if no one knows what we are. And when that word, or others like it, gets brought out—whore, slut, whatever—I get defensive and so does she. As you said, you don't understand. It's not something that can be explained."

"I won't bring it up again."

"Thank you," Tommas said, sighing. "Now, your face is fixed and we've got a few things straightened out."

Had they?

"I guess," Evelina replied.

"Well, I got a few things figured out. Smile pretty, Eve, and put your worries away for the evening."

"That's kind of hard to do, isn't it?"

"Why is that?"

"I rarely feel safe with these people anymore. After the shootings, this nonsense with my father, and now my car being burned last week? People like my father and Joel Trentini are using Theo as a scapegoat for what has happened these last few weeks while I'm the only one who knows the truth that it couldn't possibly be him."

Tommas' face remained impassive. "I'm aware of that now."

"It's starting to feel personal, Tommas."

Hell, it felt personal the moment her mother was shot in the head.

Tommas smirked. "With me, Eve, you'll have nothing to worry about."

"Forgive me, but I doubt it."

"Don't."

Why did she feel like he was telling the truth?

"You can't possibly promise me that, Tommas."

"I just did."

"Stay," Riley told Adriano. "For the night, at least. Your old room is open, son. It's been a long night, no need to drive across town if you can stay here."

Indecision wavered in Adriano's face as he passed a look to Alessa. She said nothing, but Evelina wasn't surprised. Alessa rarely spoke up in front of Riley. The man made her as uncomfortable as he made everyone else.

"Lissa?" Adriano asked.

Riley waved a hand. "Oh, I'm sure she doesn't mind."

"We can stay," Alessa said. "But we have breakfast with my parents in the morning. I don't want to miss that, Adriano."

"We won't."

"Good." Riley clapped his hands together and smiled. "All my children under our roof for Christmas. This is nice."

Riley's genuine joy felt all wrong to Evelina. Lately, her father hadn't shown much compassion or care toward his children or their happiness. The party had gone off well enough, sure, and Riley's announcement regarding Tommas and Evelina had been received well. Surely that wasn't enough to make her father seem like he'd taken a few happy pills.

Where had this man come from?

"I have a guest upstairs to deal with," Riley said, "but make yourselves at home for the evening. Maybe Courtney and I will join you later."

"Actually, I think I'll just head straight to a shower and bed if we're going to stay," Evelina said. She had no intention of spending time with Courtney. The two women would never be friends.

Riley frowned. "Eve, you could at least try with my new wife."

"No, Dad, I can't."

Even Adriano coughed out a laugh at that, but managed to hide it quickly with the palm of his hand.

"You're honest, I suppose," Riley said heavily. "I do like that about you, Eve."

"Goodnight," Evelina replied, not wanting to keep the conversation going.

Riley let her go.

Upstairs in her old bedroom, Evelina slipped out of the dress she'd chosen for the Christmas party and kicked her heels off. Standing in front of the full-length mirror, she couldn't help but run the tips of her fingers over her waist and hips where Theo had grabbed her. There was nothing to see there. He'd left no marks behind other than the tiny love bite on her neck, the one on her right breast that was hidden by her bra, and the one on her pubic bone that was covered by her lace panties.

But she still felt him.

An ache settled between her thighs.

Lovely. Heady. Deep.

She didn't need to see him to feel him.

Quickly, Evelina grabbed the old robe hanging off the back of the mirror and made her way out of the room to the bathroom down the hall. After showering, returning to her room and changing into something suitable to sleep in, she had a craving for tea or something hot to drink before bed.

Stepping out of her old bedroom, quiet murmurs down the hall drew her in that direction instead of the opposite way that would lead downstairs.

"She won't pick up my calls," Alessa said, sadness coloring her every word.

"Give her a night, babe. Maybe she's just … cooling off."

"Abriella's cooling off period never ends well, Adriano."

"She's a big girl, Lissa."

"I know that," Alessa snapped.

"Hey. Don't be pissed at me. I didn't do anything wrong here."

"Sorry, I know. I'm just … not here right now, Adriano."

"Come here." Quiet shuffles followed Adriano's order before he said, "I don't think anyone knew, Alessa. Not until the very last minute, anyway. You know how Riley is. He likes the shock factor, and he certainly got that tonight."

"Your sister must have known."

Evelina flinched at the anger in Alessa's tone.

"I asked Riley. He said she knew nothing until right before the party."

"Oh," Alessa mumbled.

"Evelina is good at this nonsense, Lissa. She's good at turning on for the crowd. That's exactly what we saw tonight. But I can bet she's not happy. Not at all."

"Does this whole thing feel motivated to you?"

"The marriage?" Adriano asked.

"Yes."

"It does. It's got to be. I don't think Riley was telling the entire truth when he announced the engagement. Not everyone was happy."

"My brother certainly wasn't," Alessa said.

Evelina wasn't the only person who noticed Joel's anger over the proposed marriage, then. That was all she needed to hear. Turning away, she left the quiet couple alone and made her way downstairs for tea. Unfortunately, she found Courtney sitting at the kitchen island with a cup of her own coffee in hand.

Crap.

Before she could make a beeline back for the upstairs, Courtney noticed Evelina's presence.

"Hi," the young woman said softly.

Evelina forced herself to smile. "Hi."

"Your father is busy. Even I can't drive him out of that office. The last time I tried tonight, he shouted at me. I'd had enough."

Courtney didn't sound all too pleased about that.

"Riley does that sometimes," Evelina explained, giving her new stepmother an olive branch. She wouldn't offer the woman much more. She couldn't do that without feeling like she was betraying her dead mother. "I've seen him stay in there for five days before he rejoined the real world."

"He does have the attached bathroom, I suppose."

"The cook leaves him a plate of food outside the door."

Courtney frowned. "I didn't realize he was so intense like he is."

"Demanding. Controlling. Obsessive. Introverted. That kind of intense?"

"I—"

"You don't have to make some excuse for him," Evelina interjected quickly. "I know what my father is like, Courtney. I grew up watching my mother at his side for twenty-two years before she died and was free from it."

"But she loved him, didn't she?"

Yes.

"Eve?" Courtney asked when Evelina stayed quiet.

"I think she loved him enough."

"Enough?"

"Enough to handle his craziness."

Courtney laughed. "Well, that's the thing, isn't it? We simply have to love them enough."

"I would rather love a man entirely. Hidden monsters, scars, secrets and all. Enough isn't just *good enough* for me. The whole point of giving your heart to someone is getting theirs in return. I don't want a piece of some man's heart. I want his whole heart, even if that means holding the pieces of it together."

Evelina almost wished she could have stopped herself from blurting those inner thoughts out, but she couldn't find it inside to regret the statement. It was true.

Courtney cleared her throat and glanced away. "That's ... a very mature way of looking at things, Eve."

"That's one way to put it."

"I know you don't approve of me."

"I really don't." Evelina sighed. "And you've not given me a lot of reasons to try, Courtney."

"No, I suppose I haven't."

"If we're being honest here, I don't like where you came from or how this all started between you and my father, either."

Courtney's cheeks pinked at Evelina's blatant statement. "I hear the whispers about me just as well as you do, Eve. And the saddest part of it all is that I can't deny any of them. I do love your father."

"I hope so. Because otherwise, you're in way over your head with him."

"I'm still drowning no matter what way we look at it." Courtney stood from the stool and pushed her tea cup aside. "My intention is not to replace the hole your mother left. I couldn't do that anyway. Mia was a pretty amazing woman."

Anger trickled down Evelina's spine in a hot drip. "You didn't know my mother. Not well, anyway."

"Actually, I did. Riley is a bastard, to be sure, but he was always upfront about the kind of bastard he could be. Your mother knew very well who I was, and what I was doing with her husband."

Evelina could only stare dumbly at Courtney. "You're serious."

"I have no reason to lie, Eve. But your mother? She never once treated me like anything other than a young woman who deserved a kind hand and respect. So yes, I know exactly the kind of woman your mother was, and I also know there is no way I could ever be like she was. I don't plan on trying, either."

"Huh."

"This is new information to you, I take it?"

"Very new."

Courtney shrugged. "She raised you and your brother well. Tonight was the perfect example of that. You didn't even bat an eye at the engagement."

"It's not my place to," Evelina said honestly.

"But you want to," Courtney replied just as fast. "Because as you said, you want a man's whole heart. You can't have that when he's the one you've been dictated to marry, right?"

"Something like that."

Courtney grinned slyly. "You and I are the same in a lot of ways, Eve. We're not particularly friendly with one another, but we don't have a lot of allies outside of our homes, either. In this life, women have to stick together or they're stuck depending on the men around them to do everything for them."

She had a point.

"What are you looking for from me?" Evelina asked.

"Nothing more than another ally, Eve. Someone who doesn't whisper behind my back and who gives me respect when I ask for it. You don't have to like me, I'm only asking for you to accept my place here."

"Don't you worry that you're just a fill-in until he finds another willing hole?"

"He already has," Courtney said quietly. "And she's a year younger than I am. Chloe Belli was here tonight with her father, actually."

"Oh."

"Riley doesn't hide the kind of bastard he is to his women."

"Just to everyone else, huh?" Evelina asked.

"People see what they want to see." Courtney pushed the stool in. "What would you like from me, Eve?"

"I don't think I need anything from you."

"We all need something."

Evelina crossed her arms, considering the woman's words. "I don't trust my father and since you're close to him, I don't trust you, either."

"You're more like your father than you think, Eve. He also doesn't trust anyone. In fact, he's so paranoid about the people around him right now that he's got his closest men fighting amongst themselves for a prize that Riley doesn't even plan to give them."

"Pardon?"

Courtney flashed a smile. "Tommas and Joel. Riley has something they both want, but he has no intention of giving it to them."

Evelina took that in for a moment before speaking again. "The only thing my father has that those men don't is a boss's seat."

"So it seems."

"He trusts them so little that he's willing to turn them against one another just to keep them from taking his seat?"

"They're more likely to kill each other than him," Courtney explained.

A heavy realization settled in Evelina's gut.

The drive-by shooting ...

Someone burned down her car ...

Engagement talk to more than one man ...

Had Riley done all of that, including putting his daughter at risk, just to keep his right and left hand men in line? Had he been willing to let someone else—someone like Theo—take the blame for those things in hopes that either Tommas or Joel would lose their life in another street war between the families?

Why?

It didn't entirely make sense. Not if Riley intended for Evelina to marry Tommas. Was tonight Riley's way of showing which man he was more likely to protect between Joel and Tommas?

Nothing felt right or true to Evelina.

"Anyone else is just a sacrifice," Evelina said quietly.

Courtney patted Evelina's arm as she passed her in the entryway.

Evelina turned fast on her heel. "Wait."

"What?" Courtney asked.

"Why are you telling me this? We're not ... We haven't exactly been friends, Courtney."

"Because, Eve, should there ever come a day when I need an ally, I expect to find one in you."

The week following the Christmas party and engagement announcement passed Evelina by in a blur of time.

"You ready?"

Evelina glanced up from the spot on the floor that she'd been staring at for the last hour to see her brother leaning in the entryway to the apartment's living room.

"Uh ..."

Adriano cocked a brow. "Are you all right? You seem out of it this week."

"I'm okay."

The last thing she wanted was for her brother to be worrying about her.

"You sure?" Adriano asked. "Because ever since the party, I don't think you've said more than ten words to me or Alessa."

"I don't know if Alessa wants me to, honestly."

Adriano frowned. "Because of Abriella and Tommas."

"Is there any other reason?"

"No. Listen, you don't get to choose what Dad wants. Alessa knows that. Hell, she was in that same position just a couple of months ago."

"And now she's marrying you, Adriano. Not exactly the same thing."

"Yeah, but—"

"It's nothing, Adriano," Evelina cut in quickly. "But there was something I wanted to talk to you about."

"What is that?"

"Me moving out."

Adriano opened his mouth, a refusal right on the tip of his tongue.

"Before you start telling me no," Evelina said before her brother could get a word out, "… think about this, Adriano. You're getting married next week. You're having a baby in May. It's time for you to start your life with Alessa and by me being here, it's only holding you two back from moving forward. You don't need to be worrying about me or watching after me, okay. I'm a big girl. Besides, isn't that Tommas' job to keep an eye on me now that we're engaged?"

"I don't have a choice but to look after you, Eve. You're my sister. I'm going to keep an eye on you regardless if you're twenty-two or eighty-eight. That's what family does."

Evelina's heart melted a little. "All right. But I still think it's time for me to get out of your way."

"And what, go back to Dad's?"

"I don't think Courtney wants to share her home. I don't blame her. Plus, Dad knows you're house shopping and whatnot, so he's probably been expecting me to say I was ready to move out. He might even have something lined up for me."

Adriano scowled. "Or he'll ship you off to live with Tommas."

Evelina shrugged. "Don't worry about me."

"I already told you."

"Yeah, yeah. You can't."

Adriano sighed heavily. "Is this really what you want?"

"Yes. I'll come stay with you for a week or something after you bring the baby home. God knows you two are going to need all the help you can get. Especially if that baby is anything like you, Adriano."

Light laughter echoed from outside in the hallway. Apparently, Alessa had been listening in. Evelina's soon-to-be sister-in-law poked her head in the doorway.

"Thanks," Alessa said with a smile.

"Yeah, ha fucking ha," Adriano grumbled. "I'm the easy target. I see how this works."

"As long as you know, little brother."

Evelina pushed up from the couch and smoothed the skirt of her body-con style dress down "I am ready."

"Should be a fun night," Alessa said.

Should being the key word.

"Tommas always did know how to throw a good New Year's party," Evelina agreed.

Adriano scoffed. "As long as nobody fucking kills anyone, that is."

Well, there was that little problem, too.

"Looks like you won't be driving with us after all," Adriano said.

Evelina looked up from the screen of her cell phone. Tommas Rossi stood just outside the locked apartment building's front entrance. Leaning against the side of a two-seater Jaguar, the man was a pillar of cool, calm, and collected.

It was no wonder why Abriella had found herself attracted to Tommas. Evelina simply couldn't bring herself to see the man in the same way.

"I wonder what he's doing here," Evelina said. "It's his party. Shouldn't he be there at the club?"

Alessa coughed and said, "Your fiancé, Eve."

"Pardon?"

"He's your fiancé. You should show up with him."

Oh.

Obviously Tommas was willing to play the part that everyone wanted to see between the two of them just to make the engagement seem all the more real. Evelina didn't like that at all, honestly. She couldn't help but wonder if showing up with Tommas would be just another nail in the coffin of the friendship that had once been between her and Abriella.

"We're going to be late," Adriano said, checking his watch. "You okay, Eve?"

"Perfect," she lied. "I'll see you at the club."

"Sure, the club."

Adriano gave his sister's hand a squeeze and a kiss on her cheek. With a silent nod to Tommas and nothing more, Adriano's arm slinked around Alessa's waist so he could put his hand to the slight roundness of her stomach and he led them toward the apartment's garage.

Evelina faced a smiling Tommas.

"Evening, Eve," he said. "I hope you don't mind driving to the club with me."

"You could have called first."

"I could have, but I didn't."

Evelina arched a brow. "So, even though you have no intention of actually making me your wife, you still expect me to jump whenever you say move?"

Tommas smirked. "I didn't say that, Eve. Are you opposed to showing up at the club in a beautiful car with a handsome man?"

"I'm opposed to making my former friend more uncomfortable than she already is."

His smile quickly fell.

"Point taken," Tommas said quietly. "But since your father demanded I take Joel off the invite list, I'm not even sure if Abriella will show up tonight."

"But she could."

"I suspect she and Joel will both show up, actually. He has a problem with following the rules."

"And her?" Evelina asked.

Tommas chuckled. "Abriella has a problem with following *my* rules."

"Interesting way to put it."

"Nonetheless, I can't say for sure if they'll show up, as I said. Abriella hasn't answered a single one of my calls since Christmas night. I don't think she would even answer a damned smoke signal if I sent one up to her."

Evelina laughed, but it came out sad and strained. "I'm sorry."

"Don't be. I made this bed. Now, can we go? The party is starting in twenty minutes and the host should be there to greet the guests."

"With his fiancée, huh?"

Tommas lifted a single shoulder like it didn't matter. "Showing up will be enough. Besides, I hear your friend was put back on the guest list, so maybe you'll get some time with him tonight."

Evelina's brow furrowed. "My friend?"

"Theo."

Oh.

A lump caught in her throat as a heat spread straight down to her sex where a wonderful ache began to pulse. Even thinking about Theo could do that to Evelina. It was crazy and wonderful at the same time. She didn't know a lot about him except for the fact that he could fuck her like nobody else, he had some kind of monsters to hide, he was the easy scapegoat ...

And he cared about her.

"Tonight wouldn't exactly be the right time for that, Tommas."

Tommas grinned. "It never is, but talking won't get you in any trouble, I'm sure."

Then, something nagged at Evelina.

"Why was Theo put back on the guest list while Joel was removed?"

"Ask your father," Tommas said. "Your guess is as good as mine."

"Because he wants to bother Joel," Evelina said, voicing her inner thoughts. "And putting someone Joel has had issues with back in Riley's good graces is a decent way to aggravate him."

Tommas turned and opened the passenger door for Evelina. "Good guess."

"Why are you letting him do that to Theo, use him like that to piss

Joel off, when you know Theo didn't do anything to deserve being someone's fall guy?"

"Eve, I'm not letting your father do a damned thing. That's the whole point."

"I don't understand."

That seemed to be her mantra lately.

Tommas waved at the car. "You don't have to. Get in."

CHAPTER FIFTEEN

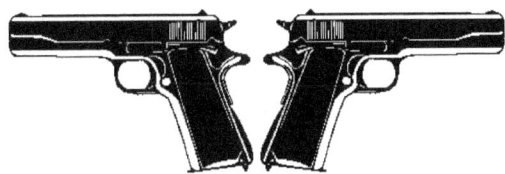

"You are coming tonight, aren't you?" Tommas asked on the other end of the phone call.

"Yes," Theo confirmed. "My sister won't shut up about it."

"I throw damn good parties and everybody knows it."

Theo laughed. "Maybe. I appreciate the call, Tommas. I'll be there."

"Good." Tommas chuckled, adding, "Riley demanded it, so I had to make sure."

"Riley demanded I come tonight?"

"Apparently. He's willing to make amends in a more public fashion than simply an invite to his Christmas party."

"Like over drinks," Theo said, sighing.

He didn't have any damned amends to make with Riley Conti. There was nothing to apologize or forgive. Not on Theo's side of things. He'd done nothing to Riley, but God knew Riley had done a few things to Theo over the years.

"Over drinks," Tommas agreed. "And there's still the little issue about Artino, you know. You haven't sat down with the boss and had a decent discussion about what happened, Theo."

"What is there to talk about, Tommas? His kid killed Artino and another one of my guys happened to be caught in the crossfire. Some scuffle happened between the crews. I talked to the only person who mattered regarding that shit, okay. Adriano. We worked it out."

"No, Walter. Not Dean."

Theo's shoulders tightened. "I don't know what you're fucking talking about."

"Sure you don't."

"Artino was working for Joel, Tommas. He had no loyalty to Riley. What difference does it make if the fool is good and gone, now, huh?"

"Exactly. Which was something Riley was well aware of. And maybe if you'd bring that up, all those little problems that your men caused on the street with Adriano's guys can be overlooked."

"Artino did that, too," Theo said.

It was the first time he'd actually admitted that to anyone. He hadn't minded the blame on him before, but now that he was being used for the fall guy in much bigger problems, Theo was done cleaning up other people's messes.

"Did he?"

"Yeah, Tommas. I had no hand in that."

"But it looked like you, Theo, and you never denied it."

"It stopped once Artino was killed, didn't it?"

"It did," Tommas said. "Nonetheless, the boss spoke. You show up tonight or don't. But if you don't, then all the hands Riley has offered out to you will be pulled back for good. There are no second chances after tonight, Theo."

Theo grit his teeth. "Playing the good little front boss and making sure Riley's happy, are you?"

"What is that supposed to mean, Theo?"

"It means you've got two faces, Tommas."

"Hey—"

"And I don't think either has good intentions."

Theo hung up the phone without saying goodbye. It would probably only piss Tommas off, but Theo couldn't find a single fuck for the man at the moment. Just because he was forced to trust Tommas in somethings didn't mean he would trust the man in all things. Nor did it mean he wanted to trust Tommas at all.

"Hey, Skip?"

"Yeah?" Theo asked, glancing up at Cole from over the top of his laptop. The young soldier leaned in the doorway with his coat slung over his arm.

"People were here last night."

Theo finished shutting down the laptop and shoved it into his leather bag. "What about it?"

"They were asking questions."

That caught Theo's attention. People came and went inside his strip club all the time. Some of those people knew him on a first name basis, some by last name only, others by Skip, and even more through a friend of a friend.

It wasn't unusual for people to ask questions regarding Theo, his whereabouts, or something about the club and business. What was unusual, was Cole bringing it up. The kid was used to getting questions about his Capo, and how to answer them.

"Again," Theo drawled, "what about it, Cole?"

"I don't know, it was kind of weird."

Theo plucked his cell phone up from the desk and shoved it into the pocket of his dress pants. "How so?"

"The guy wanted to know who had been around and who you'd been talking to. People don't usually ask that kind of stuff."

No, they didn't.

"What'd he look like?"

The two security cameras that Theo had in the club would do him no good. One was for his office and the other was for the bar directly over the cash register.

Cole raised his hand a few inches above his head. "This high, about your size, and green eyes."

Theo ran through the list of people that fit the description. None that he knew had any reason to be at his club questioning one of Theo's guys about who the Capo had been hanging around with, either.

"Has he been here before?" Theo asked.

"No," Cole answered.

"What did the guy drive?"

"I didn't see it, Skip."

Shit.

"Anything else I should know?" Theo asked as he picked his bag up from the floor.

"The guy called you DeLuca."

Not Skip. Not Theo.

DeLuca.

"And you didn't recognize him at all?" Theo asked.

"Nope."

Dammit.

It wasn't Cole's fault that someone had been in the joint and chatting up Theo's employees and probably some of the patrons, too. Theo had been busy since Christmas trying to catch up on some of his ventures with a bookie downtown, and then he'd run up to the other side of Chicago to spend a day with J and Karen.

Karen liked the pictures Dino left behind. It made the anxiety of the trip worth it, at least.

"I did say you'd be in tonight, though, if he wanted to come back," Cole said.

Theo didn't see the issue in that. "It's fine, kid."

"Except you're heading out, aren't you?"

"Yeah, I am. I've got a party to get to and I'm already late." Theo did up the three buttons on his silk vest and readjusted his tie. He hadn't had the time to run back to his place and change, plus do business at the club, and then still make it to the party, so he'd just dressed for Tommas' club ahead of time. "Is that what you're wearing?"

Cole glanced down at his T-shirt and dark jeans. "Uh …"

"You are coming with me, right?"

"Um."

"You don't have to tag along if you don't want to, Cole. It would be nice for you to meet some more people and learn some names."

Especially after this *questions* incident. Besides, it was about time Cole earned some attention for his role as Theo's middle man for the DeLuca crew. The more people and business the kid got in on, the better.

"No, I'll go," Cole said quietly.

"Then what is it with the fucking pout you're sporting?"

Cole waved between them. "One of these people does not look like the other."

"You're dressed like any other person would be at a club."

"Then why are you dressed like that?"

The kid was astute. Theo gave him that.

"Because it's an Outfit gathering, and you've got to look the part, Cole."

"I don't."

Theo tossed his navy blue Armani blazer across the room. Cole caught the item easily.

"Put it on," he demanded.

Cole shrugged the blazer on. It fit him well. The kid started doing up the buttons on the front of the blazer.

"Leave it unbuttoned," Theo said, smirking. "Looks better that way. Gives a female something to admire. Men are all about the ass, tits, and legs when it comes to admiring a beautiful woman. Women are all about the chest, shoulders, and ass when it comes to admiring a good-looking man. Women have to wear the right kind of dress, something under it, and the right heels to show off all her assets and make it look good. A man only needs the right blazer and a T-shirt underneath."

"Huh."

"It's called confidence, Cole. Get some."

"You don't have a jacket now."

"Nope. That's my favorite one and I don't carry a spare. Don't fucking ruin it."

Cole shifted on his feet. "I won't."

"Make sure of it."

Theo cringed at the sight of his sister's name flashing across the screen of his cell phone. Knowing Lily, she wouldn't stop calling him until he picked up. Ignoring her calls never worked out well for Theo.

Answering the call, he said, "Yeah, hey, Lily."

"Where are you?" his sister demanded.

Theo shrugged off his leather bag and handed it to Cole. Then, he gave the kid the keys to his cherry red Stingray, too.

"Go warm the car up and put my bag in the front seat. I'll catch up in a second."

Cole nodded. "Sure, Skip."

"Theo?" Lily asked again. "Are you ignoring me?"

"I'm here. Chill, woman."

"You went quiet. I thought the call cut out or something. Aren't you supposed to be at the club by now? We're here and you're nowhere to be found."

"I'm coming, Lily. Jesus."

Theo swore his sister had become his self-appointed babysitter. He was sure it was just her pregnancy making her usual smothering tendencies all the more apparent.

"I'm coming, little one," Theo said again. "I had a few things to finish up at the club first."

"Good. I want you here when we tell everyone about the pregnancy. You should be here, Theo."

"I will be. Stop fretting. Hasn't any of Damian's laidback attitude bled into you since you two married? Christ, I hoped it would."

"Shut up."

"Hormones," Theo teased.

"We can blame it on that if you want."

Theo chuckled. "I'll be there in less than thirty. Feed my niece or nephew some junk food while you wait for me."

"Where are you right now?"

"Just outside of my club."

"What are you going to do, fly here? Don't get pulled over speeding, Theo. That's the last thing you need."

Theo rolled his eyes and groaned. "You are going to make the—"

"What, Theo?"

"The best mother, Lily."

He could practically feel his sister's smile from all the way across the city.

"You think?" she asked softly.

"All the good mothers nag, you know."

"Asshole."

"Don't forget it. Like I said, I'll be there in thirty, Lily. I am coming, promise."

"All right—"

"Hey! It's Theo, right?"

Theo glanced over his shoulder at the sound of an unfamiliar voice calling his name. Whoever it was wasn't talking to him, but instead, the tall, dark-dressed man with his face hidden by a ball cap had directed his question to Cole.

The young solider was just starting to unlock Theo's car with the leather bag slung over his shoulder as he turned slightly to face the man. Theo opened his mouth to call out and correct the fool, but he didn't get the chance. A weapon was pulled from inside the unknown man's jacket and pointed straight at Cole's back. The handgun bloomed with light from every shot, but it only made a soft sound because of the long silencer attached.

Pop.

Pop.

Pop.

Three shots, one right after the other, entered into Cole's back before the kid could even get a word out. Cole's body jerked into the side of Theo's Stingray, the bag falling to the ground. Theo's throat contracted around the shout he wanted to let loose. Nothing but a quiet breath of air steamed in front of his face as a painful crack spider-webbed its way over his soul.

"Cole," Theo rasped.

God, *no.*

For a split second, time froze.

Theo stood as still as a rock, clenching his phone in his hand and watching the scene unfold only thirty feet away that he couldn't possibly begin to understand. Theo felt his body jerk forward, moving toward the young man on the ground in the dark parking lot, but he stumbled over his own two feet.

His body was there.

His mind wasn't.

It took Theo far too long to rejoin the two in the present time. By the time he had, the man who shot Theo's young soldier was already gone, vanished around the side of another business. The back alleyways surrounding the businesses were so thick and confusing that chances were, Theo wouldn't be able to catch the guy even if he tried.

Right then, Cole was his first and only concern. Fuck the other guy. Theo would find out who that was at another damned time. Someone would talk. Eventually.

"Cole," Theo said louder.

He finally gained his bearings and moved faster across the lot. A thin sheet of slush caused him to slip as he came closer to the Stingray, making his knee hit the pavement hard. Theo barely even registered the pain blooming in his leg as he righted himself beside Cole.

"Fuck," Theo hissed, tossing his phone aside.

Cole lay face down on the pavement with his arms tucked in under his body. The three gunshots to the kid's back bled heavily. The ground was already stained red, and Theo's pants only soaked up the thick liquid even more as he moved closer to Cole's bleeding form. Too much blood. There was far too much for Theo to help the kid.

Even calling for help wouldn't save him. It would take far too long for the ambulance to get there. Nothing would help Cole. Theo despised himself for even being able to realize those facts.

"T-Theo," Cole choked out.

Forcing back the anxiety, Theo helped Cole roll over to his back. Glassy eyed and coughing out bubbles of red saliva, Cole blinked up at Theo. Panic gripped the young man's face instantly and tears welled before they streaked lines down Cole's cheeks.

It wasn't good.

It was a terrible thing to know you were going to die.

"Hey, hey," Theo said, wiping the kid's face with his dirty hands. "None of that shit, huh? Take a breath for me, Cole."

Cole tried, but he struggled for it.

Shit.

Another coughing fit followed and more blood splattered across the kid's cheeks and mouth. An ashy tone colored Cole's face while the pink in his lips faded slowly.

"Hurts," Cole whispered.

Out of instinct alone, Theo drew Cole's shaking form closer to his body. He held tight, feeling Cole's hands fist into the side of Theo's shirt like he didn't want to let go.

Because the kid was just young. Because he was a fucking boy, not a man. Because nobody deserved to die scared and alone.

"I'm sorry," Cole mumbled.

"For what?" Theo asked.

If the kid wanted to talk, Theo would let him ramble on.

"Your jacket."

Theo laughed, but it came out strained and pained. "It's just a jacket, Cole."

"Your favorite one, Skip."

"Just a fucking jacket."

Cole's breaths came out harder, sharper. Like he couldn't take in the needed air and his lungs were struggling to keep up.

"Did you know the guy?" Theo asked quietly.

Cole nodded slowly, his stare more dazed than before.

"Who, Cole?"

"Bell. We call him Bell."

Bell.

Theo racked his brain to connect that name to someone he knew. He couldn't.

"Just Bell?"

"Bell," Cole repeated faintly.

"How'd you know him but he didn't know you?"

"Don't play with snakes, Skip. That's what you always said to me."

Twenty seconds later, Cole stopped moving. Theo held him all the while.

Theo wasn't sure how long he'd sat like that in the back parking lot of his club, resting against his Stingray with Cole's limp, unmoving body in his hands. Five minutes, maybe. It could have been ten. The cold harshness of the air bit into Theo, but he only felt numb.

The back parking lot of the club was only used for employees, Theo's vehicle, and suppliers, so no one even stepped into the lot to see what had happened. No one knew a damned thing.

Theo couldn't breathe.

Those bullets had clearly been meant for him.

Don't play with snakes, Skip.

Theo's head fell back to hit the driver's door. "Snakes."

Snakes.

Snakes. Evelina flashed into Theo's memories. The day of her eighteenth party. The fight he'd had with Dino that Evelina walked in on.

Dino's voice was far louder, but a twenty-one-year-old Theo hadn't been listening to his older brother way back then. By the time Theo had started listening to Dino, it was already too late. He'd let the snake in.

Snakes like Joel Trentini will only bite you when you're not looking.

Because a man couldn't expect to charm a snake without feeling the fangs, too.

Cole had known who the snakes were. A street kid like Cole, despite being an Artino, had limited access to other families and their business. But Cole had known all the same who he should and shouldn't be chumming with on the streets, because Theo wouldn't let his business mingle with other families.

Joel.

The ringing buzz of the cell phone broke Theo from his daze. It'd been buzzing for a while, but he had mostly ignored whoever was calling so he could get his thoughts straight.

Someone wanted to kill him. Someone had been wanting to kill him for a while. That someone was Joel, and Theo wasn't surprised. Theo had been waiting for Joel to make his move, but he'd let his guard down over the last couple of weeks.

The phone buzzed again. He reached for the phone and picked it up, pressing the wet device to his ear.

"Yeah?" Theo asked, his throat feeling sore.

"Oh, my God, Theo!"

Lily's frantic cry sliced straight through Theo's middle. He'd never hung up her phone call. It was likely she heard everything.

How long had his sister sat there listening, wondering if her brother was dead or not?

"I'm okay," Theo said quietly.

"Good," came a far darker, gruffer voice than his sister's.

"Damian?" Theo asked.

"Yeah, Theo." Damian barked something on the other end of the line before he came back to the call. "What happened?"

Theo needed help. He didn't have a lot of people he trusted to ask for it.

"Theo?" Damian asked again.

"Family first, right, D?"

Damian blew a hard breath into the phone. "You know it. How long is it going to fucking take you to figure out you've always been family to me, Theo?"

"Joel killed Dino."

"I know," Damian murmured.

Theo wasn't even surprised that Ghost knew before him.

"I think—no, I know he just tried to have someone cull me, too. He got my guy instead, thinking it was me. I don't think the guy even knew the difference."

"Where are you?" Damian demanded.

"Out back of the club."

"I'm coming. Don't move."

"Don't bring my sister," Theo said.

"I won't. Get out of the fucking cold."

Theo swallowed back his rage and nerves. "Joel wants me dead, D."

"Correction, if he had someone go at you tonight, he already thinks you are dead."

"So?"

"Family first, Theo."

"Yeah, I got that." Theo heard the sound of car door slam before an engine was gunned. "So what does that got to do with Joel, D?"

"We're going to let him think it. And I'm going to make it happen."

Theo blinked up at the dark sky, confused. "DeLuca's don't hide."

"Vacation isn't hiding, Theo. God knows you could use one."

"Sorry about your car and all," Damian said.

Theo scowled at the windshield. "I had that fucking thing since I was twenty, man."

"It's just a car."

Theo drug the tip of his fingernail along the leather covered dashboard of Damian's Porsche. It left an inch long scratch behind.

"Stop it," Damian growled.

"Just a car, man."

Point made.

"Yeah, but yours needed to go boom, Theo. I still want to drive mine."

"Still wanted to drive mine, too."

But now the Stingray was a pile of smouldering metal with a body that would look suspiciously like Theo's for a while inside.

"I gave you the choice on how to destroy it," Damian said without a lick of emotion on his face.

"Burning was the best choice. Evelina's car got burned. Maybe people will stop blaming me for that shit if mine ends up burned, too."

"Like I said, you chose."

Speaking of Evelina ...

"I don't trust your cousin," Theo said.

Damian eyed Theo from the driver's seat. "Tommas, you mean."

"I don't trust him."

"And why is that?"

"He's got motives and he's not upfront with them. I don't trust that nonsense from any man."

"We've all got motives, Theo."

"Do you?" Theo asked.

Damian straightened in his seat. "Listen, we're talking about Tommas not me."

"You're his cousin. Loyal to him like nobody else."

"Wrong. Dino came first, then Tommas, and then you. But really, I was loyal to any of you depending on who needed me the most at the time. A few months ago, it was Dino. Lately, it's been Tommas. Tonight, it's you."

Theo's gaze narrowed. "Did you tell your cousin anything before you left the club?"

"Not a word."

"On my sister's life, D, say it."

"What are you, fucking five?"

"Say it," Theo growled.

"On Lily's life, man, I didn't say a thing. What is all this nonsense with Tommas?"

Theo ignored the question and asked one of his own. "Dino started all this shit, didn't he?"

Damian took a turn and replied, "Yes."

"Because of Ben."

"Partly, I think. I don't know."

"Mostly because he wanted to feel better."

Damian quieted for a long while before he asked, "From all that shit that happened with Ben and you brothers when you were kids, right?"

"Probably."

"Explains a lot of other shit, then."

"Like what?" Theo asked.

"Like how he manipulated me into killing the boss. Terrance knew what Ben was like with you and Dino and he never did a damned thing."

"That was you, huh?"

"And Ben's death, too," Damian said quietly. "Dino pulled the strings. I let him because I was being fucking stupid."

"And loyal." Theo rubbed at the sudden ache in his wrist at the reminders of the abuse he and his brother had taken by their uncle and the men who turned cheek to it for years. "Riley knew, too."

Damian's cheek twitched. "Riley more than just knew, didn't he?"

"Nearly killed me once."

"I'm sorry, man."

Theo waved the apology off. "Don't be. I'm here. Most of them aren't."

"Neither is Dino."

"Don't turn into my therapist."

Damian cocked a brow. "Nice try, though."

"What?"

"Deflecting me. What is it about Tommas that's got you on edge?"

"What do you know about Tommas, D?"

"I know he's got something he wants bad and can't have right now.

That can sometimes make for a dangerous man who is willing to do whatever he can to get what is his."

"Does that thing happen to be a female he shouldn't be messing with?"

Damian laughed loudly. "You know about Abriella, huh?"

"I haven't known for long."

"I have," Damian admitted under his breath. "You didn't answer my question, Theo."

Taking a breath to calm his restlessness, Theo spilled his fucking guts because he needed to. He had to tell someone about the shit he knew and the stuff he didn't. Yeah, that meant outing his business with Evelina, and all the trouble that came along with it, but Theo figured maybe he'd finally get some answers.

Theo started with the day he visited Karen and Evelina's car was shot up, and ended his story with the week before at the Conti Christmas party. He didn't leave out the fact he'd been called a sacrifice for the boss or how Tommas seemed close to Riley because of what Theo learned from Evelina.

Nothing was off-limits. Damian stayed quiet and let Theo talk.

"Eve?" Damian asked when Theo finished.

"Was that all you heard in what I just said?"

"Just didn't think the girl was your type."

"What in the fuck is that supposed to mean, Damian?"

"She's friends with Lily, all right. Jesus. You're not ... messing with the girl's head, right?"

"No," Theo said. "We're not anything important."

"Yes, you are. You're just like Tommas, Theo. You like to pretend because you don't label something, it doesn't exist. It fucking exists, man."

"You're missing the whole goddamn point."

"No, I'm not." Damian sighed and rubbed at his face with one hand, never taking his eyes off the road. "Tommas isn't stupid, Theo. He knows Riley is fucking him left and right with Joel, as far as that goes. Just the fact Tommas openly told Evelina that their marriage won't happen, and he only wants the idea of the engagement to be important says a hell of a lot. I didn't know any of that shit. So is my cousin working his own angles? Probably. I don't know what they are and I don't like that you might be acting as someone else's fall guy for the games those three men are playing."

"At least someone else sees it."

Rage danced on Damian's features, but the man never admitted to his anger. Not out loud, anyway.

"But which one is it, Theo? Which one is using you, huh?"

Theo shrugged. "Joel seems like the obvious choice after tonight, doesn't he?"

"Yes."

"You don't sound like you believe it, Damian."

"Because the obvious choice is usually the wrong one, Theo."

Yeah. It was.

"And that leaves me with Tommas or Riley," Damian added quieter.

"I'm not asking you to—"

"Shut up, man. You don't have to ask. You don't get it, Theo. It's not about asking or anything. It's Lily, all right. She hurts and she fucking worries. I can't let her keep doing that."

Theo grew silent in the passenger seat. Damian said nothing for the next thirty minutes until he parked the Porsche in an airport terminal.

"Do you have cash to carry you for a while?" Damian asked.

"Cards."

"That isn't going to work. I want nothing drawing back to your name except your ID. People aren't going to look for that for a while." Damian leaned over and popped open the glove compartment. He pulled out a black credit card with gold lettering and numbers. "Here. Doesn't require ID. There's no limit."

"I—"

"Take the card or I'll break your face. This isn't a fucking democracy here, Theo. You don't get a damned vote."

Theo took the card. "Thanks."

"Don't use the regular cell number, either."

"I've got a backup."

"Text me from it," Damian said.

"All right."

"This isn't running, Theo, but you can't be here right now. Something isn't right here. This is more than Joel. I need to know what it is, man. Lily can't bury another brother. Don't make her do that."

Theo forced back the pain settling in his middle. "I'll stay away."

Damian nodded. "So … Eve, huh?"

"She doesn't know anything about me, D."

"But does she want to?"

"I'm a selfish fucker."

"Why?" Damian asked.

"Because I don't think she would care if she knew it all, D. And that makes me want to tell her."

"You'll figure out whether or not you're willing to go there with her, Theo."

Theo scoffed. "I guess I've got time to think about it all now, huh?"

"I guess so."

"By the way," Theo added as he opened the passenger door.

"What, man?"

"Does the name Bell mean anything to you?"

Damian's hands clenched around the steering wheel. "Like the Belli family?"

Belli.

Jesus H. Christ.

Why hadn't Theo thought of that?

"By the look on your face, I'd say it means something to you now." Damian glanced at Theo. "What do I need to know about the name, Theo?"

"At the restaurant when Laurent tried to shoot the boss and Abriella ended up taking a bullet to the back, wasn't it Riley who said Joel was messing around with Chloe Belli?"

Damian nodded. "He did."

"Her father is one of Joel's little rats, isn't he?"

"A snake is more like it."

"Cole recognized the guy who shot him. He said the man's name was Bell."

Damian scowled. "Shit."

"What am I missing?" Theo asked.

"Chloe has an older brother around Joel's age. He does a lot of the dirty work when Joel doesn't want people to know. Nate is the guy's name, but he keeps a low profile. Like he doesn't want to get his in to the Outfit or something, but he doesn't mind doing business and all."

"So?"

"I'm pretty sure he goes by Bell, Theo."

CHAPTER SIXTEEN

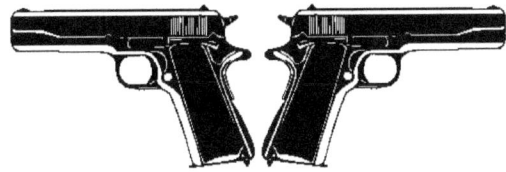

Something was wrong.

Evelina knew it the moment Damian had skipped out of the club without a single word to anyone but his wife. It didn't help Evelina's worries when Lily continued to sit in a booth with her thumb between her teeth, and a phone in her hand.

"There's your father," Tommas said quietly.

Riley entered the club with two men in smart suits coming in behind him. Courtney hung onto Riley's arm with her usual smile plastered on.

"I'll go greet him." Tommas stepped away from Evelina side. "Why don't you go talk with Lily? She looks terribly alone without Damian. I didn't even see him leave."

"He must have gone to the bathroom," Evelina lied.

"Maybe. And I should go check on my mother. God knows Serena and a club never mix well."

Tommas left Evelina alone, and she didn't mind. So far, their evening had consisted of greeting people and being polite as liquor started flowing. Evelina had never gotten along very well with drunk people unless she was one of them, too.

"Hey," Evelina said to Lily.

Lily glanced up from her phone, concern lighting up her features. "Hey, Eve."

"Where did your husband go? I don't think I've ever seen him leave you alone for more than five minutes."

"Uh … he just had to run out to get something I forgot."

Before Evelina could question her friend on the lie, Lily's phone rang. Lily jumped in the booth and quickly answered the call.

"Well?" Lily demanded.

Evelina kept one eye on her friend and one on the guests of the New Year party behind her.

"Good. So he's fine." Lily sighed loudly. "Um … Tommas, Riley. Their bunch, mostly … No, no Joel. Not yet."

Lily said a quick goodbye and something else that sounded a hell of a lot like *I love you*. There was only one man Lily would say those words to.

Damian.

Turning back to her friend, Evelina asked, "He just had to run out and get something you forgot, huh?"

Lily eyed the people behind Evelina. "Something happened."

Evelina's heart dropped. "Something bad?"

"Yeah, sort of. I mean, he's okay, but it was still bad."

"What was it?"

"Theo—"

Someone grabbed Evelina's arm and pulled, interrupting her conversation with Lily.

Theo, what?

Theo, what?

It was all Evelina could think about as she turned to meet Tommas' severe expression.

"Eve, we have guests. Be polite. Even if they make it hard."

Tommas' dark words in Evelina's ear didn't feel all that hopeful. A shiver climbed down her spine as she spun on her heel to see Joel walk in with Abriella at his side, and Chloe Belli on the other.

Great.

All Evelina really wanted to do was question the hell out of Lily until she got information on Theo. Wasn't he invited to the party? She had a cell phone number he'd given her to text or call if she needed something, but her phone was in Tommas' office with her clutch and coat.

"Let's go say hi," Tommas said, tugging Evelina along the club's floor. "It looks like your father is making his way to do that as well."

"Everybody was checked for guns at the door, right?" Evelina asked.

She was only half-joking.

Tommas shrugged. "In this life, people's loyalties only go as far as their pockets are deep. Even my people."

"Great."

"Worry not. I don't think Joel showed up for any other reason than to defy Riley. Just his presence is enough to piss off the boss."

"I never understood why Riley gave him a high position. He hates Joel."

"Because Riley wanted no more fighting and your brother knocked up Joel's sister," Tommas said simply. "It was shame all the way around the board. Bloodshed was a guarantee if Riley didn't do something to settle Joel's demands. This was the best choice until he could handle it further."

Evelina stopped walking, and jerked her elbow out of Tommas' grasp. "What in the hell does that mean?"

Tommas blinked down at her. "Pardon?"

"What was Riley going to do to handle Joel?"

"I—"

"Don't say that you don't know, Tommas."

All of Evelina's suspicions about her father came bubbling right back up with a vengeance. The shooting and her car, the marriage with Tommas and now, taking Joel off the guest list to the party just to anger the man.

Evelina squared her shoulders, determined to get some answers once and for all. "Has my father been purposely causing problems on the off-chance that Joel would be blamed, and he could take the man out without anyone making a fuss?"

And in turn, Evelina realized, *Theo was the man taking all the blame instead of Joel*.

Was that what had happened?

Evelina shoved her finger into Tommas' chest. "Is my father trying to make a reason to kill Joel, or has he been doing things that would cause Joel to put himself in a position to be killed? Is Theo the sacrifice people like you and my father were willing to make, whether it be by Joel going after him, or Theo becoming another casualty to blame, just to get what you wanted in the end?"

Tommas' jaw clenched briefly. "Not entirely."

"That doesn't make any sense. It either is or it isn't, Tommas."

"Yes, it does make sense. And some of us have been trying to fix the by-products of the mess, Eve, but Riley makes it terribly fucking hard to do when he's got his own agenda. Unfortunately, his agenda is not what he's been telling everybody else. Or at least not me. I'm trying. That is all that I can tell you. I am trying."

"Trying to do what?" she asked quietly.

"Trying to keep some people from being a goddamned sacrifice."

Theo.

"Now," Tommas added harshly, "smile for these people and do what you're good at, Evelina."

Evelina forced herself not to smack Tommas. "Go to hell."

"Surprise, sweetheart. I've been there for a while. Women like you don't make it any fucking easier."

"I suppose you have your own reasons for wanting Joel gone, don't you?" Evelina asked as she tossed a pointed look in Abriella Trentini's direction.

"I did," Tommas said. "Now, let's go."

Angrier and more confused than ever, Evelina let Tommas lead her the rest of the way across the floor to where they could greet the unwanted newcomers. Riley had made it to Joel and Abriella a few seconds before Tommas and Evelina did.

"Joel," Riley said, smiling falsely. "I'm surprised to see you here. I'm pretty sure Tommas was directed to remove your name from the guest list for this party after recent events. The last thing we need is another Trentini temper tantrum."

"I didn't get the memo until I was on my way here, Boss," Joel replied. "I figured my sister and I were already dressed up and coming, why not enjoy the evening with the rest of you. I'm sure we can put away the issues for an evening, can't we?"

Evelina tossed Abriella a wary look. Abriella didn't even act like Evelina existed. She also didn't give Tommas a passing look, either. That, however, wasn't anything new.

"Tommas?" Riley asked.

"I did what you wanted," Tommas said.

"What I wanted—"

"I passed the info along, Riley."

Riley's gaze narrowed in Tommas' direction. "Late, I see."

What had Evelina missed?

Tommas nodded politely at Joel. "Enjoy the evening, like you said. If there are any issues, I'll have you removed. Sound good to you?"

Joel flicked his old friend with a dismissive glance. "Sounds fine."

"Good."

Joel nodded at Abriella, and the two sauntered off into the crowd without a backward glance. They weren't gone more than five seconds before Riley rounded on Tommas.

"What in the hell was that?" Riley barked.

"I don't know what you're talking about," Tommas murmured.

Evelina moved aside a couple of inches away from Tommas. She didn't like the way her father looked right then. Like he was ready to blow any fucking second. She'd seen that look on him one too many times and had been privy to the mess it could create.

"Was DeLuca put back on the list like I demanded?" Riley asked.

"Yes," Tommas answered.

"And Joel was only made aware of that on his way over here then?"

Tommas shrugged. "I can't say for sure. All I know is that my message about Joel's removal was passed along. The rest is your mess to handle, Boss. Not mine."

"The whole point was for blame—"

"Your point. Mine is not the same."

Riley's teeth clenched. "I see."

What game was Tommas playing?

"You!"

The hissed, angry word was all Evelina heard before Tommas was shoved roughly from her side. She caught the shriek of surprise in her throat before it escaped, but barely. Damian grabbed Tommas by the jacket collar and practically dragged the man into the dark hallway.

On his way in, Damian pointed a finger at Evelina and growled, "You stay the fuck out here."

Evelina nodded, but she couldn't promise anything.

A few seconds later, she heard a hard thump like a body had hit a wall. Evelina poked her head around the corner only to find Tommas pinned against the wall and Damian glaring at his cousin.

"Where have you been?" Tommas asked.

"Getting Theo the hell out of town before someone tried to take another pound from him."

All the fight in Tommas seemed to leave at that statement. "He went after Theo."

"What the fuck did you do?" Damian asked. "You're so crazy over that girl that you're doing stupid shit, aren't you?"

Tommas rubbed a hand over his face and sighed. "Damian—"

Damian shoved Tommas into the wall again. "Answers or nothing, man. I'll find it out either way. You know it's the goddamn truth."

"I trusted the wrong person."

For a brief moment, Damian seemed to relax. "I know the feeling."

"I tried to fix it, D."

"Did you?"

"Tonight I tried. But mostly, I didn't know what in the hell Riley had planned. I thought something here maybe and I could keep an eye out and stop it. The whole musical chairs on the guest list was supposed to look like a favored thing for Riley between Theo and Joel."

"Bell," Damian spat.

Tommas' brow furrowed. "Who?"

"Belli—Bell. Mean something to you now?"

"Like the Belli family?"

"Yes, asshole. Them."

"Chloe is Joel's girl. I mean, if you want to call her that," Tommas said. "But mostly he just uses her to fuck whenever he feels the need. And, you know …"

"No, enlighten me."

"I've seen her around Riley the last couple of months, too."

Evelina's heart was leaping into her throat as she took all this information in. Her suspicious about her father were being confirmed right before her eyes. What was she going to do now?

"I was doing what Riley wanted," Tommas said quietly. "I was letting him think he was using me in the whole back and forth between Joel and me. I didn't care, D."

"Because you knew between the two of you, it would be you who came out on top."

"Yeah."

"And then you'd get Abriella."

Tommas sagged against the wall.

"I couldn't let Theo take the blame for it, though, not after I found out about …" Tommas trailed off with a wince. "Anyway, I couldn't let him be someone's scapegoat just in hopes that Riley would get what he wanted. I figured if Riley wanted Joel gone bad enough, he'd find a way to make it work."

"But the blame still kept being put on Theo."

Tommas nodded. "Yeah."

"Who burned the car?" Damian asked.

"Riley."

"Who tried to shoot it up the day Theo was with Eve?"

"Me," Tommas said so softly that Evelina strained to hear.

Evelina felt sick to her stomach. There was so much more involved than she had realized. She trusted no one except the man who apparently wasn't even in the city anymore if Damian's earlier words about getting Theo out had any truth to them.

"Did Riley get you to do the car job?" Damian asked.

"No. That was all me. Riley already had the seed planted in his mind to get rid of Joel. I simply thought messing around his family would push Riley into it early. Instead, Theo got blamed and it all snowballed from there."

"Theo thinks it was Joel who went after him tonight," Damian said.

"Riley probably wants everyone to think that. I know he took a trip down to Theo's territory yesterday with someone. It might have been Bell. I'm sorry, man," Tommas said. "My goal had nothing to do with Theo, but all the shit happening in the streets with Theo's crew only let the blame go straight to him first before anyone else. Joel grabbed onto that. I don't know why, but he held onto that like he was trying to find a reason to go at Theo."

Damian cleared his throat. "You know why. I told you why."

"Joel killed Dino."

"Theo knows it was Joel," Damian said. "And given the very public statement Theo made at the dinner where he told Joel that unlike Dino, he would see Joel coming tells me that maybe Joel didn't want it getting out. It makes sense that Joel would try to find a reason to get rid of an enemy. But Riley, that's where I'm lost."

"Don't be," Tommas muttered heavily. "Theo was the easy target. When the blame went Theo's way from Joel's side of things, Riley didn't mind feeding it. It was the simplest, quickest way for Riley to start something that would take Joel out."

"But Theo—"

"Was the casualty that Riley didn't mind losing in all this. You remember how close Ben was to Riley, D. Theo and Riley have bad blood from way back when Theo was a kid."

Damian stiffened. "I hadn't considered that."

"You should have. You knew Ben beat the shit out of Theo and Dino whenever he got the fucking chance, and Riley was just one of the men who helped at times. Riley nearly killed Theo once with a metal chair and Ben just stood back and let the man do it. Bad, bad blood, Damian."

Evelina disappeared around the corner. Her back hit the wall hard and she sunk down to her backside.

Abuse.

Theo had been abused. By his uncle. Likely by Evelina's father. The more she thought about Theo's issues with the dark, the nightmares he talked about, and his strange quirks, the more it made sense.

She couldn't breathe and an ache began to spread in her heart. Now, more than ever, she wished she could talk to Theo.

A few minutes later, Damian and Tommas exited the hallway. Neither man looked like they were any worse for wear after their conversation. Evelina was already standing back up and waiting for Tommas.

"Eve," he said.

Tommas offered his hand.

Evelina refused to take it.

Damian chuckled. "You've spent too much time with Theo if you're forgetting your place, Eve."

Her gaze cut to Damian. "Excuse me?"

"Theo is the rule breaker, right?" Damian flashed his white teeth in a smile. "You can only be so close to someone before their habits start bleeding over onto you."

Evelina finally understood what he was saying. Damian knew about her and Theo.

"He's okay," Damian said. "Theo, I mean. He's safe."

"Thank you."

Evelina had needed to hear that more than Damian could possibly understand.

Tommas shot Damian a look that Evelina couldn't decipher.

"What?" she asked.

"In five minutes," Tommas said, "we're all going to pretend like Theo isn't okay."

"Why?"

Damian shoved his hands in his pocket. "Someone wanted him dead tonight. We want that person to believe Theo is."

"My father, you mean."

Tommas chuckled. "You listened to everything, didn't you?"

"Yes," Evelina admitted.

"I'm sorry, Eve," Tommas said. "About the car shooting and what followed. I'm sorry."

"No, I don't think you are."

Five minutes later, Evelina watched the crowd of guests in the club begin to whisper as word of an accident and a shooting involving Theo DeLuca began to travel around. No one seemed to have the whole story. No one knew any real facts. One thing was the same all the way around the board.

Theo was dead.

"Why can't I go home with my brother?" Evelina asked.

Tommas put his car in park and cut the engine. He watched Damian park his own vehicle and then help his wife out of the car. "There might be trouble after tonight, Eve. It was your father's main goal in this entire thing. I want you to be somewhere safe. Despite what you may think about me and what I did, there was a reason that not a single bullet of mine hit you or Theo."

Evelina refused to grace that with a response.

"Damian and Lily have a safe home in DeLuca territory," Tommas said.

"My brother's wedding is in a few days."

"You'll attend with Damian and Lily."

"I really don't like you right now," Evelina said quietly.

"You don't have to. You simply have to trust me to correct this."

"From what I understand, you nearly got Theo killed tonight."

"Your father, not me," Tommas replied just as fast. "Damian is waiting. I'll have a bag brought to you tomorrow. I'm sure Alessa knows where your things are for the wedding."

Evelina didn't need to be told again. She got out of the car and slammed it much harder than necessary. She hadn't even made it to the front step and Tommas was already backing out of the gates.

"Lily went inside already," Damian informed. "She's tired."

"And worried," Evelina said.

So was she.

Terribly so.

An emptiness had settled in her heart and she hadn't expected that at all. She hadn't quite realized it until Theo was gone, but she wished he was there. It wasn't safe for him to be there now.

"Yes, I imagine you are, too," Damian murmured.

Evelina wouldn't meet the man's gaze. "How do you know anything?"

"Theo told me."

Well, then ...

"You should know," Damian added, giving Evelina a small smile, "that I think he cares about you a great deal, even if he doesn't want to admit it."

"Why is that?"

"Because Theo doesn't get involved with things that could bring him trouble, despite what he makes it look like. He's a smart man. Very smart."

"Messing around with me isn't smart at all."

"No," Damian agreed. "And if he's willing to take that risk, my guess is that he's wondering what might come of it. Do you wonder?"

"With my father alive, not at all."

Damian frowned. "And what if he wasn't alive?"

"He is, so your question doesn't matter."

"My question is hypothetical, Eve."

"I don't deal in delusions," she said, walking past him to go inside.

In her heart, the truth was screaming much louder than her words.

She wondered all the time now.

"Hey," Damian said, poking his head into the living room.

Lily glanced up from the book she was reading. "Yeah?"

"Theo just called. He's settled and safe."

Evelina felt the tension leave her body as Lily sunk into the couch. It was two in the damned morning. Lily refused to sleep until Damian gave word about Theo. Evelina wasn't in much better of a spot.

"Yeah?" Lily asked.

"Yes. Will you go to sleep now, sweetheart?"

Lily laughed. "I'll think about it."

"I will carry you upstairs, Lily," Damian warned.

She waved her husband off. "Give me a few more minutes."

"Fine."

Once Damian was gone from the doorway, Lily went back to her book.

Then, very quietly, Lily asked, "When are you going to tell me, Eve?"

Evelina looked away from the sitcom playing on the television. "About what?"

"About you and my brother."

No words formed.

Evelina tried—God, she tried—but nothing came.

"You're not even denying it," Lily noted, never once taking her eyes off her book.

"I wouldn't lie to you. You're my best friend, Lily."

Finally, Lily looked up and met Evelina's stare. "You know, you've sat in that spot for hours and barely moved. You haven't talked to me really since we got here. You've stared at your phone like you were waiting for a call. You have no romantic interest in Tommas, and anyone with two brain cells can see it. You're worried, you're unsettled, and you're fidgety. Because of someone. Just like me. The only person who deserves that right now is Theo."

Evelina swallowed the lump in her throat. "He is, you're right."

"When were you going to tell me?"

"It wasn't like we were anything. There wasn't much to tell."

"You're something," Lily said. "I know Theo. You're something, Eve. How long?"

Evelina had to think about that one. "That's hard to answer, Lily."

"Try me."

"Ever since I turned eighteen, Theo has been in the background of my life in one way or another. Flirting, pushing my boundaries, teasing me, and nonsense like that. He's asked me out and I refused him. He's approached me and I shut him down. I've even bailed on him a couple of times when I did agree to a date. So yeah, it's hard to answer that because it's been on-going for years. At least from his side of it."

"I think from your side of it, too, obviously."

Evelina glanced down at her hands. "I wanted to say yes to him every time. I wanted to let him take me out and see what would happen. But I've been stuck wearing the princess's tiara even though I never wanted it. Theo wasn't the right kind of prince and I wasn't ready to take the tiara off. When I was, it was too late."

Lily sucked in a deep breath and tossed her book aside before resting her hand on her still-flat midsection. "So when did things change?"

"Shortly before my mother died, Theo asked me out to the ballet and I agreed."

"*Giselle?*"

"Yes. You got the tickets because I flaked on him for the dinner where my mom was killed. And then last month … last month I ended up in a hotel with Theo for days."

Lily cleared her throat, asking, "And?"

"And it was the best three days of my life."

"Okay then."

Lily grabbed her book and opened it back up.

"Just like that? Okay?" Evelina asked.

"Just like that," Lily echoed softly. "I learned with Damian that sometimes, we just don't get to choose who we hand that part of ourselves over to, Eve."

"What part?"

"Our hearts."

Evelina straightened on the couch. "I'm not … in love with Theo."

Was she?

She cared about him but she wasn't in love with him.

"Sometimes, it takes you a while to figure it all out," Lily said like she knew exactly what was going through Evelina's head. "That doesn't make whatever it is any less real, Eve."

"Love is a dangerous word and not one I would use right now."

"Let me know when that changes."

Evelina fixed a smudge of eyeliner in the ornate mirror. The private room had been designated for the bride's party to get ready, but Evelina was alone in the room. Abriella had apparently decided to get ready elsewhere.

It wasn't like Evelina blamed the girl.

A knock on the door was the only warning Evelina got before Lily poked her head in.

"Hey," said her friend.

Evelina turned and waved her arms wide. "How do I look?"

"Gorgeous." Lily smiled, held out a cell phone, and said, "Here, take this. Call it a late Christmas present or whatever."

Evelina took the phone. "What for?"

"He'll call back in a minute. Five minutes until we meet at the doors, okay?"

Still confused, Evelina agreed. Lily closed the door, leaving Evelina alone once again. Thankfully, the day had gone by mostly smoothly. Her father had left her alone and Tommas kept a safe distance. Abriella didn't say two words to her, and Alessa was just hoping for a quiet wedding day.

Interestingly enough, Joel had not shown up yet to his sister's wedding. Evelina wasn't surprised. Riley was probably soaking that up.

Going back to the mirror, Evelina fixed a wayward curl. The cell phone vibrated in her hand, nearly making her jump out of her heels. Without looking at the caller ID, Evelina picked up the call.

"Hello?"

"Princess," came a familiar, honey-rich voice.

Evelina backed into the mirror with a sigh. "Theo."

"Who else, babe?"

She had known he was okay and safe. She had known the news reports about the dead, burned body found in Theo's ruined Stingray had been a lie to distract Riley. She knew all of those things.

It was only once she heard Theo's voice that Evelina finally believed it.

"Eve?" Theo asked.

She came out of her daze quickly. "Where are you?"

"A plane ride away. The wedding is today, right?"

"Yes."

"Sorry to miss you in your dress. I bet you look damn good."

Evelina laughed. "I'm sure you would have only come for me."

"Well, you'd have been the best sight, but I also would have come for wine and cake."

"You're awful."

"I know," Theo said, chuckling. "I'm sorry, Eve, I should have called before this. Lily let me know that you were worried."

"I was."

"You told my sister, huh?"

"She figured it out."

"Yeah, Lily is smart like that," Theo said quietly. "How is everything else?"

"The Outfit?"

"Yes."

"Dangerous," Evelina replied. "It's dangerous and I don't trust anyone."

"Good. You shouldn't."

"I'd trust you."

Theo grew silent for a moment before he said, "Well, who else is going to save you, princess?"

"Exactly." Evelina kept an eye on the door as she asked, "Have you talked to Damian?"

"Yes."

"So you know—"

"Everything," Theo interrupted quickly. "I'm trying to figure out what I want to do with it all right now. I was sure it was Joel. It made sense for it to be him. But I'm not surprised it was Riley, and sadly, I'm not shocked that Tommas had a hand in certain things. It's still a lot to take in."

"It was for me, too."

Then, in the background of Theo's call, Evelina heard the sound of a woman's laughter ringing out. A door was shut and it stopped. Instantly, like a shot of hot lava straight to her bloodstream, jealousy waged a war inside Evelina's body.

"What was that?" she asked.

Theo hummed. "Hmm, what?"

"I heard a woman, Theo. Who is it?"

"A friend."

Evelina choked on his answer, hurt. "A woman friend? I didn't realize you had friends who were women that you stayed with, Theo."

Suddenly, Theo barked out a laugh. "Wait, wait … are you jealous?"

"No," Evelina said.

"Liar, you are. You're jealous. That's new."

"Well …"

"Come on, Eve, you can do better than that," Theo goaded.

"Go to hell, Theo."

"Hey, listen for a second. You've got no reason to be jealous, Eve. What did I tell you the night of the Christmas party, huh?"

Evelina picked at her fingernails and used her shoulder to hold the phone. "That you cared."

"And that I was interested in you," Theo added, sounding far too smug for his own good. "I'm not looking elsewhere, Eve. We don't have to fuck around with all the title nonsense right now because it's not important, but I'm not looking at anyone but you right now."

"Who was that?"

"A friend's wife. Kim is her name."

Married.

The woman was married.

Evelina's little green monster climbed off her back. "Oh."

"And Gio would kill me if I even looked anywhere but at his wife's eyes, trust me," Theo said with not a lick of humor in his tone.

"He sounds like an interesting man."

"All the Marcellos are."

"You're in New York," she said.

"Yeah. Eve?"

"Hmm?"

"I like it when you're jealous."

Theo's voice sounded entirely wicked and it felt like sex had just washed over her senses.

Evelina wet her lips and asked. "Do you?"

"Yes, but you still don't need to be."

"Only looking at me, right?"

"Right," Theo agreed.

"Theo?"

"Yeah?"

"Why didn't you tell me about your uncle and my father?"

Theo coughed. "Tell you what?"

"About the abuse and whatnot. Why didn't you—"

"I have to go," Theo said quickly.

"No, wait a minute. Don't hang up on me just because you don't want to talk about something, Theo. This is important. You could have told me."

Theo sighed heavily. "I would have eventually. I still will someday."

"Not today?"

"Not today," he repeated. "One more thing."

"Shoot."

"Be safe."

Evelina's anxiety was back in a blink. "I'm trying."

"Good, because it's fucking killing me to know you've got nobody watching your back right now."

"You do," she whispered.

"But I'm not there, Eve."

"You'll be back."

Theo made a dark noise. "Do you remember what I said in the car driving to the hotel? About the king and the prince?"

Evelina didn't even have to think about it. Every word, every touch, and every second she spent with Theo had somehow imprinted itself on her memories. It wouldn't leave.

"Yes," she said.

"What was it, Eve?"

"That the king should have left you locked in the tower."

"He's really going to regret letting me out when I get back," Theo said.

Evelina's father was the king wearing the stolen crown, after all.

"Don't forget the princess, Theo," Evelina said.

"I thought you didn't want to be the princess anymore?"

"I'm just waiting to take off the tiara."

"And burn it," Theo muttered.

"I'll let you light the fire."

"Eve, you already did."

He was right.

CHAPTER SEVENTEEN

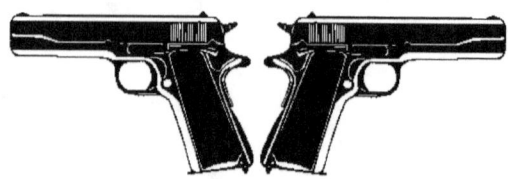

"Tell me something nobody knows about you, Theo."

Theo blinked and suddenly, Evelina was across the room, watching him with those expressive green eyes of hers. The scene felt familiar to him, and at the same time, new somehow. But in the back of his mind, he knew he'd done this with Evelina before.

A dream, maybe?

She sat on a plush bed, her back against a cushioned headboard, and with her knees drawn up to her chest. In just his dress shirt, her legs were on display for him to admire.

"You've got beautiful legs," Theo said.

Evelina shifted on the bed, letting the shirt ride up higher. The movement allowed Theo a flash of her bare sex between her thighs and the rounded shape of her ass. Evelina ran her fingers through the damp strands of her hair, mussing up the waves even more as thick lashes fanned her cheeks. *Beautiful.* The girl was goddamn beautiful and every part of Theo knew it. The more of Evelina that Theo got to see, taste, and have, the more he wanted.

He was starting to wonder how much more this girl would give. He might take whatever it was.

Two days …

They'd been in the hotel together for two days. Tomorrow evening, he would have to let Evelina go back home. At least, that's what she said after another phone call to her brother. Theo wasn't sure he was ready to let her go. It was easy to forget about the outside world when right then, it was nothing but him, her, sex, a hotel room, and quiet peace.

The monsters didn't live here.

He liked it far too much.

"I said a secret about you," Evelina said, smiling. "But thank you."

"About me, huh?"

"Something cute or funny."

Theo laughed. "All right. My first kiss was one I stole from a girl who was a couple of years older than me when I was twelve. Nobody knows that."

Evelina's nose scrunched. "That is kind of cute."

"She was also the girl I lost my virginity to when I was fifteen."

"Theo!"

"Hey, she came back for more," Theo said, smirking. "Speaks of my talent, Eve. Your turn."

Evelina's smile fell. "What, a secret?"

"Don't you have any?"

"I guess. None that are very ... worthy to tell."

Theo didn't believe that, but he wouldn't push her. "Favorite color then?"

"Yellow. It's warm."

"And bright," Theo said.

Evelina shrugged. "Somethings are meant to stand out more than others."

"I suppose that fits you quite well, then, doesn't it?"

Her lips curved with a sensual little smile, but she didn't respond to his statement.

"What about your fondest memory?" Theo asked.

"Really?"

"Yeah, give me it."

Evelina looked up at the ceiling before saying, "When I was six, Riley took us all to Bora Bora. I've always remembered it and it was one of the only vacations we ever went on."

"Why is that your favorite?"

"Because for a week, there was nothing but us. We were just a family. I don't remember my mother ever being happier, and that was the one time I think my father acted like a father and nothing else."

"And then you came back home."

"Yep," Evelina said, letting the word pop from her mouth. "What's with all the questions, Theo?"

"Curious, maybe."

"Oh?"

"Or maybe I'm trying to learn more about this woman sitting across from me," Theo admitted.

Evelina bit her lip before she pushed forward until she was on her hands and knees. Then, quietly with her stare leveled only on him, she crawled to the edge of the bed. The tight shape of her ass swayed as she moved and her delicate collarbones peeked out from under his shirt.

Theo's cock hardened. "I can't say there's ever been a woman who looks quite as good as you do on your hands and knees, Eve."

"No?"

"No." Theo took his time to admire the opening of the shirt where Evelina had left the top three buttons undone. The swells of her breasts peered out at him with her movements. He was fucking memorized by smooth, peachy skin and dark waves of hair. "Your favorite food?"

"Poutine, but it has to be authentic, not some remake."

"Isn't that like fries, gravy, and cheese all messed onto one plate?"

"Essentially," Evelina said.

"Sounds like a heart attack waiting to happen."

"Or art for the mouth." Evelina grinned at him. "Maybe I'll cook it for you someday. Come on, Theo. You can do better than that."

Theo pushed up from the chair and tugged off the T-shirt he wore without a word. He always kept a small bag for overnight in the trunk of his Stingray just in case. It'd finally came in handy for him when he needed a change of clothes. He didn't mind letting Evelina wear his other stuff.

Tossing the shirt to the couch behind him, Theo asked, "Biggest regret?"

Evelina stilled on the bed. "I've never taken a lot of risks that left me feeling guilty or ashamed, Theo."

"That's not an answer, Eve."

"You're right."

"What is your biggest regret?"

Evelina pushed back on the bed to sit on her ass as Theo came to stand at the end of the bed. "You."

That was not what he expected to hear.

"Me?" he asked.

"Well, never giving you that call when I was eighteen. I've always wondered what might have come of it, Theo. So yeah, it's probably my biggest regret."

Theo leaned down and placed his palms at the end of the bed. Like this, he was nose to nose with Evelina and was able to see every little emotion flicker in her eyes. "Don't bother regretting that anymore, babe."

"It never happened, Theo. Of course, I'm going to wonder."

"Don't. You saw what could have come of it. We're here, aren't we?"

Evelina blinked. "I hadn't thought of it that way."

"Do you often overthink things?" he asked.

"Yes."

Theo moved forward even more until his hands were on Evelina's thighs, his knees were resting at the edge of the mattress, and he was forcing her to lean back. "Do you want to just feel for a while instead?"

"Sometimes I overthink sex, too."

His chuckles came out dark, heady, and deep.

"Don't. Sex is all about the feeling and fulfilling the need, Eve."

"Not always," she whispered.

"It is right now." Theo cocked a brow. "Do you want me to fuck you until the only thing you can do is *feel?* Feel just me, my hands on you, this bed under you, my cock inside you, my mouth on your body, and nothing else? Is that what you want?"

Evelina shivered. "Do you think that's possible?"

"I know it is. It's just a matter of getting you out of that head of yours."

"Try me."

Theo wet his lips under his tongue. "I'm out of condoms, Eve. Unless you want to wait for the bellboy to run us up a pack when I call down to the desk for some."

Evelina shook her head. "I'm safe."

That was the only permission Theo needed. He lunged at Evelina and didn't give her any warning to his surprise move. Her loud yelp was drowned out by his mouth crushing hers as he took her down to the sheets. Theo wrapped a hand into her hair and bunched the strands into a tight fist, keeping her head pulled back into the pillow as he owned her mouth with his own. She widened her legs for his body to fit in between while his tongue danced with hers. It was a battle that she didn't seem to mind if she lost.

Quiet moans fell from her lips as Evelina rocked her sex against the hard ridge of Theo's erection through his pants. She was bare, no panties, and he was sure she was enjoying the feeling of rubbing against his dick.

Theo bit Evelina's bottom lip hard when she tried to pull away from his kiss for a breath. Her responding whine was answered by another one of his bruising kisses. He dragged the tips of his fingers down her chest and over the buttons of his shirt. With one grab and a hard tug, the buttons popped through the loops and he had skin.

More of her flesh to feel under his palms. More of her to taste.

Theo let her undo the zipper and button on his slacks before he kicked them off. His boxer-briefs followed the same path. Naked against her, the hardness of his body to the soft smoothness of hers, was like an electrical current was passing over every single one of his nerves.

Live wires.

"You're fucking soaked," Theo told her. "You made my pants wet rubbing on me like that."

Evelina's hand wrapped around his cock and squeezed. Then, she hooked her legs around his lower back and tightened them, making him fall into her body again. The silky wetness of her arousal smeared to his bare cock as she rocked against him again. With every tilt of her hips, his length glided through her slippery folds. Sparks of heat danced up Theo's spine.

The more her fingernails scraped and she rocked into his cock, the more his mouth found places on her to suck, kiss, and taste, the better it was.

All the better.

"Jesus," Evelina breathed, arching off the bed.

Theo pushed her hard into the bed. "This fucking bed under you, Eve."

She groaned.

He ached from her sounds.

His fingers pinched her nipples until they were hard little peaks and she was biting her lip so hard they were a rosy red. His fingertips pressed into her skin and slid down the toned path of her stomach until he was grazing the spot below her bellybutton. All over, Evelina trembled.

"My hands on you," Theo growled.

Evelina tilted her head back, giving him access to her throat. Theo took it, holding under her jaw with one hand as he nipped and licked a path over her collarbones. He could feel her swallow all her pretty little noises under his hands.

"Your mouth on me," she said, barely above a whisper.

With another lift of her hips, Theo felt the tip of his cock slide along her entrance. He flexed his hips and that was it—his cock filled her instantly. Evelina's eyes flew wide and her lips opened. The cry that tumbled out of her started from somewhere in her chest and clawed its way out.

Raw.

She was so raw like this.

Not untouched. Not pure.

Beauty always was a little dirty.

Evelina shifted her hips and widened her legs for him. Her fingers curled into the bedsheets while her back bowed off the bed.

"What's that feel like for you, Eve?" Theo asked, holding her lower body down with his hand while he hovered above her. "I've got you so full. You're soaking me all over. Fucking you is a dream."

Evelina didn't say a word. It was like she couldn't speak. Her noises were more than enough, and Theo could feel the way her pussy shuddered around his cock with every jostle of their bodies.

Another pull of his body and he was withdrawing. Evelina whimpered under him.

"Breathe," Theo murmured.

Evelina's gaze met his, stunned and dazed. She still didn't take in the air like he demanded.

"*Breathe*, Eve."

He let go of his hold on her body and widened her thighs even more until he was sure she could feel it burning in her muscles. Then, he was slamming back into her hard enough that he felt it in his goddamn bones.

Evelina sucked in a hard breath. "*Oh.*"

His pace was brutal, so ruthless. Evelina didn't, or couldn't, seem to stay still. She met the hard cracks of his body with her own and he felt his cock hitting her even deeper because of it. Her teeth found the underside of his jaw while her fingers dug into his shoulder blades.

"In you," he mumbled into her hair.

Evelina shuddered.

Theo could feel the words forming on her lips, but they came out as a nothing more than air whispering over his skin.

"All over me," Evelina gasped. "You're ruining me with this."

"Am I?" he asked.

Forcing her head back again so he could watch her while he fucked her, Theo saw the sliver of wetness fall from the corner of her eye.

"How am I supposed to feel like this again?" she asked.

Theo didn't know.

He didn't have those answers.

"What else is there right now?" he asked.

"Nothing …" Evelina's muscles clenched, her release coming quick and strong. "Just this. Don't stop, Theo."

He ran his thumb over the tear and then down to her lips. Evelina kissed the digit and the moment her mouth opened, she took his thumb in and sucked. When she did that, they both flew.

Nothing but them …

"Wake up, Theo."

Theo's eyes snapped open to an unfamiliar bedroom lightened by the large windows.

"Theo!"

Three more bangs hit the door hard.

A heavy weight settled in his stomach as he realized his cock was rock hard under the sleep pants he wore, his body ached like he'd just been fucking a woman for hours, and his mind was running a million miles a minute. Damp with sweat and out of breath, Theo stared at the ceiling, confused.

When Theo dreamed of things, it was always nightmares of his past and the people who had done him wrong. He had never dreamed of a woman. He had never relived an entire night he'd spent with a woman through his dreams.

Evelina.

Not just any woman.

Eve.

Sure, he'd thought a lot about their nights in the hotel, but since he'd been in New York, he'd dreamt about it every night in vivid detail. Theo's throat was tight and his mouth was dry. He cared about Evelina. Denying it was pointless.

But now ... what in the hell did *this* mean?

Another bang hit the bedroom door. "Are you even listening to me?"

"I'm up," Theo said hoarsely.

"It's seven," his friend said from outside the room.

"So what?"

"It's Sunday."

"Come on, Gio, stop being a little shit."

"Church," Gio said. "You've been here three weeks and not once have you gone. Antony found out you were staying with me and Kim when Lucian had a fit a couple of days ago. Antony is demanding you come to the church and show face. Dante made the final call. You're coming. Get your ass out of bed."

Theo groaned and dropped back onto the pillow. "The whole point of this is for me to stay out of the goddamn limelight."

The Marcello family might as well have been royalty in New York. They were not low profile in the city.

"It's just church, man," Gio said flippantly.

Frustrated, Theo tossed off the sheets and blankets, hit the cold hardwood floors in a fluid movement, and stalked to the door. Yanking it open just enough that he could glare at his old friend, Theo found a grinning Giovanni on the other side.

Napping over the man's shoulder was his seven-and-a-half-month old son, Andino. The baby had a thumb popped into his mouth and fist full of the hair on the nape of Gio's neck.

"I could just up and go to a hotel, you know," Theo said. "Saves me the trouble of making nice with your father."

"Or," Gio drawled, "... my father will come to you."

"He's not even the Don anymore. Dante took over, right?"

"Antony still gets his way whenever he wants." Gio leaned against the wall and said, "It's just church, like I said. Dinner after with the family. Usually we do a big one for everybody, but Ma agreed to keep it as just us brothers, the wives, and the kids this week for your benefit."

"Is your brother going to glare at me from the other side of the table all day?"

"Lucian knows how to be respectful."

"The man hates my guts," Theo said frankly.

Theo had been friends with Giovanni Marcello for a decade. He'd taken a trip to New York with his uncle back when he was a teenager to do business with the Marcello family and learn who was who in the city.

The Marcellos were fucking everything.

Theo had learned that fact fast.

But Lucian, the oldest of the brothers, had issues with the Outfit. It stemmed from some problem Joel had caused with Lucian's guys when they were supposed to be working together at the docks for shipments. Nonetheless, all the love was lost after that.

"Lucian has some trust issues," Gio said, shrugging. "It is what it is. He is who he is. He'll be good today for Ma's benefit."

"Not for mine?" Theo asked, chuckling.

"You can only ask a Marcello for so much before they start taking shit back, man."

Theo rubbed at his forehead. "Whatever. Did you get that suit dry-cleaned for me?"

"Yeah, Kim hung it in the bathroom."

He'd picked up a few essentials that he would need for his stay in New York, but nothing big. The short stay he thought it would be had turned into three weeks of wondering and guilt. He shouldn't have left Chicago. People needed him there. His family needed him. Inside, he felt like a fool for leaving. Like he'd given the bastards, Riley and Joel, exactly what they wanted.

Except he wasn't dead yet.

Little Andino's eyes popped open a second before he tugged hard on his father's hair.

"Ouch, Andino, Jesus," Gio cussed.

"Ba," Andino cooed, pulling on his father's hair some more. "Baba, *Papà.*"

"I'll get you some milk in a minute."

Theo couldn't help but grin as Gio fought to get his hair out of his son's hand.

"Kim's right. I need a fucking haircut."

"And a bar of soap for your mouth," Theo said.

Gio scoffed. "You're one to talk."

"I don't cuss in front of your kid."

"Yet," Gio muttered.

Theo went to close the door, but Gio grabbed it just as fast to stop him.

"Wait a sec," Gio said.

Little Andino was put to the floor and immediately, the baby began to scoot himself down the hallway a couple of inches at a time.

"What?" Theo asked.

"Who is she?"

Theo's back straightened like someone had shoved a stake up through his spine. "I don't know what you're talking about."

"Right," Gio said like he was talking to a small child. "Kim was asking me about you last night, and she mentioned some shit I hadn't taken notice of. But you're different, Theo, and it's not just about the nonsense happening in Chicago. You make private calls behind closed doors, you don't mention names of anybody, even family, and you're private as hell."

"Is that a problem?" Theo asked. "Because I've always been private, man."

"No, it's not. But I can see it in your face, like you're not all here most of the time. It makes me think that you want to be somewhere else, even if right here is the safest place for you to be. Maybe you want to be with someone else. Did you leave somebody behind? Is that it?"

"Mind your business, Gio."

Gio laughed. "What's her name?"

"There is nobody."

Liar.

Theo kept his expression passive, but his mind taunted him. *Liar.*

"You're a fool, then," Gio said, "because I know the look you've got, Theo. Lucian walked around like that for weeks before he finally got his shit straight."

"I don't get it."

Gio smirked. "Yeah, neither did Lucian until he learned Jordyn's name."

"I still don't know what you're talking about."

"Yes, you do. What's her name, Theo?"

Theo's grip on the door tightened until he was sure he would leave fingerprints indented in the wood. "What does it matter?"

"I find it always helps a man when he's got somebody to confess to. For whatever reason, you know."

"Eve," Theo murmured. "Her name is Eve."

Gio nodded. "And she's from Chicago?"

"Yes."

"From an *Outfit* family in Chicago," Gio pressed.

"Yes."

"There is only one daughter in Chicago that I know with that name."

Theo dropped his head slightly, just enough to keep Gio from looking at his eyes. "What about it?"

"You are so fucked, Theo."

"Tell me about it. Church?"

"Yeah. I think you need it."

Theo stood when the congregation was blessed a final time. As the parishioners began to file out, he turned to leave alongside the family he'd attended with. Antony and Dante Marcello blocked his way.

"Sit," Antony said quietly.

Theo shot a look over the older man's shoulder and watched Gio file out with his oldest brother, the wives, their handful of children, and the family matriarch, Cecelia.

"Is this one of those things where you're going to be nice, but tell me to get the hell out of your city?" Theo asked.

Dante laughed, the sound echoing in the large church above the voices and footsteps. "No. We just want to talk, Theo. Seeing as how you've had three weeks on the low at Gio's, we'd like to find out why and exactly what's been going down in Chicago. Obviously you needed a timeout from it all, and this is where you came to."

"What my son is saying," Antony said with a jerk of his thumb toward Dante, "… is that you owe us an explanation. Nothing more, Theo."

Theo sat back down in the pew. "I haven't been to church in months."

Antony took a seat beside Theo while Dante took one beside his father.

"Why is that?" Antony asked.

"My brother."

Antony lifted a single brow and nodded. "Ah, Dino. I heard about his death. Bombed in front of his family's church, right?"

"The news reports were all over that," Theo said.

"That's how we were keeping up with most of it," Dante replied from the far end. "Sometimes we made a call or two just to make sure the war wasn't going to make its way down here."

Theo shook his head. "It won't. It has nothing to do with New York."

"No, it's entirely about the Outfit." Antony passed Theo a look and asked, "Am I correct?"

"Pretty much. Greedy men who can't get enough and are never satisfied. It made for a bad situation that quickly got worse."

"What started it?" Antony asked.

"Someone was killed. It snowballed from there," Theo explained.

"I think you're leaving a lot out," Dante murmured.

"I didn't want to be a part of it."

Antony leaned back in the pew. "Yet, here you are in New York. Hiding."

Theo's guilt climbed higher. "I was told not to call it hiding. I was told it was a much needed vacation."

"Once I heard about you being in New York, I did a little bit of checking," Dante said, leaning forward so he could see Theo. "And do you know what I found?"

"Enlighten me," Theo said dully.

Antony smirked. "We found that you're supposed to be dead."

"Apparently not. Here I am."

"Who do they think it was?" Dante asked. "A shooting and then your car was burned, correct?"

"Well, somebody else burned the car and I helped. The shooting was a mistaken identity between the fool with the gun and my middle man outside of my club. I was lucky, that's all."

"Damn," Antony said quietly.

Then, the man made the sign of the cross and glanced up at the high vaulted ceiling. Swearing in church was never okay, after all.

"Damian Rossi married your sister, didn't he?" Dante asked, sounding far too casual.

"He did."

"I like him. Damian, I mean. Good man."

Theo caught Dante's gaze from the side. "He is."

"By chance, was he the one who sent you out of Chicago?" Antony asked.

Theo bit his cheek, but answered honestly. "Yeah."

"Family is not as dead there as we thought," Dante told his father. "Maybe the honorable ones are just waiting to show themselves, hmm?"

"Anything is possible," Antony agreed.

Theo watched the men, confused as hell. "You lost me."

"This war …" Dante trailed off with a disgusted sound.

"It's bad for *la famiglia* as a whole," Antony explained for his son. "They're killing whoever gets in the way without a thought because of greed and misplaced loyalty. Dante, as the boss he is, wondered if it was time for the Marcellos to pull some influence and put an end to it."

"But maybe we should wait it out and see who comes out on top," Dante said, falling back into the pew again.

"They could still come out of it, son. Better than before. Far better. All it takes is the right boss and the right men under him, Dante. You know this. I taught you this."

Antony's words were exactly why the Marcellos were as formidable of a crime family as they were. They were take-no-bullshit and cutthroat. Issues weren't even a concern because they didn't let one get whispered before they culled the problem.

"As for you, Theo," Antony said, pushing up from the pew to stand.

Theo glanced up at the man. "What about me?"

"You somehow became a target. It makes me wonder where your loyalties are."

Theo had to think about that for a second. The obvious answer was that his loyalties were to himself, to protect his territory and his crew from becoming another casualty in Chicago's war. But a different answer came out instead.

"My sister, the family she's trying to make, and her husband," Theo said quietly. "Because they're my family, and I care for them. It isn't about having the most power for me, or the best seat in the family. I've never wanted that. I simply wanted to keep my family safe and happy in the life that I chose."

Evelina, too.

Theo cared for her.

"Then what's the problem?" Antony asked. "Because you talk like there is one."

"I think I forgot what family was supposed to be for a while. I'm just now being reminded."

Dante eyed Theo from the side. "You look like a guilty man."

"That obvious?"

"Did you leave unfinished business behind?" Antony asked.

"Someone tried to kill me," Theo stated simply. "Isn't that unfinished enough?"

"But why did they do it?"

Theo already knew the answer. It wasn't a good one. He had talked enough with Damian and got all the info he needed on Riley, Tommas, and Joel.

"In a roundabout way, one snake thought I would be the easiest way to get rid of another snake."

Antony sighed. "Good men do their own work, Theo."

Theo had always thought so.

"You're welcome to stay in New York for as long as you need," Dante said, standing from the pew as well. "But I'll give you some friendly advice, Theo. From a Marcello, it means a little more than when it comes from others."

"Yes," Antony added, laughing under his breath, "I think he could use some Marcello-brand advice."

"What is it?" Theo asked. "Anything is better than nothing, I suppose."

"It is," Dante agreed. "In this life, family is the most important thing, which I think you already know. But what you might not realize is that the family are also the people who make up the life you chose. Running from those people when they have no one who will stand for them means you are leaving them behind, and with it goes any honor you have left. If you feel like the people who are supposed to care for *la famiglia* are only hurting them …"

"… then correct the problem," Antony finished for his son, "before someone else permanently corrects the problem they believe you are."

"That is easier said than done," Theo replied.

"Perhaps, but as you said, you chose this life," Dante said frankly.

"So?"

Antony waved his arms wide and smiled. "That makes it yours, Theo. Keep it that way."

"I'm a Capo, not a—"

"*La famiglia* has never been about the man holding the highest seat," Dante interrupted. "It is every man, not just one. It is yours. You wanted it. Fight for it."

Theo watched as the late January sun filtered in through the stained-glass windows of the church, sending spirals of colors throughout the floor and pews. This wasn't home, and he'd been in knots about being gone since the moment the plane lifted off the tarmac.

Chicago was calling his name.

So was someone else.

Theo figured it was time to answer.

CHAPTER EIGHTEEN

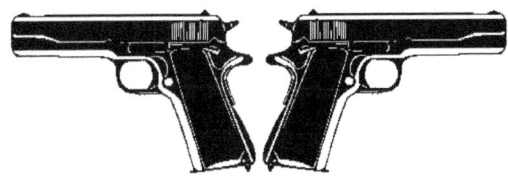

"How is the fish?" Tommas asked.

Evelina swallowed the bite of food in her mouth before saying, "It's good. Better than I thought. I'm not a fan of things with scales and fins mostly."

Tommas laughed. "When you put it that way, I understand."

Dropping her napkin to her lap, Evelina shook off the restless feeling weighing her down. She'd felt like this for weeks with no end in sight.

"Riley must have forgiven you for the guest list mix up, huh?"

Tommas flashed a brief smile. "You could say that."

"How would you say it?"

"You know how your father is, Eve. Do you need me to spell it out?"

"He's paranoid and distrustful," she said quietly.

"And Joel is on another one of his rampages now that he realizes some of the things Riley was doing," Tommas added, shrugging. "Your father's best bet is to keep the one man he believes will help him the most close to him. That, unfortunately, happens to be me. And even I'm not getting very far with Riley at the moment."

"Well, the engagement is still on," Evelina replied bitterly.

"We'll never make it to the aisle, Eve." Tommas cut another chunk off his salmon and stuck a fork in the meat as he said, "And with the belief that Theo is dead, Riley is getting what he wants."

"Blame placed on Joel."

"Exactly, but that doesn't mean he isn't pissed at me for going against his demands. For now, your father is under the belief that the safest spot for you to be is in a non-hostile territory. With Theo assumed dead, your brother has control of that end of Chicago. He has no issue with Damian and Lily having their home there and you will stay with them. Better for you to be out of the danger zone."

Evelina scoffed rudely. "My father never gave a damn about my safety before."

Tommas' expression remained passive. "You are his last hope at the moment, Eve."

"I don't get it."

"Adriano is married off to a Trentini. Riley knows that no matter what he says to his son, Adriano is not going to do something that might hurt his wife or her family regardless of how much he despises Joel."

"So?" Evelina asked.

"So, I made sure Riley was under the impression that should he end the engagement between you and me, that he would lose all and any loyalty he has with me and my crew. He didn't realize how much power he was giving up when he started playing games with me, Eve."

Evelina felt cold all over. "But you don't want to marry me."

"I don't."

"I don't understand."

Why did that feel like the story of her damned life right now?

"I'm correcting my mistakes," Tommas said quietly. "There are only so many ways I can do that and make sure we all come out unscathed."

Evelina didn't need Tommas to explain that one.

"By killing my father," she whispered.

Tommas went back to his salmon like Evelina hadn't said a thing. He didn't confirm or deny her suspicions. Not knowing what to say or do, Evelina took another bite of her own fish.

Riley was her father, for Christ's sake. Why didn't she feel anything for him over this?

In her soul, she knew the truth. She'd grown up with a mother who loved her children, and father who put on a good show. Evelina had always been one of her father's pawns and nothing more. She was simply an advantage for Riley from the day she was born until the time she was old enough that he could use her to make a move.

Evelina was the doll.

Riley moved her how he saw fit.

"He could have been a damn good boss," Tommas murmured, wiping his mouth with a napkin. "He was a good one for a while, but he's run his course."

"Who would be the right fit for the title after he's gone?"

Tommas' hands froze when he moved to cut his fish again. "Whoever wants it bad enough, I suppose."

"Seems like a dangerous job to have, given the lifespan of a boss lately."

"Anything worth keeping is worth the risk and effort it takes to have it."

"Are you talking about being the boss or having Abriella?"

Tommas chuckled. "You're a smart girl, Eve. What do you think?"

"Wouldn't you have to get one to have the other?"

"Yes," Tommas said, "I would."

"Have you spoken to Abriella yet?"

"No." Tommas flicked his napkin to the table with a little more force than he had all through the dinner. "You?"

"No. She won't answer anything from me. Lily tried, too. Nothing."

"Well, I saw her but we didn't talk."

Evelina's brow widened at the suggestive tone Tommas took on. "Excuse me? You just said—"

"I said I didn't talk to Abriella. I never said I hadn't seen her. She showed up at my club last Saturday just after closing. She always did know the hours of when the place cleared." Tommas glanced up, meeting Evelina's stare head-on and unashamed. "Of the people who would recognize her and report back, I mean."

Evelina shifted in her seat. "And?"

"She didn't talk. She wouldn't listen when I tried to explain myself yet again. The night ended the way it usually does between us."

"You had sex."

"Yes. Except it doesn't quite feel the same when the person you love fucks you like they despise you."

Evelina dropped Tommas' stare. "Oh."

"Yes, oh. But she sought me out when she could have found someone else if all she wanted was to fuck out some anger, which means Abriella either doesn't want to, or can't, stay away."

"Is that good or bad?"

Tommas laughed darkly. "It's both. With us, it has always been both."

"You're not going to invite me in, I take it?"

Damian leaned on Tommas' car. "Not tonight. Lily had a long day. I want her to rest."

Evelina let the cousins talk and got out of Tommas' car. The man didn't say goodbye to her, but she didn't exactly mind.

"That," Tommas drawled, "or you're still pissed at me, D."

Damian chuckled lowly and smacked the roof of the car with his hand. "I'm not angry with you, anymore."

"Not at all?"

"I understand, I don't approve," Damian said. "There is a difference."

"Good to know."

Evelina tightened her coat around her frame, ignoring the cold bite of the late January wind as she waited out the men's conversation.

"How is the Joel situation?" Damian asked.

"You know how Joel is. He waits and plans for what he believes is the right moment."

Evelina passed Tommas a look, knowing the truth. Tommas was more concerned about handling Riley than he was Joel. Why wasn't he telling Damian that?

"Joel will find his way into a grave eventually," Damian said.

"I'm sure. And Theo, what about him?"

Damian shrugged. "What about him?"

"Nothing, not a thing. Give me a call, all right?"

"Will do, Tommas."

Once Tommas' car disappeared beyond the gate, Damian turned to Evelina.

"We have a guest," he said with a smile.

"Didn't you just tell Tommas—"

"Yes, I lied about why he couldn't come in. Anyway, our guest is tired, but he wouldn't chill out until you got back. He had a long flight."

Flight?

Evelina's heart practically leapt out of her chest. "Theo?"

"Theo," Damian confirmed.

She was already half way toward the house before Damian started to follow behind. Beyond the dark red door, Evelina kicked off her heels and dropped her bag to the floor. She shrugged off her coat and left it slung over a side table. Following the sounds of Lily's laughter and another deeper, richer voice, Evelina found herself standing in the entryway to the large living room.

Theo was just five feet away with his back turned to her.

"Theo," Evelina said quietly.

He turned slightly, just enough to shoot her a look over his shoulder. His brown gaze fell on her and a sexy grin bloomed over his features, making the sharp lines of his face all the more handsome.

"Hey," Theo said.

Just like that, the knot of anxiety that had been plaguing Evelina for three weeks melted away. She had known he was okay, and that he was safer being out of the city. It hadn't helped her much because she still worried.

Evelina hadn't realized how much she cared for Theo until he was gone.

Dressed in dark-wash jeans slung low around his hips and a gray T-shirt, he seemed relaxed and content. The last time she'd seen him, the tension had practically radiated over him because of what was happening around them. Now, Theo seemed to have reverted back to his cool, unbothered attitude.

For some reason, Evelina couldn't move or look away as Theo took a couple of steps forward. She felt frozen to the floor when he came to stand in front of her with his usual cocky smirk.

"I didn't know you were coming back today," Evelina said.

"None of us did," Lily chimed from the couch. "He surprised us while you were out."

"What changed?" Evelina asked Theo.

Damian walked past the couple to join his wife. "That's what I would like to know, too. We had an agreement, Theo. You were supposed to stay away until we knew it was safe for you to come back. It isn't safe yet. Things are tricky between Riley, Joel, and Tommas."

Theo didn't take his eyes off of Evelina for a second. "Someone gave me a bit of advice that I needed to hear. Coming home was just a part of that."

Evelina's worries couldn't be ignored. What if Riley found out that Theo had come back, and he went after him again?

Theo glanced over his shoulder at Damian. "Dante sends his regards, by the way."

Damian's expression remained passive. "Thanks for passing along the memo."

"Theo," Evelina said, wanting his attention back on her.

She'd missed Theo. He was the only person who seemed to get her. He didn't judge her and he challenged her. Most importantly, he *affected* her. Far more than anyone else ever had.

But as much as she missed him, she would rather he stay away until everything was good and calm again, so he could come back without fear of being someone's target.

Theo's stare cut to Evelina. The intensity of it hit her in the chest like a bullet meeting glass. For a moment, she felt like the most important thing in his space. How he did that, she didn't understand.

"Yes, Eve?"

"What was so important here that you would risk your life again to come back before it was safe?"

Theo didn't even blink. "Everything worth having."

Carefully, Evelina undid the diamond necklace that she'd borrowed from

Lily for her dinner with Tommas. She placed the delicate rope of diamonds into the waiting velvet case on the dresser before doing the same to the studs in her ears. Then, she went about pulling, or trying to pull, most of the pins holding her hair up.

"You were quiet earlier," Theo said from the doorway.

Evelina damn near jumped out of her skin. "Christ, Theo."

Theo stepped into the room, arms crossed and grinning. "What?"

She wrapped her arms around her frame, tightening the thin robe she wore to her body. The bedroom door had been closed. She was sure of it.

"How long were you standing there?"

Theo lifted a single shoulder. "A minute or so."

"You could have knocked."

"I don't think you realize how interesting you are when you're doing simple things, Eve. I enjoy watching you do it."

Evelina glanced down at the floor. "Really?"

"Sure. Especially when you think you're alone."

"I'll remember that for the next time I think I am."

"Do that. What was up with earlier?" he asked.

"Nothing. You surprised me being here. That was all."

"And maybe because people were watching," he suggested.

Evelina laughed and nodded. "That, too."

Theo flashed his white teeth with one of his signature grins. "No one is watching now."

"We're in your sister's home."

"I don't care, Eve."

Theo didn't give her a chance to argue. She hadn't even taken a breath and he was on her. Evelina whined the moment his hands fisted her robe, his lips crashed down on hers, and he pulled her in close to his warm chest. The second his tongue swept her bottom lip, Evelina opened her mouth to allow him in. Theo took the offer she gave him without question, deepening the kiss until her breaths began to stutter and her legs felt weak. He didn't let her go.

When he did finally pull away, Theo rested his forehead to hers and watched her silently. Evelina didn't mind the attention. It never felt like he was searching for something, but rather, like he'd already found it.

Down at her side, Evelina felt the side of Theo's hand graze hers. It was only a brief pause before his pinky finger hooked around hers without him saying a thing.

Intimate.

This felt so intimate to Evelina and she didn't know why.

"What are you doing?" she asked.

"Trying something," Theo replied at the same quiet level.

"Let me in on the secret, okay."

"I realized when I was away that I missed you. And the longer I thought about it all, the more I missed you. It bothered me, because I wondered if I had somehow attached myself to a person who I couldn't have."

"And?"

"And I wanted to see if that's what it was, Eve."

She forced back the tightness in her throat that was threatening to keep her quiet.

"Is it?"

"It's the closest I've ever been to it. I don't mind."

But he had before. She remembered his worries about being selfish, and wanting to keep a safe distance.

"I'm still not asking you for anything, Theo," she whispered.

"No, you're not."

"Don't feel like you have to give me something."

"I don't feel like that at all," he admitted. "I feel like I wanted to come back, fix the problems that have nearly ruined me, and then try to take something from you instead. If you were willing, I mean."

Evelina wet her lips, taking in his words. Just as quick, Theo raised his hand and grazed his thumb over her mouth with the softest touch.

"Are you willing to try?" he asked.

"Don't you already know?"

"I know you care."

"So do you," she said softly.

"I want to try to be something, Eve."

"We can do that."

Theo's pinky tightened around hers. "The rest of the shit happening right now—"

"Stop," Evelina ordered firmly.

"Okay."

"Don't you know?"

"Tell me," he said.

"I would give up everything for a chance at this, Theo. To be free, to have someone who cares for me, and for a life of my own. I haven't asked you for a thing, but I've already taken everything you gave me."

"It wasn't much."

"It was enough."

Theo nodded. "It was, huh?"

"Yeah."

"You had dinner with Tommas earlier," Theo said.

It wasn't even a question.

"Maintaining the idea, Theo."

Theo's cheek ticked. "I don't like it."

Evelina pressed a quick kiss to his mouth. "Don't be jealous."

"That I can't take you out to dinner and be seen with you like a normal man would do?"

Ouch.

"I didn't mean it like that, Theo."

"That's how I meant it."

Evelina pursed her lips. "Then take me out."

"Oh?"

"Yeah. Figure it out. I want a date with you. Soon."

"I'll see what I can do," he murmured. "You're getting ready for bed, I see."

"I was going to jump into the shower, actually."

Theo let her go. Evelina wanted his hands back on her the moment they were gone.

"Go. I've got to chat with Damian some more."

Evelina drew her lip in between her teeth as she asked, "You're coming back, right?"

"I'll be back," he said with a chuckle.

Evelina let the hot spray of the shower head drive down her skin and massage away the worries. Rinsing the last bit of conditioner from her hair, she turned to reach for the tap to shut the water off, and froze mid-way.

Theo stood leaning against the closed bathroom door, watching her. Unlike earlier, he didn't scare her this time. Theo caught her eye and then his lips split with a wicked smirk.

"You're not finished, are you?" she heard him ask.

Behind the glass, his voice was muffled slightly.

"I was," Evelina said.

Theo shook his head. "No, you're not. Not yet."

"What—"

Cocking a brow, Theo flicked open the button on his jeans and quickly pulled the zipper down. Like a fucking statue, Evelina was stuck staring at the man as he lifted his shirt a little as if to give her a better view, and then he freed his cock from his boxer-briefs to his palm.

Silently, Theo stroked his hard length from the tip to the base in sure, firm tugs. Never once did he take his gaze away from Evelina's body. The water continued to pound down on her like a torrent of heavy, hot rain.

An ache pulsed between her thighs. The air in her chest caught painfully hard. The sight of Theo fisting his cock while he watched her was intoxicating.

"You're just going to watch me—"

"While I jerk myself off, yes," Theo interrupted calmly. "Look how fucking hard you made me just by standing there, Eve. It hurts—that's how goddamn hard I am. Like steel. But since you're giving such a good show, I don't want to force you out."

Evelina licked her lips. "I could take care of that, you know."

Theo kept stroking his cock. "You will, babe. Trust me."

Stunned, Evelina could only nod.

"Keep going," Theo ordered.

The demand washed over her senses with a promising intent following right behind. Evelina moved back into the spray of the shower while keeping her head turned just enough that she could enjoy the sight of Theo through the glass. He might have thought she was putting on a good show, but nothing could be better than him tugging on his cock while he got off on her.

Her body was hot all over and getting hotter.

"The hotel," Theo said.

Gruff, deep, and dark. His tone was throaty and it turned her on like nothing else.

"Hmm?"

"Eyes down there, Eve."

Evelina's gaze instantly flew down to Theo's hand and his cock. Not once had he slowed or eased up on his member while he stroked himself. She wondered how much control the man had before he would lose it and paint the tiles with his come.

"What about the hotel?" she asked, breathless and spun.

"I dreamed about it while I was away. You, me, and the bed. Fucking you, being inside you, and just feeling you, Eve. Once the dreams started, I couldn't get them to stop. It was ..."

"Yeah?"

"Distracting and amazing," he finished quieter.

"Over and over?"

"Night after night, Eve." Theo's words melted into a low groan when Evelina turned to face him again. "Let me see that pussy of yours, Eve. I want to see you touching it. I want you to tell me if you're wet and hot down there for me. I want your fingers sliding through your lips and your legs spread wide. Now."

Evelina's back hit the tiled wall of the shower with a thump. Widening her stance and lifting her foot to rest on the ledge of the tub, she drove her hand down over her stomach until her fingers danced over her clit. Just the lightest graze made her body jerk and her shoulders shudder.

Her fingers slid through the lips of her pussy slowly, taking the silky wetness she found there and smearing it up to her clit. With gentle circles, she rolled the tips of her fingers over her throbbing nub until her thighs were shaking and she couldn't catch her breath.

"Tell me what I asked for," Theo said darkly.

"I'm ..."

"Mmm?"

"Wet," she said in a moan. "So wet, Theo, and hot. Oh, my God."

"Inside. I want to see your fingers inside your pussy, Eve. Do it for me, princess. Show me how your fuck yourself when you want it to be me instead."

Evelina swallowed hard, letting her fingers glide down to the entrance of her sex. As she pushed two fingers into her clenching pussy, she watched Theo's strokes begin to pick up in pace, and his grip tightened on his length. Her body felt far too sensitive, like she was right on the cusp of an orgasm that would shatter her totally. The thrusts of her fingers came harder and deeper with each one. She wanted that bliss, and for the heat in her body to burn more.

"Theo," Evelina breathed, "I'm going to come."

"Fuck, that's hot," Theo said, satisfaction coating his every word. "Let me see you come, Eve, and then I'll fucking fill you full of me and make you do it all over again."

He broke her.

Just like that, her control was gone and the orgasm raged. Her cry bounced off the tiled walls and echoed back. It left her a shaking, trembling mess under the spray of the shower while shocks of pleasure and heat stabbed through her body with no end in sight.

Evelina wasn't sure how long she stayed like that, but she felt the shower turn off, and cool air wrapped her sensitive body a second before a towel covered her. Then, strong arms were pulling her out from the space and up into his embrace.

Dazed and high, Evelina closed her eyes and willingly drifted into her thoughts as Theo carried her from the bathroom. He said nothing when he sat her down on something soft and sturdy. Evelina was still flying high in her euphoria while a towel was run over her body until she was dry and hot all over again.

Opening her eyes, Evelina caught sight of Theo tossing the towel to the floor before he was tugging down his jeans and boxer-briefs, and yanking off his shirt. It was only then that Evelina realized Theo had set her in the window bench seat. It was high enough that he didn't have to bend down to fuck her, she realized.

He just had to spread her legs and ...

Jesus.

Evelina's head fell back and hit the curtained covered glass with a gentle thump.

"Look at me," she heard Theo order.

Evelina did as he asked. "You promised me something, Theo."

"I'm working on it. Show me your pussy. Open up those legs of yours and let me see what belongs to me, babe."

The heels of her feet rested on the edge of the ledge and her legs opened wide for him. Naked and out of breath, with her hair mussed and drenched, she was sure she looked like a damned mess. Theo looked at her like she was fucking gorgeous.

"How long are you going to stare at me, Theo?"

"A man is supposed to appreciate his beautiful things."

His. The word hit her straight in the heart, taking away her air.

"Do you want me to fuck you?" Theo asked.

"Yes."

Theo cocked a brow. "What was that?"

Evelina grinned slyly. "*Please*, Theo."

"A man wants what he wants, Eve."

"Then please take it before I switch to manual again."

"Don't. You. Fucking. Dare."

Each word had been growled out. Theo punctuated them with quick, confident strides until he was pressed between her thighs, and his rock-hard cock rested against her stomach. Evelina shivered when his fingers bit into her thighs and his dick twitched.

"Don't you fucking dare," he repeated in a rumble. His free hand wrapped up in her hair and tugged, forcing her head back so he could stare down at her. "I have thought about getting between your legs every single day for the last three weeks."

God.

Evelina ached for this man. "Every day?"

"Jesus, *yes*," Theo whispered.

The softness of his voice took her off guard.

Evelina blinked up at him, feeling his fingers loosen in her hair. "Theo?"

"So mine."

His finger trailed down along her cheekbone to her chin and then under her throat. She felt his hand grab her there with the lightest pressure, tilting her head back further. Evelina sighed at the promise of his roughness, loving how this man had never treated her like a china doll or the proper princess like everyone else seemed to do. He handled her as if she was precious, like a rare diamond, but he didn't touch her like she was breakable.

Evelina didn't want to be anyone's princess. But she would be anything for this man. The heavy realization cut through her soul in one fell swoop.

"Ask me for it, Eve."

"Fuck me, Theo."

"Just me," Theo murmured.

"Always you."

He couldn't possibly know how true those words were.

Evelina felt his hand spread her thighs wider, the sting of his fingers digging into her flesh, and then his cock filled her in one swift, hard flex of his hips. Tension fell from her body in waves as her air rushed out of her lungs in a long moan. Just as fast, he was pulling out before he slammed right back in.

There was no break for Evelina between Theo's thrusts. She barely managed to get a grip on the ledge with her hands as he spread her legs even more until her damn thighs ached. His muscles clenched and shuddered as he fucked her. Gritted teeth and fiery dark eyes watched her as his mouth came close enough to hers that their lips grazed with every exhale.

He was brutal—so relentless.

The rough pace with his hand at her throat and his mouth on hers while he fucked her raw on the bench seat made her delirious. She couldn't breathe. Her senses went on overdrive.

But goddamn, it was so good.

So, so good.

CHAPTER NINETEEN

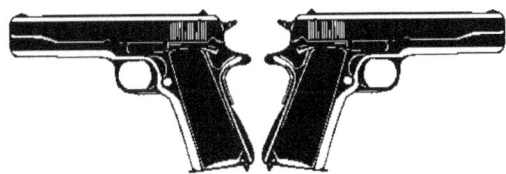

Theo smiled at the sound of Evelina's pleased but tired hum. It sounded entirely like happiness and contentment. He didn't know that it was possible for him to do that for someone else. Draped over his body on the bed, Evelina rested her cheek to the spot over his heart, and didn't move. She hadn't for the last hour, anyway.

Tracing loopy pathways on her shoulder with the tip of his finger, Theo felt the shivers roll over Evelina's frame.

"You should sleep," he said.

Evelina shrugged. "I should, but this is good, too."

He had to agree.

Leaning up, Evelina reached over, making her body wiggle over Theo's in the best way, and flicked on the bedside lamp.

"That's better," she said softly. "Right?"

"I hadn't really noticed, but I do prefer the light."

"Lily gave you the other spare room, didn't she?"

Theo nodded. "I'll stay in here. That used to be Dino's room."

"But you don't like to share—"

"I like this," Theo said pointedly, running his hand down her back to her ass. "I like this a lot, Eve."

She sunk back down into his embrace. "Okay. What are you going to do about my father?"

"Something. Or maybe someone else will do it."

"You don't like him, do you?"

"No," Theo confessed, "and I haven't for a long time."

"Because he treated you like your uncle did."

Theo stiffened at the very mention of his childhood and teenaged years of abuse. "Once or twice I had incidents with Riley."

"One that almost left you dead," she whispered.

"I prefer to leave those things in the past, Eve."

"But I don't think they are, Theo. I don't think it's something that you can ever leave behind."

"It's better than feeding the monsters," he replied.

"I wondered …"

"About what?"

"Your wrist," she said simply.

"Ben broke it once with a metal pole. Then I spent a couple of days in the trunk of a car as a punishment for trying to help Dino when Ben was beating the hell out of him." Theo cleared his throat, uncomfortable with the way Evelina had gone completely silent. "By the time Ben figured he should take me to the hospital, my wrist was the double the normal size and the bones were already trying to fuse back together in some spots. They had to re-break and set it for a cast. The doctor offered to put me out for it because I was just a kid—fourteen."

"Did they put you out for it?"

"No, Ben wouldn't sign the waver for the anesthesia."

Evelina frowned, but quickly hid it from his view. "I'm sorry."

"Don't be. It wasn't your fault. It was what it was."

"But people knew, Theo. Didn't they?"

"Lots did," he said.

"No one stepped in or did anything to help you."

"Dino did, Eve."

"Wasn't he being treated the same way?"

"Until he had enough control of his own to step out from under Ben, yes he was given the same treatment as me," Theo explained. "But for a long time, Dino kept Ben's attention on him and his faults instead of me and mine. But it was inevitable that it would turn on me the more defiant and rebellious Dino became as an adult in his own life. I blamed my brother. I hated him. I didn't realize how wrong I was about my brother until it was too late."

"Wrong about what?" she asked.

"I thought he was weak. He was far stronger than I gave him credit for."

Evelina wrapped her arm around his side. "Thank you for telling me some of this."

"There's something else," Theo said, knowing she deserved to know.

"Hmm?"

"Look at me."

Evelina shifted on his chest so she could rest her chin in her palm. "What, Theo?"

He'd talked to Damian again. He knew what Dino had done, how he'd started this war between the families, and how it unraveled far too fast for anyone to fix.

"I know who killed your mother," Theo said.

Evelina flinched away from him. He could practically feel the pain radiating off her in waves. Wounds like those never healed, not completely. They were always sore to the touch and raw on the inside.

"I don't want to know," Evelina said quickly.

"I need you to know, Eve."

"But—"

"Please," Theo murmured, "listen to me."

Evelina sucked her lower lip in between her teeth. "Okay."

"In his effort to protect his family when he knew he wouldn't be able to do it anymore, Dino went after the people he thought might hurt those he cared about. People like Ben and Terrance."

"And my father."

Theo nodded once. "I imagine he would have went after Riley if given the chance."

Evelina made a heartbroken sound that cut him to the core. Tears welled in her eyes and threatened to fall. Theo swept his thumbs under her lashes to wipe the wetness away. "My mom, though? Why my mom?"

"All I know is that it was a mistake. He hadn't meant for Mia to get caught in the crossfire. He hadn't even meant for anyone to be hurt when he shot into the restaurant. He intended for some issues to be stirred up, and nothing more. I didn't know the extent of everything until recently. It was a mistake."

"A mistake that cost me my mother, Theo."

"I know. I'm sorry, Eve."

He expected her to ask him to leave. He thought maybe she would break the intimate closeness they shared. She surprised him. Evelina usually did where he was concerned.

"Thank you for telling me the truth."

"I don't want to lie to you, Eve."

"Can we sleep now?" she asked.

He'd give her whatever she wanted. Or try, anyway.

Theo went back to tracing pathways on her naked shoulder. "Sleep, babe."

"I don't like this," Theo muttered.

Two days being home in Chicago, and Theo had no idea what he was going to do yet about his problems.

Damian glanced up from the papers on his desk. The man never seemed to stop working. How he found time to keep an eye on his wife, run his crew, and handle all his other business, Theo didn't know.

"What are you going on about?" his friend asked.

"Eve. I don't like it."

Damian cocked a brow. "She has to keep up appearances, Theo. That means going with Tommas for dinners when her father demands their presence. Especially now that Riley is trying to strengthen the ally he has in Tommas while planning to take out Joel. And just the fact that we all know he's pissed off and doesn't trust Tommas, yet he's willing to attempt to play nice with him shows just how desperate Riley really is. Then, there's the little issue about you, too."

Theo rolled his eyes. "I know, I'm supposed to be dead."

"That isn't going to fly forever. The M.E. is backed up to their eyeballs and your *body* is still chilling somewhere on a slab."

"Oh?"

"Yeah, but the moment they try to make a positive ID with dental records, it won't fly."

"Three weeks seems a bit long for them to be waiting to do that, D."

Damian smirked. "Tommas called in a favor or two."

Theo lifted a brow. "Seriously?"

"You'd be surprised who Tommas has rubbed elbows with. I know you don't trust him a whole lot right now, but give him some credit. He is helping us however he can."

"You're right, I don't trust him."

"I get it," Damian said.

"And I don't like Evelina being out with him."

"The green monster on your shoulder is roaring, Theo."

Theo glared. "Go to hell."

"He has no interest in Eve."

"I am aware of where Tommas' *interests* are, asshole," Theo spat.

Damian sighed heavily. "What is your fucking problem?"

"It's not him, D. It's her father and the fact we both know that Riley is unstable on his best days. He hides it well, but that man is insane when pushed the right way. I don't like her being around him right now."

"Tommas will watch out for Eve. He wants her to have whatever will make her happy. He decided on that the moment he knew you cared for her, Theo. Give the man a chance."

Theo glanced away. "You're asking for a lot."

"I know."

Damian went back to his papers without another word. Theo walked over to the window that overlooked the large driveway leading down to the gates.

"Does it feel weird for you to live here?" Theo asked.

The chair squeaked from across the room, letting Theo know his old friend was watching him.

"No," Damian said. "Despite how heartbroken Lily was at first, she's really come to love this house. She wants to change some things, and she's already redecorated a few rooms to her own taste. She's made it home for us, which keeps me from thinking about it as Dino's home."

"I guess."

"What, Theo?"

"Dino bought this house three years ago. I remember when he bought it because at the time, it seemed like a ridiculous expense for him to go out and purchase a house this size with all the land and everything."

"It is if you consider he was a bachelor with no family."

Theo frowned at his reflection in the glass. "But he wasn't. And if I think about the dates when he purchased this house, it was right around the time when his son was born. Maybe he wanted to raise that boy, but someone kept him from being a hands-on father. Someone like Ben. Dino would have made a good father, I think."

"He would have," Damian agreed. "On another topic, Riley is throwing a party at his bar for Courtney in a week."

"Oh?"

"When Tommas was here earlier, he mentioned that it might be time to start feeding the snakes."

Theo chewed over those words. "How so?"

"Maybe we should let the ID go through that it wasn't you in that car. Get Riley nervous and see how it goes. Plus, Lily would really be appreciative if she could quit acting like she's grieving over you. She's had to plan a fake funeral, or do the best she can, and it's not good for her, not right now."

"I get that," Theo said. "What does that have to do with this upcoming party for his wife?"

"For once, maybe I don't have to be the ghost, you can."

Theo chuckled dryly. "What, like rising from the fucking dead?"

"It would certainly be a shocker. And another thing, doesn't it interest you at all to think that maybe Joel had planted Chloe Belli in Riley's bed as a way to get info?"

"I've considered it."

"Have you considered that Riley's new wife used to be good friends with Chloe?" Damian asked quietly.

Theo turned fast on his heel. "Was she?"

"They were. Women like those tend to stick together. From what I gathered, Courtney plays a good show, but she's not to be trusted at all. She's not as innocent as she looks."

"Are you saying his wife is playing him, too?" Theo asked.

Damian shrugged. "I think we should be careful where Courtney is concerned if she's close to anyone who is close to Joel."

"But Chloe's brother and Riley … Tommas said Riley was going after me that night."

"He was. Maybe Chloe got her brother close to Riley to keep her place looking less suspicious. Who knows? That's not important."

Damian was right. Theo dropped it.

Turning back to the window, Theo's eye caught Damian's blue Porsche. The windows were tinted so dark, it was impossible to see inside even through the front windshield.

"Your car is illegal with that tint."

"I know," Damian said, a smile in his voice.

"And safe for me to drive. I want to borrow your car."

"Why?"

"I owe Eve a date."

Theo leaned against the hood of the Porsche as Evelina was shoved out the door by Lily. Just as fast, the front door slammed. He couldn't help the grin forming when he watched Evelina stomp her booted heeled foot like she was pissed.

He always had a thing for angry women in heels. Evelina wore the look well.

"What the—" Evelina's words cut off the moment her stare landed on Theo. "Oh."

Fixing the leather jacket he wore, Theo asked, "Oh, is that all you've got for me?"

"Well …"

"Hmm?"

Evelina smiled widely. "Lily wouldn't tell me why I had to wear this," Evelina said, waving at the tight, black dress under her beige trench coat. "She wouldn't tell me where you were or what was going on. What is going on, Theo?"

"A date. Wasn't that what you wanted?"

"Yes."

Theo pushed off the car. "You need the dress because we're attending a show inside a venue that has a suit and dress policy for their patrons."

Evelina smiled. "That sounds nice."

"And after, there's a little place over on Lincoln Avenue in Lincoln

Park that I think you might like. I've been going there for years but never with someone. It's a favorite spot of mine."

She took the steps carefully and slowly in her heels. The slushy, slippery snow could be dangerous with those boots she had on.

"And it's okay for you to be out on the town tonight?" Evelina asked.

Theo held out his hand and she took it instantly. "We'll be careful."

"You don't know how to be careful, Theo."

"I do know how, thank you," he said with a wink. "But tonight isn't about me, anyway. It's about you, Eve. Stop your worrying and have some fun with me."

"What kind of show?" Evelina asked.

Theo tugged her into his side. "That one is actually for me, sort of."

"Is that so?"

"A private booth, ballet, the dark, and you? Oh, yeah, that's all for me."

Evelina cocked a brow and poked him in the chest. "Isn't that the date I cancelled on you months ago?"

"New ballet," he said. "*Swan Lake* is being performed this month. I hear it's quite a production."

"I've never seen it."

"I have and it was amazing."

Evelina eyed him curiously. "Do you have a thing for ballet?"

"And opera," Theo admitted.

"I wouldn't take you for the type."

"What, cultured and gentlemanly? Mostly, I just want to get you in a private booth, and get you liquored up on cocktails. We'll see where it goes from there."

"You are awful."

Theo laughed as he pulled Evelina toward the passenger side of the car. "I'm aware."

"I've seen this place before, just driving by," Evelina said. "It's a bar, right?"

"It's more than just a bar, it's an experience, Eve."

Her laughter coated him like sweet honey.

"Show me, then."

"Gladly."

Theo intertwined their fingers together as he pushed open the front doors of the Barrelhouse Flat. Instantly, the atmosphere of the bar and restaurant surrounded Theo with comfort. The place had an old fashioned feel with a modern sentiment lingering around the edges. Leather chairs lined the walls with small tables in between. The placement forced the patrons to be close while sitting and drinking, or to lean over when people wanted to talk. Artwork lined the walls and pool tables with gorgeous woodwork rested along the right wing of the place.

"Pick a spot," Theo told Evelina. "What do you want to drink?"

"Surprise me."

Theo could have waited for a server to come to them, but he went straight to the bar. Once his drink orders were filled and in hand, he found Evelina in the far back corner, sitting in one of the butternut-colored leather chairs. She'd slung her coat around the arm of the chair and he had to admit, she looked at home and comfortable in the place.

Legs crossed, a smile playing on her lips, and with curious eyes watching him as he handed over her drink, Evelina seemed happy.

It wasn't much.

It wasn't a big thing.

Theo had needed to be terribly careful about where they went and what they did on this night out of theirs. He'd hated that he couldn't take her to a dozen other spots that would have shown her off more, or that he couldn't take her out and let her dance, but this was just as good.

Private. Intimate.

Sexy, given the way Evelina looked in her black dress and high boots. The flash of her thighs as she fixed her crossed legs made his mouth go dry.

Evelina took a sip of the drink, a curiosity lighting up her green eyes. "What is this?"

"*Madness Most Discreet*," Theo said.

"It's ... different."

"It is."

Evelina took another drink. "I like it."

"I thought you would."

"And the name," she added with a wink. "I like that, too."

Theo chuckled and lifted his own glass. "I always thought the name of a drink could sum up someone far better than anything else ever could."

Evelina leaned over in her seat and reached out to hook a finger into the collar of Theo's shirt. She pulled lightly, silently asking him to come closer. When he did, she pressed her painted red lips to his in a soft kiss. The slowness of their lips moving together soothed Theo as her thumb swept his jawline.

"You're drawing attention," Theo murmured against her lips.

"So?"

"Please, continue. I don't mind people knowing that you're happy right where you are … with me."

"Thank you for bringing me here," Evelina said softly.

"You deserve some quiet, peaceful time, babe."

"The calm before the storm, huh?"

Theo forced back his frown. "Something like that."

Evelina glanced over at the pool tables. "Will you teach me how to play?"

"I'm not sure you want to learn from a hustler, Eve. I may know how to play the game, but that doesn't mean I'll teach you anything worth learning except how to be a damned shark."

"I'm good with that."

Theo laughed. "Of course you are."

He tipped his drink up for a sip.

"What is that called?" she asked.

Theo extended the glass. "Take a taste."

Evelina reached over and dipped the tip of her pinky into his drink before sticking it into her mouth. Theo was pretty sure she did that on purpose, because he loved to watch her suck on things, especially his cock. But just the way her face screwed up said she didn't like the taste.

"Meh," Evelina muttered before she lifted her own glass and downed a good gulp. "It's okay."

"I like it."

"What it is?" she asked again.

Theo grinned. "A *Kingslayer*."

The next week passed Theo by slowly. It wasn't any wonder, considering he couldn't do a goddamn thing without taking the risk of someone seeing him. The last thing he wanted to do was bring any attention or danger to his sister and Damian. Having Evelina at the DeLuca home to keep Theo's attention occupied helped a great deal.

Leaning his back to the cold brick wall, Theo ignored the chill of the early February cold. The ground, covered in a light dusting of crusty snow, crunched under his leather shoes as he shifted to a more comfortable position.

He'd been waiting for a call for an hour. Theo was starting to think Damian had either forgotten about him being out back, or the Ghost had decided to call it quits on their plans before they could even get started.

Taking a long drag off his cigarette to finish it, Theo exhaled the thick cloud of smoke, and then tossed the butt to the ground before stubbing it. He should be nervous about what he was going to do, but he didn't really feel a thing.

Nothing.

Theo figured that, in a way, he was just finishing out the business Dino hadn't been able to do himself. Clearing out the snakes.

It was a little more than that for Theo, too. Evelina, for one. But he decided to keep those thoughts and feelings to himself until it was safer and she was free to do what she wished, with whom she wished. The only way to make that happen was to remove the man who kept her from being happy.

Riley.

Revenge was supposed to feel cold and low. Theo only felt high.

The click of the exit door just feet away had Theo moving fast. He was nearly around the side of the building when a soft, sweet voice stopped him.

"Damian said I would find you out here," Evelina said.

Theo glanced over his shoulder, finding his lover peeking her head out the back door. "He's supposed to call me."

"He can't, I guess. There's too many people and he doesn't want to take the risk of someone overhearing the conversation. So, he got Lily to pass along a message to me. I excused myself to the little girl's room and here I am to let you in."

Made sense, Theo thought.

He spun on his heel to face Evelina. She stepped out of the bar and let the door close, but still held the edge so it wouldn't lock them out.

"You do know why I'm here, right?"

Theo had tried not to hide his plans from Evelina, but he didn't go into great detail. Nonetheless, he figured the outcome of the night was obvious.

"You're here to end some unfinished business," Evelina replied quietly.

"Is that what you want to call this?"

"The Outfit is full of scars and secrets, Theo."

"It is," he agreed.

"I'm starting to wonder how much of that my father did." Before Theo could say a thing, Evelina added, "Not just with this war between the families, but even before that. To my mother, to his own kids, to you … sometimes a king just has to fall."

"He's still your father."

"I would rather have the memory of a good man than the delusion of a living one."

"I didn't expect you to say something like that," Theo said.

"You're that guy and I'm that girl, remember?"

Theo did.

He was the guy who used her to get what he wanted. She was the girl who let him do it to get what she wanted.

It was kind of perfect, really. Once this was all over, Theo was pretty damned sure he would be that guy who gave that girl whatever she wanted for the rest of her life, as long as he got to see her smile.

She had a beautiful smile.

"Is Courtney having a good birthday party in there?" he asked.

Evelina smirked. "Soaking up the attention, like usual."

"And your father?"

"He seems off."

"He should be off his game. Didn't you hear?" Theo winked. "The DeLuca *principe* wasn't the one dead and burned beyond recognition in the Stingray, or so the news reports say. No one knows where he is, though."

"I do."

Evelina opened up the back door wide for Theo to enter. He kissed her on the way by. The gun at his back, resting in the waistband of his slacks, wouldn't let him forget what he was there to do. The door clicked shut behind them, shrouding the couple in the darkness of the back hallway.

"Were you checked at the door for weapons?" Theo asked.

"Riley had everyone checked except him and Courtney."

"Did he have a gun on him?"

"He has no jacket on and I didn't see one when I talked to him."

"What about his enforcers?" he asked.

Evelina frowned. "I don't know."

It was a risk Theo would have to take.

"There was something else that Damian wanted you to know," Evelina added.

"What was it?"

"Joel showed up. Abriella came, too. Even the Trentini family showed up. Peter and Sara, I mean."

Theo cussed. "Riley didn't turn them away?"

"Apparently, he invited them last minute."

"Why?"

"Why else, Theo? My father is insane, and he still thinks he is the one controlling the games. That includes Joel."

"I think the better question is why did Joel agree to an invitation knowing how Riley feels about him?"

Evelina didn't have an answer.

Neither did Theo.

Theo stayed hidden in the shadows of the hallway at the back of the large bar. As far as he could see, the dark corridor wasn't used for anything except a back exit. No one had even come close to his hidden spot. He had the perfect view of everyone else, though.

It damn near killed him inside to let Evelina walk back out onto the floor and join the people. Something was nagging at his middle, making him want to keep her safe and hidden in the hallway while he did what needed to be done.

Shaking off the unnerving feeling, Theo found the most important people in the crowd of guests. He wanted to make sure he knew where everyone was, and to keep them constantly in his sights so that no mistakes would happen.

Damian and Lily sat at a booth at the far end of the bar. With his arm slung around Lily's shoulder, Damian chatted with his cousin, Tommas, beside him. Evelina stood beside the booth, but she was looking over her shoulder in Theo's general direction. A few booths down, Theo found Adriano sitting with his new wife. Alessa's hand rested on her rounded midsection as she watched her sister from across the room. Following Alessa's gaze, Theo found Abriella and Joel. One watched a man on one side of the bar while the other watched another man. Riley chatted with the bartender at the bar while his wife stood, pretty and quiet, at his side.

The bar held at least sixty to seventy guests.

The more people moved, danced, and talked, the more concerned Theo got. It was hard to keep track of where everyone was when it seemed like the floor was a sea of moving bodies dressed up to the nines and getting louder by the second.

When the lights dimmed more than they already were and the music turned down a few notches, Theo stepped further back into the hallway. Sparklers were handed out to the people by the servers as Riley led his young wife to the middle of the floor.

Waving a hand high, Riley said, "Tonight, we put aside our differences to celebrate the life of a beautiful woman. Happy birthday, my dear."

People began to light their sparklers. It was distracting and bright, but Theo kept his gaze trained on the man in the middle of the room. When

Riley pulled his wife in for a kiss, the lights went out and all that could be seen were the shapes of people and the sparks from the sparklers lighting up the ceiling as people held them high.

Clapping thundered in the room, making a volcano of noise. Happy birthday rang out from several voices as people started to sing for Courtney. Theo hadn't taken his eyes off where he was supposed to go, or rather, where Riley had stopped to stand with his wife.

Theo moved out of the safety that the dark hallway had provided him and moved forward as quietly and fast as he could. He weaved in and out of people who sang with their sparklers held high. No one seemed to even notice someone pushing through them.

Soon, Theo could hear Riley's voice over everyone else's.

"Happy birthday, sweetheart," Riley said.

Courtney's laughter rang out two feet in front of Theo.

Another couple of steps …

He drew the gun out, clicked off the safety, and cocked the hammer. Pulling the eight inch long silencer from his pocket, Theo screwed the device into the barrel of his gun. He wanted to make this fast and the darkness allowed him to make an easy getaway without being seen.

It was dirty as fuck, but it would be clean.

"It's so pretty," Courtney said.

"They're almost burned out, I think," Riley replied.

Theo was behind the man in a second. It almost seemed like the crowd had crushed in on them, surrounding him. Maneuvering around another person, Theo found himself directly behind Riley and Courtney.

"Riley," Theo said.

It was just loud enough for the boss to hear.

Riley turned fast on his heel. No doubt, he recognized Theo's voice. He'd probably been waiting for Theo to show, but not like this. Not tonight. Someone grabbed Courtney's arm and pulled her, drawing her into the crowd and away from her husband. Theo didn't know who it was.

Even in the darkness, Theo could see Riley's gaze widen with fear.

"Don't play with snakes," Theo said. "You always end up with a bite."

Theo's gun met Riley's forehead and he pulled the trigger. Above the clapping and the singing, the shot barely made a sound. Riley was dead before he even hit the floor. Theo was already half way back toward the hallway when the screams started.

He heard the feet hit the floor hard as people moved and rushed. Lights were turned on and the cries turned desperate and loud. Through the sea of people, no one seemed to take notice of him. People shoved and shouted, trying to make it to the doors. Several rushed right past Theo, intent on making it to the back door. Not one looked him in the face to realize who they were passing.

Suddenly, a presence was beside him. A familiar one.

"There you are," Damian said. "Give me it and I'll get it out of here."

Theo knew what his old friend was asking for. He handed the gun over. Damian had black gloves on and a rag in his other hand. The man wiped down the weapon quickly before he held it out behind his back.

Confused, Theo watched as Tommas Rossi strolled past Damian with another wave of guests, grabbed the gun, and kept on going without even looking back.

"Where is Evelina?" Theo asked.

Damian jerked his thumb toward the corner where they had been sitting. "With Lily. I told them to stay put when the lights went out, no matter what, and I left the table."

Theo looked. Evelina was not beside a frightened Lily. He couldn't find Evelina. The more he looked, the heavier his stomach felt.

"Shit," Damian growled, realizing the same thing Theo had. He pointed in two different directions. "You go that way, I'll go this way."

Theo couldn't leave the goddamn bar until he knew where Evelina was. He shoved his way back into the stampede of people and made a beeline for the direction he knew Evelina had been before the lights went out.

"It was *him*!"

"You asked me for an ally," Evelina cried.

Her shout echoed from somewhere to his left. Theo cut in that direction and saw Evelina backed into a corner. Courtney stood only a couple of feet away with a gun in her hand and the weapon pointed right at Evelina.

Theo's heart stopped.

"You asked me for an ally," Evelina repeated. "That's all I was trying to do, that's why I pulled you away, Courtney."

"You knew," Courtney hissed. "You knew what was going to happen tonight!"

Evelina's gaze darted around, and landed on Theo. He could see the terror and pleas that were right on the tip of her tongue. And he had no fucking gun.

"I just thought ... I thought—"

"That I would want to go back like I was before?" Courtney asked, spitting the words. "To being a whore and nothing else? Move on to the next man that will keep me? Was that it?"

"No," Evelina said, shaking her head.

Theo had moved a few steps closer. Another few and he could hit the bitch from behind. Evelina looked over Courtney's shoulder again at him.

Wrong move.

Theo knew it instantly.

Courtney turned on her heel to face Theo, her gun dropping slightly to her side.

"Run, Eve!" Theo shouted.

Evelina bolted to the side and Theo lurched toward Courtney. The bitch barely got out of the way. He was just a couple of feet in front of Courtney but off to the side. It gave her the perfect aim to shoot at Evelina. Out of the corner of his eye, he saw two things. Evelina shot a fleeting look over her shoulder at him, and Courtney pointed the gun at Evelina.

Theo moved faster than he thought was possible. Gunshots echoed one after the other. He felt all three bullets when they hit his back. Pain sliced through his nervous system. Theo turned slightly at the force of the bullets entering his body, making him fall on his side when he hit the floor.

Theo choked on something rusty, unable to get a proper breath. His hands slid on the floor when he tried to right himself. He glanced around, trying to find Evelina again. Instead, he watched as someone grabbed a screaming, fighting Courtney, disarmed her, and pulled her away.

Soft, familiar hands fluttered over Theo's hair, down his face, and to his jaw.

"Oh, my God," Evelina mumbled.

Theo couldn't talk. He tried, but that rusty, metallic taste just got worse.

Evelina cried above him.

Don't do that, he wanted to tell her.

He'd be okay.

He just needed to breathe.

CHAPTER TWENTY

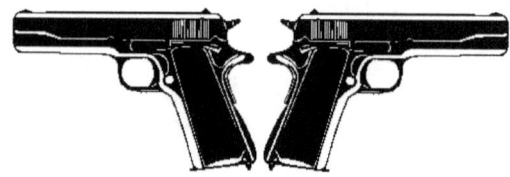

"**M**ove," Evelina heard growled at her.

A hard shove tossed her backwards from Theo.

She fought to get back. She fought hard. She wanted to hold him, to make it stop. The blood kept coming. Her white dress was stained a morbid crimson and it soaked right through to her skin. Evelina didn't care.

She just wanted to hold him.

"Let me go!" she cried.

"Eve, stop it," Adriano hissed in her ear.

Instinct drove her closer. It made her kick her brother and hit him with her fist. The desire to be closer to the man on the ground, the one who was dying for her, thrummed hard and fast in her bloodstream.

The tears streaked down her face. She couldn't wipe them away quickly enough. The coppery taste of Theo's blood on her lips made her sick to her stomach but she ignored the urge to wipe his blood away.

Adriano's grip around Evelina's waist tightened. "Stop fighting me."

Why did he keep pulling her away?

Theo's face was ashy, his lips were slack. His eyes were open but vacantness filled them. So fucking vacant. Theo gave no response. He'd stopped trying to speak, but blood still trickled from his mouth. While Damian worked on Theo, Evelina tried to comprehend how much time had passed. A minute, maybe a little more.

He couldn't be dead.

Someone had called the ambulance a few minutes earlier for Riley. She wondered if they'd make it here in time for the person who really needed it.

She barely recognized the body of her father a few feet away or the rushed movements of people as they fled the club. She didn't know where Courtney had gone, except that Joel had dragged the woman away. Evelina was far too focused on Theo.

Tommas joined his cousin on the floor, and he and Damian worked on Theo. One man pumped Theo's chest while the other forced his head back and pushed air into his lungs.

"Fuck, come on, Theo," Damian mumbled. "Please don't do this to me, man. Don't do this to Lily. Please don't do this to her."

Evelina couldn't breathe.

Apparently, neither could Theo.

"Why isn't he breathing?" Evelina demanded. "Make him breathe!"

"Get her out of here!" Damian roared.

It was only then that the background noise began to bleed through Evelina's shocked senses. Lily's screams, heartbroken and terrified, echoed above the catacomb of noise from everyone else in the club.

There was blood on the floor. Evelina's heels slipped in it as Adriano dragged her closer to the front door. It was hard to get out with all the people. Evelina felt sluggish, slow, and frozen. Her heart ached.

Cold February wind whipped around Evelina. Her coat and purse were somewhere inside. She didn't even care. The temperature barely registered. Red and white lights pulsed around Evelina. Sirens blared.

"You can't leave," a man said from behind them.

The cops had arrived. How had they gotten there already?

Adriano didn't turn around. "Fuck."

"You can't leave until you've been questioned!"

Evelina was going to be sick.

"Adriano …"

Blank.

Stunned.

Barely there.

Evelina couldn't feel a thing but the rolling sensation in her stomach, and her brother's fingers digging into her arm to keep her upright.

"Theo," Evelina said to Adriano.

"Be quiet, Eve," Adriano murmured as a man stood in front of them with an item held out.

A badge.

A cop.

Where had that man come from? How long had it taken them to get out of the club? She'd just wanted to help Courtney. She thought the girl would appreciate being away from the mess that was about to happen to her husband.

Why had she turned like that on Evelina?

Evelina blinked away her hazy vision. The cop spoke to Adriano. Evelina didn't hear a thing. She saw the man's lips move, but his words were lost to her.

"She is covered in blood," the man snapped.

"She saw nothing!" Adriano barked back.

"Miss—"

Automatic reaction forced Evelina to speak.

Nothing more.

"I saw nothing," Evelina whispered. "I slipped running out. That's all."

The cop kept arguing.

Evelina tuned him out.

She was too busy watching the man being wheeled out on the stretcher. A paramedic was on top of him, his hands beating hard into his chest. Another paramedic helped to push the stretcher.

Theo.

Theo ... Theo ... *Theo.*

People flooded out of the club again, making Evelina lose sight of Theo and the paramedics. The crowd wouldn't thin.

Evelina wavered. She swayed on her feet.

"I can't get it," she heard the paramedic say. "I can't get a beat. The bleeding won't staunch. Get the oxygen, he isn't breathing!"

Evelina didn't even feel the ground when she hit it.

But every single piece of her heart did.

"I have news."

Evelina looked up from her hands still stained red. Alessa had tried to help her clean them. Adriano had tried to help. The most Evelina managed to do was get out of her bloody dress and put on something suitable.

Even breathing felt wrong.

"What?" Evelina asked, her voice a raspy croak.

How long had it been since she spoke?

Hours.

So many hours.

"He's critical, but he's alive," Adriano said.

Evelina felt Alessa's hand rub her back soothingly. It did very little to help calm the raging torrent of grief pounding at Evelina's heart and soul.

"Alive."

"Theo got through the first surgery, Eve," Adriano explained.

"The first?"

"He was too unstable to begin the second this morning."

Morning?

Evelina glanced out the window, noting the early morning light. "Oh."

"They got the bullet out of his heart, but he's got two lodged in his lung and it's taking a toll."

"But he's alive."

Adriano nodded.

His unspoken words were louder: *barely alive.*

"Can I go to the hospital?" Evelina asked. "I want to go."

"You need to stay away. Just until this calms down. Until we bury Dad, maybe."

Riley ...

"I don't care about Riley," Evelina spat.

"Me, either, Eve. We still have to play a part."

Evelina's chest hurt. She rubbed at the spot over her heart. "I want to go to Theo."

"Soon," her brother promised. "You could have told me about you and Theo."

"You told me not to tell."

Adriano's expression didn't change. "I didn't want to refuse you something and hurt you."

"Dad did that enough."

"Yeah." Adriano sighed heavily. "What do you need, Eve?"

"Theo."

"I—"

"Can't," Evelina interrupted before her brother could get out another word. "That's all I have ever heard my whole life. *I can't. You won't. No, Eve. Don't, Eve.* Give me something. I want my own life, Adriano."

Adriano passed his quiet wife an indecipherable look. Alessa just kept rubbing Evelina's back, silent and strong. Alessa had always been that way. Right then, Evelina appreciated it more than she could explain.

"I will," Adriano said finally. "But I need you to put on your mask one last time and bury Dad with me, Eve. Do this one thing for me and I will give you whatever you want after this. To the officials, we have to be the innocent, grieving bystanders. Do this for me, and I will do anything for you."

Evelina choked on her agreement. She didn't want to be the Conti princess ever again. She let the word out anyway.

"Okay. But I see Theo right after. *Right after*, Adriano."

Adriano's façade cracked as his eyes glazed.

"Okay, Eve. I had some other news, too, but I didn't know if you would care."

"What?"

"Joel put out word that Courtney is dead. Nothing else."

"Do you believe him or do you think he's lying?"

Courtney had been friends with Chloe, after all.

"I'd say it's the truth," Adriano said.

"Why?"

"Because he left her body on Dad's front steps."

Evelina felt sick all over again.

"There's someone guarding his room," Adriano said.

Evelina's restlessness wouldn't settle. It was the uncomfortable heaviness in her stomach and the emptiness in her heart. She fidgeted with anything she could hold in her hands just to keep her mind from straying. Even while listening to her brother, she still felt like she had to get up and physically go somewhere else. Or rather, go to someone else.

Theo.

"Will they let me in?" Evelina asked.

"Yeah, probably. Just say ..."

"What, Adriano?"

Her brother wouldn't meet her gaze. "That you're his fiancée or something."

"But I'm not."

"They don't know that, Eve."

"The guard will."

"The guard knows Theo."

That was all Adriano said before he hit the red button on the wall to buzz through to the Intensive Care Unit where Theo had been situated.

"Wait, you're not coming in with me?" Evelina asked when her brother turned to leave.

Adriano smiled. "You don't need me to do this."

"But—"

"And Dad's dead, Eve. No babysitters, no rules, no princess, huh? Just ... you don't need me for this."

"Thank you."

Adriano shrugged. "Give me a call when you want a driver sent over to bring you home."

"Okay."

"ICU front desk," came a gravelly voice through the intercom on the wall. "ID number, please."

"I'm not a hospital worker," Evelina said.

"Visitation?"

"Yes."

"Which room and patient are you here to visit?"

Evelina cussed silently, not knowing Theo's room number. "Uh, it's DeLuca."

"Oh." More crackling followed on the speaker. "Theo DeLuca?"

"Yes."

"Only family has been approved—"

"I'm his fiancée," Evelina interrupted without hesitating. "I could call his sister and have her put me on whatever list, if you'd like."

"It's unit six at the very end, across from the ICU station. Please check in before you leave the unit."

"Thank you."

The door buzzed to unlock and open not five seconds later. Evelina walked into the sterile smelling, quiet ICU and tried not to let the sad atmosphere of the place take hold of her emotions. But the closer she got to the end where she knew Theo's room was, the better she felt.

Much better than she had in days, really.

This was the first time she'd been allowed to the hospital. Adriano made her wait until they'd buried Riley, and the shock of the entire situation had calmed down. Her brother talked very little about Theo, but Evelina got updates from Lily when she could.

It didn't help.

Nothing prepared Evelina.

Not to see him like that.

Evelina stood only a few feet away from the ICU room, and couldn't force her legs to move. Her heart was breaking.

Breathing tubes attached to Theo's face kept his sharp features mostly covered while leads stuck to his chest, forehead, and abdomen reflected information on four different screens hanging on the walls. A stark, rough looking hospital blanket was tucked around Theo's prone form while a rubbery looking oxygen monitor covered his right index finger. Oxygen hissed in the dimly lit room.

"It's only a shock at first," came a quiet voice.

Evelina nearly jumped out of her damn heels. "Oh, my God, Damian."

Damian Rossi glanced up at Evelina from his position on the floor. The man rested in the doorway with his foot propped up to the jamb, and his back pressed to the other side. A coffee rested in his hand while a newspaper had been set down to the floor beside him.

Evelina hadn't even noticed Damian when she approached. She wasn't surprised that he was Theo's guard. The two men had always been close.

"I … It is a shock," Evelina settled on saying.

"The good news is the bullets missed his spine," Damian said, looking back at Theo's still form in the bed. "No spinal cord damage was the best possible outcome considering the three he took to the back like that."

"What's the bad news?"

"The bad news is that he lost nearly sixty percent of his blood during the first operation to remove the bullet that entered the left side of his heart. It was just luck that the bullets hit his organs at all, but they ricocheted off bones. Twice they lost him on the table and twice they brought him back." Damian pointed to a monitor on the far wall and said, "That is his brain function."

Yellow lines scribbled across the screen.

Eve's relief was palpable. "He has brain function."

"Perfectly normal brain function, apparently."

"But he hasn't woke up yet," Evelina whispered.

Her heart clenched and broke all over again. She couldn't breathe. Her own pain was suffocating. Why wouldn't Theo wake up?

"Some people don't," Damian said quietly. "Some people enter the coma and they just don't come back out, Eve. The oxygen deprivation Theo suffered was the cause of his coma, and if he does wake up, we have to be concerned about brain damage."

"But he needs to wake up. Okay? He needs to."

The rest she could handle if he would just wake up. Theo saved her once again. Evelina needed to thank him, to hold him, and to love him. Because as she watched him stay prone in that bed, she couldn't help but know how badly she needed that man to wake up.

And she knew it then.

Right then ...

Theo was hers. He'd been hers ever since he called her a princess, and dared her to break the rules. He was hers when he couldn't stay away, and when he admitted he cared. They didn't have to be something to be one another's.

They just fucking were.

She needed him to wake up.

"He will wake up, right?" Evelina asked.

Damian wouldn't meet Evelina's eyes as he replied, "It's been a few days. There's been no improvement."

"But there's been no steps backwards, either, right?"

"No."

"He'll wake up," Evelina said. "He has to."

"Mmm." Damian pushed off the floor, scooping up the newspaper with him as he went. "Are you staying for a while?"

"I can't leave."

Not now.

Not until Theo opened his eyes.

"The nurses are kind of bitchy," Damian warned.

"That's okay."

"Lily comes around quite often."

"She'll give me someone to talk to."

Damian chuckled.

"What is so funny?" Evelina asked, annoyed.

"I was just thinking about the doctors that have been in. A lot of them are convinced that because Theo's brain function shows normal activity, he can probably hear us if he's in any kind of mentally aware state. Even if it's a state between unconsciousness and consciousness, he might not understand, but his brain knows."

"So?"

"So he'll probably be happy to hear someone else. Or you, I guess."

Evelina's heart warmed momentarily. "Oh."

"Lily nags him even like this. Asking him to wake up, and going on to herself when the monitor beeps even a little. I let her because it makes her feel better, but it isn't doing a damned thing for Theo."

"She worries and she loves him."

"I know," Damian murmured. "Be mindful of the breathing tubes. He could do without them, but the bullet he took to the right lung was bad and the respirator helps to keep him on track. It's the only life support he's currently on. His kidneys are fine, as is his heart even with the surgery."

Evelina nodded. "I will."

Taking another look at Theo, she realized most of her shock at the sight of him like he was had worn off. His chest was wrapped in gauze, and his face seemed almost peaceful, like maybe he was just sleeping.

"He doesn't like the dark," Evelina said, mostly to herself. The room was too dark. Theo wouldn't like that if he woke up to it like it was.

"You're right," Damian replied, "and that's why I was here."

"Hmm, why?"

Wasn't Damian the guard Adriano talked about?

"I didn't do a good job of looking out for him when we were teenagers, so I figure I should be here now like I should have been there with him back then."

"His uncle," Evelina said.

"Yeah. Someone has to keep his monsters away."

Three days later, Evelina watched the doctor remove the breathing tube from Theo's throat. Theo still didn't wake up. Four days later, Tommas Rossi visited with Damian outside of Theo's room. Evelina handed the man back his engagement ring without a word. Five days later, a specialist dealing in patients after they wake up from the coma came to speak with Theo's family.

He might not be the same. His temperaments may change. Some memories might be lost. Some behaviors might develop over time.

Evelina tuned the woman out. Time bled together for her. She only left the room long enough to eat, to change into clean clothes that Lily brought for her, or to shower when the ICU nurses had an open bathroom for her to use. She couldn't go. She needed to be there when Theo woke up.

Evelina propped her elbow on the side of Theo's bed and watched his eyes flicker behind his closed lids. It was supposed to be a good sign according to the doctors. It was a similar state to someone being in the midst of a vivid dream, and their body reacted. She hoped for Theo, whatever he was seeing wasn't a nightmare.

Reaching over, Evelina traced the sharp line of Theo's cheekbone with the tip of her finger. Warmth followed the path she made and she continued across his jaw and over his lips. Then, she simply rested her hand over his chest.

His heart beat.

That was all that mattered.

His heart was still beating.

"Hey."

Evelina turned at Lily's quiet greeting. "Hey."

"Nothing today?" Lily asked.

"Not yet."

Lily smiled. "Yet. I like that."

Being hopeful was better than being resigned.

"Theo is stubborn. I think he's just being selfish."

"Oh, why's that?"

"Taking some time for him, you know. And that's okay. He needs it."

Lily raised a brow like she was considering Evelina's statement. "Probably. That sounds like something my brother would do. How're you doing, Eve?"

"That's the first time you asked me that since I came to the hospital six days ago."

"I kept wondering if you were going to leave."

Evelina didn't let that offend her. "I won't, Lily."

"Good. Because he needs that. He'll need it more when he wakes up."

"I lo—"

"Don't," Lily said quickly, laughing. "I know what you're going to say and please don't. Him first and then the world, Eve. But him first. He's never had that, I don't think. Someone should give him that, and I'm happy it's someone like you."

"Okay. Him first."

"You hungry?"

"A little," Evelina admitted. "Where's Damian?"

She hadn't even noticed the man leave earlier.

"Around. Stretching his legs."

Evelina's brow furrowed. "All he does is pace."

Lily wouldn't look Evelina in the eye. "Yeah, well, he's restless and worried …"

"What is it?"

"He just thought maybe you wanted some time alone with Theo. Damian is always here, too. That's all."

Oh.

"I'll go grab a bite to eat," Evelina said.

A hesitance wavered her voice. An even bigger one held her back from leaving Theo's side. Lily didn't miss it for a second.

Lily waved a cell phone. "I'll call the very second something changes."

"Thanks."

"You know, you could have told me months ago," Lily said softly. "Back whenever it was that you two first started messing around and not so late in the game like you did."

"I already told you, there was nothing to tell."

Lily shrugged. "Anything is something. I probably would have cheered you on. I kept bothering Theo about finding someone."

"He didn't really find me. He was just always there."

"I told him he wouldn't expect it. I hoped it knocked his cocky ass down a peg or two."

Evelina grinned, but it quickly faded. "I don't really know if it's the same for him. You know what I mean? It won't change anything about what I feel if it is different for him."

Lily scoffed. "Hey, he took three bullets for you. It's the same, Eve. Trust me."

"I'll try."

With a quiet goodbye to the still man in the hospital bed, Evelina left in search of the hospital cafeteria. She checked out at the ICU front desk before leaving the unit. A few doors down, familiar voices chatted and laughed. The closer Evelina came to the room, the more confused she got.

Standing just in the doorway, the people inside didn't notice her. Tommas, Adriano, Alessa, and at least a dozen more people that Evelina recognized, and some she didn't, had set themselves up in the family waiting room. Guessing by the laptops that were set up, the overnight bags, and the garbage cans full of takeout containers, they'd been there a while.

How out of it had she been since coming to stay with Theo at the hospital? She hadn't known these people were here at all. No one mentioned it.

Those thoughts quickly drifted away as a warmth spread through Evelina's body. These people cared. They wouldn't be here otherwise. Not everything was about the show when it came to the Outfit and the families. Sometimes, like now, they simply came together for support and common need.

"Hey," Adriano said, smiling up at his sister from the recliner he sat in.

All heads turned in Evelina's direction. No judgment stared back at her. She had worried that her relationship with Theo and the fake engagement with Tommas would be the focus for people instead of Theo's medical situation. After all, look how people treated her brother and Alessa for their choices.

"Hey," Evelina greeted.

"Lily was just here," Alessa said, holding up a to-go cup. "She brought them coffee and hot chocolate for me."

Adriano pushed up from his chair and came to stand next to his sister. "You okay?"

"Yeah, Adriano."

"No change?"

"Not yet."

A man Evelina didn't recognize held a bag of takeout containers up for Evelina to see.

"You hungry, girl?" the man asked.

The guy looked vaguely familiar, but Evelina couldn't place him.

Adriano seemed to pick up on Evelina's unspoken question. "One of Theo's guys. His son worked under Theo at the club. Artino. Cole. Ring any bells?"

Barely.

"Cole was the one killed the night Theo left for New York," Adriano added.

"The one Chloe's brother mistook for Theo."

"The same one."

"Food?" the man asked again.

Evelina nodded and took another step into the room. "Sure."

For once, she didn't feel like she had to put the mask on for the crowd. These people knew her distress, they had to know her worries and pain. It wasn't about being perfect, or the emotionless little doll her father liked to take off the shelf whenever it was convenient.

She wasn't that doll anymore.

It felt like coming home.

Just like freedom.

Now, she only needed Theo to wake up, too.

"Eve?"

Evelina jerked awake in the uncomfortable hospital chair. Panic seized her throat, squeezing tight and threatening to silence her. Damian watched her from up above with a curious expression and a cocked brow.

"Bad dream?" the man asked.

"No," Evelina croaked, still half-asleep. "Those stopped the day Theo was shot."

"You dreamt of Theo being shot?"

"Me, not him. It didn't make the actual event any better, Damian."

"I guess it wouldn't."

She supposed her worst nightmare had finally come true. Unfortunately, it wasn't her who took the bullets, but someone she still adored and loved made the nightmare a reality. She'd even felt the blood in her hands like she would in her dreams.

Warm.

Wet.

Red.

Slipping right through her fingers with no end in sight.

Evelina shuddered. "Can we stop talking about it?"

"Sure." Damian jerked a thumb over his shoulder. "I woke you up because you have a visitor."

"Oh?"

"She's waiting in the café downstairs."

Evelina raised a brow. "She?"

"You ask a lot of questions."

"You could answer them."

Damian shrugged. "She asked for her visit to be kept quiet."

Still groggy, Evelina gave Theo's hand a squeeze before she passed Damian by and left the unit. After a quick elevator trip down to the second floor where the cafeteria and café was located, Evelina found her visitor.

Abriella sat at a corner table with a coffee between her hands and her head down. Large-framed sunglasses had been pushed high on Abriella's head where her hair was messily piled into a bun. Her hoodie and jeans were not the usual classed up style of Abriella Trentini. The girl looked worn.

Evelina was shocked to even see her former friend sitting there. Abriella hadn't said a single word to Evelina since the night of the fake engagement. Any attempts at contact were ignored. As far as Evelina knew, Abriella had ignored all of Tommas' attempts, too.

"Hey," Evelina said as she slid into the seat across from Abriella.

Abriella tried to smile, but it fell just as fast. "Hey."

"You could have come up to the family waiting room."

"There's a lot of people there. I heard that it's like a revolving door with guests for Theo coming in and out."

"People like Tommas?" Evelina asked.

Abriella straightened in her chair. "I know it was all for show. The engagement, I mean. I know he never meant to follow it through."

"Yeah, it was for show."

"He could have told me, Eve, not let me find out like he did."

"Ella—"

"You can't understand what that did to me. Please don't justify his choices. He made them."

"I did, too. I could have told you."

Abriella sucked in a hard breath. "You're right. You should have."

"Tommas loves you, Ella. He did it for you. He was trying to force Joel's hand and Riley's at the same time and it just ended really badly."

"Terribly," Abriella murmured. "It ended terribly. Theo—"

"Will be fine."

"Still, I'm sorry for what Tommas did to Theo, even if he did try to correct it," Abriella said.

"It wasn't just Tommas. Both Riley and Joel had their hand in things and stirred the pot. It happened. Right now, I just want to focus on Theo and getting him out of here."

Abriella frowned. "Alessa has been keeping me updated."

To Evelina, that translated to *no changes*.

"You know, I was kind of shocked to find out you and Theo ..." Abriella trailed off with a leer.

Evelina laughed. "Stop."

"Well!"

"You're just deflecting from why you're really here, Ella. What do you want?"

Abriella glanced away, her fingers tightening around her to-go cup. "I don't know if I can trust Tommas, now."

"And you came to me?"

"You seemed like the best choice. My sister is pregnant and I don't want to worry her. Lily is the same way, but Damian is forcing her to keep a distance right now because of Joel. As far as you and me ... We've been best friends since we were kids, right? People like us, we keep coming back together in the end, Eve. I need somebody right now. Please be that person for me."

Some friendships were made of straw and mud. The smallest tap could ruin everything. Other friendships were made of steel and iron. Unbreakable even through the toughest weather.

"You wouldn't answer my calls," Evelina said. "I wanted to explain."

"I needed some time. I would have been awful to you had I answered."

Fair enough.

"I trust Tommas," Evelina said after a moment.

"Even after what he did?"

"Yes."

"Joel is ..."

"What?"

Abriella cringed. "Going to go after him. Well, anyone he can hurt, maybe. Tommas for sure."

"Some people would choose the lesser of two evils, Ella."

"Which one is that?" Abriella asked. "The man who killed me without even saying a word or the one who would kill me in a heartbeat if it got him what he wanted?"

"You know, I don't think I can tell the difference between which man that is for you. Tommas would just as soon kill both you and him if it meant he got you in the next life. He'd burn this city to the ground for you, Ella."

"Maybe Tommas needs to learn that we don't always get what we want."

"You do if you want it bad enough," Evelina said quietly.

"I have a different version, Eve."

"Of what?"

"My two evils. One is choosing to hurt the person I care about the most to give him what he should have or letting him hurt everyone else so I can get what I should have."

Evelina sighed. "Give Tommas a chance to get you so you both can have what you want."

Abriella stood from the table and grabbed her coat off the back of the chair. "I might, but doing that means this whole thing keeps going."

"The war?"

"The war," her friend echoed. "Because my brother is ice cold and Tommas is the gasoline to my fire. It's never going to work without something getting destroyed. Not one of us is working toward the same thing."

"Don't you love him, though?"

"That is a word I try not to use for Tommas."

Evelina's brow furrowed. "But—"

"He's got all the control between us and that is the one thing I can keep."

Evelina didn't understand. She found herself saying that a lot where Abriella and Tommas were concerned. This, however, was something entirely different. Evelina had firsthand knowledge of how much power Abriella had over Tommas Rossi.

"I think you're wrong," Evelina said softly.

Abriella's head snapped up to meet Evelina's gaze. "Pardon?"

"What you said about the control. I think you're wrong, Ella. I don't think Tommas has any control where you're concerned."

"I should go."

"Give him a chance."

No response.

Abriella didn't even blink.

"I hope Theo wakes up for you, Eve," Abriella said instead.

"He will."

Evelina stretched her legs with a walk of the third floor outside of the ICU. The unit's nurses always got a little bitchy whenever someone was aimlessly wandering inside the ICU, so Evelina took her restlessness out of their view.

She didn't need their glares.

She also didn't like to leave Theo's side if she could help it, but Lily had practically forced Evelina out of the room. The nurses had to take care of Theo's medical needs, things that Evelina knew her lover wouldn't want her seeing, so she had gone when Lily demanded.

Now, she was just itching to get back.

Leaning against the large wall-to-wall windows that overlooked a section of the rooftop of the floor below, Evelina watched the lights of stars twinkle up above.

She knew what was going to happen. If Theo didn't begin to show signs of improvement, the doctors would begin pushing options on Lily. There was talk of trying to force Theo out of the coma with drugs, but it was dangerous and the side-effects could be permanently damaging.

And then there was simply doing nothing.

Theo had no form of life support keeping him alive. His heart beat on its own, even after taking a bullet to it. His lungs breathed without help.

He just had to wake up.

"Eve!"

Evelina turned on her heel at the muffled shout of her name. Lily barreled through the doors that connected a section of the hospital off from the one Evelina had been strolling through.

"It jumped," Lily said, breathless and teary-eyed. "It spiked. He keeps spiking."

She didn't need Lily to confirm what she was saying, but she asked anyway. "His brain function?"

Lily nodded. "Yes."

Theo's brain function had been steady. According to the doctors, it reflected a person in a deep sleep with the occasional jumps and movements that came along with the state of unconsciousness. What Theo hadn't started showing until now, was signs of his brain coming back into a more aware state.

"Yeah?" Evelina asked, pushing away from the windows.

"Yeah. He's trying to wake up, Eve."

Because Theo was ready, Evelina knew.

She wouldn't tell Lily that, though.

"Come on," Lily said, turning back toward the doors.

Evelina followed her friend without question. It took them a good five minutes to get back inside the ICU and into Theo's room. Nurses milled around, watching monitors while another chatted on the phone and asked for someone to come downstairs. By the sounds of the conversation, the nurse was asking for the main doctor on Theo's file.

Damian leaned against the far wall, his gaze trained on the monitor up above Theo's bed. He didn't act like he'd noticed Lily arrive back to the room with Evelina, but the man held his hand out to his wife. Lily took it and tucked tightly into his side.

"Keep the activity to a minimum," a nurse barked.

"Quiet and still," another one said.

The nurse on the phone hung up the call. "One familiar person in the room only, please. Choose who that's going to be now before Dr. Michaud gets down here and he decides."

Evelina looked to Lily.

"You stay," Lily said softly.

Evelina shook her head. Lily should be the one Theo woke up to. She was his family, his little sister. He adored Lily.

Her friend wasn't having it.

"You, Eve."

With that, Lily tugged a still quiet Damian out of the room. Curtains were pulled. Lights dimmed. The monitors were quieted as much as possible.

Evelina found herself beside Theo's bed, her hand wrapping up in his. She took his palm and rested it to her cheek.

Warmth.

Softness.

Home.

The nurses checked vitals and opened Theo's eyelids to shine lights and check reactions.

Normal, they said.

Everything was perfectly normal.

"Wake up, Theo."

Please wake up.

Evelina's voice was a whisper; her plea coming out so soft she was sure the man wouldn't even hear it. She couldn't make it come out any louder. Theo didn't stir. But his finger ...

His index finger stroked her cheek.

What control Evelina thought she had was lost in that moment. Her tears fell all over again. The cracks in her heart began to seal.

Please wake up. I need you here.

Evelina buried her face into Theo's slack palm and waited.

CHAPTER TWENTY-ONE

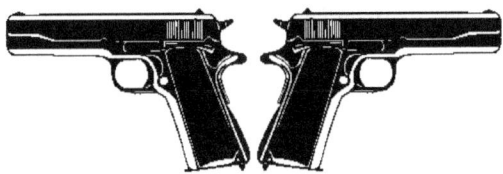

Theo turned on his heel in the dark street, seeing the flashing lights down the way. Red, white, and blue.

Something made him walk forward.

Memories, maybe.

Instinct, probably.

He'd done this before. He'd walked this street before. He'd seen those lights before.

Something tugged on his hand, and he looked down to see Lily standing beside him. He didn't have to look very far, because he wasn't all that high off the ground. Not like he usually was.

Five-year-old Lily stared up at her brother with frightened eyes. Theo took in the changes of his sister. The last time he stared at her, she was a grown woman. Now she was practically a baby again.

He'd done this before …

"Theo?" Lily whispered.

"Something ain't right," came a voice from behind them.

Damian pushed past Theo, his hand tousling little Lily's hair as he went.

"Wait up, Ghost," Theo called.

Damian didn't turn around.

"Is Damian gonna stay the night with you?" Lily asked.

"I don't know what Damian is doing, little one," Theo said.

Damian came and went a lot. Sometimes he stuck around to play, and sometimes a dark car would pick him up and go. Theo didn't even know where his friend lived.

Still quite a few steps ahead of the brother and sister, Damian didn't slow down when Theo called after him. He wished his friend would. The closer they came to the lights, the worse Theo felt.

The cars and the people were right in front of his house. The pretty, colorful walkway his mother had decorated was trampled and full of people. Theo stopped walking, and yanked his sister back to his side when she tried to continue on.

"Stop, Lily," Theo ordered.

Lily's grip on Theo tightened. "That's the police."

They weren't supposed to talk to cops.

"That's our house," Lily said.

Theo watched Damian wander into the throng of people and disappear.

Theo pulled Lily behind a car when a man turned to look in their direction. Something was wrong.

"Where's Mommy?" Lily asked.

"Shut up, Lily," Theo told her.

"The wife was in the house with him," Theo heard someone say as two figures walked past his hiding spot. "They've got kids, but nobody knows where the little ones are."

"The oldest showed up five minutes ago."

Dino?

"He's still a kid," the first guy said. "Almost seventeen, but he's still a kid."

"Theo," Lily whispered, tugging on his shirt.

"Quiet, Lily."

Theo poked his head up over the hood of the car and peered through the people. The crowd had started to thin but police tape was being put up.

"There you are!"

Theo turned to see an unknown man grab Lily around the waist and pull her away from her brother's side. Lily sucked in a deep breath and screamed for all she was worth. Her little arms and legs flew and kicked against the policeman who held her tight.

"Let me go! *Theo!*"

Theo bolted out from the car as another person came in from behind and tried to grab him.

"Give me my sister!"

"Hey, kid, calm the fuck down. We're just—"

Theo picked up a rock and whipped it at the man. It smacked the guy right in the forehead. Cursing loudly, the man dropped a struggling Lily to the ground. She hit the pavement with her knees and hands, crying out.

Theo grabbed Lily's hand and forced her up from the ground. He yanked her back into the maze of cars on the street, looking for some way out.

Where had Damian gone?

Where was Dino?

His parents?

Lily kept sniffling behind Theo, but she didn't say a word. He looked back to see his sister's knees were bloodied and her hand was scraped up. The yellow dress she wore was ripped, too.

Stupid cops.

He hoped that rock hurt.

Then, out of the corner of his eye, Theo saw a familiar form being shoved away from the cops and lights. Dino barreled right back toward the walkway again, shouting and angry.

"My parents," Dino growled. "That's my—"

Theo froze as his brother caught sight of him. Dino blinked like he didn't believe what he was seeing. Theo took a couple of hesitant steps toward his brother.

Dino stumbled forward. "Theo, Lily …"

It was barely a blink and Dino was in front of Theo. His older brother dropped to his knees and hugged Theo hard enough that it hurt. Lily got caught in the embrace, but she seemed to like it more than Theo did.

"Oh, my God," Dino said, choked and thick. "They wouldn't tell me, Theo. They wouldn't tell me if you … I'm sorry, Theo."

"Where's Dad?" Theo asked quietly.

Dino tensed all over. "We're going to go somewhere else for a couple of nights, okay?"

"To your house?" Lily asked as her oldest brother wiped her face clean of tears and snot.

Theo didn't understand why his older brother got to live outside of their house. Their dad said it was because Dino had his own stuff to handle.

"My apartment," Dino said. "It's not very big, but—"

"Where's Dad?" Theo asked again. "Mom's at Dickies, right?"

Their mother always went to Dickies on Fridays because she liked the music.

"Theo, later," Dino said quietly. "Right now, I need to get you two out of here before—"

"Right over here, Mr. DeLuca," someone said.

Dino went rigid all over. With a slowness that Theo had never seen his brother use before, Dino stood from the road with one hand on his brother and the other on his sister, and turned to face a familiar man. Their uncle Ben didn't look anything like Dino did. Dino was sad, he looked hurt, but Ben seemed almost … happy.

Theo grabbed Dino's hand tight.

"Ben," Dino said quietly as their uncle was directed over by the police.

"Dino." Ben smiled tightly. "How unfortunate that you arrived before I did."

Dino glared. "I'm sure."

Theo watched, confused and tired, as the police kept a wide berth around the DeLuca siblings and their uncle.

"I'll take them with me, of course," Ben said. "They're just children.

Better with me than the system."

Dino grabbed Theo's hand so hard it hurt. "Better with *you*? You did this, Ben!"

"Be careful, Dino, or I'll pull the system for you, too. You've got another year and a couple of months before you become of age."

"But I—"

"At sixteen, you don't honestly believe you'll have any control over your brother and sister, do you?"

Theo didn't understand what was happening. He didn't know why there were cops in front of his house, or why his brother seemed so distrustful and angry with their uncle. But he'd always listened to what Dino told him.

Always.

"I want to go with Dino," Theo said.

Ben flicked Theo with a cold look. "It isn't your choice, my boy."

With a snap of Ben's fingers, Theo found himself ripped away from Dino before he could even scream. Lily was in the same predicament. A hand covered Theo's mouth, forcing him to stay quiet. A large arm wrapped around his frame, keeping him still.

Theo still struggled with his captor, but was shoved into the backseat of a familiar Cadillac. It belonged to his aunt and uncle. Not two seconds later, a crying Lily was tossed inside on her brother, too.

The man who had grabbed Theo reached in the car, smacked Theo hard in the face with an opened palm, and then pointed at him as if to tell him to shut up. Never once had a person struck Theo. Not an adult.

Frozen, Theo looked up at the man.

"Stop your shouting and moving," the man snapped, "or you'll get another one of those, kid."

"O-okay," Theo stuttered out.

"Mind your sister, too, or she'll be the next one to get a good smack."

No way.

Theo's cheek still stung and he was pretty sure his lip was fat, now. He grabbed his sister and held her close. Lily stayed quiet but for her sniffles.

The man rolled down the window a few inches, locked the doors, and closed the car up tight. Theo turned in the seat in just enough time to watch his uncle Ben and Dino move their argument past the shine of lights and watchers.

Then, Ben snapped his fingers again. Dino was taken to the ground fast. Fists flew and hit flesh. Dino couldn't get away from the three men pummeling him on the pavement. Theo could see his brother clearly begging for the men to stop, but no one listened. Like before, the cops seemed to have turned cheek to whatever happened to the DeLuca kids once their uncle showed up on the scene.

A sick feeling made Theo want to vomit. He sucked in a hard breath and held Lily closer. A tap on his shoulder made Theo jump nearly to the roof of the car.

"Hey," came a quiet whisper.

Theo met Damian's gaze outside of the Cadillac.

"Hey," Theo said.

"You okay?"

Theo shook his head.

Damian frowned. "Me, either. I'm sorry."

"About what?"

"Your mom and dad."

Theo's eyes stung with tears.

"Somebody hit you?" Damian asked.

"Yeah."

Damian glanced down at Lily. She had her face hidden into Theo's side, and covered her ears with her hands. "Don't hit them back, Theo."

"Why?"

"Only makes it worse."

"Oh," Theo mumbled.

"I'll see you later, okay?"

"Okay, Ghost."

Damian peeked over the car. "And I'm sorry about your brother, too."

Theo blinked away his tears. DeLucas didn't cry.

"Keep an eye on Lily," Damian said.

"Nobody else does," Theo replied.

"I do sometimes."

It was true.

"Wake up, Theo."

Theo glanced around at the whisper. The voice was familiar—*her* voice.

Why did she sound like that?

Scared. Tired. Sad.

She shouldn't sound like that.

"Wake up, Theo, please."

A warmth spread on the palm of his hand, coursing down his arm and straight into his chest. He swore he could feel something soft and smooth stroking against it, too. Theo touched the invisible something back.

"Wake up."

Theo held tighter to Lily. He couldn't go yet. He was still needed here.

"Please wake up."

"I will."

"Oh, Theo, get that goddamned pen out of your mouth," Carmela chided.

Theo dropped the pen to the table and tried not to glare at his aunt. If he did, and she saw it, he would only earn himself a good smack in the side of the head. Carmela DeLuca had little to no patience for kids. Thank God she never had any of her own.

"And sit straight in that chair. Good Lord, you slouch too much."

Theo forced his shoulders straight. "Better?"

"You're getting there. Read the section back to me, now."

Chancing a glance at the digital clock on the stove, Theo noted it was well after ten at night. Tired and drowsy-eyed, he recited the section of his history textbook that his aunt asked him to read.

"Perfect," Carmela praised.

Her acceptance did nothing for him. It never had. The more Theo did right for Carmela, the more things she found wrong to criticize him with. It never ended.

"Can I go wash up for bed? I finished everything."

Carmela looked over fourteen-year-old Theo's homework with a keen eye and a severe expression.

"I suppose," she finally drawled.

"Thank you."

Mostly, Theo was just jealous as hell that his nine-year-old sister got to live away at boarding school for ten months out of the year while he was stuck here. He was glad Lily never had to deal with Carmela or Ben, though. Little Lily didn't need their special brand of love.

Theo had to pass the door that led into the garage to get to the stairwell leading to the upstairs section of the DeLuca home. His uncle was always clear about Theo staying far away from the garage when nighttime fell because sometimes Ben did business in there.

Outfit business.

"Had enough yet?"

The question made Theo pause. He noticed the garage door was opened just an inch or two. It wasn't like Ben to leave it open for someone to walk in. Usually it was locked up tight, and the shades on the door drawn.

Knowing better, but unable to stop himself, Theo pushed the door open a little more.

"Well, Dino?" Ben asked. "Have you?"

Theo's throat felt like someone had tied a noose around it and pulled as tight as they could. Dino struggled to get up from the cement floor of the garage with a bloody mouth, blackened eyes, and a swollen cheek. By the looks of the way Dino's ankle was twisted and it gave under his weight, it was probably broken. Theo grabbed the doorknob so hard he was sure he would crush it.

"What'd I fucking tell you, huh?" Ben growled.

"Don't play with snakes," Dino rasped.

"And there you go, fucking sleeping with one."

"I—"

"Oh, give it up, Dino. I told you to stay away from that family. I don't care about your feelings. They don't make a goddamn difference to me. If you can't follow my very simple fucking rules, then I will beat them into you."

Theo's heart hammered hard when Ben flicked out his wrist to showcase what he'd been hitting Dino with. A thin metal pole glinted under the light.

"You don't mess with daughters, Dino," Ben said.

Dino spat a mouthful of bloody saliva to the floor. "I know."

"Well, you surely will after tonight. As for the little whore you were running around with, I'll have that issue corrected before the morning, too."

"Don't, Ben. I'll leave it alone. She didn't do anything. She's just a girl."

"Too late," Ben murmured. "Julia Trentini will not make it home from her track and field training tonight before the brakes let go in her car. A terrible, awful accident and one that is sure to break Terrance's heart. He adores his daughter, after all. I'm sure you'll understand, Dino, in time."

Like a bolt of lightning had been shot under Dino's feet at Ben's statement, Dino was up and lunging for his uncle.

"You're a bastard, Ben!"

Without even hesitating, Ben swung the metal pole. It caught Dino right under the chin, knocking the twenty-year-old back to the floor with a sickening crack.

Theo froze. Just for a second. And then he was running into the garage and straight at his uncle's back, too.

Theo didn't even get the chance to reach Ben before the metal pole cracked him in the side. Ben had always been quick about his beatings. Theo should have known better than to think he could catch his uncle off guard.

"Stupid boy," Ben hissed as the pole snapped against Theo's wrist.

A howl caught in the back of Theo's throat. Something awful bloomed in his wrist, and he hugged his arm to his chest as he rolled to his stomach on the floor. It was the best position to save his body from a worse beating. His back was tough but his organs were not.

"Stupid, stupid child," Ben continued, the toe of his shoe catching Theo in the cheek.

Tears welled as sobs choked Theo over and over. "I'm sorry ..."

"Don't fucking touch him, Ben. Don't hurt my brother." Dino's breath was labored as he rolled onto his hands and knees, water filling his eyes and tears streaking down his bruised face. "Don't—"

"Shut your mouth!"

Theo tried to scramble away from his uncle, but every time he moved, the pain in his wrist increased until he was gagging on the bile spilling on his tongue.

Then, Ben yanked Theo back by grabbing the back of his shirt. He flung Theo to the cement floor. Instinct made Theo throw his arms out to catch himself and something snapped in his wrist. The pain increased to an unbearable point. All Theo could do was watch the pole swinging from his uncle's hand, hoping to hell it didn't hit him again.

Ben went a different route. He must have noticed that Theo was holding his wrist, because his uncle smirked cruelly before grabbing Theo's injured hand and dragging him across the garage. Theo's air left his lungs and he felt frozen to the ground as his uncle popped the trunk on the back of a black Mercedes.

Theo fought.

He fought so fucking hard that his wrist throbbed and his ankle ached. He fought hard enough to make his uncle's face bleed and to break his fingernails trying to keep Ben from shoving him into the small, dark space.

It wouldn't be the first time Ben had done this. Usually, the man favored closets.

"Ben!" Dino shouted. "Leave him be!"

Theo knew Dino was injured, but he still hated his brother for not helping him. Ben used the pole to push against Theo's stomach as he grabbed the trunk and began to close it.

"Thank your brother for this, Theo," Ben said quietly. "Three days will do you a world of good, I'm sure."

Theo opened his mouth to speak, but the trunk closed on him just as fast. He kicked and beat against his confines, but nothing helped.

What was worse ... what was worse were the sounds of his brother getting beat all over again. Dino's cries and pleads were enough to make Theo throw up on himself. The sound of metal slapping against flesh and bone were so much worse.

Hugging his knees to his chest, Theo stayed curled in his safe ball.

"I'm here, you know," came a soft voice.

His hand was so warm. Softness touched his palm over and over. It took the pain from the broken wrist away.

"All you have to do is wake up for me, Theo."

Theo let the familiar voice drown out the memories he didn't want to relive. The monsters that hid in the dark. The hell all around him.

It was gone when she spoke.

"I have something to tell you."

Theo shuddered. Dino's grunts of pain got louder. Metal clanked to cement.

"Die there for all I give a damn," Ben spat from somewhere outside of the trunk.

"Please wake up for me."

"I want to, Eve."

"Do what you will," Ben said, flicking his wrist in Theo's direction.

Dismissed.

Just like that, forgotten.

"But I didn't do anything wrong," Theo said. "Not on purpose. It was an honest mistake, Ben. I apologized to the guy. I'll stay the fuck away from the girl. It wasn't my fault she'll open her legs for a good-looking man. Maybe if the bastard treated her better, she'd stay home where she belonged."

Riley scoffed. "Women are only good for a few things, kid. If all you're looking for is to get your dick wet, Theo, find a woman who is meant just for that. She's called a whore. There's a dozen of them everywhere you look."

"I still didn't do anything wrong!"

Ben shook his head. "You started an issue with Riley's man when you slept with the guy's woman, Theo."

"I didn't know she had a fucking boyfriend!"

"Oh, well," Ben murmured as he opened the door and stepped out into the hallway. Music from the strip club's floor pumped down to the room. "I'm sure you and Riley will figure out a way to work this little problem out, Theo."

Stuck staring at his uncle as Ben closed the door, Theo didn't even see the metal chair coming. It smacked him right in the back and knocked the air out of his lungs. His knees hit the floor as a shout ricocheted out from his chest.

"Fuck," Theo snarled. "Cheap shots are for cowards, Riley."

"Just teaching you a lesson you should have already learned, DeLuca."

Theo's worst mistake was rolling over to defend himself. Riley brought the chair down on him again. The sharp end of the leg sliced through his shirt and pec, cutting him a good five inches long and deep if the amount of blood was any indication.

Just barely managing to get out of the way of the chair when Riley swung it down again, Theo scrambled to find something to fight back with. His fists were one thing, but considering Riley was coming at him with a chair, it didn't seem like they would help him much.

"Ah, there they are," Riley said, looking over Theo's shoulder and grinning coldly.

Theo made the mistake of looking back. Two men stepped inside the room and lunged for him. There was no escape this time, no way out. Theo found himself on the ground as Riley's boot landed on one of his ribs with enough force to break it. Arms barricaded him down. Fists, feet, and a chair pummeled him bloody and unconscious into the floor.

At least like that he didn't feel.

Theo wasn't entirely sure how long he stayed like that, but he vaguely recalled bouts of consciousness and pain. Hours, maybe. Days was more likely. There was so much pain in the one side of his body that he could barely breathe. The more air he tried to draw in, the worse it hurt and the less his lungs worked. He was sure he'd lost a lot of blood because he was too goddamn weak to stand, but he couldn't be sure because there was no light. But the floor around him was sticky in spots and crusty in others. The darkness of the room and the coldness of the floor was unsettling. No matter how many times he called out, no one answered him.

"Is he in there?"

Theo heard a familiar voice shout somewhere behind him. Something hard landed against something solid.

"Is he?" the voice asked again.

"Ben said to leave it be."

"Fuck you. Get out of my way or I'll give you a taste of metal when I blow your throat apart with bullets."

Light filtered into the room. Theo squinted up at the ceiling, remembering where he was and how he'd gotten there again. The pain from the light wasn't unbearable, but it wasn't comfortable, either.

"Christ ... Theo ..."

Dino leaned over him, his hands ghosting over Theo's face.

"Something's wrong," Theo told his brother.

"Yeah, man. How many fingers?"

"Six?"

"No," Dino said lowly. "There's only five fingers to a hand, Theo. What did he do?"

"Riley," Theo tried to explain.

The more he talked, the worse his face felt.

"I'll get you out of here. I think you've got some kind of internal problem."

Dino's words drifted straight past Theo.

The light kept getting brighter instead.

It was really beginning to hurt.

"Wake up, Theo."

The light flashed like a direct beam into his eye.

Someone was holding his arms down.

A hand was touching his face.

"Stop," Theo mumbled.

"It's all right," Dino said quietly. "You'll be okay, man."

"Pupil response is there," someone said. "Can you blink for me, Theo?"

Theo did what they told him to.

"Let me go," Theo croaked.

"He's trying to talk," the familiar voice whispered. "Please let him go."

"He's going to hurt himself!"

"Stop holding him down!"

Evelina.

Eve.

His.

All his.

Theo sucked in a lungful of air and struggled again. The darkness had faded finally. The room was bright and his head ached. Raw in his throat and achy in his arms and legs, Theo kept struggling.

"Stop moving, Mr. DeLuca, please."

"They usually don't wake up with this much strength," a man muttered.

"Stop holding him down!" Evelina cried. "He suffers from—"

"Hush, girl. You're not making it better."

Theo didn't recognize the room. He didn't know why there were monitors on the wall or why there were leads and tubes attached to him. He grabbed at the wires and IVs, and pulled. He wanted those fucking things off. But in the midst of the chaos, he found the most familiar thing in the room; the one thing that settled and calmed him.

Evelina …

Tears streaked down Evelina's cheeks, and she was biting down on her thumb hard enough to break the skin. A female in white scrubs had Evelina pushed into the corner, refusing to let her come any closer.

"Eve," Theo rasped.

His body sagged into something soft.

"Please," Evelina whispered. "Stop."

What happened?

She was alive.

Evelina was alive.

"Just a sedative," the man said. "Enough to calm him and make him sleep whatever this is off for a couple of hours. Sometimes this happens but it isn't usually this violent. Can you count for me, Theo? Count to ten."

Go fuck yourself.

"That's not very nice," chided a nurse.

Had he said that out loud?

A prick stung his arm.

Bastards.

He just wanted Evelina.

"Can I see her now?" Theo asked.

"Soon," the nurse replied.

A *bitchy* nurse. The woman was nasty as hell and Theo was two seconds away from telling the woman exactly that.

"Listen, I'm moving, talking, you've even taken the goddamn catheter out and I took a piss. All is good, right? I've been awake for over twenty-four hours. The physical therapist came in and checked me out. My reflexes are good. The doctor has been in and did all his tests. The brain woman came in and looked over the scan. The shrink came in and pestered the shit out of me. So if you've had enough of trying to cop a feel of my junk, I'd really like to see my girl. *Now.*"

The nurse gaped at him like a fish.

It wasn't like Theo was lying. The woman had gotten more handfuls of his cock in the last hour than he was comfortable with. He was sure she'd probably gotten a handful or two when he was unconscious, too.

The very idea of being prone in a bed, unable to help himself or take care of his basic fucking human needs, made him disgusted.

The first twenty-four hours after waking from the coma had been hell. Non-stop tests from the doctors who wanted to make sure he suffered no brain damage. Theo had felt dizzy, confused, and dazed for hours. His eyesight hadn't been able to focus until nearing the twenty-four hour mark. Sometimes, he'd just stare off into space while in the middle of a conversation. He'd talked to his sister, thankfully, but that was it. No one else had been allowed in to his room.

Theo wanted to see Evelina.

He was desperate for her.

"And when can I eat?" Theo asked. "I'm starving."

Quietly, the nurse said, "The doctor would like to wait for a certain time to pass. Sometimes, when coma patients wake up, their stomachs are sensitive. More so than usual."

"Fine."

"You're very temperamental."

"He always was," came a voice from the doorway. "It isn't a new development."

Theo relaxed into the bed. "Eve."

Evelina lifted her hand and waved two fingers. "Hey."

The nurse scowled over her shoulder. "He hasn't been approved for visitors after his episode when he woke up."

"Actually, he has," Evelina replied sweetly. "I just talked to the doctor after the man finally made time to sit down with me. We had a nice chat about why Theo reacted the way he did, like the fact he had a difficult past that was wrought with—"

"Eve," Theo said quietly.

"—abuse," his lover finished, ignoring his warning.

The nurse stiffened. "Oh."

"Yes." Evelina sighed, adding, "So when a patient begs for you to let them go, and that patient's friends and family asks you the same thing, perhaps you should listen the next time."

Theo's throat felt damn tight, but his respect for Evelina climbed higher. He didn't know how much higher it could get than it already was.

"Perhaps you should have told us beforehand."

"I tried when he was waking up. None of you listened."

The nurse's hands fluttered, dead in the air. "Well, I'll just leave you two be for a second."

Evelina smiled tightly. "Thank you."

Once the nurse was gone, Theo finally found his voice again.

"Someone doesn't like the nurses."

"I really don't," Evelina admitted.

Theo smirked. "Me, either."

"Yeah, well, you slept through most of it."

"Sleep, coma, same thing."

"Lily brought you some comfortable clothes. She'll bring them in when you're ready."

"Good. There is nothing manly about this thing," Theo said, grabbing at the flimsy piece of crap he wore. "These hospital gowns are fucking indecent."

Evelina leered. "Stand up, turn around and show me how much."

Goddamn.

"Really? Jokes?"

"One of us has to." Evelina glanced down at the floor. "You really scared me."

Theo knew what she meant. The shooting, the bullets, his coma. All of it.

"Somebody's got to save you, princess."

"You sound like you need some water."

Theo shrugged. "My throat feels like it, too."

"I'll sneak you some in. They told me not to give you anything, but …"

Hard and loud, even though it hurt like hell, Theo laughed.

"I am such a shitty influence on you," he said when his chuckles calmed.

"Bad. We'd be bad."

"I don't know. I think we're pretty good, Eve."

Evelina took another step forward and said, "You still scared me."

"I'd do it again."

"I know." Evelina bit her bottom lip and then released it just as quick. "How do you feel?"

"Like someone ran me over with an eighteen wheeler. The nurse was kind enough to show me the mess from the surgeries. I need a fucking haircut. They won't get me a toothbrush. And it took the nurse asking if I'd like to try and take a leak to realize there was a tube shoved up my dick. That's gone now, by the way. Thankfully, it's still in working order."

Evelina coughed out a quiet laugh. "So, not so good, huh?"

"Wonderful. I am wonderful because you're looking at me, Eve."

"Theo …"

"Hmm?"

"I love you."

Theo's gaze cut to Evelina's fidgeting form. "I know."

He'd known it the moment he woke up and saw her crying for him. Maybe he'd even known it for longer than that.

"Okay," Evelina said in a whisper. "I just wanted—"

"Don't do that. Don't be nervous. Don't twist your hands together and avoid looking at me like something bad is going to come now."

"But—"

"Nothing. But *nothing*, princess."

Evelina released a shuddering breath. "Okay."

Theo loved this girl, too.

"You've been mine for a while, Eve. You were mine years ago when I told you to break the rules and you did it. You were mine when you trusted me and no one else would. You were mine when I told you to get on your knees, and you didn't even hesitate to do it. You were mine when you didn't ask me for a thing. You were mine when you said you would give up everything for a chance. And you were mine when I took three bullets that were meant for you. You are *mine*, Evelina."

"Yours."

"Every single part of you."

Evelina smiled a sweet sight. "All right."

"And you're still not asking me for a thing, Eve."

"What could I ask you for that you haven't given me, Theo?"

"Three words. A proper response. The one a person usually gives back when someone says they love someone else."

"You just did," she said, "but it was even better because those three words don't mean a thing if you don't know why, Theo."

"I'm still going to say it."

"You don't have to."

Yes, he did.

"I love you, Eve." Theo swallowed hard, wishing his voice wasn't so weak and his throat didn't feel like acid had been poured down it. "Will you sneak me in the water, now?"

She laughed lightly. "Whatever you want, Theo."

"Water. You. Something decent to wear."

"In that order?"

"You first," he said.

Evelina obliged. Theo forgot about the water once she was tucked under his scratchy sheets and in his arms. He forgot about the decent clothes the second she kissed the underside of his jaw.

"Thank you," Evelina said against his skin.

"For what?"

"Waking up for me."

"I should thank you," Theo said.

"God, for what?"

"Asking me to."

CHAPTER TWENTY-TWO

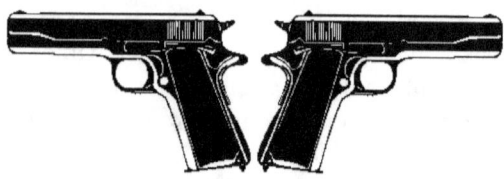

"You look ... better," Damian said lamely.

Evelina passed the usually quiet man a look. "Thanks? I didn't realize I looked terrible before."

Damian chuckled. "You looked like my wife did, I suppose."

Ah.

She got it.

"Tired and worried."

"Yeah," Damian said. "A night in a real bed does a person wonders."

"Theo didn't really give me a choice in the matter. He threatened to take me off the approved list of guests for his room if I didn't go home and get some rest."

"I'm aware. Good man."

"Something like that," Evelina muttered.

Theo had been especially difficult over the past three days since he woke up. Evelina was trying to understand his sudden attitude and snappiness, but it didn't always make sense. Last night when he demanded Evelina go to Lily's home, get some rest, and stop worrying over him, she had went because she couldn't find it in herself to argue with Theo.

Damian tossed the newspaper he'd been reading down to his lap. "He knows you've been here every single day, Eve. He knows you waited for him and that you didn't leave. That's the most important thing. Theo can only get better from here, all right."

"What are you saying?"

"Cut him some slack and let him make some rules. He'll feel like he's got some say. It's got to be hard on a person like Theo to be stuck immobile and prone in a bed for over a week, only to wake up and find out that you were that way."

"He's independent, and he just learned all of his control was taken away."

Damian nodded slowly. "Essentially. He's trying to get some back. You should have heard him with the nurses when they tried fretting over his surgery stitches this morning. I think he was mostly getting irritated because they kept touching him, and Theo ... well, you know."

"Theo doesn't like to be touched." Evelina took in Damian's spot outside of Theo's room. "Is that why you're out here in a chair?"

"Partly."

"What's the other reason?"

"My wife's having an overdue discussion with her brother. I don't do well in situations where Lily is liable to end up a crying mess. I try to find a way to fix it. She won't like it if I hit her injured, hospitalized brother for being an idiot, and for hiding their family secrets."

"Ben's abuse."

"Yes," Damian said quietly.

"How did she find out?"

"I told her shortly after she started to question why the nurses were so skittish around Theo after he woke up."

Evelina raised a brow, surprised. "Why?"

"Because I don't lie to my wife. She asked me not to. And frankly, she deserves to know the truth about her brothers. Both the living and the dead. Lily is the way she is, and she was given the freedom she had, because of the things they suffered so she wouldn't have to."

"I think he needs to talk about it for once. Honestly and openly. When I figured it out and tried asking, he shut me down. I understand why but he shouldn't do that."

Damian sighed. "Monsters can only hurt you if you keep them hidden, Eve."

"Well, mine are dead now."

Her father was gone, after all. His controlling ways and life-long goals to groom his children into the perfect mafia pets had failed. She was her own person who was capable of making her own choices.

"Lucky you." Damian looked up at her with a curiosity burning brightly. "What does that feel like?"

"Freedom," she answered instantly. "It feels like freedom."

"Oh, he's looking at her in this one," Lily said, a smile in her tone.

Theo grinned wide. "I think she was scolding him for cussing or something."

Lily laughed and Theo followed along. Evelina soaked in the siblings' happiness from her spot in the corner chair where she was pretending to read on her ereader. Lily had left the hospital earlier in the day and returned with Theo's favorite takeout, and a photo album.

Apparently, Dino had sent the family some photos to be delivered on Christmas back before the man was killed. Lily had them done up into some kind of family album, and she wanted Theo to look it over and see if he remembered anything about the day.

"Dino kind of seems like his focus was elsewhere, doesn't it?" Lily asked.

Evelina peeked over the top of her ereader and caught the sight of Theo's frown.

"Maybe he was a little unfocused. I think he had a lot going on back then. He'd just moved out of the house shortly before that."

"At sixteen?"

"Dad didn't like him being mixed up in the Outfit as much as he was."

"Oh," Lily said softly.

"Yeah, so he went out on his own to do his thing. Dad had nothing to say after that."

Lily shifted on the bed to lay back beside Theo. The tiny little hospital bed wasn't made for two people, but the siblings somehow made it work with the photo album stuck between them. Evelina would probably be jealous as hell if it were any other woman and not his sister in a close proximity to Theo, but the sweetness between the two wouldn't let her feel anything but happiness.

As much as Lily had separated from her family over the years, she missed them, too. Theo especially, Evelina knew. The two had been close when they were children even with the five-year age gap.

"Do you remember Dino ever having a girlfriend back then?" Lily asked.

"No," Theo said instantly.

"You answered that a little quickly, Theo."

Theo passed a pleading glance at Evelina. She pretended like she didn't see it.

Lily flipped a couple more pages.

"I don't think he was involved with someone publically at that time," Theo finally said after a long while.

"Privately?"

"Do you remember Julia Trentini?"

Lily's brow furrowed. "No, but I've seen her pictures in the Trentini mansion. She was Terrance's only daughter from his marriage, right?"

"Yes. She was the same age as Dino."

"That's who he ..." Lily trailed off with a wag of her brow.

Theo laughed deeply, but it faded fast. "Something like that. I think Dino cared a lot about her, but it didn't last long once Ben found out about the relationship. He beat the hell out of Dino, and then me when I tried to step in. On the same night, he had Julia killed and made it look like an accident."

Lily's face crumpled instantly. "But Terrance was Ben's friend."

"It wasn't about Terrance. It was about Dino."

"I don't understand," Lily mumbled sadly.

Evelina had heard her friend say that very sentence more times than she cared to count over the last day. Lily was confused and hurt over the past her brothers had shared under their uncle's abusive roof.

Theo flipped a page in the album as he said, "Dino couldn't have what Ben didn't give him. Julia was just one of those things."

"I thought women and children were untouchable, Theo."

"Does anything about that generation of men scream honorable to you?" he asked.

"No," Lily admitted.

"There's your answer, little one." Theo shrugged, adding, "Dino's only way of controlling what happened to you and me was by accepting Ben, and whatever the man demanded of him. That meant adhering to the rules and expectations Ben set out for all of us. More often than not, Dino failed when he tried stepping out on his own. Ben took all the pleasure he could from that, I think."

Silence fell over the siblings for a long while. Evelina watched the two while Theo and Lily continued flipping through the photo album without saying another thing. Finally, Lily closed the album up and tossed it aside.

"Why?" she asked softly.

"Why, what?"

"Why did you hate Dino so much if you knew, Theo? Why were you so distant from him for all this time?"

Theo cleared his throat. "Because I blamed him. For being weak. For not helping me. For not being strong enough and for not having control. By the time I realized that my anger and resentment towards my brother was just another one of my uncle's games, it was too late. We'd gone too far. We'd cut too many scars into one another. We hated and we loved, but we couldn't make it into something strong enough to withstand what had happened in the past."

"But you were getting there," Lily pressed, "before Dino was killed."

"We were."

"Why?"

"I learned some things that reminded me of the shit my brother had gone through with Ben separate from the shit he'd put me through. Like Julia and whatnot."

"Years later, Dino was still pining over her?" Lily asked.

"No," Theo said. "Eve, what time is it?"

Stunned that Theo remember she was in the room since she'd been so quiet, Evelina said, "Nine."

"Visiting hours are over in thirty minutes, right?"

"Yes." Evelina met Theo's stare. "Why?"

"Who is out in the waiting room today?" he asked instead of answering.

"They left after you went out and sat with them during supper," Lily told her brother. "What is up with you?"

"It wasn't about Julia," Theo said, pushing up from the bed. Every action he took was slowed and likely pained. He barely showed an ounce of his discomfort as he got up from the bed. "But I can show you better than I can explain, Lily. I need a phone. A safe one."

Suddenly, Damian was leaning in the doorway. Evelina wished she could be surprised that the man had been there and listening. He still shocked her all the same.

"I could help with that," Damian said, waving a cell phone.

Theo turned to Lily. "You can't be angry, okay."

Lily frowned. "About what?"

"Someone. Two people, actually. You can't be angry that he kept them away and safe."

"Theo—"

"Lily, this is important."

Evelina was so confused that it wasn't even funny. She had no clue what Theo was rambling on about, or why he seemed so entirely frustrated and nervous at the same time. Even with his mood swings lately, this franticness was new.

"I won't be angry," Lily whispered.

"They're not a part of this," Theo said, his tone brokering no room for argument. "They can never be a part of this, Lily. You have to understand that the most important thing is making sure they don't become integrated into this like we are. Dino didn't want that to happen."

"The Outfit?"

"That, and us."

Lily looked back at Damian. "Because we are the Outfit."

Theo nodded. "We are. They aren't."

"Visiting hours are over," a nurse said out in the hallway.

"Theo's room has had special circumstances regarding visitors since his arrival at this hospital. It's why the hospital is being paid double for the room than what the actual cost is. His afterhours visitors will not disrupt the rest of the wing, I promise, but they are unable to come during normal hours. Now, if you're done being loud while the sick people are trying to sleep, I'd like to pass by."

The nurse huffed loudly at Damian's rebuttal.

Before Evelina even got the chance to look out into the hallway to see who he'd gone downstairs to meet, a little boy with wild blond curls and big brown eyes bolted straight inside the room. The child only looked to be maybe three or four-years-old, if that. His cute little wrangler jeans and puffy jacket practically swallowed his little body whole as he tried tugging off his mittens and hat.

It was downright impossible to ignore the fact that the boy shared similar features to Theo. Like his brown eyes, light hair, and a crooked smile. Small Nike sneakers squeaked on the tile floor as the child searched the room. Then, the little boy's gaze fell on Theo who was sitting on the side of the bed.

"Hey, little man," Theo said.

The child's eyes widened with happiness. *"Chunkle Theo!"*

"Quiet, Junior," came a voice from the doorway. "There are sick people who need to sleep in the other rooms. You have to be a good boy or we'll have to leave."

Evelina turned on her heel at the new person only to come face to face with a beautiful woman. For a brief second, her heart sank. Who was this woman? Why did she have a child with her that looked like Theo in a lot of ways, even if the boy did call Theo his uncle?

Damian stood out in the hallway behind the woman.

"Yes, Mamma," Junior said.

The little boy didn't seem like he'd actually heard anything his mother said as he practically flew into Theo's waiting arms.

"I missed you," Junior said, his voice muffled into Theo's chest.

"Yeah, me too, J." Theo held the boy out and ran his hand through the child's hair. "I thought I told your mother to go get you a decent haircut."

Junior grinned. "The girls at the park like my hair."

"Screw the haircut," Theo said, chuckling.

Lily had come to stand beside Evelina. She was silent as they watched the exchange.

"Thanks for coming, Karen," Theo said, shooting the woman in the doorway a smile. "I know it was last minute, and it's late."

Karen.

Evelina remembered Theo telling her that the woman wasn't

important to him, not in a romantic way. The panic that had seized her heart in a smothering grip slowly began to subside.

Junior turned on his heel and stared at Lily with the curiosity only a child could have. "You have brown eyes like me."

Lily nodded silently. "I do."

"And you look like Daddy."

Evelina's hand ached when Lily grabbed it with her own and squeezed for all she was worth.

"That's because she's Daddy's sister," Theo said quietly.

Junior's brow knitted when he looked back at Theo. "Like you have brown eyes like mine because you're his brother?"

"Just like that."

"Oh," said the child.

This child belonged to Dino.

Karen stepped into the room and took a seat in the corner. Evelina held no animosity for the woman as she realized that Karen's relationship had been with someone else, not Theo.

"So that makes her my aunt, right?" Junior asked.

"Yes," Karen told her son.

"*Zio.*"

"*Zia,*" Theo corrected. "O's on the end for a boy, J."

"*Zia,*" the child mimicked.

"*Zia* Lily."

Junior flashed a brilliant smile. "I like that name."

Lily squeezed Evelina's hand even harder.

Evelina let her.

"Mr. DeLuca—"

"I am perfectly fucking capable of having a shower without a babysitter," Theo interrupted sharply. "I've been doing it for over twenty years without issue."

Evelina walked into Theo's private room only to find her lover in an intense staring contest with a nurse. A few days after waking up from his coma, Theo had finally been moved out of Intensive Care and into a more private section of the hospital with individual rooms that felt more like a hotel than a health care facility. He'd been in his new room for a couple of days. That made it two weeks in the hospital altogether.

Theo was over it. He was done with the hospital, the poking and prodding, the nurses, their demands and constant checking. He had started to refuse tests and request his release. Yes, Theo was ready to stop what he called madness and go back to his life.

Evelina was worried that he wasn't ready. The IV tubes had been removed. Theo no longer needed to wear leads to track his vitals, and he'd been attending physical therapy once a day to keep his strength and energy up. The doctors and specialists had been stunned at how quickly Theo bounced back after waking from his coma. In all aspects, he was healthy and perfectly fine.

Even the doctors thought so.

At the same time, Theo had opened up his surgical stitches twice on his chest when he'd attempted to do more than he should have. He'd admitted to feeling dizzy when he was on his feet for too long. The bullet wounds to his back often ached, and he was still on a heavy dose of antibiotics to fight off any infection.

So while he was doing okay, he was also at a standstill. Theo didn't give a damn. He wanted to go home.

"I can stand outside of the bathroom if you're more comfortable, but for another few days, you have to be monitored. You have shown signs of dizziness among other things, Mr. DeLuca. If, by chance, you took a spell when you were alone, we're liable."

Theo glared at the woman. The young, pretty nurse put her hands on her hips and glared right back.

Something hard and hot twisted in Evelina's gut. It wasn't something she felt often, but it always seemed like whenever Theo had to have a procedure done, the prettiest, youngest nurses jumped at the chance to do it. It wasn't like Evelina blamed them.

The man was sexy as fuck. He melted panties with a smirk. Theo could get a woman hot with a single word. He was also *hers*.

"Excuse me," Evelina said, forcing her tone to stay level.

Theo's glower melted away and his smile grew at the sight of Evelina in the doorway. "Hey, babe."

"Hey."

The nurse sighed. "Thank God."

Evelina cocked a brow. "Pardon?"

"You," the woman said, pointing at Eve. "You can handle him, yes?"

"I usually do."

Some of Evelina's jealousy started to drift away. The nurse looked like she was entirely over the conversation she'd been having with Theo.

"Good." Waving a hand at Theo, the nurse said, "He wants to shower. He needs a chaperone. His attitude is unbearable."

"It is not," Theo growled.

"Enough, Theo," Evelina said.

Theo clamped his mouth shut, but he didn't look happy about it.

"Are you fine with him?" the nurse asked.

"Perfect," Evelina assured.

"There's a buzzer in the bathroom if he takes a spell."

Theo blew out a heavy breath. "I'm not going to take a fucking *spell*."

Evelina ignored her lover's rant.

"We'll be fine, I'm sure. Thank you."

Once the nurse was out of sight, Evelina turned on her lover.

"You," she said in a hiss.

Theo's smirk melted away. "What?"

"You are acting like a spoiled man-child that had his favorite toy taken away, Theo, and I've had enough of it. Those nurses and the doctors are only trying to help you enough that you can leave this goddamn place. Don't you get that?"

"I can shower by myself, Eve."

"Maybe so, but they have policies they have to follow. Just because you demand something different doesn't mean they'll follow along, Theo. Jesus Christ."

Theo cocked a brow, amusement dancing in his gaze. "Someone's touchy today."

"Says the man who can't suck it up and follow the rules for a day just so he can get a release paper."

"Point taken."

"They are only trying to help," Evelina said.

Theo nodded. "I know, but I didn't think you'd appreciate it very much to find me soaping up my dick with a nurse just feet away. I mean, unless you're into that kind of thing."

Evelina's mouth popped open. "I—"

"Because we can try that, Eve."

"No!"

Theo laughed deeply. The sound rocked Evelina straight to her sex, making her wet and hot all at the same time. It had been far too long since she'd had this man, but she could wait a little while longer. Even if it fucking killed her.

"Stop it," Evelina said, feeling breathless. "I know what you're doing, Theo."

"Distracting you."

"Yes. So I'll stop pestering you about the nurses."

"I'll try ... being not so difficult."

"We would *all* appreciate it."

Theo crossed his arms. "I want to go home."

"You will. Soon."

"And I'm not a fucking man-child."

"In a hospital, apparently you are."

Theo scowled. "The doctor was here earlier before Lily left."

"And?"

"I'll be out by the weekend."

That was just four days away.

A realization dawned on Evelina.

"You were telling the truth."

"About not wanting to make you uncomfortable with the nurse? Yeah." Theo shrugged and added, "Because hey, if that was you and I walked in on it, I'd skin the guy alive."

Jesus.

Two people could play that game. Evelina figured if Theo was feeling up to being his usual cocky, easy-going, sexy self, then he was doing a hell of a lot better than people thought.

"And what if it was a woman in there with me?"

Theo's cheek twitched. "I need a shower."

"A cold one?"

"Stop it, Eve. The doctor said no sex for another two weeks."

"You asked?"

"Twice."

"I'm not even surprised." Evelina laughed. "I guess I'm joining you for that shower, huh?"

"Unfair, Eve. Really, really un-fucking-fair. Joining and watching are not the same thing."

"Give it as good as I get it."

"Good thing." Theo waved at the attached, private bathroom. Evelina followed his lead. As the door closed and his hand landed on her lower back, Theo said, "He didn't say I couldn't have a little fun when I got home."

Goddamn.

His hand slid down to her ass over the skinny jeans she wore. Evelina batted his hand away before things got out of control. With Theo, it didn't take very damned much for Evelina to lose all rational thought.

"Stop that, Theo."

"You like it. Too many nurses here, though. The okay was for home, not to defile the hospital every which way I could. I just have to keep the heartrate down. Nothing too strenuous. He didn't say I couldn't have a little bit of easy fun."

Evelina forced herself to breathe as Theo began undressing. "I bet he did."

Theo didn't break eye contact for a second. "I bet he didn't."

CHAPTER TWENTY-THREE

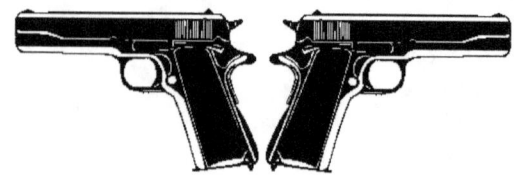

"I heard you're getting out today."

Theo shot Tommas a smirk over his shoulder. "Appropriate that you'd put it like that seeing as how this place felt like my prison for three weeks."

"You took three bullets in the back and spent a week comatose, Theo. You're lucky it wasn't longer."

"We DeLucas heal fast."

Tommas shrugged. "Or you pestered everyone enough until they let you go."

"Clean bill of health," Theo said, ignoring the ache in his chest and back.

Tommas took another step into the room and surveyed the bag Theo was packing. "How did your interviews go over with the detectives working the shooting?"

"I was shot and had no gun on me to be found in the club."

"I'm aware."

"They have to treat me like the victim in all this, Tommas. The victim who had to explain why one of his employees was found dead in his car, and burned beyond all recognition."

"So?"

"They really hate treating a DeLuca like a victim. As far as Cole's death, they're investigating but I had flight tickets showing that I left the city that night. Damian was able to give me a viable alibi. My guess is they think I did it, but they have no real proof."

"Nice."

Theo brushed it all off. "It is what it is, man. I never played well with police as it is. They had to know what they were looking at when they came in here to question me. I pretended like I didn't remember a thing from the moment I stepped inside the club. The doctor's reports will back me up on that with the coma and all."

A squeak on the floor made Theo turn around to face Tommas.

"Do you remember?" Tommas asked.

"Every last bit."

"Good to know."

Theo eyed Tommas, noting the man's gaze seemed more tired than usual, and he wasn't as well-dressed as he usually would be. Instead of the usual suit and tie apparel that Tommas was known for, the man wore a pair of dark wash jeans, a white shirt, and a leather jacket.

"Speaking of which, the car and Cole, I mean …"

"What about it?" Tommas asked.

"I'm going to give Cole's father the okay to go after Belli. It's his right after what happened."

"I'm sure no one will disagree with that."

Tommas seemed far too flippant for Theo's liking.

"What do you want, Tommas?" Theo asked.

"Not a lot, Theo. To talk, maybe."

"So talk."

"Who has handled your streets?" Tommas asked.

"Adriano. His territory borders mine. The guys know him. I suspect word about Evelina being with me, or the rumors of it, have passed around enough for it to be considered fact which makes Adriano good enough to be family. That gives the kid a little more clout. I didn't mind when he mentioned it to me. I took it as a peace offering."

"He's a good Capo. Young, but—"

"Being young doesn't have a damned thing to do with it. Adriano is good at his job. Let him be good at it and lose the judgment about his age. He deserves that, Tommas."

Tommas chuckled. "You're right. My head isn't in the right place lately, I guess."

"Women will do that to you."

The man didn't respond to that. Theo didn't need him to. He knew enough about Tommas now to suspect that Abriella Trentini had a lot to do with everything Tommas Rossi did.

"How long before Joel finds out that you've been fucking his little sister for years and goes batshit?" Theo asked.

Tommas lifted a single shoulder like he didn't give a damn. "I wouldn't be surprised if the man already knew and was trying to figure out a way to use it."

"Seriously?"

"As a heart attack. I don't believe he knows, but anything is possible. I've been terribly careful with Abriella for her sake, not mine. Joel doesn't frighten me. It doesn't matter. As of now, Joel isn't coming at me because of Abriella. He's coming at me for what I've been doing lately. And he wants the seat, you know."

"Do you want it, too?"

Tommas didn't even blink. "I want what's mine."

That answered nothing.

"What else did you come here today for?" Theo asked.

"You always were a perceptive fucker. Nonetheless, I've come for nothing more than you're willing to give me, Theo. I think with me, I've done enough where you're concerned."

"I'd say so."

"But you understand, don't you?"

"That you allowed blame to be casted on me even though you were really looking for it to go to Joel on the off-chance that Riley might take the man out once and for all? Or how about the fact that instead of seeing Riley for what he really was, you gave the man enough blind faith and completely missed the fact he was fucking with you and Joel, too? And when you did decide to give a damn, it was too late."

Tommas cleared his throat, looking entirely uncomfortable. "It was a bit more complicated than that."

"Yeah, well, I simplified shit down a bit." Theo sighed and rubbed at his forehead. "Listen, I get what you were doing. I could have handled myself, and in fact, I did several times. I appreciate that once you learned that there might have been something going on between Evelina and me, you tried to correct shit, and couldn't help that it all backfired. I know that your plans had little to do with me, and everything to do with Joel. I get it, Tommas, honestly."

"But? I can hear it in there somewhere."

"But once bitten, twice shy." Theo offered Tommas a grin. "We're not going to do this again, that's all. I refuse to be anyone else's pawn in this war, all right. I've worked my whole life to leave behind the kind of men I don't want to be. I've got more important things to worry about and keep safe than families who don't give a good goddamn about me, Tommas."

"I can't say that I blame you."

"Yeah. So hey, if you're here looking for an ally against Joel when I get out of here, look elsewhere."

Tommas' lips drew thin. "But you're not working for Joel's side of things, either."

"No, I'm working for me. I've got an entire territory to keep safe and a crew to run. I've got a man to bury and his father to apologize to. I have a woman with friends and family on your side of things and Joel's. *La famiglia* isn't war, Tommas. I refuse to put myself in the middle of it. I'm out."

"Out."

"Done. Gone. Out."

"It doesn't work that way, Theo. There is no out."

Theo nodded, knowing that all too well. "You're right, there isn't. But I'm taking one. I'm still a made man. I'm still mafia and DeLuca born and bred, but I won't feed the violence and the hatred any more than it already has been by everyone else. Why should I do that, huh? I have no part in it, and nothing to gain. I will not work for the benefit of another man's agenda, and put my family, my lover, and myself at risk like I have before. I have no chips in this game, Tommas. You're on your own."

"You might be surprised, Theo, but being alone doesn't bother me all that much. I've been this way for a long time."

"Lonely men are dangerous ones."

"They can be," Tommas agreed. "Especially when they're tired of being alone."

Theo went about packing the last bit of clothes and items he had into the small duffle bag. Evelina had gone downstairs earlier with Lily to warm up the car. After signing a dozen and one forms, Theo would be allowed to walk out of the hospital free and clear.

He was itching to go.

Soon.

"Where are you going, to your place or somewhere else?" Tommas asked.

"Trying to find out if I plan on shacking up with Eve?"

"Curious. She's still got a man heading her house even with her father dead."

She did. Adriano.

Theo figured the man didn't care. Adriano would have said something by now.

"Mind your house, Tommas, and I'll mind mine." Theo picked up the duffle bag and slung it around his shoulder. He ignored the twinge of pain in his back as the bag hit the tenderest spots. "But yeah, I'm going home. Eve will be going with me, regardless of anyone else's opinions. It was either that, or my sister would cut my balls off because I refused to go live with her for a month so she can hover over me more than she already has. Evelina was the compromise I didn't mind making."

"I suppose you wouldn't, huh?"

"Nope. She belongs with me, anyway."

Tommas gave a small smile. "You're right, she does. And once this is all over ..."

"What about it?"

"I look forward to your dues when I take the seat, Theo."

Theo stiffened at those words. "They'll be waiting for the boss, Tommas. I just won't step in to help *any* man get there."

"I don't expect you to."

"But I'll wish you luck on the way to the top."

Theo felt Evelina's glare burning into his back the moment he unlocked the apartment door. He ignored her crossed arms and tight frown as he kicked off his dress shoes, and shrugged of his suit jacket.

He'd been back at his apartment and out of the hospital for four days. Theo couldn't settle. He was restless as hell, needing to be on the move, and the feeling wouldn't go away. He had no idea what to do to correct the problem. It seemed like the perpetual knot of tension in his stomach just kept getting tighter.

"Get it out before you blow up," Theo said, turning to face Evelina.

"You are …"

"What, Eve?"

"Unbelievable, Theo."

Theo waved a hand high. "Nothing I haven't already heard."

"You know the rules. You were released early on the understanding you would take it easy, get lots of rest, and stay away from stressful things, Theo."

"I have work to do," Theo said.

Evelina scowled at him. "The doctor said—"

"Being home and wondering about all the trouble my crew is getting into when I'm not looking over their shoulders is really stressful for me, Eve. And my businesses? Yeah, I run those hands-on, too."

She clamped her mouth shut with an audible snap. Guilt ate away at Theo. He wasn't accustomed to living with someone, or needing to check in with them like he was now with Evelina. She didn't ask him to do it, but he knew she worried about him.

"I knew you'd be pissed," he said quietly.

"That you got up at five in the morning and sneaked out of the apartment without me knowing?"

"Yeah, about that. Sorry?"

"You're right. I'm pissed," she said.

Theo sighed. "I have work to do."

"I know, but you have to take it easy, Theo."

"I am. I had something to handle today."

"Like what?" Evelina asked, cocking a brow.

Shit.

Theo decided to give her the truth since he figured lying would only put him in the dog house. Now that he was living with Evelina, and they'd put titles on their relationship, lying was kind of low. Real men didn't lie, not to women they loved.

"I had a bookie that Adriano caught stealing off the bottom," Theo explained. "It had to be handled. Thieves have a disease that tends to spread when it isn't culled quickly."

Evelina's fists met her hips. "Theo!"

"I let Adriano handle it. I watched. Less work. No stress."

"Oh, my God."

Frustration wrote heavy lines over Evelina's brow. Theo's guilt climbed tenfold. Crossing the space between them in the apartment's entryway, he grabbed Evelina's wrists and pulled her into his chest before she could refuse him.

"I'm sorry," he murmured into her hair. "I didn't mean to worry you. I don't want to fight about it, Eve, but I have business to do. I can't stop it simply because you worry."

Evelina's tension released as her body sunk against his. "I had to lie to Lily when she called earlier."

"What did you say?"

"That you were napping."

Theo scoffed. "I don't nap."

"She fell for it."

Good thing.

Lily was another one who hovered and worried too much.

"She's going to worry that little baby of hers right out," Theo said.

Evelina laughed. "Don't say that."

"Well, it's a genuine concern. Damian will blame me, I know it."

"Maybe you should take away some of her stress by following the rules, Theo."

Theo put two fingers under Evelina's chin, and forced her to look up at him. Quickly, he pressed a kiss to her mouth to keep her quiet, and take away whatever worries she had left. "I'm fine, Eve."

"Are you?"

"Yes. No pain. No achiness. No dizziness. I'm good."

Evelina pouted. "You could have called."

"You might have yelled at me."

"I might have."

"See," he muttered.

"A little. Because I love you."

Theo grinned. "Good to know. Now …"

"Hmm, what?"

Before Evelina blinked, Theo spun her to the side and pinned her against the closest wall. It just happened to be the door for the coat closet. The wood shuddered under the impact. Evelina's wide, green eyes stared up at Theo with a mixture of shock and lust. Her grin deepened the moment he pressed a kiss to the tip of her nose.

"Now this," Theo said, fitting himself between her opened legs.

"Not two weeks yet," Evelina said, all the air in her voice gone.

She wasn't even fighting him. She didn't move his hands when he began tugging her wool dress up. She didn't avoid his kiss as he took her mouth with hard strikes of his tongue and scrapes of his teeth. She didn't tell him to stop when he ground the hard length of his erection into her pelvis.

Aching.

Starving.

Needing.

Theo felt all of those things for Evelina.

"No, he said to keep my heartrate down and not to do anything too strenuous," Theo said before he bit Evelina's lower lip.

She whined, and the sound melted into the sexiest moan when Theo's hand slipped between her legs to palm her hot sex through her panties. He adored how responsive this woman always was for him. She tilted her hips into his hand, matching his strokes until he was sure she was wet and fucking wanting him bad.

"Fucking me against a wall isn't strenuous to you?" Evelina asked sweetly.

Theo dropped down to his knees with a cocked brow. "Who said anything about fucking you against a wall, Eve?"

Evelina bit her bottom lip as Theo pushed her skirt up around her hips with one hand, and pulled her panties down to her ankles with the other.

"You didn't answer me," Theo said.

"Your heartrate ..."

"Hush up. My heart is fine."

"But—"

"Hush. You know you want this, Eve. You know you want me to fuck you with my mouth until you're begging, sweating, and coming all over my tongue. Don't you want my tongue and fingers all over you, babe? You look so good when you let me eat you."

Theo pulled Evelina's panties off when she stepped out of them and tossed them to the side. Evelina released a shaky breath. Her legs tightened around his hand when he slid two fingers along the seam of her wet sex. Her clit throbbed under the pad of his digit as he circled the hard nub over and over.

"Jesus, Theo."

"Feel, princess. You're wet as hell. You want this so fucking bad. Deny it."

"I want it."

"Hmm? Louder."

"I want your mouth on my pussy, Theo. Now."

"There you go, babe." Theo smirked up at her.

"You're still not supposed to be doing this, Theo."

"We're going to do this like that, huh?" he asked.

"Like what?"

"The way you like. With my dirty mouth and your easily offended sensibilities. See, this relationship of ours is all about giving to the other what they need. And I think you need this terribly bad, Eve."

"Oh?"

"Yes. So unless the next words out of your mouth are either *fuck me, Theo* or *more, Theo* … I don't want to hear it. I'm a giver when it comes to you. Shut up and take it."

Evelina swallowed hard. "*God*, that's awful."

"You love it. Just like you love it when I fuck you. Be quiet, or beg me and love it, Eve."

"I—"

"Beg me and love it, Eve."

She whimpered when he teased the slit of her sex with gentle touches.

"Please, Theo. *Please*."

"And?"

"God, you know I'll fucking love it."

He did.

Shooting her a grin, Theo thrust two fingers into her clenching sex and curled the digits hard into the wet walls. Evelina cried out loudly, sinking against the wall. Theo didn't give her any time to gather her bearings. He leaned forward and covered her clit with his mouth and sucked hard.

"Holy shit," Evelina breathed.

Theo felt her fingers find his hair. She tugged on the strands just hard enough for it to hurt. He didn't mind a damn bit. Watching her from up above, he attacked her clit with fast strokes of his tongue.

Over and over.

Fucking relentless.

Her tartly sweet arousal flooded his tongue, the flavor making him groan. Thick and deep, the sound started from somewhere in his chest and vibrated against Evelina's clit. It only made her pretty little sounds turn a little more breathless for him.

Almost …

Theo knew it.

She was almost there.

"Oh, God," Evelina mumbled.

Theo kissed the hood of her clit and kept the pace of his fingers up as he met her stare. "So close, princess. You're craving it, babe. It's right there, huh?"

"Stop teasing me, Theo. Fuck."

He curled his fingers hard again, knowing he was hitting the spot that was sure to make her shake even more.

"There, Eve. It's right there. I fucking missed this with you. Tasting you. Feeling you."

Evelina's lashes fluttered closed. "You're killing me."

"Not even close. Watch me, Eve, or this stops."

Her eyes flew open instantly.

Theo chuckled. "Good girl. Ready?"

"So ready."

Theo's mouth was back on Evelina's clit with rough, fast strikes in a blink. Evelina's cries got louder when his fingers matched the rhythm of his tongue. The sounds of her wet flesh taking him in as her thighs began to shake was fucking perfection. Evelina looked like sex on legs up above him, riding his face and fingers, chasing her orgasm.

Evelina's grip on Theo's hair tightened. He practically felt all of the tension in her body release when she came. Forcing her to stay in place so he could lap up every single drop of her arousal, Theo pushed his palm into Evelina's stomach and kept her pinned to the wall.

"*Theo!*"

"Mmm," Theo hummed, kissing Evelina's trembling thigh. "Perfect."

Evelina sucked in a deep breath as Theo stood. "You were right."

"I always am."

"Smartass."

Theo smirked. "Very. Do tell me what I'm right about this time, though."

"I missed this."

"I knew you did."

"Still not—"

Theo didn't let Evelina get her worries about his heart out. Not again. She'd said it enough. He was perfectly fucking fine.

Yanking her away from the wall, Theo pulled on Evelina's dress until it was up over her head and tossed to the floor.

"Theo, wait," Evelina said, sounding amused and annoyed at the same time.

"No."

Theo pulled her in for a kiss that burned him from the inside out. He took his time owning her mouth all over again while Evelina fisted his shirt and pulled him closer. When he did finally pull away, he felt like he couldn't fucking breathe again.

He was so in love with this woman. Because she didn't give a damn about his monsters, and she wasn't out to chase them away. She didn't think he was broken. She didn't fix him like someone else might try to. She worried too damned much about him. He liked waking up in sheets that smelled like whatever perfume she wore. The extra clothes in his closet and the frilly shit in the bathroom didn't even look out of place.

Evelina hadn't made a place in his life. She simply took the open spot that Theo hadn't known was missing someone until it was filled.

She just was.

His entirely.

Theo loved it.

"Goddamn, Eve, you're …"

Looking stunned and goddamn gorgeous in nothing but her bra, Evelina watched Theo warily.

"What, Theo?"

"You settle me. Do you know that?"

Evelina's brow puckered. "Settle you?"

"I feel so restless, and then I touch you and I'm good again."

"Oh."

"That all you got to say?"

"I didn't know that I did that for you."

"You do," he murmured. "Take it off, Eve. The rest of it needs to go."

"But—"

Theo gave her one look that shut Evelina up instantly. "Off."

Silently, Evelina hooked her thumbs around her bra straps and pulled them down until her breasts spilled free. While she unhooked the bra from the back, Theo cupped her tits in his hands and rolled his thumbs over the peaks of her nipples.

Evelina shuddered. "That feels so good."

"What do I always say, hmm?"

"It'll get so much better."

"Bang on, babe."

Then, Evelina leaned forward and pressed her lips to his. It was a much softer, sweeter kiss than he'd leveled on her. It didn't feel any less powerful, though. It still heated his blood, made his cock throb, and Theo still wanted to get down on his damned knees for this woman.

Anything.

He'd do anything for her.

"Let me," Evelina whispered.

"What, Eve?"

"Undress you."

Theo smiled wickedly. "Go for it."

Evelina returned his grin and began unbuttoning the dress shirt he wore. She took her time pulling the shirt off and then tugging down his pants until he stood in nothing but boxer-briefs and skin. Theo waited for his lover to surprise him with something, and she didn't disappoint. Her hot mouth touched down to his skin over and over while the tips of her fingers roamed over his body.

Without a word, Evelina touched and kissed all the spots and marks Theo's body owned. The old ones and the news ones became hers with a single graze of her fingers to the scars. He had far too many. His life had cut more scars into his body than he cared to count.

Evelina still took them all.

Then, her hand slipped under his boxer-briefs and wrapped around his cock in a vise-tight grip. *Sweet Jesus.*

"Couch," Theo ordered.

Evelina winked. Theo stepped forward and made her walk backwards until the backs of her legs hit the couch. Quick as lightning, Theo grabbed Evelina by the waist and turned them around so she could climb on top. Anxious in his heart and hot in his blood, he freed his cock from his boxer-briefs and let Evelina position herself the way she wanted.

The second she sunk down on his length, Theo was gone. His hands found her waist to hold her still so he could just feel her like that for a moment. Flexing around him, bare, and soaking him in the best way possible.

Leaning forward, Evelina touched her nose to Theo's. Her hair created a curtain-like barrier and suddenly, it was just them. Nothing else mattered. Nothing existed except green eyes watching him and the blissful heat of pleasure licking up his spine.

He'd never loved before.

He'd fucked.

Never loved.

When Evelina began riding him slowly, with her hair still barricading them inside their own private world, he finally figured out what the difference between fucking and loving was. It was better; rawer.

A hesitance flickered in Evelina's gaze.

Theo knew her worries before she voiced them. "Feel, Eve."

Her palm lifted from his stomach to press over his heart. Gentle, soft beats answered her touch. A steady, natural rhythm that wasn't too fast and felt just right. They'd be bad. It was what he always said.

But they were terribly good, too.

"You settle me, Eve."

"I love you, Theo."

"Love you," he echoed.

"I'm ready to cash in on that apology."

Adriano glanced up from the papers on his desk.

Theo grinned from his spot in the doorway to the restaurant's office.

"What was that?" Adriano asked.

"The apology you owe me. I'm ready to cash in on it."

Adriano cleared his throat and put the papers away. "Oh?"

"I figure we've already got it settled and all, but it'd look better on you and Eve for me to do it the proper way. And I'm all about what's best for Eve, you know."

"My sister."

"That's what I said," Theo replied, chuckling.

"You worried me there for a second."

"Eve is mine, Adriano."

The younger man didn't give a single thing away as he said, "I'm aware."

"And you're her brother, so that makes you family. I'm not out to hurt family. A lot of others would do well to learn that as well."

"I agree." Adriano pushed out his chair and stood from the desk. "Where is my sister today?"

"She went shopping with Lily."

"Ghost trailing behind?"

"Probably," Theo said. "Which is why I let her go."

It was a dangerous thing for Evelina to be chumming around in Rossi and Trentini territory. Little to nothing had been settled between Tommas and Joel. But Theo trusted Damian to take care of his girl and sister. Simple as that.

"How're you feeling lately?" Adriano asked.

"Good. Two weeks out of the hospital and not a problem to be found. I'm not going to keel over and die, kid."

Adriano laughed. "I guess not."

"Your sister and my sister worry enough over my health. Let's not add to it with our own."

"All right. So what do you have to cash in, so to speak?"

"Just a guarantee, Adriano."

"Of?"

"Evelina's status. She's free to do what she wants. No more Conti business. No more *principessa*. None of it. She's not to be used in these games anymore. She's free to do as she wishes, with whomever she wishes. Give me that guarantee, and we're good."

"I already gave that to my sister when you were comatose, Theo."

"It's different."

"How so?"

"You know how. You and I, we're not the same. We follow different rules. Give me the guarantee."

"I'm not … taking sides. Not now. I have more important things to worry about, like my wife, if that's what you're thinking, Theo."

"Actually, I wasn't."

Adriano sighed heavily. "One condition."

"What's that?"

"I want my sister to be safe, which means, I don't want anyone questioning her status or stance with a family. I don't want to even offer someone the chance to somehow use my sister in the future."

Theo felt a line of tension creep up his spine. "Me, either."

"Good. Then you'll marry her. Soon."

"I—"

"You love her, don't you?"

"Very much," Theo admitted.

"Then what's the goddamn problem?"

"I wonder if that'll feel like tying her down. To her, not to me. She's spent her whole life under someone's demands and dictations. I wouldn't want to marry Eve and it make her feel that way again."

"I guess you won't know until you ask, Theo. My guarantee is there, but you marry her."

Fair enough.

"Soon," Theo said, "but it's on her terms."

"Works for me."

"You good?" Evelina asked.

Theo nodded, but inside, he was a war raging out of control.

"Yeah," he finally said.

"You can wait a while, if you want."

"Today is good, Eve. Otherwise, I'll just keep putting it off."

"Okay."

With a squeeze of his hand to hers, Theo disappeared into the confessional room. Their church didn't have the traditional confessional box like many of the old Catholic churches had. Thankfully, their church had gone with the times and offered a room full of beautiful art, colorful tapestry and rugs, and ornate chairs for the parishioner and the priest to sit in.

Father Garner was waiting inside.

"Theo," the man greeted with a small smile.

"Father."

"Sit, Theo."

Theo shifted on his feet. "Can I stand?"

"You never did before."

"This time is different," Theo explained lamely.

Father Garner rested back into his chair with grace and years of learned patience. "And why is that?"

"Is it possible to confess for men who can no longer ask for forgiveness for their sins?"

"Do their sins leave you with burdens?"

"Every day," Theo said.

"Then yes, you absolutely can. And if their sins have been wrongs done to you, then it is your forgiveness you're giving Theo. It might not be something you need me here for unless you want to do your own confession, too."

"I'd like you here for it."

"Then I'll stay." Father Garner waved at Theo. "You can begin whenever."

Theo took a breath and it felt almost freeing.

"Forgive me, Father …"

Words spilled easily. Far easier than they ever had before.

Theo confessed for the father who had lost all his loyalty to his family and left his children as orphans. He confessed for the mother who had been nothing but an innocent bystander in games she had never wanted to play. He confessed for the aunt and uncle who had abused those they were supposed to love. He confessed for the brother who died trying to correct all the wrongs around them. He confessed for his sister. For him.

And even for Eve.

Because he needed to be free.

Completely.

Twenty minutes later, Theo walked out of the confessional room to find Evelina still leaning against the wall where he had left her. She flashed him with a brilliant smile.

"Hey," she said.

"Hey. Ready for some food?"

"As long as we get to take it back to the club. I hear the dancers have a meeting early tonight or something like that."

Theo laughed deeply. "You just like watching them dance."

"Well, you don't. At least one of us should enjoy the show."

"As long as you give me one at home."

"Maybe," Evelina said, winking.

Theo grabbed the hand she offered. It was just a piece of something beautiful, one single part of her. It was far too precious to be ignored. But she had offered it to him, and only him.

And in his own, it felt sacred.

Theo had forgotten what those things were to him.

Evelina was all of them.

As they walked out into the main floor of the church, Theo directed Evelina down the aisle between the rows of pews. Silent, the church was flooded with the winter light casting through the stained glass windows.

"Eve?"

"Hmm?" she asked softly.

"What do you want in the future?"

"You."

Theo smiled. "That's a simple answer."

"It's an honest one."

He tugged her hand to stop Evelina. "Remember when I told you that there were certain things I couldn't give to you, because it wasn't something I wanted."

"I think your words were a happily ever after, a white wedding, and children."

"Yeah ... those."

"I'm not asking for them," Evelina said, reaching out to stroke his jaw.

"You are, and so am I now. Things change, you know."

Evelina laughed. "They do."

"We're going to go that way soon."

"What way?"

"That happily ever after, maybe the wedding, whenever you're ready," Theo said, holding her hand tight in his own. "You just have to say the word and I'll give it to you."

Evelina glanced down the altar. "Yeah?"

"The very second you ask me, babe."

"But ..."

"What?" he asked.

"I don't think I want everyone else's happily ever after. I don't want to repeat my history."

Theo nodded. "Me, either."

"It's not selfish to be happy in your own way, is it?"

"No," he answered honestly.

"With just each other," she pressed.

Theo got her unspoken words. Like him, she had very little interest in having children. He didn't mind. His feelings on the topic weren't likely to change anytime soon.

"Come on," Theo murmured, pulling Evelina along the aisle again.

They walked hand in hand to the front of the church. Theo pushed the doors open to the flurry of snow and light. Flakes of snow fell in spirals to the steps.

"Theo, you didn't answer me," Evelina said quietly.

"I'm going in whatever direction you want to go, Eve."

"I just have to say the word, right?"

"That's all, Eve. Just say the word."

She stepped out of the church and into the falling snowflakes. Haloed in light, she looked like the angel he knew her to be.

Theo followed.

ABOUT THE AUTHOR

Bethany-Kris is a Canadian author, lover of much, and mother to three very young sons, one cat, and two dogs. A small town in Eastern Canada where she was born and raised is where she has always called home. With her boys under her feet, a snuggling cat, barking dogs, and a spouse calling over his shoulder, she is nearly always writing something ... when she can find the time.

Find Bethany-Kris at:
Her website www.bethanykris.com,
or on Facebook at www.facebook.com/bethanykriswrites,
on her blog at www.bethanykris.blogspot.ca,
or on Twitter - @BethanyKris.

Sign up to Bethany-Kris's New Release Newsletter here:
http://eepurl.com/bf9lzD